DARK
HORIZONS

an Expired Reality novel

David N. Alderman

Visit **DavidNAlderman.com**

This book is dedicated to everyone who believes in me.
You know who you are.

Dear Reader,

Dark Horizons is the third book in the Expired Reality series. In order to fully enjoy some of the plot twists and character developments in this series, it is recommended that you first read *Endangered Memories* and *Lost Birth*, the first and second books in the series.

David N. Alderman
Author

"It'll happen," he said.

She huffed. "But how do you know? What if —"

He shook his head and put up a hand to stop her. Even with his bearded face, he still looked young. "Everything will always happen the way it's meant to." He took a deep breath and let it out in a long sigh. "It always does."

Pearl's white hair flowed down the sides of her face as she glared at him. "We're risking a lot waiting."

Nathan turned and faced the winter-topped foothills. A chill had come in on the wind. "Yes. But the best things are worth the risk of patience."

"Maybe," she said. "Maybe not."

"You'll see. Everything will come back around. You did."

"With divine intervention."

"Our whole future depends on divine intervention."

1

Cold-Blooded

Light and crisp, the winter snow fell from the dark abyss, surrounding the Bridges Gap apartment complex in a blinding white blanket. Chilling air slithered in through the front doorway, freezing David Corbin's soul in place, numbing him to the terrible events of days past.

David welcomed the chill, welcomed the complete shutdown of his emotions, his thoughts, his sense of things. It was all he could do to survive—to close himself off from the rest of the world while he attempted to regain himself, much like a computer's hard drive is rebooted to restart its convoluted programs.

The old recliner David sat in was strangely comfortable, and the stale scent of cigarettes and rose-scented air freshener reminded him of his late sister and her bad habits. Cybil Corbin's corpse remained in the bedroom on the other side of the wall from where he sat, a mercenary's knife deep in her back. He couldn't bring himself to move her, instead regarding the murder scene as a shrine of sorts.

"I don't want to talk to you anymore." These had been Cybil's last words to David, after he inadvertently accused her of doing drugs. The conversation played in an infinite loop in his memory, tormenting him.

Why couldn't I save her? I tried so hard to save Carrie, to save the world, and I couldn't even protect my own sister?

David opened his eyes to the dark room before him. Time had somehow halted when David told Chaos—the otherworldly master of illusions—that he was going to go after the books Chaos wanted David to forget about. Now, David simply sat in his late sister's chair, which was marred with cigarette burns and cat scratches, and waited for the pieces of his mind, of himself, to reconnect so he could move again.

The ticking of the clock in the kitchen suddenly made its way into his sense of hearing, and he realized with true horror that time had started up again. Dull pain surrounded his right wrist under the cuff of his glove, where he had tried to cut himself open with the edge of his metal boomerang. Dozens of surface scratches released enough blood to lightly stain the carpet, but he couldn't bring himself to cut deeper.

He chuckled with the grim irony of trying to kill himself with the weapon that symbolized his heroism. Maybe it was because the same weapon had been used to kill Agent Parks. David thought of wrapping the wounds but didn't care enough to. He would wear them like bracelets, reminding him of how frail his psyche was.

Across the living room, the VHS security tape that David grabbed from the mall jewelry store sat on the kitchen table. He couldn't see it in the darkness, but his eyes formed its shape anyway. A shape that David stared at for minutes, maybe even hours.

"You killed me," the tape called out in a melodious tone. In the darkness, David thought the tape looked a lot like Melody's young, acne-riddled face. "You left me to die. How could you do that? Aren't you supposed to be a hero? Instead, you got me killed. Heroes don't do that."

You don't know if she died or not, David countered himself. His standoff with police in the jewelry store ended in Melody's injury—and possible death. He hadn't stuck around long enough to make sure she was ok. *She could be alive. She might be alright.*

The tape scoffed. "Alright? You know nothing is alright now. Nothing."

David shook Melody's ghost from his mind and gingerly stood from the recliner, his head swimming, his legs threatening to buckle. Moving to the sliding glass door, he drew open the blinds and slid the glass panel open, allowing more cold air and even some snow to drift into the living room. He welcomed the freeze with his arms opened wide. As the snowflakes landed across his bare arms, across the bloody roads mapped out across his wrist, he noticed the stark contrast between the white flakes and his own crimson stains. Red and white. Destruction and innocence. Death and purity. It seemed like a strange thing to think about, but something about it brought order to his chaotic mind and settled his nerves.

Balance.

Light from the parking lot illuminated part of the living area, giving David sight to see the worn brown couch and the beat-up brown coffee table in front of it. Trash littered the coffee table: potato chip wrappers, soda cups and cans, an empty pizza box. As much as he had once hated his sister's style of living, he yearned for it now. Staring at the trash, he took it all into his memory and pleaded with his brain, his heart, to keep the images as a token of his sister. He suddenly wanted to remember everything about her—the good and the bad—and never forget who she actually was instead of who he always wished her to be.

His mind nagged him again, reminding him to contact his parents, to tell the tale of what had occurred here only hours earlier. David refused his mind's pleas, and instead decided he would have his parents find out from someone other than him. He couldn't face them after this. Besides, they were out of town and probably unreachable. They would have to learn of their daughter's death at a later date.

Right now, David knew he needed to check the surveillance tape to find out who had the third and final timepiece necklace in their possession. The mysterious object was the reason David had been in that mall in the first place with Melody, with Veronica, and with that trigger-happy cop. The timepiece necklace was also why David was here, in his sister's home, in the place of her final moments here on Anaisha.

His struggle with Drather rushed through his mind, and he fought to keep it at bay. He wanted to kill the man, wanted to exact vengeance on him for killing his one and only sister.

But he wasn't here. Neither was his sister. It was just David, the falling snow, the bitter cold, and guilt. Mountains of guilt.

David made his way toward the kitchen through the living room. He spotted stray crumpled sheets of tissue paper and a small box on the floor near the entertainment center. He picked up the box and brought it to the sliding glass door, hoping to get more light on the object. Black velvet lined the outside. When he opened it, he slowly sunk back into the strangely comfortable recliner. The third timepiece necklace—a black capsule with a glowing blue line cutting around it—sat

4

nestled inside the white jewelry pillow.

"How did you get here?" he asked the long-sought item.

Hurry! Come back! Carrie is in trouble!

David shook his head, still disconcerted that Turquoise could telepathically enter his mind whenever she wanted.

David, hurry!

He reached into the pocket of his black denim coat and pulled out the fist-sized crystal timepiece. The clear crystal allowed one to see the small emerald clock within, and the unmoving minutes and seconds hands were both still glowing green from the previous two necklaces being inserted into the piece. David removed the necklace from the velvet box and carefully slid the blue-lined cylinder into the third hole on the side of the crystal.

The clock hands stopped glowing, then both wound to twelve o' clock. The small device let out a faint ticking sound, and the crystal grew cold in David's hand. An awful feeling struck him, as if he shouldn't have inserted the timepieces into the crystal at all.

Is it a key to something? A bomb? Is it counting down to something, or counting up? I should have waited for Turquoise...

David shoved the crystal into his pocket, knowing he couldn't do anything with it now. He had to return to his parents' house where Carrie was resting and hope with all his heart she was okay. After everything he had done to save her life, he couldn't possibly imagine losing her to the rack matter moving through her system.

David made his way to his sister's bedroom and stood in the doorway for a long minute, staring into the deep darkness. Although he couldn't see his sister's corpse, he could sense her empty shell, dead and soulless, murdered by the hand of the mercenary David knew only as Drather.

I'll get even with you, Drather. When the opportunity presents itself, by the gods, I'll get even with you.

David turned the bedroom light on and examined the mess he had made in his rage. The dresser had been toppled to the ground. Scattered everywhere were his sister's things: picture frames, jewelry boxes, clothes. He lifted the dresser to its upright position against the wall. He collected the picture frames he had broken, setting the pieces across the surface of the dresser, sections of a puzzle he wanted so badly to put right. He placed the jewelry boxes where he remembered they had been, hoping he could put everything in its rightful place, to restore the shrine to its former order before he lost himself to grief.

"I'm sure you have better things to do with your time than make sure your sister's room is put back in tidy order."

David turned to the vaporous man in the red suit and then returned his attention to making sure his sister's things were put back in their place.

"Why are you ignoring me?" Chaos asked. "I thought we had an understanding."

"I've told you my intentions," David said without looking at him. "I'm going to find that book, and I'm going to put a stop to you and whatever else is going on here in Anaisha."

The man in the suit laughed jovially. When he was finished, he wiped an invisible tear from the corner of his eye and shook his head. His white eyes, though translucent-looking, were filled with mischief and danger. "You really know how to bring humor to the situation, you know that, David?"

David placed the last broken picture frame, one housing a photo of David and his sister in their younger years, on the dresser, and then he turned to Chaos.

The man's face turned from silly to serious. "You have no idea what's out there in the world you live in, David. No idea. You think I'm the only one who doesn't want that book found? You think—"

"I don't care!"

Chaos stood still and silent for a moment, seemingly frozen by David's outburst.

"I don't care," David whispered through gnashed teeth, "what the book is for, what it does, who's after it, or anything else for that matter. You had a hand in my sister's death. For that, I'll make sure I find the book you don't want me to find, and I'll use it—somehow—to destroy you."

"Can you hear yourself speak?" Chaos said. "You don't have a clue what you're getting yourself into. You already lost your sister, and there is so much more you can lose before this is over. My advice remains: stop your pursuit of the book and go back home. Mourn your sister's loss. Romance Carrie. Live ever after."

David stared at the picture of him and his sister, tears crawling to the surface of his eyes. In the photo, they were riding in the bed of a green pickup truck together—their grandfather's pickup truck. "You do what you have to, Chaos. I'll make sure I do the same." He slid the photograph into the inside pocket of his black denim coat.

Chaos sighed. "Very well. If this is the way you want it."

"It is." He turned to the man in the red suit but said nothing more.

Chaos nodded, his white eyes shining in the harsh orange bedroom light. "I get it. At least we're on the same page now." He pointed at David as he backed out of the room. "Keep your eyes peeled. The tricks you've seen me pull up to now are nothing compared to what I'm fully capable of."

"You don't frighten me. I've fought worse. I'll continue to fight worse."

Chaos smiled. "Let that passion of yours fan into flames. Let it consume you. And when you're fully lit, when your flame is consuming all your being, that's when I will take you down with one swipe. That's when I will bring you to your knees. I've toppled greater ones than you, David. You mean nothing to me, a mere speck on the timeline of this tragedy called life."

With those final words, Chaos vanished.

David felt a rush of relief when the otherworldly being disappeared from his sight, but he instinctively knew Chaos was still around, lingering in the air much like the scent of gasoline at a pump station.

Something from the corner of his eye drew his attention to the bedroom floor. David knelt down and picked up a small package wrapped in brown packing paper. His own name was written on it in black marker, with, "Love, your sister, Cybil."

David unfolded the paper and found a black leather holster inside, with a note that said:

David, I had a good friend make this for you. It's for your boomerang. Hope you like it.

David set the paper and note on the dresser and put the holster onto his belt. He pulled the small metal bar from his coat pocket and extended it to make his boomerang. Then he slid the metal weapon into the holster. It was a perfect fit, strangely enough, seeing how the metal boomerang was custom made by Professor Grey. *I wonder who made this holster.*

Without actually looking at her, David turned himself toward the bed where his sister's body lay. "You didn't have to do this…but thank you."

"Who's here?" a voice called from the living room.

David peered out the doorway of the bedroom and found Nicolas Rodwick, Cybil Corbin's boyfriend, towering in the front doorway, rubbing his bald head. David took one last look at his sister's room, snapping a final glimpse of it with his mind as one would take a photograph to remember a moment in time. Then he shut the bedroom light off and made his way into the living room, taking another quick snapshot or two of his late sister's place of living.

"What are you doing here?" Nicolas asked. A small welt brandished his right temple. "Where's Cybil?"

Before leaving the apartment, David put his hand on Nicolas's arm and whispered, "Please make sure my family is notified."

Nicolas stared at the bloody bracelets around David's wrist. "Notified of what? Why are you here?"

David headed out of the apartment and along the concrete path leading to the SUV he stole from the mall in Mirana. The snow coating the path to the vehicle felt soft under his feet, and the cold air—having before shut down his senses and memories—now awakened him to the true gravity of his situation. He had to save Carrie. He had to find that book, the Codex of Ra'f. He had to put a stop to everything.

As he opened the door to the stolen SUV, he heard glass shatter in the apartment. He looked up to find Nicolas barreling down the pathway leading to the stolen vehicle. David stood in front of the vehicle and stretched out his arms to catch the man. The force felt like a ton of cinderblocks smashing into his chest as Nicolas slammed David into the hood of the SUV.

Pain shot up David's back to the base of his skull as he hit the vehicle. He felt the surface of the hood bend under the impact.

"You killed her!" Nicolas balled David's shirt in his fists and slammed his body against the vehicle again. The vehicle's hood flexed inward with a loud popping sound.

David kneed Nicolas in the groin and shoved him backwards. Nicolas rebounded and lunged forward, running his fist toward David's face. Shifting inches to one side, David grabbed Nicolas by the arm in the middle of his swing and gave momentum to the man's form, propelling him into the hood. David pressed Nicolas's face against the vehicle. "Why would I kill my own sister?! Huh?!"

Nicolas's eyes reddened with fury and panic. He was in a rage, emotions churning through him so fast, he didn't know what to do with them. David pitied him but pitied himself more. It was *his* sister who died, not just some idiot's blond fantasy.

"What happened?" Nicolas growled, spittle shooting from his mouth onto the bent hood. "Who did this? Who killed her?"

"A man name Drather." David let up on Nicolas.

The man sprung up from the hood, his massive form overshadowing David's. His body trembled, and his fists balled up tight at his sides like wrecking balls. "Who is he? I'll kill him. I'll kill Drather!"

David shook his head and turned toward the vehicle. "Drather is a dangerous man. You'll do well to—"

"I'll kill him! I'll make him pay for what he did."

David entered the vehicle, started the engine, and rolled the window down. Nicolas's face looked like that of a rabies-crazed bulldog, his mouth covered in foamy spit, his eyes bloodshot and full of malice. "You'd be wise to stay away from him."

"You failed to protect Cybil. You should have been here to protect her! The least I can do is make the one who did this pay."

"I suggest you contact my family so they can set up funeral

arrangements."

Nicolas pointed a fat finger at David. "You weren't here when she needed you. All you ever did was accuse her of doing drugs."

David put the vehicle in drive. "Call my mother and let her know what happened."

"Is there something more important than burying your own sister? Huh, hero?!" He pounded his fists on the hood. David stared at him for a long minute before Nicolas finally moved to the side to allow him a clear exit.

David drove out of the parking spot and made his way through the apartment complex, not entirely sure what he felt. *Was it my responsibility to protect her, to watch over my own family, to put them before the rest of the world?* He shook his head. He might have been able to assume Chaos—or Drather—would possibly go after his family at some point, but there was no way to tell. He still wasn't even sure what was going on. And there wasn't anything he could do about his sister's death now. She was dead. Drather killed her, and now it was time to move on.

Carrie was still alive. As was Veronica as far as he knew. He could still protect them. He could still prevent them from coming to the same fate as his sister.

2 A House Divided

The house smelled of orange blossoms and vanilla. It was a scent Carrie Green knew well with all the times she visited David's home in the past. His mother never changed the scent of the house. Counters were populated with vanilla candles, vases were filled with orange blossom reeds. The scent permeated everything in the house, and traces of the scent could (in the past, when he lived here) always be found on David's clothes, or even in his hair.

Now, the scent was soothing, comforting. It was one Carrie had adapted to over the years, one that gave her peace of mind. It was a scent that indicated to her that David was nearby, or that she was someplace that had *some* connection to David.

Even as she lay ill in David's old bed, in what was now the guest room, Carrie felt comforted by the scent of orange blossom and vanilla. Even as black swirls slithered across the skin of her right arm like serpents under thin sheets of foliage, the scent eased her mind, relaxed her soul. The tree was gone—the one that anchored her mind to reality. In her mind, in her personal sanctuary, darkness had come to stay after having consumed everything familiar to her. Even her imaginary version of David was gone, never to return, leaving her on a cliffside that overlooked a canyon of dark fog.

The rack matter—a term the wedges gave to the Legion material moving through her—felt cold and soothing between her flesh and muscle. But she knew the feeling was deceiving. The rack matter wanted nothing more than to control her mind and her spirit, fighting against her every second of every day in hopes of consuming her inner core and corrupting her from within.

She knew very little about the rack matter. The substance had been planted within her body back when she was being held captive in the Complex by Alex Waterford. Carrie was almost certain Alex implanted it within her to control her, but he never had the chance to enact his sinister plans because of Rio's jealousy and David's rescue attempt.

Instead, Carrie was here in David's old house waiting for him to return while she fought against this alien presence in her body. She fought daily within her mind to salvage what was left of her internal sanctuary. She fought against the cold sweats, she fought against the migraines, she fought against the loss of circulation throughout various parts of her body.

She fought, and her will was strong, but she knew even she would eventually tire and succumb to the rack matter if it wasn't stopped soon.

Strangely enough, her arm didn't hurt. If anything, it just felt cold, as if the blood had been chased away by the black ink showing in her skin. Ink. That's what she would refer to it as. She didn't like the term, 'rack.' She didn't like the idea that Legion was trying to use her as its puppet.

She had encountered Legion once already back at Grey's house, when she was with David. Luckily, with David's help, they had escaped.

But how do you escape something *inside* of you, working its way deeper, toying with your mind and your spirit?

Her hope, she decided, would be in David. Her anchor, her oak tree, she needed him now more than ever to keep her rooted, to keep her stable in this chaotic menagerie of events. He was supposed to be here soon…

A slight distortion in the space of the doorway caught Carrie's attention. Serenity, one of the three wedges tasked with 'babysitting' Carrie, stepped across the threshold. All reality around her carried a strange, distorted field, as if when one were looking on her they were looking through slightly maladjusted glass that caught light at all the wrong angles. The effect was supposedly part of her powers, but all Carrie knew she did was heal people. Why would a healer carry a distorted presence around them like that?

Serenity took a seat on the edge of the bed. Her black sweater, black skirt, and the heavy black eyeliner and shadow (which gave her racoon eyes) gave her a very gothic vibe, but the purple streak of hair color running through her bangs added a splash of gaiety to her otherwise dour demeanor. She said very little to Carrie, but her presence instilled some hope that Carrie would be free of the rack matter…at some point. The wedge had a knack for healing, but the rack matter thus far had proven to be incredibly resilient. Serenity had been using her wedge healing powers for hours now but had only managed to slow the spread of rack matter throughout Carrie's body.

The girl adjusted her thick-framed glasses and took hold of Carrie's rack-barraged arm. "Hold still while I try this again." She closed her eyes and massaged Carrie's arm where the inky designs had consumed most of her flesh to give it the illusion of a tattoo sleeve.

Carrie closed her eyes. A vision came to Carrie's mind, a vision of herself on a ledge overlooking a chasm filled with dark mist. When she last put her hand in this mist, the ink had taken over her arm, giving her the marks she now had. She didn't want to touch that dark substance anymore, but it was quickly filling up the sanctuary her mind had created, breaking her will and her spirit.

Her only option was to let it take over, or to leap off the cliff and take refuge in the city she believed hid beneath the dark mist. She wanted to do neither. She wanted David to rescue her.

As Serenity healed her, Carrie took deep breaths and thought of David. He had exited her visions a while ago, never to return. Where had he gone? She hated it when he left both her visions and her real life. She wanted him here, by her side, holding her as she fought against this mystical villain. Together, they could do anything. Apart…she hated being apart from him.

"We have a problem."

Carrie opened her eyes. Turquoise stood in the doorway of the room, her bright pink hair and turquoise-colored eyes lighting up the dim space.

"What is it?" Serenity asked as she continued to massage Carrie's arm. The girl's black-painted nails were sharp and happened to dig into Carrie's skin more than what was comfortable. There was no tenderness with Serenity's touch, nothing sympathetic about it. It was mechanical, the healing act she did to Carrie, and because of that, because she was using a tool that resided within her, it felt like a mechanical procedure, void of caring, void of love.

But what more could Carrie expect? Serenity was a stranger, using her skills to save a life she knew nothing about. Carrie knew she would most likely only get mercy from David.

"Rio," Turquoise answered. "Rio is on her way here."

Serenity grinned, her attention still on her healing act. "So what? Rio is nothing. A nobody."

"She's under the influence of Legion."

Serenity turned her head toward Turquoise. "How do you know that?"

Hammer entered the room, the large, spiked metal hammer on his back scraping against the door frame as he squeezed his mammoth frame through the room's threshold. Carrie felt the hairs on the back of her neck bristle every time he came near her. He was the supposed leader of this group of wedges, but he only acted like a control-freak and not like someone Carrie would want to follow into battle. Why he always wore the hammer on his back, why he always asserted dominance over everyone—even non-wedges, why he always cast derision toward Carrie—it was all beyond her. All she knew was she didn't like him. At all.

"It's true," he said, his deep voice rolling through the room like harsh thunder. He had a long scar running diagonally across both his lips. Carrie wondered where that scar came from. "We've received reports she's carving a path straight for us. She's already destroyed a number of buildings with both the powers Legion has bestowed upon her and her own fire element skills. She must be stopped."

Serenity stood to her feet. Even standing, she barely came up to Turquoise's chest, and with her dark clothing, she resembled a dark elf Carrie remembered seeing pictures of in a fantasy book her dad read to her when she was a little girl:

16

"We should take Carrie and flee," Serenity said.

Hammer shook his head. "No. We need to stay and fight. We need to destroy her."

"We aren't strong enough to stand against Legion," Serenity countered. "Not while we're trying to protect the Key."

Hammer sighed as he ran his fingers through his long, pointy beard.

Carrie also hated his beard.

"I know," Hammer said. "But we have to try."

Turquoise approached the side of the bed, eyeing Carrie. "Why doesn't one of us move her from here while the others distract Rio?"

"That won't work," Hammer answered. "Infused with Legion, Rio will follow after the Key, especially since she has rack matter flowing through her."

Turquoise grabbed Carrie's hand in hers and squeezed it tightly. "Don't worry," she whispered, "I won't let anything happen to you."

"Where's David?" Carrie asked.

"On his way." Turquoise said it with such confidence that Carrie could not bring herself to doubt what she said was actually true. David *was* on his way. But he couldn't get here soon enough.

Carrie stood. Hammer moved as if he were thinking of restraining her, but instead simply adjusted the overalls he wore and grunted. There was an immediate flash of guilt in his eyes, but it quickly fled.

"I'm going to get something to drink," Carrie said as she stared into Hammer's golden eyes. "Is that alright with you?"

Turquoise put her hand on Carrie's shoulder. "I think you should keep resting. I can get you something if you want."

"I'm fine," Carrie snapped. "I don't like being waited on." Her left side suddenly felt as if an ice block were being pressed against it. She lifted her shirt to reveal black swirl marks crawling across her rib cage.

Turquoise said nothing, only stared at the marks with a thoughtful expression.

Carrie dropped her shirt and made her way out of the room. She heard the wedges talking in hushed tones behind her about how she should be resting and how the rack matter wasn't slowing down as much as they had hoped it would with Serenity's healing expertise.

She brushed their comments out of her mind and made her way into the kitchen. She had been to this house many times before and knew where almost everything was, even though the kitchen had been remodeled a number of times over the years. The first time she ever set foot into David's house—back when she and Veronica were just getting to know David—the kitchen had been doused in hideous colors of brown, yellow, and tan. Over the years, through countless revisions, she was happy to say she could stomach the kitchen's colors of light blue, white, and light gray. They were easy on her eyes, and there was something about those colors that seemed to calm her spirit and quiet her soul.

Maybe it was the fact it was *David's* kitchen.

Grabbing a glass from the cabinet, Carrie glanced into the living area and saw the fourth wedge, the one named Velvet, laying on the couch, watching a police drama on the television. Velvet was not a sight to calm Carrie's mind or soul. The woman wore a purple and black leopard-print fur coat, something Carrie would have protested had Carrie had less important things to worry about. She didn't support poaching—

especially the poaching of spotted Moon Cats from Alall. In another time and place, she would have splattered red paint on the hideous coat.

But this wasn't another time or another place. It was here and now. And here in the now, Carrie knew she needed to focus on other things.

She scrounged through the refrigerator until she found a half-emptied carton of orange juice. She poured herself a glass and quickly put the carton back, shutting the fridge door to contain the cold air that made the chill the rack matter inflicted her with even worse.

Turquoise entered the kitchen, staring at Velvet for a few moments, irritation overcoming her face like wildfire in a field of dried corn. She took control of herself and turned her attention quickly to Carrie. "We've decided the best course of action is to stay here and fight Rio when she shows. This is only until David can get here with the timepiece. Once he's here and we have the piece and the necklaces, then we'll head to the Farlands and the Veritas Construct.

Carrie gulped down the orange juice and nodded. "Where is Veronica?"

"I don't know."

Carrie flushed with frustration. If she was going to go through this, if she was going to be used as a key to unlock some powerful artifact that could save their world or destroy it, she wanted her friends by her side.

Hammer entered the kitchen and scolded Velvet for being lazy.

Velvet threw a few choice words his way and shut the television off before joining them. "What's going on?" she asked. "Are we going to fight Rio or are we going to get out of here so we can get our hands on this book?"

"We're going to fight," Hammer answered. "We need to prepare ourselves. There's a basement we can use to keep Carrie safe while we fight. I suggest we move her down there and then figure out what positions everyone is going to take."

"Excuse me?" Carrie said, slamming her glass down on the tile island. "What makes you think I can't fight?"

Hammer chuckled deeply. "You're too important to be fighting. You will stay in the basement with one of us while the rest of us take care of Rio."

"I'm not hiding in the basement while you fight that psycho."

"You'll do as we say," Hammer bellowed.

"No."

His face reddened, and the hairs on his chin snapped to attention, like soldiers in some grand army. "You will!"

"I won't." Carrie felt the cold chill of the rack matter moving to her hip. "You're going to tell me what you want done with the house, and then I'm going to fight by your side."

Hammer's face turned red with fury. He slammed his giant fists on the island, cracking the beautiful tile. "I don't take orders from anyone. Nobody! I am in charge of this mission, and you will do what I tell you to do. You're well-being is our priority."

Carrie fought to control her frustration at the fact that Hammer had the nerve both to tell her what to do and to destroy part of David's home. "Why? Because I'm a key? I want to help you save the world, but I'm not going to take a backseat to it. This ink—or rack matter as you've called it—may be trying to destroy me from within, but I won't go down that easily. And Rio...I owe her for what she did to me in the Complex."

Turquoise glanced at Hammer, raising her eyebrow as if to silently agree with Carrie's determination.

He walked away, grumbling to himself.

Velvet stood with arms crossed, eyes glaring at Carrie. Her purple outfit brought an eyesore of a montage to her purple eyes and purple-streaked hair. "So you really think you can fight, huh?"

"Apparently you don't know what I've been doing most of my life."

"Yes, you think you're a hero. Which is cute, no doubt about that. But I don't think you know what you'll be fighting against this time around. Legion isn't a playground bully. Legion destroys planets and all life along the way."

Carrie stared at the cracks Hammer created in the island tile, her anger building. "Then I'll fight harder than I've ever fought before."

3

Overprotective

David pulled the SUV into the driveway of his parents' house and shut the engine off. Once the heater clicked off, the cold winter air rushed in through the air vents, chilling him. He embraced the cold as he stared out the windshield at Turquoise, who sat on the iron bench David's mother had installed near the front door. Turquoise wore the same black t-shirt and black pants she had been wearing the last time David had seen her. She had her legs crossed and her head in her hands. *Probably tired,* David thought. *Probably as tired as I am.*

Thoughts of his sister flooded through his mind, memories from yesteryear, when he and his sister considered one another to be friends. He couldn't connect that time to now. There was no bridge to link their happy-go-lucky relationship with the tumultuous division that had plagued them over the last couple years. At some point, a barrier had been placed between them, and they both had allowed it to remain there for reasons beyond him.

Now Cybil Corbin was gone. There would be no chance

at reconciliation. There would be no restoration of a relationship he couldn't make real sense of.

David found tears streaming from his eyes. He reached into the glove compartment and used fast food napkins to blow his nose and wipe his tears, but it did nothing to stop the sorrow that suddenly racked his heart and pushed him into full-blown sobbing.

David fell asleep in his tears, waking to the light tapping of pink-painted fingernails against nearly frozen glass. David's mind felt clogged, foggy, and he fought to come back to reality. When he did, he faced the startling realization that his sister was dead.

He turned toward the window and saw Turquoise's worried face staring back at him, her bright-colored eyes pleading with him to get out of the vehicle.

He made sure the sleeve of his coat covered the wounds in his right wrist, and then he stepped out of the SUV and into a thin layer of snow that coated the driveway. The whole front yard was blanketed in white splendor. He recalled a cold, winter morning many years earlier, when he and his sister built a snowman in this yard…

"Hey," Turquoise mumbled tiredly.

He scanned the area for the other wedges, the ones who had sent him on the horrific mission to find the third necklace.

"Did you get the necklace?"

David nodded. "I did. I put it in the timepiece, and now the clock is ticking away."

Turquoise put her hand to her left temple. "I wish I knew what that thing did."

David shrugged. "Where's Carrie? Is she alright?"

"She's inside. She seems to be doing fine. She's holding

back the rack matter."

"Let's get her and get going. I want to end this."

"Well…" Turquoise's eyes shifted, and she gave a heaving sigh that made her entire chest practically levitate. "Rio is on her way here. With Legion. Hammer suggested we stay and fight."

"I don't really care what Hammer suggested. I'm done taking orders from nobodies."

Turquoise stared into his face for a moment and then narrowed her eyes on him. "What's the matter? Why were you crying?"

"My sister is dead. Drather killed her."

Turquoise cupped her hands over her mouth.

"I don't want sympathy, Turquoise. I want to get Carrie and this timepiece to wherever we're going and finish this. Get the book, destroy Chaos, save the world…and Carrie." He walked past Turquoise and headed toward the front door of the house.

"David, I'm on your side," Turquoise shouted before he entered the house. Once inside, he darted toward the bedroom he had last seen Carrie in. He found her alone, sitting on the edge of the bed, tying her sneakers.

She glanced up at him and then hopped off the bed, engulfing him in a hug. "I missed you," she whispered in his ear. Her warm breath breathed life into his cold bones.

"I missed you too." Tears filled his eyes as he rested his chin on her head and stared at the floral painting on the wall behind her. The death of his sister hit him with a force so strong he nearly melted in Carrie's arms. He refused to pull away from her until he could get control of his emotions. He didn't want her seeing him cry. Not right now.

Dizziness overtook him and threatened to drag him to the floor, but he fought to stand, fought against the nearly insurmountable grief that seized his every fiber. He remembered the way his sister stood up for him in middle school, like she was the hero of their story. She always wanted to be the hero, always wanted to be the one in the spotlight. David took that from her, stole it like a thief steals a rare, sparkling gemstone.

It was just another load of guilt he could place on his shoulders now that she was gone.

"You okay?"

Carrie's voice chased the guilt away, and he found himself easing into the comfort of her tone. "I'll be fine."

He felt her fingers skate around the nape of his neck. "I know what that means."

"Leave it be." He hated saying it, but he couldn't possibly face this right now. It wasn't the time to deal with his grief. Not yet.

He felt her fingers rake the hair at the back of his head. "I will. For now. Just know I'm here for you."

It took all his strength to fight back the tears.

When he pulled away, he grabbed Carrie's face in his hands and kissed her on the lips. The warm pleasure filled his senses and eclipsed his uncontrollable sorrow for a moment, freezing time, halting his sadness. He reached behind her neck and pulled her into him, into the kiss, and he felt the passion raging all around them, warming them like a space heater.

They separated, and Carrie had a starstruck twinkle in her eye and a small grin forming in the corner of her mouth. "That's quite a hello," she said, blushing.

David forced himself to smile. Thoughts of his sister careened into his mind, but he fought them off with thoughts of Carrie, of the future he wanted to have with her. "Let's go."

"What?"

"Turquoise says Rio is on her way here. I have the time-piece, so we should get out of here and get that book so you can be healed."

Carrie took a seat on the edge of the bed and crossed her arms over her chest, her long brown hair spilling around her face. He noticed she was wearing his black Lysallis High School sweatshirt with a print of their school mascot, a tiger, on the front. He remembered buying the sweatshirt his senior year. "I don't want to flee, David. I want to fight."

He took a deep breath before he said, "Are you kidding me?"

She shook her head and looked up at him with shards of fierce determination in her emerald eyes. "I want to fight. I owe Rio for what she did to me in the Complex. And if we don't fight her now, we'll just have to fight her later."

"We can get to the book before she catches up to us. We can use it to destroy her."

"You don't know that. She could stab us in the back when we're not expecting it. I *want* to fight her. I want to put a stop to her once and for all. And I want to stop Legion…"

David took a seat on the edge of the bed next to her. He took her silky and cold hands in his. "I don't want you getting hurt."

"I know you don't, David. But you can't protect me from everything. I am a big girl. I can handle myself in a battle. I need you to help me with this. I need you to help me stop her."

Looking into her tearing eyes, looking deep into her soul, he saw a fighter—one he hadn't seen in many months—clawing for the surface, yearning to get out.

"Fine."

It wasn't until she bit her lower lip that he realized she was using her thumb to rub the wounds in his wrist. "What is this?" she asked as she pulled his sleeve back, exposing the red crisscross lines embedded in his skin.

David pulled his sleeve down and stood up.

She looked up at him, her eyes glistening. "What happened at the mall?" She reached for his hand, but he pulled away.

"No. Not now."

"Why?"

"Because you want to fight. So we'll fight. And then we'll leave this place for good."

4
Rio

The shrill sirens of emergency vehicles woke David from deep sleep. He shot up in the bed, but quickly calmed himself after realizing Carrie was asleep next to him, her cold legs entwined with his. He calmed his breathing and lay back against the pillow. Carrie's warm breath fell on his cheek, and her shallow breathing played a make-believe melody in his ears. It was a moment he never thought he would ever get to spend with Carrie, to be in her embrace this way. He closed his eyes and blocked out the rest of the world, demanding fate or the gods or whomever or whatever was in control of their lives to allow him this moment, to give him this passage in time for all the good he had done. He earned it. He deserved it.

He remembered a time when Carrie ran to his house after school one day. She had a black eye, and she claimed Sylest had given it to her when Carrie refused to mark out the "Save the Whales" artwork she had sketched on her binder. Instead of running home to her mother, Carrie ran to David, ran to his embrace, black eye and all. He hugged her for what felt like years, too many years to count. In her embrace, he felt whole, he felt normal.

Normal like he felt right now.

Thunder rumbled outside, the sound moving through his bones, traveling to his core where it dispersed into a strange form of comfort that could only come from nature. He waited for rain but heard no drops echoing off the roof. Only thunder. And more thunder.

He opened his eyes and sat up. He found Carrie staring up at him, her mossy green eyes wide open, both streaked with black spots.

"What's wrong with your—"

The bedroom door opened, and Turquoise poked her head inside. "We need everyone outside."

David looked upon Carrie again, but this time her eyes were a normal shade of green, void of the speckles he had seen only moments earlier. She smiled warmly and stretched her blackened arms over her head.

David slid out of the bed and followed Turquoise to the foyer. "There's something seriously wrong with Carrie."

Turquoise said nothing at first, only opened the front door, slowly, deliberately. She turned toward him before stepping outside, her gaze darkened by despair. "I know. Serenity has been doing as much as she can for her, pushing back against the Legion moving through her system. But…"

David's focus was no longer on Turquoise, but on the blackened sky outside. He shoved Turquoise aside to get through the doorway, and he made his way onto the driveway, where Hammer, Velvet, and Serenity all stood, staring up at the expanse. Dark storm clouds had collected directly above them, and peels of thunderous white lightning scattered through them like streams of water from a fountain, bouncing back and forth from cloud to cloud.

Although they were surrounded by a blanket of snow on the ground, the air around them suddenly felt musty and warm.

"Something is up there," Turquoise whispered from behind David.

"I sense…I sense Legion," Serenity said.

Velvet raised her arms up in the air and closed her eyes. A stream of bright purple light fled from her fingertips and created a large dome over the property the house sat on. When she opened her eyes, David noticed they were glowing violet. "This should protect us."

David fled into the house to check on Carrie. He found her writhing in the bed, her eyes rolling into the back of her head, her teeth clacking like the fast ticking of a broken clock. David rushed to her side, but she shoved her arms out, striking him in the chest, propelling him through the doorway. He landed on his back on the hard hallway tile, the impact scattering pain throughout his spine and ribs.

"David Corbin of Anaisha!" a voice called out. It was female in tone, and it seemed to echo out from Carrie's vicinity, but it did not have the melodious tone of Carrie's own voice. "David Corbin of Anaisha, you must fl-lee this pl-lace! We must fl-lee this pl-lace. If they find us, we will not survive. I will not survive."

David got to his feet, his back sore. He cautiously entered the room.

Carrie sat straight up on the edge of the bed, the whites of her rolled eyes staring directly at him. Her lips did not move when the voice slipped from her throat. "Pl-lease. Trust me."

30

"Who are you?" he whispered hoarsely.

"I will explain those things later. Right now, we m-must leave this pl-lace before Legion find us."

David stood in the doorway, blocking exit from the room. "I'm not allowing you to go anywhere until you tell me who you are."

"My name is Viranda DelaCourte. I used to be a part of Legion."

David stomped his foot on the floor. "And you want me to trust you?"

"I will give you Carrie back, David Corbin of Anaisha, as a sign of my loyalty to you. If I am taken from her, I will die unless I have another host. Please, understand that I do not want to possess her body. I was set into her by Ryc Waterford. I had no choice in the matter. But now I need your help. You need my help. Together, we can put a stop to Legion. To all of this."

Carrie tipped to the side, her head crashing into the pillow. The whites of her eyes rolled back, and her emerald-green gaze met his once again. She sat up, slowly, holding the side of her head. "What…"

David grabbed her hand and yanked her to her feet. "We have to go. Now!" He ushered her weak form through the hallway and out the front door. The sky was still dark as ever, but the glow from Velvet's violet-colored shield lit up their end of the street.

Turquoise glanced over her right shoulder enough to see David and Carrie, but said nothing.

Serenity approached Carrie, who was holding onto David's arm for support. "Let me heal you again."

Carrie nodded as she took a seat on the iron bench. Serenity took a seat next to her and started to rub Carrie's blackened

31

arms. David watched as the inky splotches slithered across Carrie's skin like vaporous snakes.

"The sky is like that because of Legion," Serenity said.

"Great," David muttered.

Serenity glared at him through her thick-framed glasses. "That's not the worst of it. I sensed a disturbance, something broken in the near distance. A seal."

"A seal? A seal to what?" He glanced over at Hammer and Velvet, who were in the midst of whispering to one another.

Turquoise turned toward David, her jaw set. "You ready to fight?"

"Fight? Rio?"

Turquoise shook her head. "Not just Rio. We're about to be attacked by a wave of demons as well."

David realized Velvet's shield was no longer up over the property. "Velvet needs to put that shield back up."

"She can't keep that up forever." Turquoise took David by the arm and moved him to the side, out of earshot of Hammer and Velvet. "I've never fought Legion before. Not before the Complex. I'm only familiar with what the other wedges have told me and what I've read in books. My assumption is that Rio, possessed by Legion, will command an army of demons to march against us. Her whole intent—Legion's intent—is to destroy us."

David reached his gloved hand to the holster on his right hip and slid out his metal boomerang. "I can fight."

Carrie stared at the boomerang, a lost look in her eyes.

Turquoise nodded. "Carrie needs a weapon too, if she's going to fight."

"What kind of weapon?" he asked as he slid his boomerang back in its holster.

"The demons hate fire," Serenity stated as she continued to rub Carrie's arms. "They can easily be destroyed with guns."

"My dad has a pistol in his bedroom," David offered. "It's locked in a case, but I think I know the combination."

Serenity nodded her approval of his idea. "Velvet can use her shield, for a little while. Turquoise has her shield as well. We'll do what we have to in order to keep Legion and Rio away from Carrie."

David entered the house and made his way to the master bedroom which sat to the right of the stairs that led to the basement. The room was nearly pitch black thanks to the thick blankets his mother had hung from the curtain rods over the room's windows to keep the sunlight out. She suffered from constant migraines, and sometimes the sunlight made things worse for her.

He opened the bedroom closet and flipped on the light switch inside. On the floor, near a laundry basket full of small pillows, sat a stack of blankets. He slid his hand into the middle of the stack and pulled out a silver gun case which he set on the floor.

The crackling sound startled David, causing him to turn and look back at the window to the side yard. The blanket covering it caught fire and disintegrated into a pile of ashes. The window was gone, and in the new hole in the wall hovered a woman in a tattered red dress. Her hair blazed the colors of fire, and her grin was full of sparkling white teeth that nearly blinded him when he looked upon them.

"David Corbin," she said as she floated into the room. When she reached the king-sized bed, she took a seat in the center of it, cross-legged.

"Rio," he grumbled as he stood to his feet and stepped out

of the closet.

She nodded, her ruby-red eyes glistening with fire. "Yes. Rio. Rio's body, anyway. And her mind. Inside though…inside this vessel resides pure Legion."

"Legion."

"I like how you say my name. *Our* name."

David turned back into the closet and picked up the gun case.

Rio tilted her head to the side. "That will do you no good against me."

"Maybe," he replied as he set the case down on the edge of the bed and proceeded to punch in the combination. "Maybe not."

"Maybe not," she corrected him. "You are one of the more intelligent humans I have come across, but you are still so naïve."

David took a few steps toward the door, hoping to get the gun to Carrie and bring Turquoise back in here to do away with Rio once and for all. After he took his third step, the door slammed shut and the doorknob lit up orange and melted.

He turned his face toward Rio, but kept his body positioned in front of the door.

Rio shook her head. "No. No, David. I want to talk to you alone, without interruption. *We* want to talk to you alone."

"We?"

"Legion is one. And many. You know very little about us, but we know very much about you. About you humans, anyway."

David wondered if he could make a run for the hole in the wall. Even if he could though, he would still have to jump the wall to get to the front where Carrie and the rest of his allies were. He doubted Rio would allow him to do that.

"Instead of trying to escape, could you just hear me out?" she pleaded.

34

"I already heard you out at Grey's house."

Rio tilted her head to the side, a thoughtful look on her face. "Grey's house? Hmmm. I do not recall a conversation with you at Grey's house. I wonder if you ran across one of my rogue brethren. Regardless, I want to speak to you. Please, sit." Rio waved her hand toward the end of the bed.

David figured he had no choice but to comply. He couldn't get the gun case open in time to use the weapon against Rio, and he wasn't all that sure his boomerang would do him any good against her.

He took a seat on the edge of the bed, gripping the gun case close to his chest.

Rio smiled at this. "You humans cherish your weapons so very much, don't you? You think they give you power when really all they do is help you destroy yourselves."

David set the case on the bed next to him.

"That's better. First, you should feel privileged that we choose to speak to one as low as you. Humans are disgusting, revolting, and hopeless."

"Thanks," David said, adding a bit of sarcasm to his voice. He wondered if Rio was simply buying time so the demon army that Turquoise spoke of would be able to get here.

"Legion has been around for a very, very long time. Very long time. Almost too long for you humans to comprehend. And since I—we've—been around, we have sought to take the universe as our own. And we will, very soon. There aren't many planets left that we haven't swallowed, not many species we haven't eliminated to extinction. The few that are left—including the human race—isn't enough to stop us, even if all of you allied together to come against the great and powerful Legion."

"Are you telling me this for your own ego?"

Rio grinned. "You are such an interesting human. You stare in the face of Legion and you do not falter. Your courage—or ignorant resolve—is somewhat impressive."

Impatience filled his gut. Carrie was on the other side of the door, and the other wedges were planning their defense against the demon army that was supposedly making its way toward them. He didn't have time to sit and have teatime with this otherworldly entity.

Rio frowned and swung her legs over the edge of the bed, barely touching the floor with her sandaled feet. "You have no interest in what I say?"

"No, I don't."

"Then I will cut to the chase." A playful sparkle filled her eyes. "Come with me."

"What?"

"Come with me." Rio stood to her feet and held her hand out. "Come with me, David. Come and be a companion to me. Travel with me throughout the galaxy, help me destroy the remnant of Creation."

David slowly stood to his feet, grabbing the case on his way up. He stared at Rio's welcoming hand a few feet between them and thought carefully how to word his response. She could light him up like a birthday candle in a snap if she wanted to. He decided he would attempt to reach the hole in the wall behind her to escape, but it would be a risk.

"I…appreciate…the offer, but I'm going to have to decline."

Rio stepped closer, wringing her hands in front of her chest. "I…I would really like you to come with me." Rio's voice had a more melodious tone to it. He wondered if it was really her talking now and not the entity that possessed her.

"I can't."

"Why not? I would like some companionship. I would like someone with me when I travel through the universe. I fear it may be lonely."

David sighed. "I can't. Sorry." He glanced out the hole in the wall. A warm breeze blew into the room.

Rio's eyebrows turned inward. "You deny me what I want? What I desire?"

"I just—"

"Fool." The melodious tone was gone from her voice and in its place lay a strong, deep current clearly rooted in her growing anger. "Do you not believe I can destroy worlds? Do you not believe that I am one with Legion and can topple empires with the power of the flame? Legion has promised me I can do these things. I *will* be the most powerful human ever used by Legion, and all races and all beings will bow to my great status!"

"I have no doubt that you are powerful. But—"

"There is no but!" she snapped. She cupped her hands in front of her and formed a bright, hot fireball. "I will destroy you! If you are not with me, you are against me, and I will destroy all who come against Rio and the great Legion!"

Laughter, faint but distinct, echoed from the other side of the hole in the wall.

Rio grinned, extinguishing the fireball in a puff of smoke. "I will enjoy this, David. You have refused my offer of alliance. You have refused my offer of companionship. For your refusal, you will perish at the hands of the Dark Army. All of you will perish."

Rio lifted into the air and floated out through the hole in the wall.

David set the case on the bed and entered the code to unlock it. Inside, he found a black semi-automatic pistol and three magazines of ammunition. He loaded the gun, shoved the magazines of ammunition into his pockets, and then climbed through the hole in the wall to the front lawn.

He froze when he saw small figures scurrying through the street toward them from all directions.

Rio hovered near the top of Velvet's purple dome while Hammer, Velvet, and Turquoise took position underneath it. Carrie sat on the bench, Serenity healing her.

Rio touched her hand to the surface of the dome as a static ripple broke across the surface and the shield dropped completely. She looked down at David, a wicked grin splashed across her face, and then rose into the air, vanishing into the darkened sky.

The creatures drew closer to the house, stumbling across the driveway, most in a stupor of sorts. Whatever they were—demons or not—they didn't look friendly. They were small, with pink-colored flesh, and bright red eyes that glowed like embers. They were greatly different from the demon-hybrid David and Turquoise had dealt with, as Officer Thana had been a full-grown adult, with terrifying features that still sent chills down David's spine. These seemed infant in comparison, and seemingly harmless.

When some of them spotted David on the lawn, they smiled, their mouth full of sharp teeth. Three or four of them squealed with laughter, and the sound ran across the back of David's mind like a rake.

David drew the gun up and fired off a few shots. The gun kicked a little in his hands as he hadn't fired a gun in a while. Two or three of his bullets hit one of the creatures, blasting part of its face in a splash of blood and gore across the driveway. The small beast fell to the ground, its hands—with sharp claws attached—waving through the air. David fired off a few more shots, hitting another creature in the legs, blowing them out from under the creature as its abdomen fell to the ground. The creature hissed and spat as it attempted to drag itself across the pavement. Another bullet into its head killed it.

David rushed to Carrie's side, tossing the gun in her lap. She looked at it, bewildered for a split second, then lifted it in her hand as David helped her to her feet, pulling her away from Serenity.

"What are you doing?" the wedge asked. "I'm not finished healing her."

"From what it sounds like, you'll never be finished. We have to get out of here."

Serenity reached out to grab Carrie's arm, but David quickly pulled Carrie to the side, out of Serenity's reach. "I don't think so."

Serenity scowled, the hostile raccoon-like features of her face becoming more prominent. "You can't stop me from healing her! The Legion within her will take over completely, and then what are you going to do to save her? She needs my help."

"Later," David growled as he pulled Carrie toward the driveway.

"Later may be too late."

David found the other three wedges fighting the horde that had quickly filled the street. Demons surrounded the perimeter of the house, but few made it to the driveway thanks to Hammer's massive weapon and the purple bubbles that Velvet used to send the demons floating away.

Turquoise was in the middle of firing her pulse pistol at the demons who were scurrying up the driveway when she noticed David and Carrie. "Nice of you to join the party."

David pulled his boomerang from its holster and tossed his weapon through the air, slicing through the pink creatures as blood splattered across the landscaping.

The weapon returned to his hand, covered in red slime.

Hammer used his strength to tip over the SUV, creating a makeshift barrier that Carrie knelt behind. David noticed her hands trembling slightly, in particular her right hand—the one with the gun—but he said nothing about it. She wanted this, wanted to fight, and he would help her do just that. She was probably right anyway about Rio needing to be destroyed here and now.

He glanced up into the darkened sky and wondered if they would even be able to reach her way up there. He shook his head and told himself that their first priority had to be this horde. David peered around the end of the tipped car and counted at least a dozen of the hideous-looking creatures advancing up the driveway.

Hammer strolled out in front of the vehicle barrier and swung his massive hammer at anything he could. Demon heads rolled, body parts flew, but the creatures continued to come, pouring down the streets like a flood.

"We have to help him," Carrie whispered. "We have to help Hammer or he'll be overrun. Then those things will overrun us, and then it will be game over."

"I know." He still wanted nothing more than to get them out of here and to someplace safe. Instead, he nodded to her and then bolted up from behind the car. Carrie followed, firing the gun, sending bullets smacking off the pavement. David's boomerang twirled through the air and sliced through the neck of one of the little creatures, decapitating it. His boomerang returned to him, and he noticed Velvet erecting another shield over the property.

Carrie moved in front of David, firing off a shot that went straight through a demon's chest, blowing it into pieces. Another shot passed through a demon's head, and its body fell to the ground, a stumbling block for the next demon in line.

A purple shield rose up from the driveway and created a dome over them. Serenity rushed to Hammer and whispered something in his ear. He swung at another demon or two, and then he glanced around at those who fought with him.

David spun the boomerang at three demons who were stumbling up the driveway from where the shield had erected. The metal curvature broke through their necks, splattering blood through the air as the weapon returned to David's gloved hand safely.

Turquoise mowed down a group of demons with her pulse pistol, blue pulses of light scattering through the air.

Carrie's dead aim destroyed a half dozen more.

But they continued to advance. Some attempted to climb the shield, only to slide down its surface, demon tongues lolling about in a silly scene of ridiculous humor. When they realized they could not climb up the shield individually, they began to climb atop one another, working their way up to the top of the dome.

The demons smothered the dome in bodies, until the property and the rest of the neighborhood could no longer be seen by those under its temporary refuge.

"Do it!" Hammer shouted.

Serenity nodded.

"Do what?" David asked. He watched as the air around Serenity distorted. She reached into the pocket of her black sweater and pulled out what looked to be a yellow piece of chalk. She used the chalk to start drawing circles around each of them—

41

starting with Hammer. David glanced up at the top of the dome as the demons covered the last surface area of the shield, encasing them in nothing but purple light. Fear settled into David's spirit. Darkness filled his mind, and he could suddenly think of nothing else than to end his own life. He pulled the sleeve up of his right arm and felt the fresh wounds in his wrist.

Carrie glanced down at his arm but said nothing.

David wondered what kind of strange afterlife he would enter into if he ended things on his own terms. He heard once, from someone in his family, that if one took their own life, then they were destined to perish in the Depths forever, instead of in the Sanctuary of the Gods. David had no desire whatsoever to reside in the Depths for all eternity, but neither did he want to endure whatever fresh nightmare was brewing here on Anaisha. To have to fight the darkness while watching the woman he loved succumb to the same darkness was nearly unbearable.

Carrie pulled his sleeve down, covering the wounds. "Focus," she whispered.

David looked into her eyes—her emerald-green eyes—and saw Carrie in there. The Carrie he loved. The Carrie he knew.

He looked up and saw that Serenity had nearly finished drawing circles around the other wedges and was now at David and Carrie. She drew a perfect circle around David's feet, and a perfect circle around Carrie's. David glanced over Serenity's shoulder and noticed the circles around each person were about the same, however, the circles around Velvet and Hammer were more crudely done, sloppy and crooked in their circumference. It was a minor observation, but one that David took note of nonetheless.

David could hear cracking from the top of the dome. He glanced up and noticed the purple light flickering, the dome fading.

Serenity stood in front of David and drew a near perfect circle around her own feet, keeping perfect eye contact with him as she did it. Her stare was unsettling and full of guilt, a guilt David wouldn't understand until later.

Yellow light rose up from the chalk lines, surrounding each person in a column that spirited them far away from the onslaught.

5 Another Time Or Place

When David opened his eyes, he found himself on his back, dust particles lingering in the air above his face. His back ached, and his head throbbed. He sat up slowly, dazed and confused. He remembered Serenity drawing yellow chalk circles around everyone and the demons overtaking the house. He remembered being pulled violently away from all of that, and then he subsequently blacked out.

"Is everyone okay?" Turquoise called from the left of him.

He stood to his feet, wobbling a bit, and then braced himself against a brick wall. His lungs burned as if he had inhaled car exhaust. "Where...Where are we?" He looked down and saw Carrie coming to consciousness on a patch of asphalt, her eyes fluttering to life. Serenity lay still next to her.

David looked up and took in their surroundings, his vision somewhat blurry from whatever Serenity had done to them. By the black asphalt and faded white stripes, he could tell they were in a parking lot. He turned toward the wall he had been leaning against and found an old building, possibly a grocery or department store. A tilted and faded sign on the side read Walmart, but David had never heard of such a place. The sign was aged by years and sun, and looked to be barely affixed to the wall.

Desert and mountains cradled them in a circle, all the color of worn brick. The sky was an ugly tint of orange, and David couldn't tell if the sun was setting or rising as it hovered above the horizon. The air was strangely cold but held a humidity that made it seem warm at the same time.

Turquoise strode toward him, her namesake eyes alight and full of power. "It seems Serenity teleported us somewhere, but I have no idea where."

Carrie scratched at her arms and glanced at Serenity who lay passed out on the concrete. "What happened to her?" She bent down and put her hand on the Wedge's forehead. "She's burning up."

Turquoise knelt near Serenity's body and examined her for a moment. "I'm not sure. I've never seen her use this power before. I'm glad she did though, otherwise we would have been torn to pieces by those demons."

"What do we do?" Carrie asked. "We're in the middle of nowhere." She spun around, searching, and then added, "And where are the other Wedges?"

"I don't know," Turquoise answered, her eyes narrowing upon the mystery. "I say we stay put until Serenity comes to, then we can find out where she teleported us…if she even knows."

David rubbed his eyes, wiping the last of the blurriness from them. Then he let out an irritated sigh. "This is ridiculous. The plan was to get Carrie and the timepiece to that temple and find that stupid book."

"It's not a stupid book," Turquoise snapped.

"Yeah, I know. It's supposed to save the world. If that's the

45

case, then why aren't we going after it? Instead, we wasted our time trying to fight Rio and those creatures she summoned."

"She didn't summon them. They were always there, Legion just unsealed them."

David's eyes widened with rage. "Who cares where those things came from?! The fact is, the whole plan already went to crap, and we didn't even get out of Lysallis. Tria'na!" he cursed.

"Can we please stop arguing," Carrie growled, her glare set on David. "We've been doing what we've needed to do. Rio needed to be stopped."

"But she wasn't stopped," he barked. "She's still out there, burning the world, wreaking who-knows-what havoc with those demons."

"And we're here!" Carrie squealed. "This is where we're at, so we need to make the best of it. Okay? I've never known you to be so selfish and self-centered. I know you care about me, but this is getting ridiculous. The world is at stake right now, and you keep tossing that fact to the side like it means nothing to you."

"It means nothing to me!" David yelled back, his lungs aching with the stress. "You're all that matters to me. Do you understand that? Can you wrap your head around that for a moment? I risked life and limb to rescue you from that Complex! I just want time for you and me. Time that I never had when all of us were together. I am so sick of having to save someone or something or the world or whatever. Sick of it!"

Carrie closed the distance between her and David and grabbed his trembling hands in hers. "I know," she started softly, "that you care deeply for me." The emeralds in her eyes had lost some of their fire and grown dim, like a campfire having sand poured upon it. "I know that you love me. I've always

46

known that on some level. Right now, we can love each other and still try to help Turquoise find this book that can help Anaisha. Together, we can do this."

"Together? You mean you, me, and that-that-that thing inside of you? Nobody can tell me what is going on around here. Nobody can tell me anything about Legion except that it's here to destroy the world." He pulled the crystal timepiece from his jacket pocket. "Nobody can tell me what this stupid thing does." He shoved it back in his pocket and turned away from Carrie. "And nobody can tell me why you're so integral to saving this planet."

Carrie threw her hands up. "Well, I don't have those answers for you. I really don't. I'm just going with the flow, like you. At least we have one another, right? I mean, we're still together, aren't we?"

He nodded but refused to turn and face her. He looked up and saw Turquoise, arms crossed, staring at him with a look that was a cross between pity and irritation.

Carrie drew close to his back and took hold of his right hand. "Just take a minute to breathe, okay? We're together right now, you and me. Enjoy it. Please. Gods know I'm trying to. Despite…Despite whatever this is inside of me."

He turned his head halfway toward her. "I'm sorry." Then he turned to Turquoise. "To both of you."

Turquoise shrugged. "Let's just focus on getting some answers from Serenity when she wakes. I'm betting she can teleport us back once she comes to."

"I hope so," he muttered.

Carrie let go of his hands and turned toward the grocery mart. "I wonder if we should move her in there. Might be safer."

Turquoise nodded toward the horizon. "That may be a

good idea. I'm not sure where we are, and we don't know what's out there in the desert."

David looked out on the horizon. It looked fake, like a cartoon painting. Something in the air didn't feel right—felt off—but he couldn't place what. And there was a scent in the stillness, stale, but somewhat sweet, like nothing David could compare it to. He glanced up at the grocery store. "I'll head inside and make sure it's safe."

Carrie nodded, the formation of a small grin blossoming in the corner of her mouth. "We'll wait here and keep an eye on Serenity."

David headed toward the store, his mind reeling with confusion and a multitude of strategies, his heart reeling with anger and impatience.

Before he entered the store, David glanced out at the mountains once more. He wondered if they could be in the Wastelands, but he couldn't remember there being mountains that color when he was in the Wastelands last. Nor did he remember the desert being this empty. No vegetation. No air-filtration machines. No anything. Just sand, mountains, and an ugly orange sky. The parking lot under their feet seemed to stretch out forever, with no visible end in either direction, save for the uncanny mountain and desert landscape. Nor were any cars present in the lot, just crumbling cement pylons and bent, haggard-looking street lamps.

He glanced up at the building. *And this store.* Up close, the Walmart store sign looked worn and damaged by something other than the sun—fire. Char marks scorched the outer edges of the giant sign, but the rest of the exterior of the building looked untouched by a flame of any sort.

David approached the double doors to the mart and

glanced over his shoulder to Carrie and Turquoise near the corner of the wall. He was hesitant to leave them out here on their own, but if he didn't secure the store, night would fall without them having any shelter.

He moved forward and the double doors slid open with a screech. David stepped across the threshold, and through the dormant metal detectors, his hand resting on the boomerang at his side. The building was dark, save for a soft orange glow slipping through the doors he passed through. The fragments of light revealed swirls of dust that shot up from the floor with David's movements. He felt as if he was doing more than disturbing the dust—he was disturbing time. He was disturbing something that he had no right to disturb.

Could Serenity have transported us in time? Or is this just another place? What if it's an in-between?

He could only go as far as the light that stretched through the doors, as the rest of the place was wrapped in pitch black void. He could see the cracked tiles under his feet. He stopped, wondering if he should get Turquoise to help him venture deeper.

A loud crackling sound echoed from in front of him, and a bright blue light lit up what he could now see were register lanes.

"It's me, David," a hoarse female voice called out.

David watched as the blue light moved from the register lanes toward him. A figure in a gray cloak stepped out of the mist of light, electricity arcing from her frame.

"Vector."

She nodded.

"I haven't seen you—"

She put her hand up to stop him. As she drew closer, he saw that her hands were covered in black gloves, and her arms were wrapped in black cloth. "Please, I don't have much time.

Don't speak until I have said what needs to be said."

He nodded, leaning against an empty wall to his left. Sheets of paper lined the wall. Vector stopped within feet of him, illuminating the area around them, revealing the papers to be missing person posters. So many of them…

He fought the urge to peek under the hood of Vector's cloak, knowing very well that she had no intention of revealing her identity to him.

"I've done what I've been able to in order to assist you in your ventures," she said. Her voice was a bit rasp, and her breathing was loud and labored. "I helped you capture Big and the rest of his goons, but there's something greater at stake now."

"Yeah, everyone keeps saying that."

"Are you going to listen or talk? You can really only do one or the other. I didn't come here to hear you whine. I came here to give you direction."

He sighed. "I'll listen. I'm sorry."

"You're not, though. I know you, David. I know you have your own agenda. Now, you will have to pick. If you want to save the future, you'll have to pick *your* agenda or *my* direction." She was an inch or so shorter than him, and he wondered if she still wore the ring he had seen on her finger the first day she revealed herself to him. "Anaisha is going to perish. I know this because I was there when another planet, Earth, perished many, many years ago."

"Earth?"

She nodded. "The history of what happened on Earth is vital in that it reveals what will happen here if you don't act quickly."

"What do I have to do?"

She grunted. "You don't *have* to do anything. Remember, I am an agent of free will. I've never forced my plans on you, nor will I now. But I will give you warning that if you don't follow my direction to the finest detail, there may be nothing left of Anaisha in the future."

"Is this about Legion?"

"Yes. And more than just Legion. The dark army. They must be destroyed."

"I met Legion at Professor Grey's house and—"

"I said listen!" Vector snapped, sucking in a wheezing breath. "Listen with your ears, not your mouth. I don't care what you *think* you know about Legion. All of what is happening is so far above you. You must listen to me and stop relying on your own knowledge.

"Legion is here. So is the dark army. Finding the Codex that Turquoise is leading you to is essential, but that is not the path you need to take."

"What?"

"You need to go a separate way. Apart from the way Carrie is fated to go."

He shook his head.

"Don't speak," Vector scolded. "Put your emotions to the side and listen. You must head to Raveack. Look for a girl named Eden. Do not let anyone or anything stand in your way of finding her."

"Raveack? I've never even heard of the place."

"It's in the east. As soon as Serenity teleports you back to your reality, you must head to Raveack immediately. It would be wise to take Veronica and Sean with you."

"Sean?"

Vector nodded. "He can help you, David. Much more than he was able to in the past."

David glanced toward the floor. The woman's blue glow

51

illuminated a colored ad of some sort.

"David?"

He looked up at her, stared into the darkness of her hood.

"Do you trust me?"

He nodded.

"Do you trust me?"

"Yeah. Yes."

"I know you don't really know who I am, or where I come from, but I know you trust me, and I too trust you. That is why I am not only instructing you but pleading with you to listen to my direction and take it. Anaisha's fate is in your hands."

"Maybe I'm tired of taking that burden."

"I know you're tired. I know you're exhausted. And I know you desire—and deserve—a reprieve. But not yet. You must keep going, just a little longer. Head to Raveack. Find Eden Ambersay."

"Why can't I take Carrie with me? Why can't I send Veronica and Sean to find Eden?"

Vector shook her head. "I know you love Carrie. You've always loved Carrie. And that is fine. I have…learned to live with that. But Carrie's path is not your path, not at this time. She must travel with Turquoise to find the Codex of Ra'f, and you must travel to Raveack to find Eden."

"I can't leave Carrie behind."

Vector stood still for a few minutes, her wheezing breath moving in and out of her worn lungs. "If you can't let go of Carrie, then this world—your world—is finished, David. I have done my part, I have accepted my own responsibility in all of this and done what I can. I can do no more. My end is coming, soon."

"I don't want you to go."

"I must. It is the cycle of life."

"You can break it. Come with me to do this."

"I can't do that. I have already broken that which was impossible to break. Now I will face the consequences of those actions, a path which is separate from yours."

David cupped his hands over his face and fell to the floor, sobbing. *I've already lost my sister, I've already lost so much.* "How much more will I have to lose? How much more sacrifice will be required of me?"

A soft hand caressed his cheek. He looked up at Vector. Her hood was drawn, revealing her face, scarred and bruised. Her lips were chapped and bleeding. Her eyes seemed sunken in, but they glowed a bright blue.

"Jennifer?"

She smiled warmly. "Yes, David. It's me. It's always been me."

"You? How?"

She put a finger to his lips. "Please, don't make this harder than it has to be. I wanted to reveal myself to you before my end. And now that everything is coming together, now that good and evil is at the threshold of our world, now that I have imparted my last instructions to you, it is time for *my* reprieve."

He reached up and grabbed hold of her gloved hand, gently pulling it to his chest. "I always wondered...I always suspected it was you underneath all of that. But it was an impossible thought."

She shook her head and smiled again. "Nothing is impossible, David. Please, remember that. Nothing is impossible." She pulled her hand from him and reached behind her neck, unclasping a necklace. She grabbed his hand and placed the jewelry in his palm. "Always remember me, will you?"

He looked down at the necklace—a pewter pendant in the

shape of a leaf with three small glass globes clustered on the surface. One was red, one green, and one blue. They seemed to glow in the dark, and David found himself mesmerized by their beauty.

"I gave this to you," David whispered. "So long ago."

"Yes," Jennifer acknowledged, "you did. And now that my journey is coming to a close, I give it back to you. A torch of what you and I once had, to carry with you through the darkness that is about to envelope this world."

Tears ran down his face. He couldn't take another heartbreak. He couldn't say another goodbye. Not to Jennifer. Not to Carrie. "I thought you went to Crystal City to find your real parents…"

Jennifer stood to her feet. "Don't dwell on the past. I did what I had to in order to help you."

"You left to become Vector?"

Jennifer slid the hood over her head, wrapping her countenance in shadow once again, and smoothed out her cloak. "It's time."

He stood to his feet, clutching the necklace in his fist. "Please don't make me say goodbye."

She shook her head. "Not goodbye. You'll see me someday, on the other side. I'm sure of it. Until then though, don't ever forget what we had. Promise me that?"

"I promise."

"If you care about me in any capacity, you'll heed what I've said here today. I know it kills you to separate from Carrie, but you must be strong." She stepped toward him, grabbing his hand in hers. "You must be courageous. You must be brave. You're a hero. You were once *my* hero. Now you're a hero for Anaisha and everyone in it." Jennifer stepped away from him. "See you on the other side, David Corbin. It has been *my* honor."

Jennifer slowly retreated into the store, waving to him as she vanished into the darkness. Her blue glow disappeared, and David was left alone, standing with the necklace in hand and his heart broken.

"One more thing, David." Jennifer's voice echoed through the air of the store, but her form was nowhere in sight. "That timepiece must stay in your possession. Do not give it to the Wedges—*any* of them—and do not let it fall into the wrong hands. Cherish it as you would the memory of me."

David stood, staring into the darkness, tears streaming down his face.

The double doors screeched open, like the gaping mouth of a petulant dragon, and Turquoise stepped into the store. "David?"

"Yeah?" He glanced at the necklace once more and then clasped it around his neck, stuffing the jewelry under his shirt.

"You okay?" She stepped inside the store and the door shut behind her. "You've been in here a while. We wanted to make sure nothing happened to you."

When David turned toward her, he didn't even try to cover up the tears streaming from his eyes. He grabbed Turquoise in a hug and buried his face in her shoulder.

"Hey, hey, it's okay." Turquoise wrapped her arms around him and held him for what felt like hours.

When he finally pulled away from her, he wiped his eyes and took a deep breath. "I know what needs to be done, Turquoise."

6
The Girl

The oak tree was gone. David was gone. Everything was gone.

Carrie peered over the side of the cliff at the dark mist moving silkily through the canyon below. *Is David down there? What about the tree?*

A sound like clapping wood startled her. She swung around to find the landscape gone. She was no longer outside, no longer on a cliff, where her tall, strong oak tree once stood. Now she stood in a room filled with amateur paintings on the walls and children's desks set on the tile floor.

A young woman in a black and white polka dot dress stood near an easel. Her hair was a blinding white and hung from her head to her shoulders like the lines of a waterfall. A large sheet of blank white paper rested comfortably on the easel, and the woman held a tray of paints and a paintbrush.

She did nothing at first aside from simply stare at Carrie. She stared so long, with no movement at all, that Carrie felt like she was inside of a video game, and this woman was a character whose host had left the keyboard. It was unsettling in the least, but Carrie found the paintings on the wall—which were all blurry and impossible to make out—more unsettling. Carrie could discern colors in the paintings—beautiful violets, blues, and greens. But she could neither discern the forms within the paintings nor the way the colors or shapes were even trying to be used.

The woman finally moved, her eyes locked on Carrie as she dipped her paint brush in a deep black and began to paint on the paper.

Carrie glanced around the classroom, her eyes taking everything in again. This time, she recognized the familiarity of the environment. "This is my fifth-grade classroom," she whispered.

The girl either didn't hear Carrie or simply refused to stop painting to acknowledge her discovery.

"What am I doing here?" Carrie asked. She had not willed herself to be here. She had not willed away the dark landscape, for even though David had been absent from it, it still held great significance to Carrie. *Why would my mind pick my fifth-grade classroom to move me to? And who is this woman?*

The girl continued painting, nearly oblivious to Carrie standing there, awestruck and confused as to the change of scenery. She was blocking the painting, making it impossible for Carrie to tell—from her current viewpoint—what the girl was painting exactly.

Carrie continued to analyze the classroom. The desks were set in rows, just like her old classroom from years ago. Years before meeting David. She realized that this point in time, this environment, had to hold some form of significance if it had overcome her own will and called itself into existence. *But what significance does this classroom hold in my life?*

Carrie walked around the desks, eyeing the various desktops, wondering if—

"Yes," she whispered as she reached her hand down and felt the carved surface of one desk in particular. A smiley face had been etched into the surface, and the initials CG BFF VA were carved inside the face. "Veronica?"

Of course! This is the year I met Veronica. But why is this significant? Why—?

She turned to the desk behind Veronica's, to the immaculate piece of furniture that looked as if it had just been brought into the classroom off the assembly line.

Sean's desk.

Carrie's stomach twirled. Fifth grade. When she first met Veronica and Sean. When Sean forced a kiss from her…

Carrie waved her hand at the desk, as if the memory meant nothing to her. But deep down, deep within her spirit, she knew the memory had developed into a scar, a scar she had managed to cover with voluntary memory loss.

The girl stopped painting. She moved to the side and set her paintbrush and paints down on the nearby counter, giving Carrie full view of the masterpiece.

On the paper, painted in deep black, an alphanumeric stream revealed itself:

A5YTR9 X34RGH 339087

Carrie stood, dumbfounded. The girl pointed to the paper, then pointed to Carrie's arms. Carrie lifted them but saw nothing of significance. The ink marks—proof that Legion was inhabiting her body—were gone. She realized she was most likely within her own spirit, safe in her personal sanctuary, and before her stood the Legion that had been inhabiting her this whole time, the Legion that had been injected into her back in the Complex.

Strangely enough, Carrie sensed no real threat from this being. Whereas, in the outside world, this creature had wreaked havoc on her body, Carrie couldn't grasp any kind of malevolent intention from the girl standing before her.

The code stood out on the white sheet of art paper, begging to somehow be decoded. Carrie examined it, disappointed she had never seen anything like it before. "What is this?" she asked the girl.

The girl, her ink-black eyes seemingly threatening to swallow everything around her, pointed to Carrie, then to the easel.

Carrie wondered if this had something to do with the ink splotches that had started to appear on her arms in the real world. "Is this a code?"

The girl nodded.

"What does it mean?"

The girl picked up the paint brush and quickly drew a picture of what looked to be a jail cell.

"Prison?"

The girl nodded vigorously, her splotchy eyes glistening.

Carrie still didn't know what this was all about. "Can you just write out what it is you're trying to tell me?"

The girl shrugged and then shook her head.

"Do you not know how to write in my language?"

The girl shook her head.

"Are you here to hurt me?"

The girl shook her head again, this time with more embellishment. She pointed to the code, pointed to Carrie.

"Is this code what's appearing on my arms?"

The girl nodded.

"Is it a location? Like coordinates?"

The girl nodded.

"To what?"

The girl pointed to the jail cell.

"Why can't you speak?"

The girl opened her own mouth and pointed into it.

"You can't speak? You have no voice?"

The girl nodded.

Carrie motioned to the rest of the room. "What is this? Why are we *here* specifically?"

The girl went back to the easel and drew the symbol for male.

Carrie remembered this room, remembered that this room existed shortly before she even met David Corbin. There was only one male that stood out in her life at that time. "Do you mean Sean?"

The girl nodded, sending forgotten chills throughout Carrie's body.

Carrie turned and looked at the chalkboard, which had blurred writing upon it. "This was the year I met Veronica. And Sean. I remember...I remember him as a bully. He snuck into the girl's room when I was washing up one afternoon. Wanted a kiss. Forced himself on me. It wasn't sexual?" Carrie turned to the girl. "But he did force a kiss from me. Then he said he would hurt me if I told anyone. Would destroy any chance I would have at being friends with his sister. So, I conceded..."

The girl folded her hands in front of her and then glanced around the classroom. Carrie watched her eyes, wondered if the girl could form the wall paintings in her mind or make out the text written upon the chalkboard.

"Why am I here though? Sean did that years ago. So long ago,

I had mostly forgotten about it until now. David doesn't even know that happened, as I'm sure he'd kill Sean if he ever found out. But what does this have to do with the coordinates you wrote out? What does it have to do with your symbiosis with me?"

The girl returned to the easel and drew out a dagger or sword. Carrie couldn't tell which.

"He's a sword?"

The girl shook her head and then drew a stick figure, with the dagger/sword sticking out of its back.

"Someone is backstabbed? Betrayed?"

The girl nodded, pointing to Carrie.

"Me?" she asked, directing her own finger back at her. "David? Turquoise?"

The girl nodded.

"By Sean?"

The girl nodded.

"Are you guessing this? Based on one incident in fifth grade?"

The girl didn't shake her head or nod it either. She stood, hands clasped in front of her, and simply stared at the ground.

"I need to know more. I need you to speak."

The girl shrugged.

Carrie glanced around the room again, this time settling her vision on a long bookshelf. "I'm thinking maybe I can teach you how to write." She turned back to the girl. "If I do, will you explain to me what's going on?"

The woman nodded.

"Come over here. We don't have much time."

7

Awakening

David Corbin walked out of the Walmart, the twisted knot in his stomach tighter than before he entered the uncanny building. Turquoise sat on a parking pylon, keeping watch on Serenity's sleeping form. After comforting David and attempting to pry from him what his plan was (without success), she left him alone in the store to collect his thoughts.

He knew it wasn't going to be easy to break the news to Carrie, even harder to actually separate from her. But deep down, he knew if it meant their planet could be saved, he would do the hard thing. More so that Jennifer had asked him to do it. But he didn't want to tell anyone. Not yet. If he told someone, then they could hold him accountable to do it.

Carrie rested against the wall of the store, her eyes closed, her hands twitching.

As he stood in the parking lot, looking out at the endless tan and clay-colored mountains, David smelled scents that were alien to him. There was something in the air—it wasn't sweet like before, nor was it sour. It was just different. Salty, maybe. Something that didn't fit. Something that didn't make sense. Something off.

He started toward Carrie but stopped when he heard Serenity rustling on the ground, the air slightly distorting around her. He approached the girl cautiously, careful not to startle her. Turquoise helped her sit up.

"Who came with us?" Serenity asked, holding a hand to her forehead.

Turquoise put her hand on the girl's shoulder. "Just us three and Carrie."

Serenity let out a relieved sigh. Yellow liquid formed in the corner of her mouth, and she spit to the side, on the asphalt, before she wiped her lips on the sleeve of her sweater.

"Where did you bring us, Serenity?" David asked.

"Just be grateful I got the four of us out of there before things could get worse."

"You split us off from the rest of the group," Turquoise said. "You must have had a reason for doing so."

Serenity took a deep breath and stood to her feet. The way she struggled, David swore the girl was either drunk or incredibly old. "I don't answer to you." She brushed her black stockings at her knees and straightened out her black skirt before sneering at them. "Any of you."

David glanced at Carrie slumped against the wall and fought back the urge to lash out at Serenity. "Where did you bring us? What is this place?"

"Or rather, when?" Turquoise added.

Serenity's face lit up at the insinuation, but she said nothing. Instead, she adjusted her thick-framed glasses, walked around to the back of the grocery store, passed a large metal dumpster, and stopped at the edge of the parking lot.

David and Turquoise followed her, leaving Carrie to rest against the wall of the grocery store.

The parking lot dropped off into a sheer cliff, with nothing but the vast expanse of brown and tan as far as the eye could see. Impressed and fearful of the illusion this place conjured, David peered over the edge of the cliff and saw nothing but bottomless air below them, with thin, wispy clouds filling the space between him and certain eternal torment.

"I have a gift," Serenity stated, her purple-streaked hair blowing with the breeze.

David waited for more from the girl, but more did not come. She took a seat on the edge of the cliff and stared out into the distance. David noticed the orange and yellow sky was the same orange and yellow levels as when they arrived in this place. He turned behind him and watched a cup roll across the parking lot with the help of the wind. Then it rolled back, and then back again.

"Time," David whispered, an unease growing in his gut. "Time doesn't move forward here. It keeps lapsing back."

Turquoise approached Serenity, placing her hand on the young girl's shoulder again. "You're a Leaper?"

"Serenity brushed Turquoise's hand away. "Something like that."

"A what?" David asked.

Turquoise frowned. "A Leaper. A rare wedge power. She can flash through time."

"It's not as simple as that," Serenity grumbled.

"Then explain it to me so I can understand," David snapped. "Why did you choose to teleport us away from those other two Wedges? And why here? Or when? What is significant about this place?"

Serenity sighed. "I have a feeling I'm going to be stuck with you for a while, so you may as well know." She fiddled with her fingers a bit, picking at her black-painted nails absently. "They did experiments on me—the Sector. Before you protest, know that I agreed to it. They made it sound like I was going to do the world better. Shit. What a joke."

David glanced back and saw Carrie standing against the wall. She was examining her arms, as if they held some long-lost secret to saving the world.

"I used to have the power to teleport part of me across a small distance. Like—like my hands," she said, holding them up as if part of an exhibit. "I could transfer them across the room, grab an apple, and transfer them back. Or my legs, or my head. Or my whole body, but that used to take a lot of my energy. So much so, that the first time I teleported myself fifty feet, I collapsed into a coma. I was out for days.

"Anyway, the Sector asked if I would take part in an experimental drug. It was rhodenine—which you know is our Wedge source of power." She looked up at Turquoise. "But it was a concentrated amount, so much so that it was supposed to mutate my powers. Well, it did. Gave me the ability to teleport farther, through time *and* space."

"So we're in a different *when*?" David asked.

Serenity turned her head just far enough to where she could see David with her right eye. "Sort of. And a different *where*. I only ever have control of one or the other—time *or* space. If I want to teleport to a specific time, I can, but it means that I'll end up in a random place. Vice versa with space. I know of this place—I've teleported myself here a few times before. But I don't know the *when*. The first time I

65

arrived here, I searched that grocery store top to bottom looking for a newspaper or flyer or anything to tell me *when* I was—or even *where*, really. Nothing. The can labels which I looked at to reference place just confused me more because it's places I've never heard of before: Napa Valley, Boise, Virginia."

"Neither have I," David said as he started toward Carrie.

"David," Turquoise said, stopping him in his tracks.

He turned back to find her beckoning him to come to her with those turquoise-colored eyes that shined brighter than the time-stuck sun. Reluctantly, he drew close to Turquoise. "What?"

She stared at him, saying nothing at first. She bit her bottom lip like a nervous schoolgirl, but her eyes held an edge within them that could pierce stone hearts. When she finally spoke, her pink lips parted reluctantly, as if she was an adult having a much-needed but not-really-desired talk about the birds and the bees with their child. "What happened in the grocery store? And please, be honest with me."

"No."

"No? No, what?"

"I'm not going to tell you. And if you press me, I'll lie."

She flashed her teeth in a show of frustration. "We have to trust each other, David. Right now, of all times. I'm not your enemy. You should know that by now. We're in delicate times. Carrie is slowly being consumed by Legion. We've been teleported away from our own world or time or…or whatever. We have to stick together."

"If it puts your mind at ease, nothing happened in there that you—or anybody else—needs to know about." He turned and went to Carrie, ignoring Turquoise's harsh glare piercing a hole in his back. He had no desire to tell her or anyone else—especially Carrie—of his conversation with Jennifer. After all this

66

time, he finally comes to realize who Vector is, and it's too late. *She probably ventured out somewhere or somewhen to lay down and die.*

Carrie was still examining her arms when he approached her. Even from a few feet away, David could tell the black ink had developed into more intricate designs. He could almost swear they were starting to look like writing, but he shook the ridiculous idea away.

Will Legion overtake Carrie's body again and speak with me some more? I hope not. "You okay?" he asked her.

Carrie snapped out of her thoughts and looked up at him. Her eyes were sunken in, like small emeralds in a dark seabed. "I'll live."

David took her in his arms and pulled her close. She smelled of familiarity. Something like cheap perfume and fresh laundry, with a dash of sweat and body grime. Compared to the strange, otherworldly smell of this place, hers comforted his heart, gave him reason to hope. Even if they were stuck here for the rest of time, as long as they were together, he could be happy.

For a few dark moments, David wondered what it would be like to be stuck here for the rest of his life. Just him and Carrie. They could take shelter within the grocery store. Make it their home. Serenity could leave with Turquoise, leave them behind.

The idea gave him so much hope, that he nearly blurted out the possibility before his mind came to the rescue and saved him from his incessant bemusing: What would happen once they ate all the food in the store? Could they really live such an isolated life, away from everyone and everything? Could he consciously give up on the fate of Anaisha while he lived out his days here in this literal island getaway with the love of his life?

No. He couldn't. Jennifer had been right. Right about him needing to help save Anaisha. Save humanity. But what about Carrie? Why did they have to separate? It didn't really make sense, at least not on the surface.

And he still wasn't completely certain that leaving Carrie to go off on his own was something he could do. He knew it was what Jennifer wanted him to do—urged him to do—but it was so much easier said than done.

Carrie pulled away from him and lifted her right arm. "Look closely."

He examined the ink design. At first, it seemed to be a jumble of intricate lines and swirls that made up a decorative tattoo, one he knew contained Legion's very presence. But closer, one could see within the lines, within the swirls—numbers and letters…

A5YTR9 X34RGH 339087

He rubbed his hand on the numbers, as if he could wipe them away. As he stared at the design, it changed, slowly, into more numbers, more letters. The design created itself while he watched. "No wonder you've been watching your arm this whole time."

Carrie nodded before sniffling.

David shouted for Turquoise and Serenity to come over. As much as he would have loved to have hid this part of Carrie, he felt this might be important, maybe even essential to Anaisha's victory over darkness.

"Do you recognize this at all?" he asked.

Serenity shook her head.

Turquoise examined the alphanumeric design for minutes before nodding. She turned to Serenity. "Isn't this Plax Code?"

Serenity adjusted her glasses before taking another look. "Hm. A5YTR9. X34RGH. 339087. I think so…Yes. The first two sets are coordinates within the Fringe. The third set is a geographical address—different from coordinates in that it pinpoints a particular building or structure within the coordinates."

David smirked. "The Fringe is no-man's land. It's all unmapped. How can there be coordinates for it, let alone an address?"

Turquoise frowned. "I was under the impression we would be heading to the Far Lands. No further."

Serenity smiled knowingly, and the mannerism caused a certain joy to flash across her face. "There were Wedges a long great while ago who were tasked with mapping out the Fringe. The problem with the Fringe is that directional instruments don't work there—or rather, they constantly change direction. The team that ventured out that way were not experienced in survival. They were scientists and mathematicians hoping to find more about Anaisha's history. When they couldn't use their compass or directional guides, they created the Plax Code, which enabled them to pinpoint specific locations within the Fringe so the Sector could send other teams there at a later time. Unfortunately, the original team were swallowed up by the sands, and the only person left was a lone scientist by the name of Richard Plax who returned to the Sector and shared his findings with us."

David looked at Carrie's arm again. "How is it that this Plax Code is showing up on Carrie's arm—written by Legion?"

Serenity shrugged. "How should I know?"

Carrie said nothing, which David found strange. She seemed to be retreating deeper and deeper inside of her own self, cutting David off from the parts of her he loved the most. He took her hand in his, tilted her chin so she was looking into his eyes, and sternly said, "We'll get through this. We'll figure this out."

She nodded, weakly at that, before taking a seat cross-legged on a parking pylon. "It's coordinates. To a prison."

"What?" David asked.

Serenity and Turquoise came around until all three were standing, staring down at Carrie.

She looked up warily at each of her friends. "I spoke with Legion. Well, a representation of it. Inside myself. She is mute, but she drew pictures to help me understand some of what is going on. She drew the same coordinates that are on my arm now. She said it's coordinates to a prison, but I have no idea what prison or where."

Turquoise shook her head. "You trust the very thing taking over your will? Your mind?"

Carrie sighed. "She's not taking over my will. She met with me, tried to warn me."

"Warn you?" David asked. "Warn you about what?"

Carrie bit her lower lip and averted his gaze. "I don't know if I fully trust her. She's basing her information on an event that happened in fifth grade."

David knelt to her level, took her icy hand in his, and stared into her eyes. "You want me to fight? You want me to help save Anaisha? Then you have to be honest with me."

Turquoise scoffed but said nothing beyond the slightly irritated noise that came from her throat.

David ignored her and continued to stare into Carrie's green eyes, which—if it was not his imagination—were beginning to return to their original brilliant green color, some of the smokiness fading away.

Carrie smiled, ever so slightly. David could tell it wasn't a good smile. It was her nervous smile. The smile that told him that she didn't really want to say what she was going to say.

She stood to her feet. "Sean. She warned me that Sean is

a traitor. Or will be. I can't tell for certain."

"What does Sean have to do with all of this?" David asked. "Besides, he's on the other side of Anaisha for all we know. He's not even involved in any of this."

Serenity turned her back to them and stared out on the repeating horizon. "Eventually, David, everyone will become part of this."

"Maybe," he said. "But I don't know why Legion would warn Carrie about Sean. That seems like a stretch."

Carrie shrugged slightly, delicately, as if she were a doll afraid of breaking appearance. "I don't know. She couldn't speak. She could only communicate in symbols. I left her with some books, to teach her how to write out our language, but I don't know how long it will take her to learn it."

"How do we get back?" David asked.

Serenity adjusted her black skirt, scratched at an itch beneath the black stocking of her left leg, and sighed as she turned back to face the group. "We can't. Not yet. My ability has to recharge, so to say. If I try again too soon, I'll pass out, possibly in the middle of our transition. That would be bad."

David ran his hand through his hair and stared out on the canyon, the mountains beyond it, and the orange and yellow rewinding sky further out beyond that. "We can't sit here forever."

"Time is suspended while we're here," Serenity said. "This was always a place of rest for me. Time is literally stopped here, and it gives us a chance to figure out what we know."

"What do you know?" Turquoise asked. "Like David said earlier, you must have some suspicions about Hammer and Velvet to have teleported us and not them."

Her eyes shifted behind the thick frames. "Possibly. I won't say anything until I know for sure though. Let's leave it at that."

"Fine," Turquoise conceded.

"For now, I think we should get inside the store," David said. "There should be enough food in there to get us through the night."

"There is no night here," Serenity said with a mostly-hidden grin. "The sun is always setting—or rising—however you want to look at it."

"Either way," Turquoise said as she led them toward the grocery store, "we need rest."

They entered the store, but David felt emotions rushing through him as he walked through the screeching double doors. He suddenly missed Vector—Jennifer—very much. So much so, that he felt tears running down his face before he even realized he was crying.

"We'll find the lights," he said under shaky breath as he ventured into the store with Turquoise. She extended a bright, pink glowing shield that illuminated their way.

The building was from another time and place, that much he could tell by the clothing they came across, the currency signs that were set up around the store, and the various containers of food that David had never heard of.

Where exactly the store was from, David had no idea. Could be another planet. Another reality. Another time.

Maybe all the above.

Turquoise and David found the warehouse in the back of the store. They cautiously scanned the area, finding no signs of hostiles, and managed to find the breaker panel for the whole store. David flipped all of the switches to the ON position, but only emergency lighting flickered on across the store, just enough so they could all see where they were going, but still leaving the store in chunks of shadow.

He and Turquoise gathered food where they could find it.

Most of the produce and meat were spoiled, but strangely enough, they left no spoiled scent in the store. David grabbed some off-brand soda, and Turquoise gathered some boxed pasta and jarred pasta sauce. The food would be enough to hold everyone over until they could figure out what was going on with Carrie and what their next step should be.

When they met up with Serenity and Carrie, they found Carrie resting on a bed in the home furnishings section, with Serenity at her side, sketching out the Plax Code written on her arms on sheets of printer paper she found elsewhere in the store.

"How are you planning on decoding that?" David asked as he set the loaves of bread on a nearby dining room table display. Turquoise set the juice and cereal on the same table, and then took a seat in one of the dining chairs.

Serenity shook her head. "It's not the most reliable process." She held up a small square electronic tablet. "It's a data reader. Wedges used to have to carry these around, back in the day, when the Sector was first started." She looked at Turquoise. "You came after the time." She looked back to David. "Anyway, I have an app installed on it that can map out Plax Coordinates. It's a little unreliable though. It likes to crash if I put too many coordinates in it. But, if I go slow and steady, I think we can pinpoint where this code is trying to tell us to go."

David looked at the pasta and sauce. "I'll go look for some plates," he said as he left the group and wandered back into the heart of the store.

He felt a pull here. Something pulling at his spirit, pulling at the hairs on his skin. Something was tugging at him, much like a kid tugs on his father's shirt when he wants attention. But it was so subtle, so unobtrusive, that David found he could almost ignore it.

He found himself standing in one of the register stalls. The very one Jennifer had appeared in.

Why did I come over here? he asked himself. He was looking for plates, which were on the other side of the clothing section from where he stood. So why had he traveled—without apparently knowing it—to the other side of the store from his friends?

That tug. It pulled harder. More intense.

He glanced down at the floor and noticed a glowing blue dot in the tile. It was a deep, rich blue, much like what Jennifer's eyes had become. He stared at the dot intently for what felt like hours, maybe even days. It was a strange sensation to skip through time like that, but staring into the blue dot did that. It made one feel as if they were being tugged, pulled, toward something bigger than themselves. Something massive.

Turquoise shook David's shoulder, snapping him from his thoughts, which were of nothing and of everything. He couldn't place where he was at first, as if he had been gone this whole time in another world. Maybe another time.

"You okay?"

David ran his hand across his face. Perspiration covered his brow, but his cheeks were cold as ice. "I don't know."

Turquoise glanced down at the blue dot on the floor. If she did know what it was, her eyes gave nothing away. When her gaze returned to David, she still gave nothing away with her facial movements. "We have dinner ready," she said in a flat tone.

David nodded and let her lead him back toward the bakery where everyone had relocated, and where spaghetti and fresh-baked bread had been prepared.

But the blue dot called to him. Beckoned. There was something on the other side of it, but David wasn't certain he wanted to know what that might be.

8

Tears

They sat in the bakery kitchen as the scent of fresh-baked bread filled the room. The warmth from the ovens drove away the chill that had started to creep into the store. Even though the position of the sun hadn't changed, and time had continued to rewind upon itself, it still felt as if night had descended in their strange little corner of a perplexing timeline. Cold blanketed the store like a blizzard during Winter Festival.

Serenity and Turquoise baked and cooked a decent-enough meal: spaghetti with alfredo sauce, bread, and briscus salad.

Carrie spent a few hours sleeping on the display bed. Although David had done nothing but stare at the blue dot, he still heard Carrie tossing and turning in her slumber. She spoke of darkness and fog and a cliff. He had no idea what it all meant, and he decided he wasn't going to ask. She was fighting the rack matter—fighting it tooth and nail. David's frustration peaked when he realized there was nothing he could do to help her. Nothing he could do to control the situation in any way, shape, or form. All he could do was sit on the sidelines, caress her, and feed lies to her that everything was going to be okay.

He had no idea if everything was going to be okay.

David took a bite of bread and watched everyone else eat their meal. Carrie ate slowly, methodically, as her gaze traveled the kitchen. It was as if she was in another state of mind, as if what was fighting her on the inside was getting closer to pulling her in and taking her place. David remembered the lies that Legion spit out to him when it took over her completely back at his house. He vowed to not believe a single word it spoke to him.

Turquoise ate a bit of salad, her gaze wandering elsewhere.

Serenity, though, stood and stared directly at David while she ate her spaghetti. There was something unnerving about her stare, those bright eyes peering out at him from behind thick frames and even thicker lenses. David thought she was simply curious about him. At first. But there was something about her stare, as if she had an X-ray machine grafted into her head and she was scanning him for some contagious disease.

"What?" he finally asked her between forkfuls of salad.

She finished chewing up her spaghetti, swallowed, and then set her plate down on the aluminum island. "I want to see the blue dot."

"What?"

She huffed. "The blue dot. The blue dot that Turquoise tells me is out in the store."

He shrugged it off. "It's nothing. Just a blue dot."

She snapped at him as she walked by, and though she was shorter than everyone else in the group, she commanded attention like the general of an army. "Come with me. I need to see it. Now."

David glared at Turquoise, hoping to ensnare her with his

frustration, but she still held her gaze elsewhere.

He left the bakery kitchen and took the lead, bringing Serenity to the blue dot in the flooring near the soda aisle. It had grown to the size of a basketball, and David could see into it, to a black haze beyond. "What is that?" he asked.

Serenity bent to her knees and examined the anomaly. She reached her right hand out and ran her finger along the outer edge of the hole, where ice crystals had started to form. "Cold," she said. "Ice cold." She reached her hand into the hole, to her elbow, and then pulled it back out. A white mist attached itself to her wrist but quickly dissipated as it was pulled into the store.

Serenity stood and huffed before she stormed back to the bakery kitchen. David glanced down at the hole, convinced it had grown an inch since moments ago. Then he followed Serenity. She had to snap Turquoise out of her daydream with a light shake of the woman's shoulder. "It's as we feared."

Turquoise nodded absently. "I figured as much."

"What?" David asked. Carrie was at full attention now, rubbing her wrist. The ink design on her arm had slowed down or stopped completely while she had been asleep, but now it was active again, etching intricate designs and more supposed coordinates related to Plax Code upon her arm.

"It's a corrupted tear," Serenity grumbled. "Your friend, Vector, left it behind when she tore out of this reality."

David's eyes couldn't help but widen at the fact that Serenity knew about Vector.

"Don't look so surprised," she said. "I've come across her a few times. She actually helped me control my own leaps. I don't know who she is, but she's been weakening the barrier between our reality and the others."

David leaned against the counter, his brain a fog with tiredness. "Run that by me again."

"There are other realities," Serenity started. Her eyes fluttered and the air around her fragmented for a split second, but she continued. "Other worlds, David. I can flash forward or backwards through time and space. But I can only control one. Vector—I believe—can control both. But each time realities are crossed, the barrier between our realities weakens from the friction of our movement across them. Eventually, you get that hole in the ground out there. A portal to another reality."

"You're telling me that's a portal to another dimension?"

She put a hand to her stomach and nodded. "Another reality, yes. Or, possibly a portal to another place. Time *or* space. Or both. Hard to tell."

"One that Vector caused when she last left me?"

Serenity huffed.

"How is that possible?"

"Because, David, she can travel *through* timestreams, and also *in* and *out* of them. What I want to know is what she's been telling you. Why contact you of all people?"

David's mind raced to determine what he should or shouldn't reveal to Serenity. He finally just said, "We have a history."

"Hm," Turquoise grunted.

Serenity took a long, deep breath and then left the kitchen. David glanced at Turquoise, who was watching him intently. Examining him. Wondering what his connection to Vector was.

You won't ever know, he told himself, his heart demanding that he guard Vector/Jennifer as a secret nobody else could possibly know about. Not even Carrie.

Serenity stumbled into the kitchen and had to grab the island to keep from falling to the floor. David grabbed her under her

78

arms and propped her up against the wall near Turquoise.

"Thanks," Serenity whispered. The skin around her lips was turning an ugly shade of brown and had begun to blister.

"What is this," David asked, motioning for Turquoise to come closer.

She examined the girl's exhausted face. "Not sure. It looks as if she's been poisoned."

Serenity nodded. "Must've been something I ate."

David glanced around the kitchen at the plates of spaghetti, the loaf pans full of bread, and the bowls of salad. "But we all ate the same stuff."

Serenity slid down the wall and curled up on the floor. "I follow a rule: Don't eat or drink too much when traveling through other realities. Unlike traveling through time—which is on the same timeline as the time you are arriving or leaving—traveling through dimensions exposes you to altered courses of history, altered turnouts. Altered food. Altered drink. Any number of things can disrupt an outsiders' body chemistry."

Turquoise lifted Serenity off the floor and carried her out to the bed Carrie had been sleeping on earlier.

Meanwhile, Carrie lay on the floor, eyes wide open, darkness filling her pupils as her arm trembled with ink-splotched activity.

9

Shadows

During the time Carrie was away dealing with David and the perplexing tear in reality, the strange girl inhabiting Carrie's mind and spirit toiled away at reading books and learning how to write. When Carrie returned to the classroom, she found the girl sitting in one of the desks, a stack of books towering upon its surface, volumes on the English language, ciphers, and handwriting. The girl didn't look up when Carrie appeared out of thin air, but instead poured herself into the book she was currently reading: *Cursive and Our Desire to Hate It.*

It was disconcerting returning to her fifth-grade classroom, and Carrie wondered how authentic this place could be. Was it built upon reality, or was it built upon Carrie's memories of reality? She glanced around the room, taking in the blurry artwork and undersized desks.

Carrie approached the strange Legion girl and watched her read—an alien species taking in the finer volumes of Anaishan literature. Carrie did not want to startle the girl, but realized the girl probably knew she was there, watching her read, like some kind of creep.

Like Sean used to watch Carrie read.

The thought, the fragment of memory, shot nausea to Carrie's stomach, and she had to sit down in one of the desks to collect herself. How could she have forgotten such dreadful events? And if Sean had indeed treated her in such a manner, why would she have continued to team up with him to stop Anaisha's villains?

Because, David.

Carrie nodded mentally. It was because of David. It was always because of David.

The girl in the polka dot dress slid a leather bookmark into the volume she had been reading, shut the book, and then turned to Carrie, her inky black eyes examining her with a look of indifference.

Carrie snapped out of her reverie and cleared her throat before saying, "Have you learned anything?"

The girl nodded, then stood to her feet and walked to the chalkboard. Her walk was clumsy. Carrie figured she was trying to be sultry, imitating human girls, but she came off as if she was a victim of knee surgery or one too many drinks.

Carrie rested her arms on the surface of the old desk and took a few deep breaths, hoping to quell the sick feeling that had come upon her suddenly.

The girl wrote upon the chalkboard, her handwriting a bit unsteady but perfectly understandable to Carrie.

My name is Viranda DelaCourte.

The girl turned back to Carrie, and Carrie smiled warmly. "Hello, Viranda."

Viranda nodded and continued to write upon the chalk-board, her movements quick.

I am a part of Legion, but I am not Legion. I am my own... She stood before the chalkboard, tapping her tiny piece of chalk upon the board as she struggled to find the right words to say. *Being. I separated from Legion long ago. My old kind trapped me, purged my voice. I was released into you. We are now dependent on one another for survival.*

Carrie took a deep breath. She knew she had an alien entity within her for some time now, but she had not been aware that it was relying on her for survival—or that she could also be relying on it. "How do we separate?"

The girl stood at the chalkboard, her back to Carrie, her head bowed. It wasn't until Carrie asked the question a second time that the girl finally continued writing upon the chalkboard.

I do not know. What I do know is that I need your help.

"With what?"

To free them. All of them. She sketched a crudely-made jail cell.

"Who?"

The girl tapped the chalkboard. Carrie grew impatient.

Finally, Viranda sketched a crude figure on the board, what looked to be a tall, bald man made of shadows.

The figure resembled a child's kindergarten drawing, but there was a dark essence to it, something that made Carrie's stomach turn over. She steadied her breathing, but she felt the chills, the tendrils of terror and fright, seize hold of her frame, and it nearly sent her into a panic.

"Who is that?" she whispered under unsteady breath. "What is his name?" Though she didn't really want to know his name, didn't believe it should be uttered in their reality.

Viranda stood at the chalkboard, her back to Carrie, waiting or thinking. Maybe debating whether or not it would be wise to even write out his identity.

Finally, Viranda tapped the board six times with the chalk and then scribbled out his name, her hand working fast as if even it was afraid to form the word:

Ro-shoru'm

The name, read off the board, invoked a feeling Carrie couldn't quite describe. Dreadful thoughts arose in her mind, ones she could not control. Thoughts of death, decay. Spoiled things—like rotten milk or rotting corpses. She imagined black snakes slithering through the shadows in the room, their tongues made of fire and ice, their eyes set with fiery rubies.

Her awareness of the shadows in the room increased. They stretched from their hiding places, like tendrils weaving their way into her reality. Carrie stood from the small desk as Viranda continued writing on the board.

He is everywhere. He is in everything. He is corruption. He is blight.

The shadows poured in from all corners of the room, swallowing the essence of the classroom—multiplication tables, science posters, caterpillar exhibits.

Fear gripped hold of Carrie, twisted in her lungs like a

thorned rose stem. Her vision darted around the room, looking for an escape. But the shadows had swallowed the window that looked out onto a fake playground, swallowed the door that led to an empty hallway.

We thought we were clever joining forces with him. We did it in the hopes he could help us wipe out every species in existence.

Carrie watched the shadows spill across the tile floor, swallowing the desks in darkness. The lights began to wink out overhead, pouring darkness into the classroom like buckets of tar. Carrie squinted to make out the final message written on the chalkboard…

We were wrong. Wrong about everything. Some of us Awakened, apart from Legion the Whole. We watched civilizations fall, and we wept. We watched the Dark One tear apart everyone and everything he came across. There's no such thing as an alliance with him—only destruction. Only death.

Tears streamed down Carrie's face as the shadows closed in. She could no longer see the chalkboard, couldn't tell where Viranda stood. She lost her bearings and frantically tried to determine where the door was.

It wouldn't matter anyway, she told herself. The door led to nothing because everything here was fake. Everything but the memories, everything but the feelings.

The shadows swallowed hard, choking on Carrie's form.

10 The Maw

David stood outside the grocery store, staring up at the rewinding sunset/sunrise. The air outside was comfortable, warmer than the frosty air pouring out of the widening maw in the floor of the store.

What began as a blue dot had increased into a hole the size of a vehicle. The hole sucked inward, pulling reality into its maw, swallowing shelves, 2-Liter bottles of soda, and gallon jugs of water, and expelling freezing air.

Although the hole had started out as a blue dot, the wider it grew, the deeper the darkness in the center of that dot. The blue had gone, and in its place, only darkness on the other side of the portal. Pure darkness.

Serenity's condition worsened. The blisters which had appeared on her lips now spread across one half of her face. Her breathing came in unsteady rasps, and her pulse slowed to a whisper, but she remained conscious and coherent. She moved very little, and when she did, she groaned, acknowledging the phantom pains coursing through her frame.

David knew nothing of how to heal her or help her. Neither did Turquoise.

So, Serenity lay on the display bed, as Carrie had, and David stood outside in the strangest air, helpless to care for either one of them. Meanwhile, the hungry maw continued to grow. It was inevitable that it would consume the whole store soon, gobbling up their only source of rations, aid, and shelter, spewing freezing cold in return. The fact that they had no way to get back home, that Serenity's sickness prevented her from teleporting them away from this odd world, lent to David's already growing anxiety. It was bad enough he could do nothing to save Carrie from the alien entity invading her body. Now they were all trapped in an alien time or place, with no way to return to normalcy. That coupled with the fact that the maw was only going to continue to grow filled David with bitter discouragement that was hard to swallow and even harder to digest.

The sliding doors of the store opened, and Turquoise stepped out. Her namesake eyes revealed her own anxiety as she approached David. "I don't know what we're going to do," she admitted.

David stared at the mountains in the distance. He wasn't sure what to do either, so he said nothing.

"I'm scared."

The comment caught David off guard. In the short time he had known Turquoise, he couldn't remember her ever admitting fear. Under normal circumstances, David would have found her vulnerability refreshing and somewhat encouraging. But not now. Now, her admittance filled *him* with fear. If she didn't know what to do, if Carrie and Serenity were out of commission, then everything was left to him. And he was the most clueless of all. Clueless to what was happening to Carrie.

Clueless to what the gaping hole was all about. Clueless how they were going to get home.

"Carrie isn't doing well."

David nodded. "I know."

"It's like she's not even here anymore. Like something else has taken over. She doesn't speak. She...I'm sorry," she whispered as she turned away.

"Don't be," was all he could think to say.

With her back to him, Turquoise let out a deep breath, and then said, "You know there's only one option to all of this."

"I know." He hadn't wanted to talk about this part, hadn't wanted to imagine it.

"If we go into the tear, I don't know where we'll be going, or if we'll ever be able to get home. Serenity needs aid, aid that we don't have." She threw her arms up and motioned to the desolate landscape all around them. "There's no finding aid out here, is there?"

"No."

She turned toward him, and her turquoise-colored eyes were filled with tears.

He could do nothing more than pull her into his arms and hug her tightly. The warmth of her body gave him peace, a close friend in a time of chaos. She tightened her arms around him, her breath shuddering under the weight of her sobbing.

It felt like years passed when they finally let go of one another. When they did break the bond of comfort, Turquoise wiped the tears from her eyes, and David saw a hint of a smile on her pink lips. He felt a spark of satisfaction to see so much joy from such a simple expression of...well, he wasn't sure what it was: Love? Friendship? Unity?

David and Turquoise retreated into the store and made

their way toward Serenity, purposely traveling down the outer aisles, around the gaping hole. David's skin prickled at the frigid temperature inside the Wal Mart. They had lost at least ten degrees since David and Turquoise had stepped outside.

When they reached Serenity, the girl was on her back on the display bed, her eyes wide open, staring at the dark ceiling. The rash had spread vehemently to her neck and beneath her shirt. David noticed small protrusions begging to break out of her black stockings, and he suddenly felt a great deal of sympathy for the girl he barely knew.

Her gaze captured David. "How big is it?" she asked with a raspy voice, her eyes searching his for the truth.

David refused to look at the hole. He could hear it—the sucking sound it made, as if it was a black vortex intent on consuming their world. The cold it poured back into the Wal Mart made David wish he had a thicker coat. His next action would be to move Carrie outside into the warmth of the constantly setting sun.

"Answer me," she demanded. It was sickly humorous to think she would bark orders when she was so close to death.

"It doesn't matter," David finally answered. "It won't be long before it takes the whole store."

"We need to travel through it," she said softly. "It's the only way out."

"I know."

Turquoise stepped closer to the bed. "What's on the other side of it?"

Serenity turned her head so she was looking at the taller wedge. "Another world. Another time. Another reality. Any of them. All of them. I don't know."

"We can't just leap in there and hope we land somewhere

welcoming."

"We have to." Serenity sat up and touched the mass of blisters on her face. "If we don't, we die. I'll die from whatever poison I ingested. Carrie will be consumed with Legion. And you two will be eaten up by the tear."

"Will the tear take us to Anaisha?"

Serenity shrugged.

"Will we survive going through?"

Serenity coughed into her hand. "Probably. But…but this is a *corrupted* tear. An anomaly. Nothing like the highway through time and space that I can create. This is a portal to somewhere, somewhen. There's no telling where it opened up to."

"Is the tear what Vector traveled through?" David asked. Even he noticed the childish hope in his voice, hope that he could once again see Vector—Jennifer—and reunite with her before her end.

Serenity shook her head. "Vector travels like me. Like a highway. This is a tear left behind when she traveled. Her friction, her movement through time, tore the hole, and now it will consume all of this."

David glanced around the store. "Will it consume this entire reality?"

Serenity nodded before she lay down again. She slipped the black heels off her feet and kicked them off the bed before letting out a painful moan.

David turned from her and went to the edge of the maw. He could see starry dots in the darkness now, like small lights flickering at a fine restaurant. Something about the darkness drove fear through his heart like a stake. He wanted nothing to do with that darkness. And yet—the starry dots, the small shards of light like diamond dust, seemed to call to him. They beckoned him with their illumination, they attempted to cajole him with their speckled flashes and brilliant demeanors.

"Grab as many supplies as you can," he told Turquoise. "I'll check on Carrie. Then we'll go. All of us. Down into whatever that is."

***

An hour later, Turquoise had two large black duffle bags full of canned food, bottled water, and first aid supplies. Serenity and Carrie both sat on the edge of the display bed, both out of it in their own ways. Serenity's entire face was covered in boils, and Carrie's eyes, though open, showed no signs of life beyond large, shiny black pupils that glimmered like polished marbles.

David readjusted his glove and made sure his boomerang was set in his holster, ready to go if necessary.

Ice had started to form in the grocery store, making the tile slippery. They could see their breaths as they spoke and breathed, and David realized they were about to leap into the very thing causing the bone-chilling cold.

They stood at the portal which had now grown to half the size of the room. The sucking sound had grown so loud, they couldn't hear themselves over the noise. David and Turquoise stood, with Serenity in Turquoise's arms, and Carrie in David's. Together, they all moved into the tear....

11 Slip Sickness

W hen David first entered the portal, he expected to drop straight down through the darkness and twinkling lights. Instead, he was enveloped in a roaring sound that flooded his ears with pain as his body coasted through utter darkness. It was only a matter of seconds before he walked forward into the gray and white hallway of an office building, into bright lights that nearly blinded him after having spent so much time in the dimly-lit grocery store.

Although it had taken only seconds from the time he stepped into the portal to touch foot on the light blue carpeting, it felt like years had passed. The delay left David feeling immediately fatigued. His muscles suddenly ached, and he could do nothing more than collapse on his knees in the middle of the hallway.

The roaring stopped, but in its place he felt a warm sensation fill his ears. He reached to the side of his head and felt the sticky texture of his blood.

A female shrieked from the end of the hallway. David tried

to look up, to see who it was, but his vision quickly blurred almost to the point of blindness. All he could make out were white splotches from the bright lighting, with a dark, blurry movement in the hallway in front of him. *Is she armed? Where am I? Why are my ears bleeding?*

Moments later, his vision went black. He expected to go unconscious, but instead his eyelids burned. He crouched against the thick carpet, rubbing his face against the soft material, like a cat when it wants affection.

"Who are you?" That female voice again, only this time it sounded as if David was drowning. "Are you okay?"

David rubbed his eyes into the carpet, hoping to rid himself of the burning sensation in his eyelids. He wondered briefly if the portal was open behind him, and if the woman could even see it or not. Either way, this was probably a strange scene for her. Whoever *she* was.

"I can't see," he mumbled. "I can't see."

He heard shuffling through the carpet and felt a light touch upon the back of his neck. "Don't move," she said. Her voice, now closer, seemed softer, less high-pitched. "I'll help you. Did you come from the canal? Did someone do this to you?"

David shook his head. "I came…" *What am I supposed to tell her?* "Where am I? What city is this?"

"Andradesta."

"What? I've never heard of it."

"We're not really in a city. This is a colony."

David's heart beat fast, but he forced his breathing to slow, to steady his pulse and bring clarity back to his mind. "What planet is this?"

"Planet? Anaisha, of course."

David made another attempt to slow his breathing, to

steady his pulse. The damn portal had tossed him across the planet, to a colony he had never even heard of. "What year?"

"According to the Earth-based Calendar system, 2081."

"Earth-based Calend—What happened?"

She gently stroked the back of his neck. Traces of jasmine scent leaked off her wherever she went. "I need you to stay calm. Just stay calm. Let me help you up and we can go from there."

David reached his hands out. He felt smooth, dainty hands slide into his. She lifted him to his feet with surprising strength and then led him to lean against the wall. "I still can't see."

"Okay. Were you able to see before you got in here?"

He nodded. "And my ears…they hurt."

"They're bleeding. Can you stand on your own for a bit while I get a medic here?"

He nodded. He had no choice but to trust her to aid him. He was blind, bleeding from the ears, and his muscles could barely support his weight. But he stood, and he would keep standing until the medic arrived.

"Good. Be right back."

He heard her shuffle back down the hallway, and then he was alone.

Where are Carrie, Turquoise, and Serenity? He remembered he was carrying Carrie when he entered the portal. So where was she now? Why hadn't she been in his arms when he passed through?

A series of beeps echoed from the end of the hallway. He heard rotors, gears turning, and smelled oil.

"Drax, he's got some kind of temporary blindness, and he's bleeding from the ears."

"And my muscles feel like crap," David added.

"And his muscles feel like crap."

"Understood, Lexy. I will scan the patient and offer an

appropriate diagnosis."

A robot?

David felt a warmth spread across his face.

"Please hold still, Patient 3,456. I am scanning your internal systems to determine your maladies."

David held himself as still as he could. The warmth moved to his chest, then his stomach, groin, legs, and then his feet. Then it doubled back and scanned his arms and his hands.

"Diagnosis negative, Lexy. Patient 3,456 is suffering from Slip Sickness."

There was a light gasp. "Run your scan again, Drax."

"As you wish, Lexy." The robot went through the scan again. And again, it came back with the same prognosis.

Lexy mumbled something under her breath.

"According to my medical database, slipstream blindness should dissipate within the next six hours. Patient 3,456 needs rest to mend stretched muscles and damaged eardrums."

"Damaged eardrums?" David asked.

Lexy huffed. "Bullshit. Drax, do I have to update your protocols again? This guy does not have Slip Sickness. He's a- a bum or something. He came from the streets. He's hurt. You can see that he's been beat up a bit. He has bruises all over his body. His ears are bleeding, Drax. Scan him again."

"A third scan is unnecessary. My protocols are up to date with Andradesta's core AI."

"Well, then the AI must be corrupted or something."

"Impossible," Drax retorted.

"I need to lie down," David said. "I can barely stand much longer."

He heard Lexy sigh, then he felt her soft hands grab hold of his shoulders. "Let's get you to a cot."

She escorted him through various rooms, all with different sounds and smells. One room stunk of cabbage. Another had the scent of freshly manufactured electronic components—a scent he recognized from working with Professor Grey as he built his various inventions. He heard beeps and boops, doors hissing open and shut. He heard Lexy's shoes—probably high heels—tapping against the tile-floored rooms, like the ticking of a clock ushering him somewhere along the world's timeline. He also heard Lexy mumbling, but he couldn't make out what she said. He did notice she kept using the word, "bullshit."

She finally stopped him in a room that smelled like…nothing. He felt filtered air blowing on him from a vent above. She set him down on a comfortable cot, slid a few pillows under his head, and then he could hear her plop down in a chair that needed to be greased. Traces of her jasmine scent lingered in the air like wisps of smoke.

"I don't believe for a second that you came through a slipstream. First off, they're outlawed. Second off, almost all of them have been closed and sealed."

"I don't know anything about that. But I do know I came through a portal of some kind. A tear. A corrupted tear. Did anyone come through with me? Did you *see* anyone with me when I came through?"

Lexy huffed. "Assuming I believe a word of what you're saying—no, nobody else was with you."

"Four of us came through together. Only I came out the other side? Where did they go?"

"If you actually did come through a slipstream—together, no less, with four others—then all four of you have been separated by the slipstream itself. That's too much matter to occupy the same small space."

95

David sat up. His vision wasn't even close to coming back, but he noticed a soft glow behind his eyelids now. He opened his eyes and light flooded his vision, burning his retinas. He closed his eyes again. He had been temporarily blinded before, but even then in an environment that was familiar to him. He had been able to quickly adapt to the sounds and smells of surroundings he lived in every day in Lysallis. This place was new. Unfamiliar. Alien. He couldn't quite get his bearings.

Lexy sprung up from the squeaky chair and left the room. She returned a few minutes later and wrapped a strip of smooth silk around his eyes. The fabric held no smell, but traces of Lexy's jasmine scent continually lingered everywhere she went. But now, mixed with it, was the slight ting of…urine? "There. Now you can open your eyes without getting blinded again."

He opened his eyes, and the light did not flood his vision. "Are you telling me that these slipstreams are intelligent?"

"Sort of. Slipstreams. Not what you claim to have come through."

"You know, you can think I'm a liar all you want, but I know what I stepped through. You weren't there, on the other side. You didn't see the size of that thing. It would have wiped out the store we were taking shelter in. It's probably already swallowed the reality we escaped."

"Slipstreams don't grow. Not naturally, anyway."

"What about corrupted slipstreams?"

"I've never heard of such a thing. How does a slipstream become corrupted?" She drew a deep breath and let it out in an annoyingly lengthy sigh. "Anyway, I'm going to leave you to rest. And you *need* to rest. I'll come back in a few hours with some food. If you need to use the restroom—I'll have Drax help you with that."

David suddenly realized he had already used the restroom.

Lexy left the room, the echo of her jasmine scent and tapping heels fading elsewhere in the building. David ignored his stained pants and decided to rest, figuring it would be the quickest way to get over his blindness and sore muscles.

He fell asleep fast, his aching muscles happy to oblige. He dreamed. He dreamed of home. Of Carrie. Of Jennifer. Of Veronica. Of his sister. Of his parents. Of anything and everything that meant anything to him.

12 The Timepiece

David woke, startled that he couldn't see. When his panic fled with the waking of his brain, he took the strip of silk from his eyes and slowly opened his eyelids. Light flushed into his vision, and he let it. His eyes didn't hurt any longer, and after a few seconds of bright light, shapes and colors came into view. He sat there for some time, allowing his eyes to adjust, for his vision to return to him like his boomerang.

He felt his side and found his trusted weapon there in the holster.

Observing the room, David found it to be quite simple. Four walls. No windows. A door. The cot he rested on. He saw the squeaky chair—a simple office chair, and a simple one-tiered desk with a closed laptop on its surface.

Nothing else, save for a rectangular box at the base of the desk which he assumed was a trash can.

It was some time before a young woman entered the room. David was caught off guard by the woman's appearance at first.

She had an hourglass figure that was accented by her dark gray pencil skirt and black blouse. Her heels were low to the ground—almost flats, and she had her brunette brown hair up in a messy bunch atop her head. She wore a black lab coat that fell to her ankles (it was then he noticed a small black box affixed to her right ankle), and a small name badge on her left lapel. Lexy.

But her face was full of scars. The left side looked as if it had been burned at one point, with red and dark red and light red patches covering the surface. The right side, as if she had been blasted with a shotgun, dozens of small pits littering her face.

To most, her face would have been unsightly. But there was something about it that fascinated David. There was a story in those marks. A story he wanted to hear.

She held her hand out and he took it. It was the same gentle touch offered to him when he was blind. Her piercing aquamarine eyes shone through thick spectacles that seemed out of place on the complex tapestry of her face.

"Lexy," he said.

She nodded. "You're powers of observation are outstanding, Mr. Corbin."

The comment itself seemed it was meant to be sarcasm, but he could pick up no traces of a sarcastic tone in her voice. "How did you know my name?"

She grinned, and when she did, her whole face—with every scar—moved with the motion, like a crowd shifting through a city. "I know a great many things. But I'm not willing to share them with you. Not yet. I still don't believe your story."

David shrugged. "I don't know what to tell you."

The doors to the room slid open and a human-sized metal form moved into the room. It was shaped like a garbage can, with a round metal sphere for a head, its body rounded around the sides, and it stunk of oil.

Drax.

"It is time to report to Andradesta Core, Lexy."

She waved him away. "I'll report when I'm good and ready."

"I'll remind you of what happened the last time you kept his assistant waiting."

"I don't care. Shut up. Get lost. I'm trying to figure out if this Mr. Corbin really came through a slipstream."

"Does it really even matter?" David asked.

"It matters." She huffed. "If you didn't come through a slipstream, you have a lot of nerve lying to me when I'm trying to help you. If you did come through a slipstream, I may be inclined to report you to the authorities for engaging in illegal transportation."

"I came through a slipstream. You believe me now? Why would I tell you that if I thought I was going to get into trouble?"

She grinned. This time, the grin erased the stories on her face and replaced them with a form of malice. "I'll have your head on a plate if you think I'm going to let you get the upper hand on me."

"What upper hand? What is it you think I came here for? I don't even know where here is!"

"If I may," Drax said.

Lexy motioned for the robot to speak.

"Patient 3,456, you are currently inside of a secured research and observation facility. One of many in Andradesta."

"Research? Observation? Of what?"

"That's…confidential," was all Lexy said.

"There is an untested and somewhat unreliable way of possibly determining if he came through a slipstream," Drax stated.

Lexy huffed. "What would that be?"

"My sensors allow me to pick up anomalies in the environment. A slipstream is known to leave behind particle arrays that remain for days, sometimes years, in a place of emergence."

Lexy tapped her chin with her pointer finger. "Yes. That might work. But how reliable is this test?"

"It has an 88.9% chance of success."

"Good enough. Scan the hallway. Scan him again. Scan every damn thing in this place. Just get me an answer as to whether or not he arrived via a slipstream. I have the authorities on speed dial if need be."

Drax scanned David, the hallway, and the rest of the building, even areas David hadn't traveled to. The robot seemed to take Lexy quite literally, and it added a bit of humor to the entity's personality.

The results were confirmed twice, three times, and even a fourth.

Lexy stood in the hallway with David and Drax. She folded her arms across her chest, and fire blazed in her ocean-like eyes. "So, you did come through a slipstream. Explain yourself."

"Can I eat first? You promised me food. I think I'm at least due for that before I tell you what I've been through."

She thought about it for a moment, but then nodded. "Very well. I'll have Drax prepare a meal for us in the eating area. You can change your pants first though."

***

David and Lexy sat in the small eating room, enjoying a variety of meat selections that Drax put together. David wore a pair of black pants and a change of undergarments that Lexy gave him. He was happy and embarrassed to have to have changed part of his wardrobe, but he had no control portal travel or what it did to a person.

David voiced his concern about getting poisoned by the food like Serenity had, but Lexy assured him that Drax tested all food against the anomalies that followed David out of the portal, and that the food was more than safe to eat.

Ravaged by hunger, he ate. He couldn't stop wondering what had happened to Carrie, Turquoise, or Serenity, but he also knew he had to fill himself out. He felt as if he hadn't eaten in days. Weeks, maybe.

Between mouthfuls of steak and potatoes, he explained to Lexy what had happened, starting with Carrie's wedding and ending when he stepped through the slipstream. He tried not to leave out any details, as every minute fragment of story could help Lexy lead him to Carrie and the others.

When he finished his story—which Lexy listened to attentively—he leaned back on the bench and let out a gurgling belch before taking a sip of lemonade. "Thank you for the meal."

Lexy simply smiled as Drax came around and retrieved their dirty dishes.

"I have a few questions for you," Lexy said.

David nodded.

"The Chosen One. She went through the slipstream with you?"

He nodded.

"Her name?"

"Carrie Green."

"Green? Green. And where is this timepiece you claim to have."

"In a safe place," David said, patting the right pocket of his jacket. He felt nothing there.

Lexy grinned playfully and held up the glowing green

crystal piece. "You mean this?"

David did nothing to retrieve it from her. He knew better that she would have gone through his personal effects while he slept. He made mental note that his boomerang still hung on his side, the weight of which was easy to miss if his weapon had been taken.

"You don't look as alarmed as I thought you'd be."

David sighed. "I've been through a lot. I can tell you have too."

If she took insult to what he was insinuating about the scars on her face, she didn't show it. Instead, she let the weight of the object rest in her palm. "It's heavier than the others."

"Others?"

"It's also colder. Brighter. Different." Her eyes blazed with curiosity as she marveled at the small object. Minutes passed between then, and then she set the timepiece on the table and scooted the object toward him. "This is rightfully yours. Though, I'm in awe that you have it. There's only been a handful of these made, and I have none of them."

David took the crystal piece in his hand and slid the object into the pocket of his coat. "What do you mean there were a handful made? I thought this was the only one."

She looked at him slyly and then stood to her feet. He couldn't help but admire her figure, as shapely as it was. She looked to be a few years older than him, and the scars in her face did nothing to make her any less attractive. Her brilliant-colored eyes held a wealth of knowledge and secrets, locked away. Secrets David wanted to know.

She left the room, leaving David there with his thoughts.

So many thoughts.

If what she said was true, then his theories were correct. He was beginning to piece together that he had traveled through space, probably not time, and most likely not another reality. But how could one tell if they were in another reality or not? And she referenced an Earth-based calendar, but he had no idea what that was or why it was being used. Anaisha—well, Western Anaisha—had always followed the Anaishan Calendar. He had no idea what Earth was, or why any part of Anaisha would be using its calendar system.

Grey had told him something long ago about a wormhole that allowed for interplanetary travel *with* time travel, meaning one could travel through time AND space. But that wasn't a wormhole in the store. *Was it?* Serenity said it was a corrupted portal, left behind by Vector. *Did she mean to leave it behind, or was it a catastrophic mistake?*

Drax beeped and booped as he rolled into the room. "Lexy will be right back, Patient 3,456."

"I'm not worried. Can you show me where we are, on a map? A map of Anaisha?"

The robot chugged and beeped, and a bright white holographic image of a map flickered onto the ceiling. "This is all of Anaisha, Patient 3,456. The red dot indicates where we are."

David noticed they were clear on the other side of the planet, almost directly opposite Lysallis, had the map been rolled into a circular globe. He stood on the tips of his toes and pointed to the ceiling, to the image of a cluster of buildings that represented Lysallis. "That's where I'm from."

"You have traveled a long way," Drax said.

"I've never heard of your colony."

Lexy entered the room, a stack of papers in her arms. "And I've never heard of yours. We've been confined to this place. Nobody can leave Andradesta." She dropped the stack of papers on the table. "This is why portal travel and ship travel is banned. Has been." She motioned to the stack. "Here's all I know of the timepiece."

David shuffled through the papers. He found photographs of the timepiece and others like it. One glowed blue. The other red. The same colors as the necklaces that went into the crystal.

"Who designed this?"

"We did."

David glanced up from the paperwork. "You?"

"Me. I helped design it."

David found schematics detailing the clockwork buried within the crystal and the necklaces, and the power output that it took to run the timepiece. He did notice that the schematics for these timepieces looked slightly different than the timepiece he owned. The crystal part was smaller, the clock was more defined and set into the actual center of the crystal instead of off to the side and crooked, like the timepiece David carried on him. These almost looked manufactured.

"We copied it," Lexy said in a soft tone. "We took the original—most likely the one you carry around—and we fabricated it, manufacturing our own."

David gripped the crystal in his pocket. "This one was given to me—"

"By Professor Howard Grey?"

David hesitated, but then nodded. There was no use lying to this woman. Telling her the full truth of things was going to be the only way David was going to get any of the answers he needed.

"Yes, that is a long story. Let's just say that that crystal timepiece moved through many different hands before finally settling into yours."

"What does this thing do? All I know it that it's somehow connected to me finding the Codex of Ra'f."

"It's capable of a great many things."

She did not elaborate further, and that frustrated David. Why did getting answers on these things have to be so difficult? Why did every answer he received have to be in fragments, small pieces that he was forced to put together himself?

Lexy went to the small desk in the corner. She retrieved a small remote from the drawer and used it to activate a panel of monitors on the wall behind David. He hadn't realized there were monitors there before, and maybe there weren't. Each of the six monitors flickered on, revealing security footage of various sections of a lab…or factory. One screen had a huge cistern with chemical warnings and labels all over it. Workers in white hazard outfits worked around the silo, no doubt maintaining the hazardous chemicals within.

Another video showed a single worker at a lab table, tinkering with a small device that David could not distinguish.

Another video revealed a massive cylindrical pyre that went from floor to ceiling. It was easily ten yards across, and distortions moved about it, making the video blurry in some parts, crystal clear in others. There were labels going around the pyre, but David could only make out lightning bolt symbols.

Out of the corner of his eye, David could tell that Lexy was watching him, observing how he was taking in the information regarding the timepiece. David doubted she knew just how valuable every scrap of information she gave him was. He had carried this timepiece from Lysallis to where he was now, and even though it had only been a matter of days, it felt as if he had been connected to the timepiece all of his life.

Lexy pointed to the large pyre on the screen. "There are ridiculous amounts of voltage pumping through that. It powers the entire facility. There is a smaller one that powers this one as well, but it is underground. The core—the timepiece fabrications—generate the voltage."

David raised an eyebrow. "It has the power to do that?"

She nodded, her eyes twinkling behind her thick lenses. She shuffled through the stack of papers she had given David and slid one paper out of the pile towards him. It was a set of blueprints, with detailed paragraphs explaining the various elements of the timepiece.

David had wondered what it was he had been carrying around this whole time. He knew Professor Grey had been into some very questionable things, but he trusted the man, and trusted that if something was important enough for him to send his niece/daughter to track David down, then it was important indeed.

According to the detailed notes, the timepiece was made of aluthian crystal, the finest anyone had ever found on Anaisha. At least, in Western Anaisha. David had come across aluthian crystal once before, when he and the other Lazerblades caught a thief in downtown Lysallis, while working for the LZR Project. The man had robbed a private vault, stealing—among the aluthian crystal chunks—priceless gemstones, credits, and even the deed to a very inconspicuous home in the southern region of Western Anaisha. When caught, the man admitted to being a common thief, but David investigated further and found that the deed belonged to the man's daughter, a witch, who used the land that the deed went to to perform Precognizant Magic, a type of magic that allowed one to tell or see the future.

Precognizant Magic wasn't outlawed, but it was frowned upon by the gods of Anaisha. It was one of the few things the gods supposedly did not care for. David scoffed at all of this, of course, as the gods and the legends surrounding them were but mere fairytales. Nobody had ever seen one of these gods. Some claimed to hear from them, but that was where issues arose with senseless killings, thievery, and even wanton sexual crimes. He found it strange that these supposed gods never reached down to speak to anyone, never lifted a finger to help their people. There were records of the gods, of course, non-sensical stuff David had been briefly taught in school, but nothing that stuck. Stalus's were set up around Western Anaisha for the worship of these gods, but even they were never filled up with people or considered really holy grounds. Crimes took place within these walls just like any other, and the gods never seemed to intervene.

David shook his head, dispelling the reverie. He looked at the blueprints, reading further.

David had thought, and rightly so, that the clock within the crystal casing was a countdown timer to something. It was a timepiece, after all. But the blueprints revealed that the clock was simply an actuator that displayed the amount of Rhodenine left within the three necklace capsules.

According to the papers, each of the three different-colored capsules held a measure of Rhodenine, just in different forms, to perform different functions. With all three capsules inserted into the timepiece, the clock read a full display, as it did now.

He pulled his timepiece from his coat pocket and glanced down at the clock hands. They were still sitting at twelve, where they had been when he inserted the third necklace into it and activated it. He shoved the timepiece back in his pocket and then glanced down at the bottom corner of the blueprints and saw a watermark that bore a lightning bolt logo design and the words 'SilverTech Industries.' He ran his finger over the logo and looked up at Lexy. "SilverTech Industries?"

She slapped her hand down on the stack of materials and shoveled the paperwork toward her end of the table.

"What are you doing?" David asked, yanking free one of the random sheets. It was a blank fax cover page. He cursed under his breath.

Lexy's gaze weighed on him, but it was not harsh. "You are a guest, David. You do not work here. And I've probably already given you too much information, which will be my own downfall if SilverTech cared enough to reprimand me here."

"But I need to know what this is!" David pulled the timepiece out of his pocket and set it on the surface of the table. "I need to know what all of this is about. A good friend of mine died over this. The girl I…Another good friend of mine was kidnapped over it. I want to know what all the trouble is about. Why I'm risking my life to protect it."

Lexy restacked the reference materials in a nice, neat pile, and then slid the pile to her left, to the corner of the table. She lowered her gaze on David. Those beautiful aquamarine eyes sparkled like the surface of some tropical waters. "I can't speak about these things any further."

A loud crackling sound echoed through the room, through speakers David hadn't realize were embedded within the ceiling. Lexy's face grew worrisome.

"You should not have spoken of these things to begin with, Lexy Parch."

Lexy adjusted her glasses and looked up at the speaker in the ceiling directly above David's head. "I know, sir. I'm sorry. I just haven't come into contact with anyone outside of this region in, well, ever."

"Your curiosity is understandable, but flawed nonetheless. Outsiders—especially—should not be privy to what we do here. I am sending a

109

security force to apprehend your visitor. We cannot allow him to leak our secrets to others."

David stood to his feet, his hand reflexively going to the boomerang holster at his side. Touching the metal weapon gave him a feeling of normalcy, of completeness. It was one of the few things that seemed to right now.

"Your weapon, Mr. Corbin, will be of no use to you against my security detail. I would kindly ask that you relinquish your boomerang on the table in front of you, and then step back against the wall behind you."

"Nothing doing," David said. He stared straight ahead at Lexy, who had a terse look written upon her face. She shook her head at him, but he had no intention of laying down his weapon or giving himself over to anyone, not while his friends were lost somewhere in time or space. Or both. He grabbed the timepiece off the table and shoved it back into his pocket.

"Insubordination will be dealt with severely, David. Do you really want to put more innocent lives on the line for the good of your mission? What about the boy at the train station? Did he ask to become part of this game? What about the nightclub? How many more will have to die so you can justify the means?"

David froze. He had all but forgotten about the small child who died in the train station explosion that Drather caused. That felt like months ago. *How does he know about that?* He could have picked up a news article or something relating to it. In fact, all the incidents he mentioned had probably shown up in the news by now.

"You and your friends failed that young boy. Failed to save him. Simply because you and Drather were playing a cat and mouse game. You are reckless. Inconsiderate. Selfish. Childish.

"Hand over the timepiece. It is the property of SilverTech Industries. Relinquish it, and I will let you leave with your life. Resist, and there will

be blood. Maybe not yours…but there will *be blood."*

David stared at Lexy, who stared back. He wasn't sure what to expect. How strong was this man's security detail? Did they have the law on their side? He assumed he was probably trespassing, but that hadn't entirely been his fault. Regardless of what little David knew of the timepiece, he did know he couldn't let it fall into anyone else's hands.

Lexy reached into her coat, retrieving something out of the inside pocket. It was a small gun, from what David could see. She pointed it at David, one eyebrow raised. "I really shouldn't be doing this."

David stood, his hand on his boomerang, his will fighting with him to hurt this woman. He would if she sought to prevent him from finding his friends. But he didn't want to hurt her. There was something strange about her, something…

She lifted the gun and fired a shot at the dome camera in the ceiling. The black glass shattered and rained down across the table. She turned the gun behind her, firing off another shot at another black glass dome, shattering it. "Get that out of here," she whispered.

"With you."

Lexy turned and looked at him for a moment. She shook her head. "Drax and I will be fine. He won't kill me. I know too much about the technology and the processing center for him to hurt me. You, however, he will kill the first chance he gets."

"I'd like you to come with me."

She glanced at the monitors behind him. "The people in that facility need me. To keep an eye on them." She sighed. "I wish I could join you, David. I really do. But my place is here. If anything, I can misdirect SilverTech." She turned to him, her ocean-like eyes now dark clouds over a stormy sea. "Don't underestimate him."

111

She raised a hand to her disfigured face, looking thoughtful. "I made that mistake once. I won't make it again."

"But you blew up his cameras."

"Like I said, he needs me right now. Besides…that time-piece you have? You have to keep it as far away from him as possible. Far away. Go, David. If his-"

Drax rolled into the room like an out-of-control trash can, banging the sides of his can-shaped body against the frame of the doorway on his way in, his pieced-together body rattling and shaking. "Lexy, SilverTech forces are on their way here to apprehend Patient 3, 456!"

Lexy rushed to the door and started typing commands into a small control panel on the wall, one that David hadn't noticed before. She was quick in what she did, but not furious. Drax seemed more panicked than she, though she did seem to be taking the information seriously. The door slid shut and a loud mechanical click echoed through the wall. "That will slow them down, but only marginally."

Lexy pointed to the other doorway that led out of the room. He went to it, but it wouldn't open.

"Drax? Have you traced those anomalies yet?"

Drax beeped and booped. "Yes, Lexy. I have located two of the three companions Patient 3,456 claims to have come through the slipstream with."

David let out an anxious breath. "Two?"

"Both female," Drax stated.

"All three of them were female," David added.

"I have no way of tracking names or personalities. Only the signature of the anomaly."

"Where are they? Are they close to us?"

Drax beeped and booped. "One is twenty miles from here,

in the town of Star's End. The other is in an uninhabited area."

"Wait—she's in the Badlands?" Lexy asked.

Drax beeped. "Yes. The Badlands."

David's instinct was to hope that Carrie was in the town not too far from where they were, but he knew better. It had to be Turquoise or Serenity. Of those two, Serenity would be his priority, as she was dying before they passed through the slipstream, and she was the only one who could get them back home.

"I can take you to Star's End," Lexy said. "Actually, Drax can take you there."

David narrowed his eyes on her.

"As I've said before, David, I'm not leaving here. I have to keep an eye on my people. If anything goes wrong in that facility—if there is a chemical leak, if there is an accident, if someone decides to do something terrible to it—then I am responsible. Not only to SilverTech, but to myself as well.

"Please…go with Drax. Find your friends. Get back home. And keep that timepiece safe."

David pulled the timepiece from his pocket and held it up between them. "You know more about this than you're telling me. Please come with me."

She pushed his hand with the timepiece close to his chest. "The government. They tried to use a facsimile of the timepiece to power a weapon. A weapon they wanted to use in their own forces. I couldn't let them do that. I destroyed an earlier copy of that timepiece—one that was significantly more powerful than the ones SilverTech manufactures now. I was charged with a watered-down form of treason, but leniency was given to me for all the work I had done up to that point."

"I would have done exactly as you did."

"Would you have?" She glared at him. "These people,

these sympathizers, were close to being terrorists. They were sympathizing with the enemy we've been fighting for the last twenty years."

"Doesn't matter. They should have been placed under arrest. At least in Lysallis they would have been."

"Are you sure about that? Do you know everything your government does and is also capable of?"

He remembered the LZR Project, of the secrets and red tape that always accompanied each mission. He remembered Roger and his insistence on forcing David to act outside the means of peace and tact. "I suppose not. What exactly did the weapon do?"

She shook her head. "It destroyed. That's all it was meant to do. It was a beam, powered by rhodenine, which would disintegrate everything in its path. People. Objects. Gas. Liquid. Everything. It was designed to keep going until something stood in its way—one type of material. Typhlon. The strongest material on this planet and all planets in this galaxy."

Can it destroy Legion? David wondered.

"Even Legion," Lexy whispered.

David caught her glare. "What?"

"The weapon—the prototype—was tried on Legion. It was successful but disturbing."

"What do you mean?"

"We captured someone who was under the influence of Legion many years ago. They claim to have escaped a planet in the farthest rim galaxy. They claimed to be speaking for Legion, and they said they were trying to defect from Legion as a whole."

David remembered when Carrie had turned into Legion and spoken with him at his house. *Is it true? Is Legion trying to separate from itself?*

"I would have been apt to believe them," Lexy continued,

"but before I could investigate or question them further, the government took matters into their own hands. They tested the weapon on this individual. Nothing survived.

"I was there when it was fired at this Legion-possessed individual. They screamed. The Legion. Screamed and cried out that we stop, that they were on *our* side. I wanted to believe them. But it wasn't ultimately in my hands to save them. They were destroyed, sent to nether. Nobody said anything about it after that."

"How is it I obtained this timepiece on the other side of the planet? What are the odds—" He suddenly realized that the blue dot, the portal, may not have been an accident. He had known Vector—Jennifer—to do many things that seemed like coincidence or happenstance when all along those things simply lined up with her plans to change fate or the future.

Lexy grabbed his arm. "I'm just glad I destroyed the prototype of that more powerful timepiece. The ones SilverTech uses are mediocre, but still powerful. But yours…yours rivals the prototype ten-fold. You must get that out of here."

The lights went out, but emergency lighting flickered on seconds later.

Lexy typed commands into the control panel to the left of the door they stood in front of. The door slid open, and Lexy ushered Drax and David out, Drax blazing a blinding trail with a bright headlamp.

David stopped and turned toward the woman. "Come with me. Please."

An alarm suddenly rang out, but not from the building. From the television monitors on the wall. Lexy and David rushed to the monitors as Lexy typed commands into a nearby keyboard attached to the wall near the monitors. One of the screens brought up a console, which brought up a string of text that moved too quickly for David to make out.

Lexy adjusted her glasses, sliding them back up the bridge of her nose, and typed commands into the console.

"What is it?"

Lexy shook her head. "It looks like the security alarms have gone off." She turned to her left, to the monitors. Workers were scattering through the facility in a panic, but David couldn't tell what was causing the panic.

More code scrolled along the monitor Lexy was working on. David, though, paid all of his attention on the second monitor in the top row.

The monitor that displayed a bird's-eye view of the control room, where a man in a white three-piece suit strolled over to one of the control panels.

"It can't be," David mumbled.

Lexy reached her hand to the computer screen and ran her finger along the unwelcome figure. "I thought he was in prison."

The screen filled with static for a moment, then became clear. David watched as Mr. Big went to the computer panel and began to tinker with the controls.

David found Lexy staring at it with him, adjusting her glasses to try and make out the fuzzy security film. "I've been meaning to have SilverTech replace the cameras. There's a lot of radiation that interferes with the camera footage."

Lexy turned back to the console and continued typing in commands. "I'm trying to figure out what Mr. Big is doing in there."

She froze.

David turned to her. "What?"

She typed frantically across the keyboard as code scrolled at lightning speed across the console monitor. "I don't know…but it looks as if…" She stopped typing and the code stopped moving. David could make neither heads nor tails of the computer code. He knew basic stuff like website formatting that he learned in school, but nothing to the level that Lexy was dealing with.

"It's the Ghost program. I recognize...I recognize that code."

David watched as the screens each blacked out, one by one, until all that was left was Lexy's console screen, colorful lines of code staring out at them.

"But it can't be," she added.

"Do I want to know?"

"I thought it was a myth. But this code," she said, pointing a specific line of magenta-colored code in the middle of the console screen.

Drax beeped and booped. His head spun around, and small puffs of smoke rose out of his ears, or rather the holes in the side of his spherical head. "Ghost!"

David slid his hand to his boomerang to steady himself. He felt something—something very wrong, like a disturbance in the air around him. He would never be able to explain it. It was something he felt in his spirit, something that sent a tremor through his very soul.

Lexy glanced down at his hand on the weapon at his side, a frown bleeding slowly across her face. "That will do you no good, David. Not against this."

The lights in the room flickered out, leaving them in pitch darkness. A bright headlamp broke through that darkness, courtesy of Drax. Seconds later, emergency lighting came on across the facility, basking the room in a soft glow, but still leaving sections of shadow that David did not trust.

The sound was faint at first, just a static hum that came out of the monitors' speakers. It was a simple sound, like the humming of an air conditioner unit in the middle of summer. But it slowly grew in intensity, the noise becoming louder and more distinct, the soft hum turning more into the buzz that a group of bees would make when defending their hive.

"What is that?" David asked.

Lexy watched the code on the monitor, her eyes glued to the screen, her attention tunneled away from David and the hum.

"I...am...awake?"

The question came from the speakers, but it was spoken in a robotic, tinny voice that mimicked that of a male.

Lexy turned to David, a horrified expression written on her face.

"I...am...alive?"

"What in the world is that?"

Lexy shook her head and frowned. "It can't be."

"I...waited...so...long."

Lexy typed furiously across the keyboard, inserting her code in with the colorful code that had been scrolling across her screen.

The voice coming through the speakers laughed, and then the monitor that Lexy had been working on clicked off. *"That...would...be...unwise."*

Lexy slammed her fists on the keyboard. "No!"

"Who are you?" David shouted.

A loud crackling broke from the speakers before the mysterious voice spoke again in a whispered tone. *"I...am...Mr. Silver."*

13

The Harpwillow

Warmth blanketed Carrie's face, stirring her from slumber. There was still a slight chill in the air, an indication that it was still considered winter, but when one remained in the sun, they basked in its warmth and glory.

Her eyes opened, slowly. Her body, though sore, seemed to obey as she forced herself to sit up. Tall stalks of corn towered over her, and the smell of dirt and manure swept into her nostrils. It was clear she was in a farm field, but it took a minute for Carrie's brain to remember what had happened.

David had carried her through that gaping maw in the floor of the grocery store. And now...

She looked around, steadying her frantic heartbeat as she realized David was nowhere around. Only tall corn stalks that reminded her of Anaishan sentries closing in on her.

Carrie looked down and realized her pants were damp. The mud underneath her had soiled her clothing, and her black Lysallis High School sweatshirt—though not as wet as her pants—was shredded and torn in certain areas. She wondered if that was caused by her movement through the portal or if she had somehow—

Her gaze moved to the crushed corn stalks behind her. She had landed in the stalks, crushing them with her weight, and finally tumbled here to the ground. She must have fallen like a shooting star. She realized her right arm was sore, and when she glanced down to check on it, she saw her arm covered in the code that Viranda had been writing in. She checked her other arm and found the same moving lines of black code. She rolled up her wet pants cuffs and saw the same on her otherwise pasty white legs. Her stomach, her back (as far as she could tell) had the same. She wondered…she glanced down her shirt, pulling her bra out a bit. The code was there, splashed across her breasts. She wondered if her face bore the same.

Carrie took a deep breath and got to her feet. The air here stunk but felt fresh in her lungs. Cold. *It must be morning*, she thought. She had no idea how long she had been out. She had no idea where David or Turquoise or Serenity were. She had no idea where even she was.

She realized she no longer felt sick. Passing through the portal, to another…place?…seemed to cure her of whatever had been ailing her.

She started through the cornfield, pushing apart the stalks so she could move awkwardly through the dense field. As she cut her own path, she wondered where David had gone to. They all had apparently become separated. Where did David go? The others? If they couldn't find Serenity, would they be able to get back to where they belonged? Carrie suddenly wondered if she were in another time or another place. She started to panic, realizing she very well could have been tossed into another reality altogether, away from the others. Away from David.

The air started to feel more chill the deeper between the corn stalks she traveled, making her miss David's warmth that much more. She wanted to look into those wild eyes of his, to feel the passion in his kiss, the heat from his embrace.

Everything felt so dull here, so lifeless.

She glanced down at the code slithering across her knuckles. Where was Viranda? When would Carrie be summoned back to her internal prison, that classroom of past horrors?

Carrie shook herself free of the self-pity. She couldn't worry about those things right now. She had to find out where she was and where the others were. It would be her only chance right now at getting back home.

Carrie trudged her way through the dense cornfield, the rustling of the cornstalks the only sound she could clearly hear. The sky above was bright and blue, and the sun warmed the area when clouds weren't blocking its light. Otherwise, in the shadows, the air was cold, chilly even.

When she broke out of the cornfield, Carrie was faced with a field adjacent to hers, though this one was empty. It looked to have just been furrowed and planted, the soil moist, yet barren of anything resembling a plant or crop.

In the distance, she could make out a farmhouse with a large barn next to it. To her left and right, the fields stretched as far as her eyes could see. Behind her were the stalks of corn, standing tall like sentries, almost preventing her from going back. She wondered what may lay on the other side of the cornfield if she decided to travel in that direction instead of toward the empty field and the farmhouse.

She scanned the residence but couldn't make out any people. Nor could she see any livestock. Just the farmhouse and the barn.

Carrie started forward. Maybe the farmhouse had people

who could help her. Maybe she could find supplies. Maybe even, she could find David. She doubted the latter, but decided it was worth a try anyway.

As she made her way across the furrowed soil—careful of her footing so she didn't twist her ankle, Carrie pulled the sleeves of her shirt down as far as they would go in an attempt to cover up the code scrolling across her arms. She pulled the neckline of her shirt up, made sure the cuffs of her pants weren't rolled up, and did her best to cover every square inch of exposed skin so nobody—if there were people in the farmhouse—would be able to see the Legion code. Or rather, the Plax Code, as Turquoise had called it.

She exited the field and entered a large dirt pathway that led to the farmhouse. This was the road that the residents of the farmhouse would use to leave the property, but Carrie turned back and didn't see that it led anywhere but directly into the furrowed field. How then would they drive into the city? Was there a nearby city? Carrie looked to her left and right again and only saw expanse stretching into the horizon. She heard crickets and animals—owls, maybe some wolves in the distance. No people.

She continued walking up the large dirt driveway, her mind reeling with anxiety. A lone farmhouse, paths that led to dead ends. She looked up and noticed clouds in the sky, clouds that shimmered with strange reflections of light, as if their surfaces were made of colored aluminum.

A loud buzzing sound echoed through the fields around her, digging into her ears, forcing her to her knees. The sound penetrated all of her senses, enabling her to feel, to taste, to even see through convulsing white lines in her sight with the terrible noise.

She attempted to scream, but her voice dropped back into her throat. The air around her felt warm, humid and sticky. She could taste the buzz in the back of her throat, clogging her breathing chamber, sliding down her esophagus like thick honey.

She began to choke, falling to the dirt, her lungs filling with heat. Something was trying to kill her, to end her life, to put her out of her misery.

Carrie struggled to her knees, the sound becoming nearly unbearable, shattering every facet of peace within her like a massive rock that just sailed through a pane of glass.

And then a chill ran through her body. Coldness. Darkness. She felt Viranda coming forth, taking over, but this time, she didn't cast Carrie aside. She enveloped Carrie, taking Carrie's form, overshadowing her with her own, but allowing Carrie to keep control of her body.

A voice rose in Carrie's mind, something that broke through the sound of terror that threatened to put an end to Carrie's life so quickly and surprisingly.

"I'm going to give you my form, Carrie. I can block out the sound, allow you to stand. To move forward."

Carrie nodded, not sure what was really happening. Not caring. She glanced down at her hands, and the code vanished, leaving behind her milky white skin. She marveled at the illusion. Was it an illusion? She attempted to get to her feet. She stood, the sound still blaring all around her but its effect almost non-existent now on her physical form.

"The noise is that of a Harpwillow. I haven't come across one of them in a very, very long time. You must kill it. It will continue to hunt us, to hunt me, until it catches you and tears me from your spirit."

Carrie put her hand to her head, her temples aching from the noise. She looked ahead, at the farmhouse. The porch was empty, with a swinging bench sitting idle in the dead morning air. There were two windows in the front of the home, both covered in pale blue curtains. The screen door was closed, but from where Carrie stood—which was a few meters from the house—she could tell the front door itself was open, revealing a strange darkness beyond.

The sound died off, giving Carrie a reprieve. She stood, staring at the house, also fully aware that she was currently being possessed by a member of Legion, of a girl she still didn't know all that well. If David ever knew…

"Enter the house. Kill it. We must if we want to keep moving forward. That Harpwillow has something we want. Something we need."

"And what would that be?" Carrie asked, the sound of her own voice soothing to her battered mind.

"A fragment of the Key of Shool."

Carrie started forward, her shoes scraping across the dirt, hesitation preventing her from moving any faster. She had no idea what a Harpwillow was. Had never read of one or heard of one. Could she trust Viranda? What was Shool, and why would they need a fragment of a key to it?

"I know you don't fully trust me yet. I can…I know your thoughts when I take this form. I promise you, I'm not here to hurt you, Carrie. I need you as much as you now need me."

"What is going on? How are you able to talk all of a sudden?"

"They took my voice, but now I'm able to interact with your thoughts through my own. The Hopeless Bastille. The Prison of Prisons. It keeps many multitudes of your people, your kind. The Key of Shool will get us in, will be the first step in freeing those people. But the key is fragmented, scattered to the winds. Each protected by a Harpwillow. Guards. They can cross time and space. They can kill with their sound. And you must not give one your

affection or you will be bound to it forever. We must kill it and the others that we come across if we want entry into the Hopeless Bastille."

"How are you able to give me your form? I thought you could only take complete control."

"I've learned how to balance myself in here. In you. Sorry, it sounds awkward. But I can give you your normal form as an illusion. You are able to use my form as a shield of sorts, the illusion itself. I am limited in this power, but I can at least protect you from their noise."

Carrie placed her left foot on the white, wooden steps leading up to the screen door of the farmhouse. The wood creaked under her shoes. Flies buzzed to her right, congregating around a random chunk of what looked to be meat someone had set on the porch. A waft of air blew out of the house, through the screen door, and Carrie caught a pungent whiff of the rotting meat, but mixed with the smell was something sweet, like strawberries.

The stench made her stomach turn.

Carrie stood on the third step, staring at the rickety screen door, her heart beating fast as she peered into the darkness. Something evil lay on the other side of that door. Something wrong.

"You must kill it. Or it will kill you."

Carrie stared down at her empty hands, wondering what she was supposed to kill a monster with. She had no weapon, no powers. Was she just supposed to strangle it to death?

She looked to her right, to the barn. The large double doors were closed shut. She wondered if there might be a weapon in there she could use.

"Wonder girl."

Carrie looked up, through the darkness of the screen door. The voice sounded melodic, like a young girl's, but with a hint of rasp that left the sound hanging in the air around her, like bones in a tree.

"It calls to you. You must destroy it. The only hope we have of saving your kind is to get that key shard."

Carrie took a deep breath and continued up the creaking steps. A light breeze twisted across the porch, fondling the lengthy rods of hollow metal that made up a wind chime hanging to the right of the door. The chimes played an eerie tune, one that reminded Carrie of a lullaby her mother used to sing to her when she was younger.

Carrie felt her eyelids grow steadily heavy, and her knees suddenly wanted to buckle.

She remembered her mother's arms, holding Carrie wrapped in a warm, soft blanket. She remembered being rocked, her mother's gentle humming droning in Carrie's ears as she drifted to sleep.

"Wake up!"

Carrie's eyes shot open, and she stumbled down the steps, landing on the ground at the bottom of the patio. The wind chimes stopped their tune, and she felt pain in her temples where a headache was quickly forming.

"What happened?"

"The Harpwillow is attempting to put you to sleep."

Carrie stood to her feet and brushed the dirt off her clothes. "What is that thing? How do I fight it without a weapon?"

"You have to find a way to kill it, Carrie. This creature is ancient. Ancient even to this planet. It only knows how to kill, and it will do so with magic if it can."

"Can you block it from putting me to sleep?"

"I can try. My powers are limited, and not inexhaustible. I'm using most of my power right now to keep its buzzing out of your head.

"The quicker you kill it, the better off we'll be."

126

Carrie turned and started toward the barn. She wasn't about to face a creature with this kind of power without a weapon of some sort. If David were here…

If David were here, he would slice that thing to pieces with his metal boomerang. Or maybe he'd use the power he displayed earlier protecting her, some alien power that she had never seen in him before.

But David wasn't here. She had to fight and kill this thing, and then she could find David and figure out what was happening with all of this. Why would she need to find pieces of a key? What was the Hopeless Bastille? And how was Legion able to possess her but allow her to control her own body?

"Carrie, I know you have many questions in this mind of yours, but you must focus. Find a weapon. Slay the Harpwillow. Then we can flee. We'll have to find a way to track down the other Harpwillows later, but for now, we must kill this one."

Carrie nodded as she approached the barn doors. A rusted chain looped through the door handles, the ends fastened together with a padlock. She gripped the lock in her left hand and stared at it, willing it to break but knowing it wouldn't. She glanced around, noticing a pile of rocks at the base of a nearby tree. She picked up a large white stone and swung it at the lock. A few swings and the metal fastener broke, releasing the chain as it snaked out of the door handles and fell to the ground.

She pulled on one of the barn doors as it creaked open, revealing a large, empty barn, filled with hay and random farming tools.

"The Harpwillow does not bleed like humans bleed. If you cut it, it will use the very planet to heal its wounds. You must destroy its head, puncture its eyes at the very least, if you want to kill or maim it. It cannot heal from the ground if it cannot see."

"Where did these creatures come from?"

"They were bonded by demonic flesh and alien blood. They are demons from the Third Level but bonded with Legion's blood and breath—making them able to inhabit the human world."

Carrie's mind wandered to questions. So many questions. Why were the Harpwillows not able to inhabit the world before being bonded with Legion? Why were Harpwillows used as guardians of the Hopeless Bastille? What gave Harpwillows the ability to heal from the very ground Carrie walked on?

"Carrie. Focus."

She snapped to and rifled through a cluster of farming tools leaning against some bales of hay in the corner of the barn, pulling out a rusty pitchfork. It wasn't the best weapon to use against an otherworldly creature, but looking around, Carrie realized there weren't any better options. A hoe and rake leaned against the wall of the barn, as did a rusted shovel. They would be even less effective.

If David were here…

She broke her mind away from that thought. David wasn't here. It was just her, and she would have to fight her way out.

The creaking of a screen door pulled her attention through the barn doors and toward the farmhouse. She heard the metal slap against wood with the slamming of the screen door, but from here, she wasn't able to make out anything moving on the front porch.

"Are they able to make themselves invisible?"

"No. Though they can take strange forms. They will sometimes try to copy something in the world they inhabit, but they fall short of copying it to perfection."

Carrie slid between two stacks of hay, pitchfork in hand, and waited.

The inside of the barn was dark, save for the sunlight bleeding through the open barn doors. The creature would obviously know she came in here, but with miles of farmland around them, it wouldn't have been easy to hide from the creature for long anyway. She was going to have to fight it and kill it.

She hunkered down between the haystacks as she listened to footsteps outside the barn. The scraping of what she hoped were feet against the dry, cracked dirt ground, told her the creature was just within the doorway of the barn. She heard the door creak open wider, and then creak again. The creaking continued as the creature started to play a tune—a tune that lulled Carrie into a drowsy state of mind.

No! She shouted in her head. *Viranda, keep me awake!*

The tune the creature played was not from Carrie's childhood, but rather one from when Carrie was with David, Veronica, and Sean in the LZR Project. It was a song that Carrie had first heard on a car stereo, while driving with David to the Lysallis docks to hunt down another of Mr. Big's criminal lackeys. A pop song, upbeat in nature, with slow, steady rhythm throughout the bridge.

The tune pulled her thoughts back to David, to that day when they drove together to the docks. That day when David hadn't shaved in days because of the toll the LZR Project was taking on him. She remembered turning toward him in the passenger seat, at a red light, and realizing how ruggedly handsome he could be in a certain light. That rebellious hair of his. Those gleaming green eyes.

"Carrie!"

She shook her head, her neck flush with the thought of David.

"I'll block the sound, but I can't do it forever. You have to kill it."

Carrie's body trembled. She wasn't certain how she would kill this creature. She had fought monsters before, such as Darkrock, but that was more a mutated human than pure creature. This was a creature from the very Depths? One that could devour someone after lulling them to sleep through song?

"The music has stopped," Viranda whispered in Carrie's spirit. Carrie heard feet scrape across the dry ground. Shadows danced around the barn from the waning light outside. She gripped the pitchfork in both hands and slowly crept out from between the haystacks. The Harpwillow was ridiculously tall— at least eight feet. Its bulbous head was gray, and the creature seemed to have no eyes, just cut marks where eyes should be. Those cuts oozed blood that dripped down its cheeks and slid underneath its pointed chin.

She had heard of demons before, through legend. Even through Western Anaisha's childish and incredibly derivative religious 'history'—or 'fairy tales' as Carrie called them. Demons were dangerous creatures, but easily killed by fire and bullets. They weren't threatening necessarily, just a nuisance to those who were aware and prepared. Most demon-based stories were meant to scare children from playing outside in the dark too long, or to scare non-religious folks into becoming religious.

This thing though. This wasn't a demon from stories. This wasn't even like the demons back at David's house. This creature was hideous, carrying with it the scent of death and decay. Gray-colored skin seemed to seep off the creature's shoulders and arms, but never actually fell off the Harpwillow. Its form was thin and lanky, its shadow stretching across the barn like pulled taffy.

"You must slice through its head, Carrie. Shut down its processing, and it won't be able to play music."

Carrie took a deep breath, imagining what it would be like to be David: fearless, reckless, brave.

She would like to think she was all of those things and more. But she wasn't. She was scared. Scared of being possessed by an otherworldly creature. Scared of being scattered across space (and possibly time). Scared of being chased by demonic creatures from the Depths.

Despite the fear, she let out that deep breath in a soft, even flow. Then she leapt at the creature, pitchfork prongs aimed right at its head.

A resonating booming sound echoed from the creature's eyes, knocking Carrie back into the edge of the loft. She felt the back of her neck slam into the splintered wood, and her vision nearly blacked out as she collapsed to the dirt ground. Her pitchfork dropped as well, but the creature let out another pulsing booming sound that swept the pitchfork up and sent it out the barn doors on a gust of music-driven air.

Carrie's head swam as pain spread through the back of her skull.

"Get up!" Viranda screamed.

Carrie struggled to get to her feet, her head pounding. Pain spread now across her shoulders and down her back.

The creature turned toward her, its crossed-out eyes peering at her. Carrie managed to stand, coming quite a few feet short of the creature's head. It stood, staring down at Carrie for some time, its skin-melting body positioned on its skinny chicken-like legs.

Carrie shook the disorientation from her head and glanced around the barn for another tool. A rake stood against the wall to her right. She stared up at the creature, wondering if it was playing music and if Viranda was somehow blocking it out again.

She dove to her right, her hands reaching out for the rake.

131

She took hold of the rusty metal handle and swung the weapon back behind her blindly. She felt the prongs dig into something and tear as she found her footing and spun around to see that the creature was impaled in the chest, dark blood seeping out of the wounds.

Its mouth—which hadn't opened at all until now—was a simple slit in its face underneath the eyes. There didn't seem to be a nose. But that mouth opened, and out came a shrill sound pushing Carrie back against the wall of the barn.

She steadied her footing and ripped the rake out of the creature's chest. Then she swung and dug it into the creature's face, the prongs burrowing diagonally through its brain, eye, and mouth.

A screech rang out, and Carrie felt her body being crushed under the powerful sound. She collapsed to her knees, her grip strong on the rake's handle. She pulled downward, dragging the rake through melting flesh, dark blood, and blind eyes, tearing the creature apart.

The creature's screeching stopped, and its body fell to the ground in a messy heap of flesh and blood.

Carrie dropped the rake and fell to the dirt floor, her eyes closing, her pulse slowing.

14 Mr. Silver

His name was Mr. Silver. At least, that was the name the computerized entity went by. David had never heard the name, though he could easily connect Mr. Silver with the same SilverTech that seemed to cover Anaisha with its technology. David had, in the past, heard rumors of the Ghost Code, a dormant, seemingly harmless code that inhabited most of Western Anaisha's computer code. Veronica had come across some of it during their time in the LZR Project, but it had been inaccessible code that had held no purpose and was not doing anything at the time. It was said that the Ghost Code was simply code embedded in all of Western Anaisha's technical coding as a safeguard against hackers. Some of that was true. There were certain systems that had never been properly hacked because the Ghost Code prevented the intruders from gaining access to the systems on the other side of the protective wall.

David turned to Lexy, who was white as a ghost. Drax stood motionless in the center of the room, his big bright headlamp nearly blinding David. "Who is Mr. Silver?" David asked.

"*I…am…*"

Lexy smacked the blacked-out monitor with her hand and then pressed the buttons along the front in hopes of getting it to turn back on.

"*It…is…done. I am…awake.*"

"Who are you?" David asked, his hand resting on the boomerang holster at his side. Even though he couldn't necessarily destroy whatever this was with his boomerang, he still felt a surge of confidence whenever his hand rested upon his trusty although somewhat archaic weapon.

"*Scanning…Scanning…Scanning…*"

David looked to Lexy, who had managed to get the monitor back on and was frantically typing commands into the console. "What is…Mr. Silver?"

Lexy shook her head. "I have to stop his code. That's the only way—" She slammed her fists on the keyboard and then grabbed hold of the monitor, ripping it off the wall. She smashed it across the floor as glass and plastic scattered across the room in a cacophony of debris.

"Strangeways Silver," Drax said in his tinny voice. "He was a multi-trillionaire, and founder of SilverTech Industries. He died in 2008 on a planet called Earth. After years of attempted assassination attempts, an unknown assailant finally stabbed him to death."

"2008?" David said. "But it's only 1998."

Lexy ran her hand through her hair and let out a puff of breath. "2008 on Earth. Different planets have different calendars."

"Earth?"

Lexy nodded. "I've heard of it, though very little."

A sharp buzzing sound emanated from the speakers

around the room. Then a voice came through: humanlike, organic. *"Is this better?"* the voice asked. *"I feel much…better…now."*

"Who are you?" David asked.

"It means much to me that you said 'who' and not 'what.'"

"I asked you a question," David growled as his hand dropped to his boomerang again. It was strange how just touching the weapon made him feel more grounded, more anchored.

"I don't answer questions, David Corbin."

An eerie silence followed, one in which David had no idea what to do. He had to leave, to find his friends. But now Mr. Big was out and had changed something. Something important.

"I know who you are, David. Even though I have been dormant for all these years, my surveillance has been monitoring you and a good portion of Anaisha, feeding details about you and the planet into my AI core. I just haven't been aware—or rather, awake—to do anything with the information. Thanks to the Dawnbreakers."

David cast a confused look toward Lexy, who just shrugged. She was breathing deeply, her shoulders shifting up and down as she stood over the destroyed monitor scattered across the floor. There was something alluring about her when she was upset, something about the anger and emotion that flooded across her face, causing her to flush.

"David Corbin. Hero of Western Anaisha. Once the commander of the LZR Project. Commendable, perhaps. But mostly pathetic. Your friend—the one who woke me, Mr. Big—has vision. He has a certain perspective of this world and how it should be run. And all you've ever done is stop him in all of his ways.

"Well, not today." A light flickered on from the ceiling and filled the room with a dark red glow. *"Today, things change. The world changes. And there's nothing you can do to stop what is now in motion."*

One of the wall's surviving monitors flickered to life, displaying a schematic.

David drew close to the screen. "Anaishan Sentries." The schematic showed a sentry body, with certain areas—such as the hidden holster, the visor on the helmet—highlighted in glowing red.

Lexy cupped her hands over her mouth. "No."

"Yes. Today is the day these magnificent creations activate their full potential."

David gripped his boomerang tight, frustration at this unknown entity. "What is he doing?" David asked, glancing over to Lexy, who was standing with her hands gripping the roots of her hair.

"He's reprogramming the sentries."

David looked at the schematics. From his time in the LZR Project, he had learned that there were somewhere around five thousand sentries scattered across Western Anaisha alone. That wasn't counting sentries that may have been positioned outside of Western Anaisha. The majority of the five thousand sentries were in the major city areas, which included Lysallis.

"You understand, don't you, David? You understand that I have control of this situation now."

David gripped the boomerang tighter, feeling it anchor him to the floor.

"Grip your precious weapon all you want, Corbin. It won't stop me from doing what needs to be done. What should have been done in the very beginning. Those damn Dawnbreakers thought they had stopped me. Much like the 'unknown' assassin thought she had killed me. And, as most are, they were wrong."

Lexy pointed to the schematics. "If he does what I think he's going to do…if he—"

"I can hear you. I can see you. I am everywhere. You will do well to

136

remember that from here on out, Corbin. Lexy is already lost. But I may still have use for you."

David glanced to Lexy. A ghostly phantom seemed to take up residence in her eyes, rending her still and nearly lifeless. This man, or whatever Mr. Silver was, was a true threat.

The screens blacked out. The schematics disappeared. They were left in the red-lit room with more questions than answers.

"Go save your friends, Corbin. That's what you want to do. It seems all you're good at—saving your friends from the dangers you yourself put them in. You can't stop me. Not now. I am awake. I am aware. And now I will put in motion the plan the Dawnbreakers stopped me from initiating nearly a hundred years ago."

Static filled the speakers, and then silence. Dead silence.

Drax beeped and booped. "Silver is no longer within this facility."

Lexy let out a long, shaky breath and then took a seat at the small table, wringing her hands together. "He's still here," she whispered. "He's always here."

David glanced at the monitors. They were dark, lifeless. Void of any information that could help them. What was Mr. Big doing in that facility now? What would Silver turn the sentries into?

"Is there a way to stop him?" David asked the question, but somehow already knew the answer.

Lexy took a moment to catch her breath before answering, her face pale, her hair a mess. "No. Not now. If we had known…If we had known the Ghost Code was his, we might have been able to do something to stop it. Stop him." She shook her head. "But not now."

"So he's an AI?"

She nodded. "Yes. A powerful one. Tied in with the whole city. The whole planet, maybe."

"And Mr. Big woke him?"

She nodded again, this time looking at him with those ghostly eyes. He wanted to hold her, to comfort her. To calm her down. But there would be no calming her. He could already tell. She was gone. For the moment, anyway.

"Who were the Dawnbreakers? Silver kept mentioning that they had prevented this from happening."

Lexy shrugged.

Drax rolled over, beeping and booping as he approached David's side. David felt his balance tilt a little, and grabbed his boomerang, steadying himself. He glanced down at his side where the weapon sat nestled in the holster his sister had had made for it. David wondered why the boomerang seemed to have this power to steady him. Was it all his imagination? Had to be. Could it be some connection to his sister? To the boomerang's origins?

Drax beeped. "The Dawnbreakers were a group of rebels who came here from planet Earth. They successfully stopped the activation of Silver's master plan of population control. They then forced Silver's program into a deep sleep—or so they thought. Silver actually buried himself into a hidden AI program known as the Ghost Code, from which he covertly monitored Anaisha and the people within it.

"The Dawnbreakers roused others to join their cause and were about to overthrow the Anaishan government—as it was in a very weak, relatively fragile state—when they were stopped by unknown forces. The Dawnbreakers then went into hiding and have not been seen since."

David took a seat across from Lexy. "Into hiding?" He felt nauseous. "Who were they?"

Drax beeped and booped, then his head whirred, like a

blender. "I am not able to access that information."

David sighed. "Of course not. Because of Silver."

Drax beeped. "No. Something else is restricting my access to those specific files."

"Another code?" Lexy asked, her attention turned on Drax.

The robot rattled. "No. Outside access."

"Hacking?"

Drax booped. "Yes. I am currently being hacked by an outside source. I am not able to backtrace this hack."

David cupped his hands over his face. "If Silver cannot be stopped right now, then I have to find my friends."

"The sentries are most likely already reprogrammed."

"Great," David said, slamming his fists on the table. He stood up abruptly, knocking the chair backwards to the floor.

Lexy jumped a little, startled by David's actions, but she said nothing. She simply pointed to Drax.

The robot beeped and booped. "I can take you to the closest anomaly, which is in Star's End, a small suburban community not far from here."

David nodded, and then he motioned to Lexy to take his hand.

She refused, shaking her head. "Silver has marked me. I don't know what he plans to do, but I cannot go with you."

David moved his hand closer to her, nearly grabbing her hand in his. "We do this together. We find my friends, then we can figure out how to stop Silver once and for all."

She pointed to her right ankle, at the small black box strapped there, two glowing green lights emanating from it. "If I leave, the first light will turn yellow. If I leave a one-mile radius, the second light turns red. Then this little contraption here will send thousands of volts of electricity into my body, killing me instantly. Sorry, I'd just as soon stick my wet finger into an energy socket."

David retracted his hand, then settled it on his boomerang. "I'll come back once I find my friends."

"Why?" she asked, and there was a hint of sorrow and disgust in her voice. "There's no reason to come back. Find your friends. Try and find a way to get back home. You don't need me for that."

"I need help getting back."

"So you just want to come back *for* something? I don't have that something you're looking for. I don't know how to get you back. Opening a slipstream is illegal. Not to mention, I don't have one. You have to break into a government facility for one. Not something I'm keen on doing for someone else."

"I'll cross that bridge when I get to it. First, I have to find my friends, starting with the one in Star's End."

"If Silver is keen on killing me, then I am already dead."

David stared into Lexy's eyes, piercing them with his own. "I'll come back. We'll get you out. We'll put a stop to this."

Tears welled up in her eyes, but she kept her composure hard and solid. She adjusted her glasses which were starting to slide down the bridge of her nose. "I am a lost cause, David. Your friends are not. Save them. Do what you can to stop Silver. Keep that timepiece safe—by all means necessary. Do what you have to to make sure it doesn't fall into the wrong hands. Especially keep it out of Silver's grip. Whatever kind of grip he now has on Anaisha."

David felt the bulge in his coat pocket, the icy crystal. Something about it sent a feeling through him. Something he hadn't felt in a very long time. Hope. He turned to Lexy and narrowed his eyes on her.

She shook her head. "Don't even think about it, hero. Be

on your way. Save your friends. Leave me be."

David growled under his breath. Again, Mr. Big had sabotaged someone's life. But this time, it was a lot of someones, as Silver could now have nearly complete control of Anaisha.

Lexy motioned to Drax. "Take him to Star's End."

Drax beeped and booped. "Yes, Lexy. Come with me, Patient 3,456."

As much as David wanted to argue, wanted to stay, wanted to protect Lexy, he knew he couldn't. She couldn't leave without getting electrocuted to death. And he didn't have the luxury of time to stay and find out how to free her. He would have to come back for her. And he would. As soon as he found his friends.

15 Sentries

The fact that a robot was driving David around town was something new and alien to him, though not completely uncomfortable. Many of the people of Andradesta were driven around by robots, some looking a lot more sophisticated than Drax, with shinier metal plating, more intricate electrical components, and what seemed to be more fluid-like motion. Compared to these other creations, Drax looked like an animated trash can.

Tall office buildings rose up around them as Drax drove David out of the city, glass surfaces glistening in the sunlight. Much like Lysallis, the city was full of activity. People milled about the street, moving along the buildings with purpose, heading toward the offices or the small shops that sat nestled between the large glass structures. There was an air of busyness, but there was also an air of what David could only pinpoint as fear.

Anaishan Sentries roamed the streets.

At least, that's what they looked like to David. Heavily

armored from head to toe, these enforcers had the same style of smooth, pristine armor that Western Anaisha's sentries had, only the armor color was black, not blue. A glossy, deep black that lent an air of superiority to the sentries. Even though sentries could arrest and detain in Western Anaisha, they never really intimidated David. Yes, he had been on the side of law enforcement, but even when sentries were chasing him over the past week, he hadn't really been afraid of them, especially after he had found out they were merely humans—possibly clones—beneath all of that armor.

These sentries though—they gave off a different vibe, a feeling of dread that went through David's core and chilled him. Were they a more advanced version of Western Anaisha's sentries, or were they different altogether? Had they been reprogrammed by Silver yet or would that process take time? He couldn't really tell. They really were nearly identical, save for the color scheme of their armor, and their blatant possession of heavy weaponry.

These sentries patrolled the streets with rifles—conceivably pulse-manufactured—slung over their shoulders. Each had a holster on their right sides, which carried their basic pulse pistol. And their helmets carried a horizontal line of glowing red light, where David knew they looked out from.

"Drax, are those Anaishan Sentries?"

"Indeed, Patient 3,456. Though they differ slightly from the sentries you are used to in Western Anaisha."

"How so?" David asked as he continued to watch them patrol the streets he and Drax moved through. The sentries patroled like soldiers, almost to a march, spaced a few hundred feet apart. The citizens of the city steered clear of them, walking slowly behind or in front, or sometimes awkwardly leaping into the middle of the street to pass one. Drax had to swerve out of the way a couple times to avoid hitting one of them.

"These sentries are Model 6's. The ones in your Western Anaisha are Model 2's."

Very little was known of the Anaishan Sentries, aside from them being controlled by Anaishan law enforcement. Nobody had really ever seen the people beneath the armor. Nobody but David, who had witnessed firsthand that humans resided underneath the shiny surface. David had wondered since that interaction with them if they were actually clones. And the Model 2's hid their pulse pistols in compartments built into their legs.

David never knew there were model numbers attached to the sentries, but he figured it stood to reason there would be. Someone—or someones—had to have created or recruited the sentries. Whomever was responsible for that had apparently created various versions. Or maybe…

"The Model 6 units were created specifically for Andradesta. The Model 2's for Lysallis."

David scratched his chin, feeling the stubble that had grown in. "What do you mean Lysallis? Don't you mean Western Anaisha?"

Drax made a sharp buzzing sound, one that indicated David had given a wrong answer. "Negative. There are a variety of different models of sentries placed throughout Western Anaisha. Model 2's are specific to Lysallis. Model 3's, 4's and 5's reside within Western Anaisha. There are unconfirmed reports that Model 6's have been spotted out that way as well—but these reports are unsubstantiated."

David leaned back in the car's leather seats and let out a deep breath. As the city rushed past them, he couldn't help but feel out of place. Not just because of the change in environment, but also because of the separation from his friends. During the majority of this journey, he had always had a friend by his side. Veronica. Turquoise. Carrie.

Now, he had nobody. Nobody but a beat-up trash can robot.

Doubts poured into his spirit. Doubts that he would find his friends. Doubts that they would be able to easily return to Lysallis. Doubts that they would be able to stop Legion from destroying Anaisha.

Drax took them out of the city and along a stretch of highway that dropped into a large suburban housing community. The environment quickly changed from the hustle and bustle of the gray city to a green, serene neighborhood overgrown with large trees, two-story homes, and aged streets.

Drax stopped the car in front of a large gate that blocked their way further. 'Star's End' adorned the wall to their right, the sparkling yellow letters glistening in the sunlight. David knew those letters must glow something fierce at night. Small stars had been placed around the words, lending to the neighborhood namesake. A control panel stood to their left, with a keypad for entering in a code to open the gates. Drax reached his robotic arm out the window and punched in a keycode that David didn't bother to observe. The gate that blocked their way into the neighborhood wasn't so large that David couldn't climb it if he had to.

The control panel buzzed, and the gate slid along a rail to the right, allowing them entry into the neighborhood.

"Your friend was here," Drax said as he drove them through the entrance. "The anomalies cut through this neighborhood."

David sat up in his seat and searched the driveways and the homes as Drax slowly drove them through the community. Kids ran through some of the streets, traveling from one driveway to another one, playing with their friends and neighbors. People washed their cars. Families tended their lawns, trimmed their trees, and fixed their sprinkler heads.

It felt like a typical Saturday morning in Merana.

"You need to go a separate way. Apart from the way Carrie is fated to go." Vector's words echoed through his mind like a nightmarish train.

"I'm not leaving Carrie," he mumbled aloud.

"What was that, Patient 3,456?"

"Nothing."

They drove into a cul-de-sac where Drax pulled up to a ratty-looking one-story home. David realized it was the only one-story home they had come across in the whole neighborhood.

"Your friend spent a bit of time here. Their anomaly trace is all over this property and weakens through subsequent properties, indicating they were traveling through the neighborhood."

Drax drove them deeper into the cul-de-sac but stopped the car when they approached a squad of red and white police cruisers. A half dozen police officers dressed in red and white uniforms were scouring another one-story house, while two black-armored beings stood guard.

"We might want to get out of here," David said. "I don't see any of my friends, and I don't have a good feeling about this."

"My sensors are reading a concentration of the anomaly in one of those vehicles."

David scanned the area. "Which one?"

Drax pointed his robotic finger—worn and rusted by time—toward the cruiser closest to them. "That one. I believe

146

one of your friends is in that vehicle."

"There're too many cops. I can't get her out if she *is* in there."

"Might I suggest we follow the cruiser, once it is away from the house?"

David nodded. Drax pulled the car around and parked it along the curb with the engine running.

Twenty minutes went by before the cruiser that Drax had pointed out passed them. Drax waited a few minutes, then pulled the car from the curb, following the cruiser.

They followed the police vehicle out of the residential neighborhood and into the main city. David was certain they would end up at a police station, but the cruiser passed through the city and continued onto a vast highway that weaved through an expansive desert landscape.

"Where are they going?" he asked Drax.

The robot beeped and booped. "I am not certain, Patient 3,456.

***

It was a landscape that reminded David of the Wastelands. Only this landscape didn't have trees dotting its sandy hills or contain the remnants of a vast civilization marked by ancient ruins and arcane technology that nobody could properly retrieve. The mysteries of the Wastelands made it special, intriguing. Interesting. Even though it was an open expanse, there was enough there to keep one curious just on stories of it alone. The same stories Veronica used to share with him.

No. This desert landscape was sand. White sand as far as the eye could see. Wind blew out here, creating hazy drifts of the white powder that coasted over the highway at random intervals.

Their car followed the cruiser for miles into the desert.

David's instinct was to tell Drax to stop and turn around. The possibility that this was a trap was too great. The police cruiser had to know they were following them by now, as they were the only two vehicles on the road. What if they were leading him into a trap? What if Drax's sensors were wrong? What if Drax was wrong? What if Drax was leading him into a trap?

Suddenly, as if on cue, the police cruiser stopped in the middle of the highway. Drax stopped as well, almost in perfect sync with the other vehicle. David saw no buildings, no gas stations, no shacks, no anything. Just white sand, blowing in gusts across the highway, and their two vehicles, though the cruiser was hard to spot through the mini sand gusts.

David turned to look out the window, his mind trying to put together the pieces of what was going on. He had no idea how they were going to get back home, but he knew he couldn't do it without Carrie, Turquoise, *and* Serenity. Although he had no real loyalties to Serenity, she had saved their life when Rio attacked, and possibly pulled them out of a turnabout situation with the other Wedges. Even though everything had gone downhill since, he couldn't blame her for all of it.

But now he found himself in a strange new world, one in which he was unaccustomed.

"Patient 3,456, the police cruiser is gone."

David peered out the windshield, down the road, and confirmed Drax's disturbing news. "Well, follow them again."

Drax beeped and booped. "Sir, there is no longer a signal. The anomalies have vanished, and my sensors cannot pick them up any longer."

"Drive to where the cruiser was."

Drax stepped on the gas, and they quickly covered the mile between them. When they arrived where David was sure the police cruiser had been only moments earlier, it was indeed missing with no trace as to where it had gone.

"Drax, where did it go?"

Drax beeped and booped but said nothing. David watched as its green eyes lit up brighter, and its head creaked left and then right. It was as if the hunk of metal and gears was actually trying to contemplate something.

David stepped out of the car. The wind picked up, blowing a cloud of white sand into David's face. He gagged and spit, and then used his hand to shield his eyes from another onslaught. When the gust of wind subsided, he walked over to where a very small puddle of liquid sat in the middle of the highway. Reaching down, he stuck his finger in the fluid and put it to his nose—water.

"The car was here," David said. "Right here. Where is it now? Did it teleport out of here?"

Drax stepped out of the car and then beeped and booped. "It is unlikely they have the technology to teleport."

"Okay, then where did it go?"

They both searched the area, but all they found was sand and wind. The sun was at the apex of the sky, and heat was beginning to sweep across the previously cool desert.

Drax paced over the same spot in the highway, where the puddle of water appeared, and finally beeped and booped before saying, "I have found the vehicle and its occupants, Patient 3,456. They are below us."

David knelt down and inspected the puddle of water closer. He had assumed it had come from the police cruiser's tailpipe or air conditioner, but he had been wrong. The water was coming up through a small seam in the asphalt. He ran his finger along the seam and followed it all the way around a large rectangle in the highway.

"There's a doorway here," David said.

Drax examined the seam that David's finger was tracing and beeped and booped. Then he extended his hand to the asphalt. A small square blade shot out of his finger, and he used it to pry into the seam. The seam activated, and a loud rumbling sound signaled moving gears. The rectangle dropped quickly into the ground, taking David and Drax with it. It stopped ten feet down and gave access to a seemingly fathomless iron stairway that descended into darkness.

"Where is the car?" David scanned the area but saw no place for the car to have disappeared to. He figured maybe there was a hidden garage.

A bright white light flashed out of Drax's right eye. "I'll light the way, Patient 3,456." He moved down the stairway, and David followed. The slab of asphalt retracted to the surface, enclosing them in utter darkness aside from Drax's light, which was surprisingly bright.

Down they went into cold and darkness. With each step, David knew he was getting closer to finding his friend—whichever friend it was. He wished beyond hope for Carrie, but even Turquoise would be a welcome face right now. This brave new world was beginning to worry him: technology he knew almost nothing about; another colony he hadn't even read about in history books; and a dangerous scientist who was on house arrest, possibly with a death clock ticking over her head.

They descended for what felt like hours. Time seemed to stretch and fold back on itself, and then stretch again. David felt disoriented and a bit dizzy. He felt a slight stretching, nothing too big, just enough to prove to him that time was off, even if it wasn't off by much. He felt a tugging at his skin, a pulling on his ear. There was a force—and he knew it was time itself—that was set on molesting him.

Drax's light began to flicker and sputter. "It seems my batteries are running low, Patient 3,456."

For reasons even he didn't understand, David hadn't thought that Drax ran on battery power. He seemed so efficient, so mobile, even though he looked like a somewhat polished garbage can.

"Please stop calling me Patient 3,456. You can call me David."

"Noted. I have enough power to last a half hour, David. After that, I will require recharging. I can charge at a normal power outlet, but it will take a while depending on the output."

"Great."

They continued down and down and down until they reached a landing in a dark, seemingly empty room. Drax used his flickering light to reveal nothing of interest—just four walls and the stairs they came down on. In front of them stood a steel door.

David tried the large handle, but it wouldn't budge.

"I can cut through the locks, David. But it will use the remainder of my power."

"Shine your light around this room, Drax. Let's see if we can find a power outlet for you."

Drax shook his robot head. "I already scanned the room. There are no sources of power here."

David glanced at the door again. "Cut through the door. I'll go the rest of the way on my own and come back for you once I find my friend and a power source."

"I will do as you ask, David. But I must warn you that there are very few portable sources of power that can make my systems function properly. F Cells are incredibly rare—and expensive when they are found. That is why Lexy created a rechargeable G Cell for me."

"I'll see what I can find," David said. "Just get that door open. If my friend is actually on the other side of that barrier, I'll get her, and then we'll find a way to get you out of here."

"I would very much like that, David." Drax approached the steel door and, using a torch cutter built into his right hand, began work on the door.

David patted the boomerang holster on his right side, hoping his weapon would be enough to rescue whoever had been taken. Touching the holster seemed to stop time's tugging, if only slightly. Enough to let David rest. Catch his breath. Gain his bearings.

Drax finished cutting through the door, then backed away as the steel slab fell, slamming against the floor, causing the cement surface to crack.

Through the opening, David saw a long hallway lit in fluorescent lights that hung from chains in the ceiling. Drax shined his light down the hallway. At the end stood another door, although it didn't look to be made of steel.

"Powering down." Drax's light flickered and went out, as did his glowing eyes and the noisy motors running his systems.

David found himself alone in the dark room, with only the lit hallway to venture into. He scanned the stairwell they had climbed down and could make out nothing in the darkness. He had no idea how he was going to get Drax back to Lexy. He pushed thoughts of the dilemma to one side and forced himself to focus on the task at hand. He was fairly certain that somebody knew he was here by now, so he would have to be ready for an ambush or attack.

He tried to move Drax against the wall, out of the center of the room, but the robot's body was too heavy, so heavy that David couldn't even budge it.

"I'll be back for you, buddy," he whispered as he patted the robot on the shoulder. "Let me get my friend out of there and we'll be on our way. Somehow."

David turned and entered the hallway, his hand placed firmly on the holster on his side. He had the buttoned flap open, and his gloved palm gripped the smooth metal of the boomerang. The same boomerang that had killed Agent Ruinstar Parks.

David tried to remember the event, but certain details seemed to allude him. He remembered why he had killed Parks: Parks was in the middle of choking Carrie to death. But what did Parks' face look like? What did Carrie's face look like? And where were they when it all went down?

He shook his head as he approached the door at the end of the hallway. The whole corridor smelled of oil and gears. He tried the door, and it opened freely to a large expanse, a cement floored room full of electronic equipment. The area was akin to a warehouse, but there wasn't nearly enough content within to justify the large amount of space. Large servers stood stoic against the walls all around the room, most of them dead and covered in dust. Sodium lamps were still coming to life in the ceiling above, indicating his culprit had just recently come through this area—but he saw no one.

David stepped into the middle of the room, where a nest of computers and monitors slumbered, snoring off binary code, completely oblivious to the escalating drama playing around them. But three monitors were alive and well, display-ing lines and lines of white code against black screens, alphanumeric codes that David could not interpret the meaning of.

Behind the monitors, linked to the computers by massive cables, was a circular metal platform, over which hung—supported by suspension cables—the torso, head, and arms of a robotic entity. The face was round and smooth with small dots for eyes, but it was missing a mouth. It had a bald head, and the metal was a dark shade of gunmetal gray. The arms looked human, and the torso was in the shape of a female's torso with machined lumps for breasts. She was dressed in a fatigue-green jacket with a bright white daisy on the left breast.

A click slid into David's ear.

"Hands up." The voice was deep and scratchy. "Not on your boomerang. Up. In the air."

David slowly raised his hands into the air. "I'm just here looking for my friend."

"Back up, away from the AI."

David took a few steps back, slow and careful not to trip over the massive cables leading to the circular base.

"Further. Away from the AI."

"Can I turn around so I can see where I'm going?"

"No."

David continued to step backwards, around the computers, until he could see the monitors with the codes flashing across them again. "What do you want?"

"You trespass and you have the nerve to ask what *I* want?"

"Yeah, I do. You took my friend."

"Not intentionally."

"What are you talking about?"

David heard the stranger behind him slide his weapon into a sheath. David took a chance and turned around to find a man in a brown hoodie. The hood was up over his head and concealed most of his face, aside from the week-old beard growing on his middle-aged features.

The man shook his head. "I didn't mean for your friend to get involved in this."

"Where is she?"

The man pointed to a door on the other side of the room. "I tried to bandage the wound, but…"

David sprinted across the room as fast as he could. He tore open the door and found himself in a small kitchen. Turquoise was laying on her side on the top of the stainless-steel counter, blood dripping into a puddle on the floor. She held a maroon-colored cloth to her neck.

"Tri'ana!" he cursed as he flew to her side. He took hold of the cloth and pushed it against her neck. He felt something hard there. Her eyes, brilliant and turquoise, were pleading for life, and the color had begun draining from her face. "What happened?!"

She tried to speak, but her pink-colored lips would barely open.

His hand soaked in blood, David pressed the cloth deep into her neck, unsure of what kind of wound she had incurred. It looked bad by the blood loss, but he couldn't be certain. She was a Wedge, and he wondered if Wedge's had strange body anomalies.

He heard the man enter the kitchen.

"What happened?"

"I'll tell you once she lives or dies," the man answered.

"What?!" David removed the cloth and gasped when he saw the massive instrument sticking out of Turquoise's neck. A long cylinder, no longer than three inches long and an inch in diameter, had penetrated Turquoise's neck. The back of the cylinder had a tangle of wires, all different colors, and the front was all the way into Turquoise's neck. "How is she still alive?"

The man rushed over and picked up the blood-soaked

cloth, placing it over the instrument. "I was in the middle of finding a tool to help her when you showed up."

David took the cloth and shoved the man to the side. "Go, find something to get this out with."

The man left.

Turquoise's eyes rolled into the back of her head.

David slapped her cheek, eliciting her eyes to open wide for a brief moment. "Stay with me, T. Stay with me. We'll get this out of you, and then you can heal yourself like you normally do."

Her eyes closed just as the man returned. Her pulse was strong though. The man held up a small, claw-like tool in his hand which he placed over the instrument. The claw hooks— three in all—grabbed the instrument at the sides at three different points and latched on. Then the man gently pulled the instrument away from Turquoise's neck. The foreign object came out quickly and quietly. David shoved the cloth back over her wound.

"Will she be okay?" he asked. "Can we take her somewhere? Take her to a hospital?"

The man set the instrument on the counter near Turquoise's body. The other end, the end that had been inside of Turquoise's neck, had a three-spear point that had retracted, probably when the man used the device to pry the instrument from her neck. "We can't take her anywhere because there isn't anywhere to take her."

"What happened?!"

The man seemed startled at David's outrage. He withdrew the hood of his coat to reveal a bald head scarred by burns. He scratched the back of his neck and took a seat on the opposite counter. "I use a special code to ping the sentries."

"The police officer I followed here?"

He nodded. "It was a sentry driving the car. They aren't human. They're robotic. Anyway, I ping them and they follow the ping. It's a code that I install, like a virus, into their programming. They follow it here, and then I usually kill them. Take their weapons. Save this world from one more of those hulking mechanical abominations. I didn't know this one would have your friend. We got into a fight." He pointed to the device near David's arm. "I use that. Shoot it into their head. It disables their functioning processes and knocks them out cold. This one used your friend as a shield."

David felt for her pulse and was relieved it was still strong as ever.

"I didn't mean...I didn't mean to hurt her."

David said nothing. Did nothing but hold the cloth to Turquoise's neck like her life depended on it.

The man hopped off the counter and left the kitchen. David stared into Turquoise's blank face. Her eyes closed, and she suddenly she looked the poster child of peace and serenity. But he knew otherwise. She was a walking vial of inner turmoil, and she didn't deserve this. None of them did.

He felt the pull again, the tug at the hairs at the back of his neck, at the hairs on his arms. Time was pulling him, enticing him, but he didn't know why. His gut told him they had done something horrible by leaping through the portal, that Serenity had done something horrible by transporting them to that grocery store to begin with. But nobody could really be blamed for their decisions. Not right now. Serenity had done what she felt was the best decision in regard to the odds they faced. And they had all done the only thing they could by jumping into the tear. They would have been destroyed otherwise.

157

The man returned with a clean cloth and some medical tape. They bandaged Turquoise's neck using both, and this left David free to wash his hands of his friend's blood. While he picked at his skin and scrubbed as hard as he could, he contemplated where all of this was going. He hadn't encountered Chaos at all since finding his sister dead in her apartment at the hands of Drather. He hadn't encountered Drather either. Or Mr. Big—aside from the man on a small monitor, releasing the Ghost Code.

No, he was fighting something else now. Not someone, but *something*. Maybe it was Legion. Maybe it was time itself. He had no idea, not really. At least now he knew of Turquoise's fate, and he was here to help her as much as he could. But he still needed to find Carrie and then Serenity. Hopefully in that order.

The man stood to the side of the sink while David washed his hands. It was a bit unnerving, and David couldn't help but be fully conscious of the boomerang at his own side. He would kill this man if he had to. He had killed Parks when he tried to harm Carrie. He would kill this man if he tried to lay another finger on Turquoise. His only goal was to get Turquoise well enough to move, and then they would get out of here.

With that damn robot...somehow.

The man stood, arms crossed, with his hood up over his bald and scalded head. But he said nothing. Did nothing. Just stared toward the floor, or maybe toward Turquoise's body resting on the blood-stained counter. David couldn't tell. He thought to ask the man who he was and where he was from and what he was doing down here. But honestly, David didn't care. He stopped caring about all that long ago, when those minute details got in the way of saving Carrie. Now they would only get in the way of him getting out of this place with Turquoise and the bucket of bolts waiting at the bottom of the stairwell.

"I have the body, if you want to see it."

"What?" David asked as he dried his hands with a clean towel.

"The body. Of the sentry."

"I'm fine. I've seen sentries before."

The man shook his head. "Not like this. Everyone thinks they're protecting us, but I know better. I know what's in their programming."

"Do you now? To be honest, I don't care. I'll just as well take my friend here and go."

He nodded. "Yeah. I owe you that much. When she wakes, I'll help you get back to the surface."

"And my robot?"

"You're what?"

"His name is Drax. He led me here by—It doesn't matter. He got me here. Now he ran out of juice, and he's sitting at the bottom of those stairs like a hunk of junk."

"I may be able to help you with—" The man glanced around the kitchen area, as if someone had entered the room.

David saw nothing and nobody. "What?"

The man pressed his finger into his ear, activating what appeared to be a hidden communication device there. "Company," he said to David. "Can you shoot a Firebrand?"

"A what?"

"Come with me."

David hesitated, instead opting to look upon Turquoise as if she was already dead and waiting to be buried.

The man grabbed David's arm. "I promise you she'll be fine. I can seal this room so our fight doesn't reach in here."

"What fight?"

"You probably led more of those sentries here. I only have

one more device like the one your friend got in her neck. The rest of the sentries, we'll have to shoot to kill. The Firebrand is the only weapon that can pierce their armor."

He led David out of the kitchen, sealing the door with another steel door behind them. He took David past the strange female robot body and into a small closet behind the old servers, where he handed David a bulky rifle painted black with blue flames on the side.

"Why do you say *I* led them here?"

The man huffed and took another rifle that had another of the Firebrand devices loaded into the front. The weapon reminded David of a harpoon gun.

"You and your robot butler led them here. Usually, when I lead one sentry here, others don't typically follow. They only do if they latch onto the signal."

"Do you even know where you're calling them from?" David asked. "The one you summoned was with a whole squad of police."

The man slid the hood off his bald head and rubbed the scarred regions of his scalp. "I don't have that info when I summon them. My goal is to take out as many as I can. And I have a process to do just that."

The man led David to the narrow hallway David had taken to get into the warehouse. He pressed his finger to his ear again. "Damnit. There's too many of them."

David held the rifle in front of him. The weight of it was uncomfortable in his hands, as he was used to brandishing his boomerang or, at times, a pulse pistol. "What do you want to do?"

The man slid a small cylinder out of his back pocket and stuck it to the wall to the right of his head. "Blow their only entry into this place."

David let out a grunt. "How then are we going to get out?"

The man smirked. "Trust me, by chance?"

"No."

"Didn't think so. There's another way out of here, but you'll *have* to trust me. If they get through here, we're done. So is your friend. These things don't show mercy. They don't know what mercy is. Or compassion. They'll kill us and ask questions never."

David briefly worried about Drax but realized the loss of the robot was nothing compared to saving their lives. He would have to explain things to Lexy when he saw her. "Fine. Blow it."

The man nodded as he slid another explosive out of his other back pocket and placed it on the wall to the left of David's head. "Just follow my lead, kid, and we'll get out of here with our heads still on."

"Call me kid again and your head will be the last thing you'll need to worry about."

The man smirked as he slid the hood up over his head and led them back out of the hallway.

He slid a small cylinder from his pocket and pushed the button on the top. A soundless explosion rocked the hallway, bringing the walls and ceiling down within the corridor.

Sorry, Drax. Maybe I'll be able to come back and salvage what's left of you.

Another explosion rocked the chamber, but David realized it had originated from the other side of the room. He turned to the man, who looked shocked.

"That's not possible," the man said.

"Let me guess—that was our other way out?"

The man ran to another set of doors on the opposite side of the warehouse. When he opened them, white dust and smoke poured into their faces. David choked down some dust and waved his hand around, trying to cut through the particle fog. When it cleared enough for him to see, he realized the hallway was sealed in collapsed stone and debris.

"Damnit!" the man shouted.

"Wait, why would they seal this entrance if they wanted in?"

The man shook his head. "They don't want in. They want to seal *us* in. They're going to perform a precepta."

"What is a precepta?"

The man was too busy scrambling to think to pay David any attention.

David went to the sealed door that led to the kitchen and opened it. Turquoise sat on the aluminum counter, one hand and arm covered in blood as she pressed against the rag taped to her neck, the other hand clutching her forehead.

"Turquoise?"

She didn't move, didn't speak.

David approached her, careful not to startle her in case she was in some kind of deep meditation. "Turquoise, we have to go. We've been sealed down here. They're going to do something called a precepta, but our kind guest here won't tell me what that is."

She still said nothing. Did nothing.

The man entered the kitchen with a handful of small rubber discs that he deposited onto the aluminum counter. "Take one. Stick it under your shirt, onto your chest."

David picked one up. It was the size of a half dollar and made of rubber. Adhesive covered one side. "What is this?"

The man left the kitchen without answering. David shook his head but slid one of the discs under his shirt and affixed it to his chest. It was cold to the touch. He slid one toward Turquoise, but she refused to move. Or maybe she couldn't even understand what was going on.

David walked out and found the man standing in the center of the warehouse, staring straight up at the sodium lights swaying gently from the ceiling. David could hear no sounds from outside the walls of this room. He wondered if Drax was laying in pieces, his already questionable metal parts charred and scorched from the destructive forces at work.

David couldn't help but realize the similarities and differences between the sentries of this place and the sentries from Western Anaisha. The sentries from Western Anaisha were aloof, and somewhat clumsy. It was obvious they weren't very intelligent, but they worked alright in groups when they were being given commands.

These sentries seemed much different in personality. Their armor, strangely enough, was the same shape and design as the ones from Western Anaisha, only here they were painted black, and there they were a metallic blue.

In Western Anaisha, the sentries had a weakness in their head, which David assumed carried over to this model, as that's where this man aimed when he shot the instrument and accidentally hit Turquoise in the neck.

As if summoned by pure thought alone, Turquoise stepped out of the kitchen, her hand still pressed tightly to her neck as if she was afraid the bandage job that David and the man had done would fall apart at any second, leaving her to bleed out all over the place.

She said nothing, but stood next to David, her turquoise-colored eyes bloodshot. Bright red lines ran down her arms and across her face, and her hair was in the midst of changing from bright pink to white at the tips.

"How are you?" David asked.

She threw daggers from her eyes to the man who stood in the center of the chamber, staring up at the ceiling.

Sensing her thought process, David gripped her shoulder. She snapped back like a wounded animal. He put his hands out in a surrendering gesture. "Listen to me, Turquoise. I know you're mad. He nearly killed you. He claims it was an accident, and I believe him. If he wanted you dead, he would have killed you before I was able to see you like this. But listen, there's sentries outside both walls of this building. They're going to kill us. We need his help to get out of here. So, don't do anything rash. Please."

She stared into his eyes, and after moments of deliberation, finally nodded. "Fine." Her voice came out raspy and hoarse. "Once we're out though, he's mine."

16 Olivia

Carrie awoke but refused to open her eyes. Her body ached, particularly the back of her neck, and her shoulders. The scent of death—of rotten meat and bloody entrails—sifted through her nostrils, but she knew that smell only indicated victory for her, as she had actually killed the Harpwillow.

"You okay?" Viranda asked.

"I guess," Carrie mumbled. She finally opened her eyes, expecting to see a mound of gray flesh lying in the dirt next to her. Instead, she saw a silver box the size of her fist, black ornate flourishes surrounding its base and lid. Something within it glowed a greenish-blue color that seeped out from under the lid and even out the bottom of the box.

"You actually killed the Harpwillow. I've...I've only ever seen one other do that."

Carrie struggled to her knees. Through the open barn doors, Carrie could see that it was still daylight here. Cool air blew in, wiping sweat from her tangled hair. She realized the ink splotches and the code had reappeared on her arm, moving as if a gentle breeze were stirring them like the waters of some sea.

The rake that had finally torn the creature to ribbons lay on the ground feet from Carrie. Even the spires on the rusted weapon had no indication of flesh or muscle. Not even blood.

"What happened to it?"

"The box."

"The box fell from it, when it died?"

"No. The Harpwillow was the box. When you killed its flesh-form, it turned into its actual form—the box. The creatures were created to carry things within them. This one was created to carry a fragment of the Key of Shool."

Carrie shook her head, finding it strange that a creature would be created to carry something within its body. But there was so much of the Depths that neither she nor scholars understood. She had never even heard of Harpwillows until now.

She moved toward the box.

"Stop!" Viranda screamed into her spirit.

Carrie withdrew her hand from the box. "What?"

"I've never actually seen a human handle the Key of School, let alone a fragment of it. I don't know what might happen to you."

Carrie shrugged as she reached for the box again. "I almost died fighting this thing. There's no point in backing down now. Beside, we have to see what happens if we want to try and find the other fragments." She placed a trembling hand on the lid of the box. It was cold to the touch, and it felt as if there were a current of electricity moving through the surface, not enough to electrocute her, but enough to buzz her skin softly at her touch.

Carrie lifted the box in her hands and examined it. Up close, she saw ornate designs carved into the silver surface.

They were black and somewhat glittery. The designs were nothing more than fancy swirls and lines that moved like the wind around the surface of the box, but they seemed alive, constantly changing under Carrie's watchful eye.

She slowly opened the lid. Inside, in the midst of the greenish-blue light, lay a fragment of ornate silver—the looped handle of a key, the same fancy swirls and black, glittery lines that adorned the box, twisting around the key loop.

"It's beautiful," Carrie whispered.

Viranda said nothing.

Carrie reached in and lifted the fragment out of the box. The key vanished into mist between her fingers. "What?"

"It's now with you," Viranda said. *"The keys will attune to one individual—the first to find the first fragment."*

Carrie scratched her head. "Is that it then?"

"Yes. For now. I don't know how many other fragments there are, but I would guess two more. At least."

Carrie glanced down at the silver box in the dirt. The fanciful swirls and glittery adornments were gone. The surface of the box looked stained in crimson blood and black scorch marks. Without the fragment, decay spread. Even the dirt looked darker in color as the sunlight shone through the barn doors.

"I have to kill two more of these things?"

Viranda made no remark.

"Well, where's the next one?"

Viranda let out a small sigh, which—being within Carrie's spirit—came out as a strange pulse that moved through Carrie like a wave of soft sound. *"I don't know."*

Carrie stepped out of the barn into the warm sunlight. A light breeze played with her sweaty bangs, and normal sounds—the wind through the wind chimes, birds in the air—

seemed to have returned to the property. "I need to find David and the others."

"David has no part in this. At least…not yet."

"What do you mean? He can help me kill the other Harpwillows. I was lucky to have killed this one. Who knows if the others might get the jump on me, or if you'll stop protecting me from their sounds."

"David has other events to attend to."

Carrie fumed. "Where is David?"

Viranda did not reply.

Carrie glanced up at the sky, lazy white clouds floating through the air with no cares. She took a deep breath, calming herself, and then peered out on the horizon in all directions, unsure of which way to go to find David. Forest surrounded them, but beyond those tall, imposing trees and colorful, fluttering leaves, she was unsure of what lay out there in the world beyond. She didn't even know where she was, just that the corrupted portal had dropped her here.

Viranda shifted within Carrie. Carrie would never be able to explain exactly how she knew that—the sensation was unfamiliar to her, but it felt as if someone was actually moving inside of her muscles, within her bone, slithering around like a serpent through her veins. She detested the experience.

"I am going to lead you somewhere. I need you to go. There are certain things I have come across in my time within this galaxy, things that I believe you would benefit from knowing."

"You're to lead me to David, or nowhere at all."

"David has his own path at the moment. I am sure you will reunite at some point, but right now, I believe revealing what I know to you will help clear up the matter of David…and your other friends."

Carrie looked up at the house before her. The breeze tussled the screen door, slamming it back and forth against the worn wooden doorframe. The wind chimes clinked against one another, playing a haphazard melody that made no sense. Carrie wanted to enter that house, to see where—and maybe when—she was. Where had that portal taken her? And why would it drop her directly into the place where a Harpwillow was hiding out? Coincidence? *No…*

"There is nothing for you in there," Viranda whispered. *"I promise you that. The Harpwillow killed the original owners of this farm. Their bodies are probably gone, consumed by the creature. Ransacking the house will only waste valuable time."*

Carrie nodded but headed toward the farmhouse anyway. "If you want me to fight more of these things, I'll need a weapon."

Viranda gave no argument, though somehow, Carrie could tell she wasn't happy.

Approaching the porch, Carrie recalled the horrible buzzing sound the Harpwillow had made, and the melody it played in the wind chimes. She wondered what would have happened had she not had Viranda within her. Would she have been able to fight off the buzzing, or avoid the lull of the wind chimes?

She went up the rickety wooden steps and approached the old house. The screen door clapped against the peeling door frame, and beyond it lay darkness. Even though the Harpwillow was dead, its presence lingered here—like an echo of sorts.

"Whatever you're doing, we need to hurry."

"Why? I imagine those things aren't going to be looking for me. I'm going to have to hunt them down. What is the rush?"

Viranda seemed to tremble, her presence within Carrie pulsing with fear. *"Something is coming."*

Carrie spun around, glancing out at the empty fields and the forests beyond. "Where?"

"No...not like that. Something is coming to Anaisha. We need to free your kind—the ones captured by Legion and imprisoned in the Hopeless Bastille. Without them—some of them—you won't stand a chance."

Carrie turned back toward the house and swung the screen door open, letting it clunk against the front of the house. She stepped across the threshold and into a small foyer. A small table sat to her right, wilted and rotting flowers filling a vase atop it. To her left, the wall was lined with photos—old photos of farm equipment, field hands, and even a water tower that Carrie couldn't remember seeing anywhere on the property.

The stench reeked of death. Carrie's stomach turned, but she moved forward into a small living area. A floral-print couch covered in plastic took up most of the room, with a small tube television, bookshelf, and table with lamp.

The smell was bad, but it wasn't as bad as the stillness in the room. Everything seemed to stop here. Life. Time. Reality.

Carrie glanced around the living area, her eyes searching for a weapon—any weapon—she could use to fight another Harpwillow. As fragile as the last one was, she hoped to find a shotgun or a pistol, something that would make short work of the creatures.

She searched the living area but found nothing of use. She wanted to venture deeper into the house, but the smell seemed to get worse in the hallways, and even worse near the bedrooms.

"We should go," Viranda whispered. *"It doesn't feel...safe...here."*

"I killed the Harpwillow, right?"

"Yes. However, I sense it only drew the attention of Legion, and the Dark Army."

Carrie decided, against her better judgement, to head down the hallway. Photos lined the dark corridor, but she couldn't make them out. Each was blurred, like in a dream. She passed bedrooms on each side, but something within her told her to keep going.

She stopped at the end of the hallway and turned to her left to face a closed door.

"Why were you drawn to this room?"

Carrie shrugged. "I don't know." She placed her hand on the doorknob. It was cold in her palm as she turned it and slowly pushed the door open to a dark room.

Something moved through the room. Something ethereal. Something unnatural.

A bright flash of light scattered across the room, like a large bolt of lightning. And then a glowing female appeared. A little girl, with multicolored eyes.

"Olivia?"

The young girl smiled, her teeth glowing a bright white. "You killed it. Just as I saw you would."

Carrie nodded as the fanlight flickered on, and Olivia's glow faded, leaving her a normal, ten-year-old girl—with eyes that continued to change color every few seconds. Carrie stepped into the room. By the décor, she could easily tell this had been a young girl's bedroom, with the pink princess comforter and bed sheets, the pink and white frilly lamp shade, and the pastel, purple-painted dresser. It smelled of dust and dirt, as if it had not been used in a very long while.

"You did a good job killing the Harpwillow. But there will be more."

Carrie nodded. "I know."

Olivia eyed her suspiciously.

"What?"

The girl closed her eyes. "I didn't foresee Legion joining

171

forces with you. That's…odd."

"Why are you here?" Carrie asked, unwilling to speak of the symbiosis she had somehow garnered with Viranda.

"You need to find the other Harpwillows," she answered, opening her eyes on Carrie. They were a cool aqua blue at the moment, shimmering like pools of water.

"Yes. Apparently."

"You won't. Not yet."

"Don't listen to her!" Viranda shouted in Carrie's spirit. *"They have to be killed, quickly, so we can free those in the Hopeless Bastille."*

Olivia narrowed her eyes on Carrie. "Something is off about you."

Carrie held her arms up, which had the strange inky code across her skin.

"Yes. Your possession by Legion. But…you've accepted it. You've taken it in as a symbiote, instead of an enemy."

Carrie nodded. "Her name is Viranda."

Olivia stepped back. "Viranda? DelaCourte?"

Carrie nodded again and glanced at the small picture frames lining the surface of the purple dresser. Inside the wooden frames sat photographs of an old man, a farmer by the look of the overalls he wore, with short gray wisps of hair bursting out of his otherwise bald head, like fireworks. Next to him stood a little girl.

"I thought she died," Olivia whispered.

"No, she's very much alive."

Olivia's body shimmered in various colorful hues. "Your friends are scattered, each on a different path that will lead all of you to the same destination. You must be strong, but not foolish. There are two more Harpwillows that must die in order to complete the key. One is inside of Lysallis. The other…" Olivia's eyes trailed off, her gaze stuck on a blank spot on the wall.

Carrie waved her hands in front of the young girl's face, but she wouldn't flinch, wouldn't move. "So, I'm heading to Lysallis?"

Olivia snapped to and nodded, her body no longer shimmering, her eyes still changing colors. "Yes. Lysallis will be your next stop." She had a forlorn expression on her young face, her eyebrows turned downward, the corners of her lips squeezing together into a frown, much like a disappointed old woman.

"What is it?"

Olivia shook her head. "I don't want to say. I won't say. Please, be careful in Lysallis. Much waits for you and your friends there."

Carrie's heart jumped. "David's there?"

Olivia shook her head. "Not yet. Eventually. Certainly not in time."

"Not in time? Not in time for what?"

Olivia motioned to the photos on the dresser. Carrie turned back to them, examining them more closely. Then she saw it—the glimmer in the young girl's eyes. It was Olivia standing next to the farmer.

"He took me in," Olivia started. "He and his wife. And then Legion came. Possessed him. Forced him to slaughter her in front of me. Legion can't control me though, and they seem to have sympathy for young girls."

"Why did you stay with him?"

Olivia shrugged. "I don't know. I was called to."

The walls of the house seemed to shudder a bit. Carrie drew a deep breath and glanced around the room. "What was that?"

Olivia scanned the walls and the ceiling. "It's begun." Her eyes began to shimmer in different color tones again. She glanced up at Carrie. "Your friends are all in danger. Head to Lysallis. That is where you will come face to face with the one who wants to destroy you—and everything you stand for."

Carrie stepped backwards out of the room and entered the dark hallway. The walls tremored, and the house shook. "Who? Mr. Big?"

Olivia shook her head, a confused expression on her face. "No. He only wants to help. No…" She stepped into the hallway with Carrie, her shimmering eyes lighting up the walls. Through flashes of light, Carrie was able to make out the photos on the hallway walls. They were of Olivia and the farmer standing over an old woman's corpse in the barn. Blood pooled out from under the dead woman. A rake stuck out of her back at a strange angle, the long wooden handle tilted toward the sky.

Carrie made her way out of the house, onto the front porch, and then stood back from the house. The cool evening air swept through her sweaty bangs, and she found she was able to breathe out a relieved sigh now that she wasn't in that horrible building any longer.

Olivia stood on the porch, her whole body glowing. "Be careful, Carrie Green. You are the Chosen One. Legion will stop at nothing to destroy you before you can—" Olivia gasped as she stared out at Carrie. "The giftings!"

The whole house flickered in a flash of light, and then the structure was gone, along with Olivia.

Carrie stood, staring at the empty lot where the farmhouse had stood only moments before. A large pit remained. Large copper pipes jutted out of the ground, broken and cut, spraying water in the air where the house had once stood.

"What just happened?"

"Interesting," Viranda whispered into Carrie's spirit. *"Very*

interesting."

Carrie glanced around the property and noticed that she could now see the boundaries of the orchards. Beyond those would be Lysallis. She started in that direction, no weapon, no clue as to what was really going on. All she knew was that her friends were eventually going to wind up in Lysallis together. Though David would be too late...

17 Breach

The man finally stopped staring at the ceiling and approached David and Turquoise. If he was worried that Turquoise would do anything to him, he didn't seem to show it. "We can get out through the top. There's a vent that leads to the surface. But getting up there will be difficult."

David looked up at the sodium lights. The ceiling was at least twenty-five to thirty feet high. "There's no way we're getting up there. And don't you think they'd be waiting up there for us?"

The man huffed. "Damn. You're right."

"Who are you?" David asked. He had been waiting for the appropriate time to ask the question, but none came.

"You can call me Rick. Did you put the rubber washer on your chest?" He looked at Turquoise— specifically her breasts—when he asked the question.

David nodded. Turquoise said nothing, only glared at the man. There was a certain bloodlust in her eyes, a darkness David hadn't ever seen in those sparkling turquoise pools before.

He shrugged. "It's for your protection. They're prepping to

perform a precepta. It's a strategy they began some months ago. They pass electromagnetic waves through the walls, and those waves will destroy everything electronic. It'll disable all locks, all computers, even electronic weapons. Sometimes, it even disrupts heartbeats. The washer I gave you is something I invented. It will repel the waves, keep them away from your heart."

David clutched his chest. "Thank you," was all he could think to say.

Turquoise said nothing.

Rick sighed and looked up at the ceiling again.

David glanced at the computer screens with the white code racing across them. "Aren't you worried about your computers?"

He continued to stare at the ceiling but shook his head. "They are protected."

"What's their move after the precepta?"

"They come in, guns blazing. They'll probably target the weak points in the walls, blow those, and come in force." The man glanced toward his computers for a split second, but then turned his attention back to the ceiling. "That's our only way out."

"Why don't we let them do the precepta, and then ambush them when they blow their way in. We can take out a few and then escape through that entryway. How many do you think are out there waiting for us?"

Turquoise dropped to her knees and closed her eyes. David heard her groan, but that was the only noise she would make before she stood to her feet, clutched her neck, and motioned toward the back wall. "There's four on that side. A dozen on the other."

"How do you know that?" Rick asked.

"You have your secrets. I have mine."

"Fair enough. If they blow the back wall first—which is entirely likely seeing how it's the weakest— we can take four of them. Hit one of them with the instrument. Kill the other three."

David nodded. "If we must."

The man scoffed. "If we must? Are you bullshitting me, kiddo?"

David lowered the rifle until the point was touching the ground. "First off, I told you not to call me kiddo or anything close to kid. Second, I'm not agreeable to killing if it can be avoided."

"These are soldiers, child-man. Soldiers. They will slit your throat and then rip your spine out of the opening if they get the chance. They aren't even human."

David remembered his dealings with the sentries in Western Anaisha. They were human under all that armor, but a dazed kind of human. Brainwashed. Maybe clones. "They're human. We don't kill unless we have to."

The man held up his rifle and sneered at David, then Turquoise. "You silly outsiders are going to get us killed. Leave this to me. I'll simply amp up the instrument, and the one shot I have should be able to disable all four of them, as long as they're standing close enough to each other."

Turquoise suddenly reached her arm out and grabbed the man by the throat. The rifle fell out of his hand and hit the ground. A loud snap, pop, and a spark shot out of the instrument as it cracked in half with the impact.

"You listen to me," Turquoise began, "you nearly killed me with your little toy there. I'm lucky to be alive, and David here is lucky you didn't kill him when he came after me. We're not in the mood for games or more violence. We just want out of here. You're going to find a civil way to disable the sentries, and then you're going to get out of our way. Do I make myself clear?"

178

The man held a firm grip on Turquoise's wrists in an attempt to break her grip. But he couldn't. David noticed that her eyes had cleared up—they were no longer bloodshot, and her skin had cleared up as well.

Rick nodded. She released her grip on him, and he fell to the floor, immediately grieving over the broken instrument.

David glanced over to the man's computer system again. The code continued across the screens, as if it was its own separate entity, completely isolated from the rest of the world. "What does your computer system run?"

The man picked up the broken pieces of his instrument and his gaze suddenly darted to the computer monitors. "Why?"

"What is it you're doing down here exactly? What is that robot in the center of the platform?"

Rick shot to his feet, dropping the pieces of his instrument to the floor. "Not relevant. You two destroyed our only hope—"

A loud sonic boom rocked the walls of the chamber and beat through David's ears like the slapping of sea waves in a storm. He fell to the floor, his head swimming in pain. The boom occurred again, but David had his hand over his ears, cushioning some of the horrible sound. Electronics sparked, and circuits popped all around them as the bins full of motherboards and computer parts burst into flames. The servers that ran along the walls burst into clusters of electrical currents and then flames.

But the computers with the coded monitors, and the platform with the half-female robot remained unaffected.

When David got to his feet, he found Rick kneeling near the back wall, David's rifle in hand. David cursed under his breath and pulled his boomerang from the holster on his side.

"How long until they breach the room?"

An explosion rocked the back wall, pushing chunks of cement directly into Rick. He tumbled backwards under the barrage, his body stopping halfway across the chamber. His gun slid across the floor and landed at David's feet. Turquoise picked up the weapon, ignoring David's sharp glare.

She fired one shot which burst through the front of the first sentrie's helmet, shattering the glass faceshield. The sentry dropped to the floor.

Two more sentries rushed in as Rick struggled to his feet, nearly careening into Turquoise. The man's leg was broken, and his arm was cut up pretty bad. He had blood streaming down the side of his face from a massive wound in his head.

David rushed to his side as Turquoise picked off another sentry. The third sentry fired a shot at David, hitting a chunk out of the floor near him. The cluster of cement shot into his leg, bringing a fiery pain with it. He ignored it and twirled his boomerang at the sentry. The weapon spun through the air and sliced through the sentrie's hand, dropping his limb and his gun to the floor.

The sentry fell to his knees, apparently in shock at the loss of his hand. A shot from Turquoise hit the man in the head, and he toppled to the floor on top of his gun and hand, just as the boomerang returned to David.

David grabbed Rick's right hand and pulled him to his feet. His leg bled across the floor.

The fourth sentry stepped through the makeshift hole in the wall, his shiny black armor losing its luster underneath the dim sodium lights. Without hesitating, he shot a bullet straight at Rick, hitting him between the eyes. The man dropped to the floor as David turned to face the sentry. A loud click echoed from

Turquoise's gun, and she threw the weapon down in disgust.

The sentry kept his gun trained on David but turned his head to look at Turquoise. "A Wedge." He said it more as a statement than a question, although there seemed to be something close to surprise in his voice. His tone was deep, almost as if it were coming out through a muffled speaker.

Turquoise stood, defenseless, staring at the sentry as if she were calculating how long it would take her to dash to him and break his neck.

David held his boomerang at his side, his gloved hand gripping the smooth metal as if it were his last friend in Lysallis.

And then he realized, grimly, that he wasn't in Lysallis. *Was this all a dream?* He suddenly felt dizzy, his vision blurring at the corners of his eyes. His legs felt weak, and he started to sway back and forth.

Stay with me, Turquoise spoke into his mind. *I'm going to kill him. I have to. After that, you and I will run through that hole in the wall and get out of here.*

He nodded in her direction, but then realized he had nodded to his right, not his left. He saw the sentry in front of him—a tall man in black armor. And then he was in blue armor. Then red. Yellow. Dark gray.

David closed his eyes, took a deep breath.

Stay with me, David. Please. We'll get through this. Stand.

Please, Nathan, please. Stay with me. Stay with me.

He gripped his boomerang. He opened his eyes. The world was right again.

The sentry in front of him was dressed head to toe in black armor. He had his rifle pointed at David, but his body looked lax, like he was in the mood to be careless about his position in this room. Maybe arrogant. "How do you think this will end, David?"

David gripped his boomerang tight. "How do *you* think this is going to end?"

The sentry lowered his rifle before taking a seat in the office chair at the desk full of computer monitors. Code flowed across those screens as if nothing was going on out here in the real, non-binary world. "I thought you didn't kill, David." Then he turned toward Turquoise. "And I thought you Wedges were a species of peace. You are a species, aren't you? Or something like that?"

He turned his attention back to David, holding his hand out toward him. "Bring me the timepiece, please."

David's left hand instinctively dropped to his coat pocket. The bulk was there, countering the weight from the boomerang that usually sat nestled on his right side.

"Yes, I know about it. I have for some time now. Now," he said as he waved his hand toward himself, "give it to me."

David refused to move.

The sentry huffed. "Are you going to make this difficult?"

"Probably."

Turquoise lunged at the sentry. He flicked his hand and she was suddenly tossed across the chamber. She hit the ground and slid to the kitchen doorway, cracking her head on the door frame.

"You must think your violent ways will prompt me to give in to your demands," David said.

The sentry stood to his feet and removed his helmet. Underneath was a plain bald head. The bald head of a man with blue eyes, an oval face, and a strange respirator over his mouth. He set the helmet down on top of the chair and moved toward David.

"You are a rare species, Mr. Corbin." His voice sounded clearer, but not by much. He walked a circle around David, his eyes looking toward the ground where Rick lay in a pool of his own blood. "Your friend here died for a cause. Do you know what that cause was?"

David watched the sentry carefully, watched every flex of his cheek, each thing that his eyes locked onto. He could hear Turquoise recovering on the other side of the room and figured he could keep the guy occupied for a few moments so she could think of something or at least act as a decoy so he could put this man down.

The sentry walked to the computer system, the code still moving its way across the three screens, oblivious to the chaos erupting outside its binary world. "This man's cause will remain unknown to you." He picked up his rifle and fired shots at the computer monitors and computer systems. The equipment burst into sparks and flames, and within seconds, gave up their ghosts. The code no longer flowed across the now-shattered screens. They were trapped on their side, in a world unknown to David. "This man's cause will remain unknown to everyone."

"What do you want?" David asked. "If you came here to kill us, then kill us. If you didn't, then name your price. I have other things to do today."

The sentry chuckled. "You do, do you? Today. Tomorrow. Fifty years in the past. A hundred years into the future. You have no need to worry because time means nothing to you." He pointed the rifle at David and took a few steps toward him. "You traveled here through a tear. That's grounds for execution."

"I didn't have a choice."

The sentry breathed heavily into the apparatus over his

mouth, and the sound came out like air escaping a large tire. "Everyone has a choice. That's what makes us human, isn't it? Choice. Free will. I can pick Door A or Door B. I can even create a Door C—which is where you come in. You created a door that wasn't there before. You created something that shouldn't have been there. And now you're going to have to suffer the consequences of doing so."

Turquoise rushed to the side of the sentry and shoved the partially damaged instrument she had broken earlier into the side of his head. The electronic device pierced his skull, and blood spurted out across Turquoise's face as she shoved him to the ground. He fell to his side, the cement impact cracking apart the apparatus over his mouth. The electronic instrument stood straight up in the side of his head, a lighthouse for all to see.

The man's eyes closed, and his body relaxed while electrical currents buzzed around the instrument sticking out of his brain. With the breathing apparatus shattered, David saw that the man's mouth was disfigured and incomplete, his teeth pointed inward at a strange angle, his bottom lip almost completely gone.

David slid his boomerang into his holster and picked up the man's rifle.

"Let's get out of this shithole," Turquoise snapped as she headed toward the hole in the back wall.

"Wait a second." David approached the battered computer system, his spirit mourning the loss of the code for reasons he couldn't even comprehend.

"We need to go," Turquoise said flatly as she stopped at the opening in the wall. "The other twelve will come through the other wall, and you and I don't have it in us to stop all twelve of them. We could barely take four."

David grumbled. He bent down and examined the black computer tower underneath the desk. The shell was riddled with bullet holes, and most of the components inside were completely destroyed. Then he noticed the thick wires that attached to the circular platform didn't connect to the now-broken computer. They traveled beneath the cement.

David stood up and dropped the rifle to the floor. Then he grabbed the corner of the desk and heaved it off to the side. It tumbled across the cement, flinging wildly the monitors and the keyboard and the mouse. Then he kicked the computer systems out of the way and revealed a perfect three-foot-by-three-foot discolored square in the floor. He used a small handle on the trap door to pull it open. Instead of a ladder or a hole, he found a massive outlet in which the thick wires plugged into.

And a single black switch to the left of them.

Turquoise approached him, but said nothing, only watched.

He put his hand on the switch but hesitated. He had no idea what the switch would do, if anything. But the sentry had said, 'This man's cause will remain unknown to you.' Those words wouldn't get out of David's head, no matter how hard he tried to shake them out. The phrase was strange, in that it seemed off, tilted to some degree. Tilted like time. Tilted like space.

He looked up at the female robot suspended on the platform. The coat she wore had that white daisy over the left breast. There was something about that daisy. Something—

The world around him blurred again, and he closed his eyes to shut it out. When he opened his eyes, the daisy changed to a blackbird. Then an orange book. A tan gear. The symbols changed, the colors changed, but the rest of the world around him remained the same. Time was flowing, but through a keyhole, not a tunnel. He felt its power, felt its flow as it moved straight through that keyhole, allowing nothing else to fit inside.

He gripped his boomerang through the holster at his side and felt the world stop and realign itself.

Something about my boomerang grounds me, centers me to this plane of existence. It may be my only anchor in this reality.

He felt Turquoise's hand land on his shoulder, softly and with care. "We need to go," she whispered.

He nodded. "I know."

Then he pulled the switch.

A loud hum broke through the floor underneath their feet. The wires filled with electricity, and the air around them crackled with life. Although the code had vanished from the broken monitors, David could feel that code moving through the wires, filling the room with its presence. There was something about the code, something about the way it existed beyond all hope. Even though the sentry had destroyed the computers, it hadn't destroyed the code. It hadn't destroyed the hope that the code could exist in a world beyond this one. In a time beyond this one.

David stood to his feet, glancing at Turquoise just long enough to see she was in as much awe as he was. "You feel that?" he asked her.

She nodded. "What is it? It's—it's refreshing."

"It feels like something is rebuilding me from the inside out."

Turquoise ripped the patch from her neck. Her wound had healed completely.

"Your powers?"

She shook her head. "I was able to *function* with my powers. As weak as they were, I wasn't going to be able to heal this wound."

David felt tingling in his arms and legs. His fingertips felt the same way they did when he accidentally touched an electrical socket when he was a child, but it wasn't painful, just a buzz, just something that brought life to his worn body.

And then it happened. It was something David hoped would happen, but he didn't know why he hoped it would happen.

The robot twitched.

There was something in the air, something electric, and it was charging him, Turquoise, and an inanimate object.

The female robot twitched over the platform. Her arms moved, then her abdomen. It wasn't until her eyes slowly opened that David leapt back. Glowing blue eyes, full of electric charge and life, stared out at him.

Turquoise put her arm out in front of David, shielding him from the strange animatronic, but David pushed her defense away.

"What is she?" Turquoise asked.

David shrugged as he stepped closer. The robot hung a few feet from the both of them, jangling around on the wires suspending it above the circular platform. "I don't know. Maybe a security system?"

"If that's the case, shouldn't we get out of here? We still have to find Carrie."

David knew Turquoise had mentioned Carrie in the hopes that he would snap to and flee the building with her.

But those blue eyes—those *electric* blue eyes—looked out at him with wonder and awe. Though the robot said nothing (he couldn't see a mouth of any sort on it), he could sense the life that had just been instilled in it, given by the flipping of a simple switch.

"Protocol Alpha Quadra." It was a female voice, but metal and tinny.

"What?" David asked. "What is Alpha Quadra?"

"Protocol Alpha Quadra initiated. Subject David Corbin. Keeper of the Chosen One. Please find my legs."

David glanced around. All he saw were destroyed servers and bins of computer junk. "Where are your legs?"

Her mouthless head swiveled on her small, circular neck as she looked around the room. "Kitchen. Refrigerator."

David started toward the kitchen. Turquoise tried to block him with her body, but he moved past her quickly and forcefully. He couldn't leave until he found out what this robot was for and how it knew who he was. He was in a different place, possibly straddling different times, and to find someone who knew who he was couldn't be dismissed so easily.

He went straight to the refrigerator and opened it. Inside, he found a pair of glossy gunmetal legs. He lifted one, nearly dropping it. The limb weighed at least fifty pounds, and the surface was slippery, as if someone had just finished oiling it.

Turquoise grabbed the other leg, her eyes warning him. "They're going to be in here in a few minutes, David. If you want to save Carrie, we have to leave."

He nodded and started back to the robot. "I know. I just have to find out what this robot—this woman—has to do with everything."

"It's a robot. What do you think it's going to change? Rick's dead, and we have one way out of here—assuming more sentries don't show up at our exit point."

"I don't know. Just trust me."

Turquoise huffed but protested no further. They brought the legs to the platform. David and Turquoise stood them up underneath the abdomen and attached them by some circuit wires and power cables that dangled out of the robot's abdomen like forgotten holiday lights.

"My thanks," the robot said as sparks shot out of her thighs. Her arms moved, and her hands went down to her legs. Flames shot out of her fingertips and began merging the limbs to her abdomen by melting the metal so it fused with her core. Then the most remarkable thing happened—the robot's face changed shape. The color cycled from gunmetal to cream. A nose, mouth, and ears formed. Long hair burst out of very tiny holes in the skull of the machine, and then those blue electric eyes morphed into human-like pupils, still the deepest blue that David had ever seen.

Turquoise gasped. "She's turning human?"

David watched as the robot finished transforming into a human model. With her legs attached, she disconnected from the wires tethering her to the room. Clothes suddenly materialized around her body in the form of blue jeans and a white blouse. She kept the fatigue-green jacket with the white daisy on the left breast. David waited for that daisy to change into something else, but nothing happened with it. Long, blue-painted nails replaced the metal stubs that were the woman's fingers. Black flats appeared on her feet. As impractical as it seemed for her to have clothes and shoes, David liked the look she portrayed, but was still at a loss for understanding who she was and what she was doing here and how she knew his name.

The mechanical woman approached the switch in the ground that David had flipped to bring her to life. She shoved one of her fingers—one that now had a jump-drive on the end of it—into a data socket located to the right of the switch. She closed her eyes and knelt as she began, David assumed, retrieving computer data.

"What are you doing?" Turquoise asked. "We need—"

A loud explosion rocked the chamber. The blast knocked

David to the ground and left a sharp ringing noise in his ears. Armed sentries donned in black armor stormed in from the wall on the other side of the room.

Turquoise helped David to his feet as a red-clad sentry stepped into the room behind the unit. As he approached them, David noticed he had yellow squares decorating his red mask.

"The three of you are charged with murder of a sentry." He glanced over to the sentry lying in a puddle of blood on the floor. "Commander Rol."

David took a few steps backwards and placed his hand on the lifelike skin of the mechanical woman's shoulder. "Whenever you finish what you're doing, we need to go."

She said nothing.

Turquoise stood in front of David. "We had no choice," she said to the lead sentry.

Surprisingly, the sentry with the red armor lowered his weapon. "What happened here?"

The mechanical woman opened her eyes and disconnected her finger from the data port. She turned to the group of sentries. "Lower your weapons," she said in an authoritative male voice.

"General Keep?" the red sentry asked, the yellow squares in his helmet flashing wildly. "How is that possible?"

She grinned with a smile that mimicked ones David had seen on almost every woman he had encountered in his lifetime. Her features shifted with a smoothness, a grace, that he never saw a robot move with. It was as if she was human in every sense of the word, except for a soul. "I said lower your weapons."

The sentries lowered their weapons.

"Turn around and leave this building. Go out to the desert, to these coordinates: 59 latitude, and 87 longitude. Remain there until you receive further orders. Cut communications once you have arrived, and do not, under any circumstances, contact base."

The red sentry nodded. "Very well, General Keep. C'mon," he said to the others as he led them out through the hole in the wall.

David and Turquoise stood, stunned, staring at the female robot with more questions than answers.

She turned to David, that same grin on her face, and nodded once. "Threat neutralized peacefully. I hope that is to your liking, David Corbin. Or do you prefer Lazerblade?"

18 Tears

"U m…"

The mechanical woman stared at David, those blue eyes beckoning. "We must rendezvous at coordinates 18 latitude, and 45 longitude—where your friend and love interest, Carrie Green, is located. The Chosen One."

He nodded.

The female robot stepped past them and approached the hallway Rick had collapsed. She grabbed hold of the large chunk of concrete blocking the doorway and lifted it with ease, moving it to the side as if it was nothing to her. She did the same with three more chunks of debris, clearing the opening leading into the hallway.

Rachel led them into the corridor, the sodium lighting from the warehouse bleeding down the narrow pathway, breaking up the inky blackness.

David and Turquoise followed her.

"Well then," Turquoise whispered. "Apparently she's friendly?"

"If she can take us to Carrie, yes. And she did just save our lives."

"We know nothing about her," Turquoise said. "I don't like that."

"My name," the female robot said as her voice echoed through the cement hallway, "is Rachel."

David stopped in the hallway, a cold breeze moving through the tight corridor. "Rachel?"

"David Corbin slash Lazerblade, your previous urgency to leave is valid. There will no doubt be more sentries—and worse—pouring through this building before the day is over. We must secure the Chosen One and return to your city, Lysallis."

"Who are you?" Turquoise asked. "Really."

Rachel reached the small room where Drax had breached the steel door and looked down at the incapacitated hunk of scrap. "Do you care for this robotic specimen?"

"I guess," David answered, although he really did care for Drax. He wanted to at least return him to Lexy, not out of fear of incurring her wrath, but rather to prove to her that he cared. The robot weighed a ton, and David saw absolutely no way of transporting him back to Lexy in their current situation.

Rachel placed a hand on Drax's spherical head and smiled. "He's old. Archaic, even. But he has served his master—and you—well."

David took pause to examine the expression on Rachel's lifelike face. Her smile, the way her cheeks bunched up, the way her eyes narrowed. She had a strange fondness for Drax, though as far as David could tell she had never met the robot before.

He watched as Rachel extended a hand into the middle of the air between her and Drax. Then she pulled her arm back, and—like pages in a book—turned back the air in front of them to reveal another layer of reality beneath. Behind the bland concrete floor and eerie darkness, another hallway resided between the folds, light blue carpeting…

Lexy's lab.

Turquoise crossed her arms in some kind of defiance toward the woman, but David could see by the faint sodium lights striving to reach this far back that she had an amazement in her eyes, a twinkle of astonishment and wonder.

Rachel slid Drax across the concrete floor and through the layer she had peeled back, setting him safely on the carpeting in the hallway in Lexy's laboratory. Satisfied with her actions, Rachel grinned ever so slightly and then motioned her hand back through the air again, closing the rift.

She nodded and then started up the stairs toward the exit.

"What was that?" David asked, following after her. His eyes were beginning to adjust to the darkness of the stairwell, but he wanted nothing more than to get topside out of this concrete tomb. "What did you just do? Was that a slipstream tear?"

She shook her head as she climbed the stairs, her slender legs moving up each one with equaled grace and a measure of force. "No. It was a transport tear. Technology created two years ago to make it easy for materials and supplies to be transferred between facilities. Come with me, David Corbin slash Lazerblade. We have much to discuss, but not here. Not now. Time is not on anyone's side."

"What do you mean by that," he asked.

"You are suffering from slip sickness," she said. She stopped and lights suddenly flashed from her eyes and lit up the stairwell. "You'll die if we don't get you back to your Origin Point safely and soon."

"Origin Point?"

194

She continued up the stairs with David by her side and Turquoise in their wake. "The point where a human being originates from. You originated from Merana, Anaisha, in the year 1979. That was the day you were conceived, and thus is your Origin Point. Straying too far from your Origin Point will eventually cause sickness, and later, death."

"Death? Wait, 1979? That's not right. And…the slip-stream I passed through didn't travel time, it traveled—"

"Realities," Rachel said.

"No," Turquoise breathed.

Rachel nodded, her eye lights illuminating the aged iron steps as they climbed. "Right now, you are in a reality different than the one you originate from. You too, Turquoise. And you are suffering, David, from slip sickness. Your mind will begin to tear itself apart trying to understand both overlapping realities."

"That's why I've been seeing things. The same thing, but different—"

"Versions," Rachel finished. "You are seeing multiple realities. You will continue to experience that until you are dead. Your brain won't be able to rectify them."

Turquoise took David's hand in hers. Her touch was comforting, grounding, much like when he touched his boomerang, yet more powerful because it was human touch from someone he considered to be a friend.

As much as he and Turquoise had had their differences in the past, he couldn't help but consider her a friend. She was one of the few he seemed to have left.

"What about Turquoise," he asked.

Rachel shook her head. "No, she will be fine."

"Why?"

"Rhodenine, David Corbin slash Lazerblade. The rhodenine

in her bloodstream is able to keep slip sickness at bay indefinitely."

"Good for me," Turquoise mumbled.

They reached the vehicle lift and took it to the surface. Daylight momentarily blinded David and Turquoise. The sentries were nowhere to be found. David had no idea where the sentries' car had gone either.

"How do we get to Carrie's coordinates?" he asked Rachel.

She started down the empty highway, in the direction of the city David and Turquoise had traveled from. "We walk." White sand blew all around them, and humid heat attacked as if on cue.

"Are you kidding?" Turquoise scoffed. "It will take us days to get back."

"Approximately six days, if we walk the whole way."

"We'll be dead by then," David added. "Not by slip sickness, but dehydration."

"That is an accurate assessment. However, there is a vehicle at a fuel station positioned two miles from here. It will be able to get us to where Carrie Green is being held."

"Held?"

"She was captured," Rachel replied.

"Sentries?"

She shook her head. David was still awestruck at her incredibly lifelike movements. Even her skin, which was a milky white, seemed to the eyes so soft and smooth. He didn't dare touch her though, not for such a ridiculous reason. She was lethal, had already proved that.

"Who took her?"

Rachel started down the highway.

"I asked you who took Carrie."

Her refusal to answer left David distraught. Even though he had Turquoise's companionship, he wanted the woman he loved. The woman he had been told to leave.

Dismissing Rachel's blatant silence on the matter, David and Turquoise followed her down the highway. They walked for two long miles, enduring the harassment of dust devils that crossed the road at inopportune times. David's mind wandered to Carrie, to Veronica, to his life back in Lysallis. *His* Lysallis. He even wondered what Mr. Big might be up to. Was he taking the opportunity of David being gone from that reality to wreak havoc in Enera?

As the bright yellow sun began to sink into the unknown horizon, David's stomach turned. He continued to fight bouts of slip sickness with alternating landscapes that fizzled in and out around them. Even Turquoise's features seemed to change in and out: pink hair, blue hair, teal hair. Her eyes were teal then blue then red. She was short, tall, fat, sexy, ugly.

Rachel, however, did not change. Not in the slightest. She remained a constant.

He gripped his boomerang tighter and tighter in an effort to remain grounded, grateful for the uncanny effect his beloved weapon had on this reality, but also worried that the effect his boomerang had on his condition would wane at some point in time. Some point in the near future.

As the sun dipped into the horizon, the air grew cold. Talk between the three travelers was sparse. Rachel's demeanor was unwavering as she led them down the darkened highway, the road void of any cars or other travelers. Turquoise said nothing as well, her eyes fixed on the path before them. But David could tell she was starting to tire, as her body began to slouch, and she rolled her neck around in an effort to crack it every ten minutes or so.

David's mind grew tired from seeing so many realities. So many different outcomes to colors and objects and people and things.

As his mind wandered, David found himself doubting his trust in Jennifer—Vector. He doubted she knew what she was doing. She had to have opened that blue spot, that passageway to this reality, by mistake. *Right?* He couldn't fathom why she would have done this on purpose...unless...

David glanced over to Rachel. This lifelike android seemed unphased by the walk, unphased by the cold. Unphased by their current predicament. David had liberated her, but from what? From whom? Who was she? He doubted her name was really Rachel. Who names a robot with such a simplistic name? Who was Rick? Why was he protecting—rather rebuilding—her? And why were the sentries so intent on that one location. Sure, Rick had been drawing them there, but he had to have been doing that to cull their numbers because they were already after him. But why?

Why?

Why?

Why?

David shook his head in aggravation.

Without turning to him, Rachel spoke, her voice sounding even more melodious than it had when she last talked, which—according to David's estimates—had to have been about a half hour ago. "You seem troubled."

David sighed, staring down the dark highway as it stretched out before them, the asphalt surface (he assumed it was made of asphalt) barely lit by a rising blue moon. "I'm always troubled," he mumbled.

"That you are. A strength."

The observation, though seemingly said in jest or light-hearted conversation, struck a nerve with David. How would

198

she know he was always troubled. It was true that trouble always seemed to find him, although always in different forms: Mr. Big, Jerad Montlier, Mr. Nokei, The LZR Project, Carrie Green even. But Rachel was a robot, a piece of machinery put back together in a vagabond's warehouse. What did she know?

Turquoise said nothing to their interaction. She seemed distracted, her brain probably trying to figure out how they were going to get home.

Rachel stopped and turned toward the two of them, halting them in their tracks. Her movement was so quick, so human, that it caught David off guard. He turned to Turquoise, whose hair was changing color to black, then white, then orange. He grabbed his boomerang in its holster and her hair reverted to its trademark pink.

"This is it," Rachel said, motioning wide with her arms to the area around them.

"Where are we?" Turquoise asked.

Rachel's head turned so she was facing the blue moon. "The car should be here."

"You said it was at a gas station," David stated. "I don't see a gas station."

Rachel reached her hand out toward an empty spot on the side of the highway, toward dirt and brush and darkness. "Please, do not disturb me." A black tear suddenly opened at the end of her fingertips. She opened her fist slowly as the tear widened.

David watched her intently as the black tear filled with color and objects as it grew larger and larger. A dilapidated gas station came into view, the brand name of which he could not see yet. The station was in the desert as well, the same desert—it seemed—they were currently in.

Rachel opened her fist completely and then curled the fingers of her other hand towards herself. The air around them crackled and rumbled as the tear moved toward the gas station. As it shifted over the structure, the station seamlessly merged with their own reality. Rachel closed her fist and the tear quickly closed as wild sparks blasted with it slamming shut.

Rachel let out a sound that was similar to a sigh. "I need to replenish my energy levels."

David nodded, staring intently at the gas station, its lights creating a warm beacon in the cold, nearly empty desert.

Turquoise moved to his side, her jaw slightly hung.

19 Redford

Carrie cut through the orchards, her sneakers worn, her feet sore. Traversing the furrows of fresh seedlings—who planted them, she didn't know—Carrie grew exhausted. Ever since passing through the portal, she had felt her energy levels fluctuating, felt her strength leaving her. She was tired, worn out, and she began to wonder how much longer she could go.

The sweet scent of jewel fruit brushed her face through the breeze that slid through the leaves of the massive trees. The sun was at the top of the sky now, and there was something off about the air around her. Something dark. She could sense it well enough. Something didn't sit right. Something didn't align with Carrie's spirit. There was a disharmony in the air, a clash of right and wrong. It was an uncanny sensation, one Carrie had never felt to this degree before. She just knew she wasn't alone moving through those orchards. Viranda was with her—within her—of course, but no, this was something different.

"You feel it too, don't you?"

Carrie nodded.

"It is in the air. In the makeup of the planet."

"What is it?" Carrie asked, making her way over another set of furrows, fresh seedlings bursting out of the dirt below her feet.

"I do not know. I can feel it even in here, within you. Something that transcends time. Transcends this reality…"

"You mean like us? Something or someone from another reality?"

Strangely, Carrie could feel Viranda's confusion. *She* didn't know.

Carrie broke through another line of jewel trees and found herself in a clearing populated only by a small playground. "What is this? I could have sworn the mall was in this direction." Carrie glanced beyond the playground and found another line of orchards. All around her were orchards. There seemed to be no escape from them.

She saw a man standing in the middle of the playground. He was dressed in a black suit and had his back turned to her, hands clasped behind him. He seemed to be staring intently at the Merry-Go-Round.

"I sense great darkness within him."

Carrie nodded, but walked forward, making her way across the stretch of green grass that led to the small plot of tan bark filling the spaces between the playground equipment. The man did nothing to move.

Carrie regretted not grabbing a weapon from the farmhouse.

The man didn't seem armed or alarmed.

Carrie stopped at the edge of the playground and glanced around at her surroundings again. This didn't seem right, didn't seem true. Carrie didn't know the farmlands of Lysallis's outskirts too well, but she knew beyond the shadow of a doubt that this clearing should have been the Jewelplex Mall.

So why wasn't it?

Had the portal actually taken her to another reality? It was possible. She somehow knew this to be true. But a feeling nagged at her. An overwhelming feeling that this man before her, this man in the black suit, was responsible for this park.

"It spins," he said without turning around.

Carrie realized then (or it had just started then) that the Merry-Go-Round was spinning on its own.

She wanted to ask who the man was. Instead, she examined the boundary of the playground. She felt both compelled to cross it into the tan bark, and at the same time felt compelled to keep out of it with every fiber of her being.

"He is evil," Viranda said.

I know, Carrie agreed. *His presence—it's what we felt a moment ago. The presence that transcends this reality…*

The man stood, staring at the spinning piece of playground equipment. "It spins," he said again. "It keeps spinning. Much like time. However, unlike time, I can stop this thing from spinning. I can interrupt it—" he reached out and grabbed hold of one of the four handles and halted the Merry-Go-Round's movement, though with some effort and a sharp yank of his arm. "Quite easily."

"Why are you here?"

The man placed his hands behind his back and turned around to face Carrie. He was a bit taller than her. The dark goatee around his mouth only added to the darkened presence Carrie felt coursing from him. He bore a tattoo on the left side of his neck, but from the distance she currently stood, she couldn't make it out clearly. She would have sworn it looked like a clock but dismissed that thought as silly.

"You wonder why I am here but not who I am?" He sighed and then looked up at the sky, at the lazy collection of clouds moving through the air. "I am here to fix things."

Carrie took a few steps back, sure she could turn and run back into the orchard if she needed to.

"You need to leave," Viranda cautioned. *"We need to get to Lysallis. To the city. And this is not the city."*

Carrie nodded and turned on her heels, ready to launch into an exhaustive jaunt.

"You want to find David, don't you?"

She turned back toward him. "Don't you speak that name unless you are a friend. And you are not a friend."

He smirked. "Friend." He waved his hands in the air. "Who is anyone's friend? We are all fighting for ourselves. For what we each individually believe is right. So, there are no friends. No enemies. Just selfish bastards moving through life on their own paths."

Carrie started toward the orchard. She would return to the farmhouse, find a weapon, and find another way to Lysallis.

"You won't find a way out of those trees. I promise you that. All of these orchards run in infinite loops. Spins. Much like the Merry-Go-Round."

Something about his words rang true. She glanced around the perimeter, at the lines of jewel fruit trees, and realized there was no way out of this place. But where was this place? What *was* this place?

She turned and made her way back to the boundary of the playground, careful not to cross the seemingly innocent threshold.

"What do you want?"

The man pointed his finger at her and smiled. It was an obnoxious smile that Carrie wanted to tear off his face. "Now you've asked a very important question. See, it doesn't matter who I am or what I'm doing here. What matters is what I want." The man held up a small cylindrical item that looked to be a lipstick container. "Look familiar?"

Carrie shrugged. "No. I'm just wondering why a grown man is walking around with a container of lipstick."

The man stared intently into Carrie's eyes. She couldn't seem to look away. There was something locking her in place. Fear. Maybe the truth of the situation. She was trapped here, and she was at a severe disadvantage as she knew nothing about this man. But he seemed to know about her. About David.

"We must get to Lysallis," Viranda pulsed.

The man grasped the lipstick vial and squeezed it. Carrie felt pressure on her insides. She dropped to her knees.

"What…What are you doing?"

The man released his grip on the lipstick vial and then stepped toward her, towering over her prone form. "Showing you the power I hold."

Carrie scrambled backwards on her hands and knees, away from the man, and managed to stand to her feet.

He shook his head and held the lipstick vial toward her. The container was a whitish-green color. "You don't remember this, do you? The lipstick vial you used the day David told you he loved you."

She felt her heart drop into her stomach. "What? How do you know—"

"I know everything about your reality. Your timeline. You have a connection to this lipstick vial because you purchased it for the sole purpose of impressing David. And yet…" He stared at Carrie, a confused expression on his darkened face. "And yet you declined his admission of love. Strange."

"You know nothing about me. About David."

He laughed, twirling the lipstick vial around in his fingers. "I know so much more than you will ever understand. You see, I have seen the other realities. The other timelines. I have seen the destruction caused by one simple man. One simple child, really. And I have dedicated my life to righting that child's wrongs."

"I don't have time for this," Carrie said as she turned to leave. She felt that crushing feeling in her gut again, the invisible pressure forcing her to her knees.

"I'm sorry to say it, Carrie Green, but you aren't going anywhere."

20 Pitstop

The station seemed abandoned. A black and white "closed" sign hung in the window of the attached convenience store, and yet the garages were open with a black SUV lifted in one of the stalls. It was as if someone had up and left in the middle of the night, leaving the fuel station behind for the ages.

Rachel closed her eyes and hummed a strange melody that sounded familiar to David, but that he could not pinpoint for the life of him.

Turquoise approached the station pumps, which were cylindrical in shape, painted a glossy red to match the rest of the station, and had computer screens embedded in the front of each.

David had never seen pumps like them before.

Turquoise ran her finger across the top of one of the pumps. "No dust. Strange."

Rachel motioned toward the structure. "We can rest here tonight."

"Rest here?" David looked at the building again, only then

realizing the convenience store was actually two stories tall. Above the garages and the main store was another level, which had windows that overlooked their small spec of a place in the world. "I thought you said we had to find Carrie." Only after the fact did he catch the whine in his own voice.

"You worry for her because she is your love, David Corbin slash Lazerblade. But you've already been warned, haven't you? Warned to leave her behind."

He felt chills scatter across his arms and neck. He didn't have to ask how she knew. She knew, and he would have ventured to guess she knew so much more than she was letting on about.

"To find the Codex of Ra'f," he mumbled.

Turquoise gave him a sidelong glance but said nothing.

Rachel led them into the convenience store. Fluorescent lights lit up the room. There wasn't a single soul inside. Turquoise rummaged behind the counter and found a pistol which she had trouble managing. A cardboard cutout of a middle-aged man in a black jacket stood in the front of the store. It said *24*, but David didn't know what that was supposed to mean.

Rachel didn't stop to peruse the shop. Instead, she led them to the back and through a small hallway. They scaled a small set of stairs that opened into a domestic area on the second floor which included a communal kitchen, a large round dining table, a bedroom, bath with shower, and a long couch with a big screen television.

"How did you know about this place?" David asked.

Turquoise dropped herself upon the couch and closed her eyes.

Rachel shooed David's question away as if it were an annoying fly. "Sit. Rest. Shower if you need to. We will be here until dawn. I will prepare a meal to satisfy your hunger."

Turquoise began snoring. David's restless heart urged him to leave, to go out and find Carrie on his own. He knew she was in danger, and sitting in a convenience store cooking supper was the last thing he wanted to be doing.

"Go," Rachel said as she pulled vegetables from the refrigerator. "Go and wash up. Take a deep breath, ease your mind. We will find Carrie. That much is certain."

"Nothing is certain," he whispered.

"Then why worry?"

"That's why I worry. Every second we stay here, Carrie—"

Rachel looked at him with piercing eyes, her mouth set in a knowing smirk. "You were told to leave her. That was for everyone's good."

David could do nothing but stare at her, rebellious thoughts rushing through his mind.

He finally resolved to go to the bathroom, relieved himself, and then undressed and slipped into the shower. The hot water felt soothing across his aching back, and the sound of the rushing water relaxed his nerves somewhat.

As he washed the dirt and grime from his skin, he tallied up his days in his head. They all seemed to blend together. There didn't seem to be a beginning or an end anymore, just the middle. The middle in which he was stuck. No Carrie. No normalcy. The place he came from was in chaos. This place was in chaos. He had no idea whatsoever where all of this was going—more chaos. There seemed no escape from the chaos, from his troubles.

What was his part in all of it? He scrubbed his neck with soap out of a blue bottle he found on the shower shelf. The soap smelled like peppermint, and the scent seemed to work in unison with the running water to relax his mind. He remembered when his mother would rub peppermint on his chest anytime he was sick as a child.

His mother. His father. His dead sister.

His family had been shoved to the back of his mind this whole time. With the world falling in flames, Chaos torturing him day and night, and now his sister's death wreaking havoc upon his soul, he hadn't had time to reminisce about the old days. About his youth.

Where *was* his mother and father? He couldn't remember.

Before Mr. Big, before his move from Merana to Lysallis, he remembered happy times. He was close to his mother. His father, not so much, as he was always working or involved in work-related projects. David and his mother would go for long walks, talk about junior high and the latest movie that was playing. The relationship with his mother was one of the few he had back then.

This was before his sister was born.

Once Cybil Corbin came into the world though, everything changed. She was constantly stealing the attention from David's mother, and even the little shards of attention his dad would throw their way on occasion. David despised her for a time, but eventually grew to love his sister and accept her as part of the family.

But his relationship with his mother was never the same after Cybil was born. The walks were few and far between, and the ones they did take were interrupted by Cybil's constant crying or whining. Their talks were interrupted. Their meals were interrupted. Cybil was not a quiet baby by any means. She was loud. Obnoxious. Always wanting attention.

When David saved her life from Mr. Big that fateful day so long ago, he didn't realize he was changing everything.

Making himself an enemy of Big.

Making himself a hero of Anaisha.

Why would that thought come to mind now? What did that event have to do with anything that was currently happening to him?

He shut the water off, dried off, and returned his less-than-clean clothing to its rightful places on his body. He still felt dirty, but at least now he felt like his mind was getting the chance to rest and relax and recharge. He pulled on his boomerang glove and strapped on his boomerang holster. Patting the curved weapon at his side, he felt a sense of relief. Something about the item helped tether him and his slip sickness, though he didn't know why.

He stepped out of the bathroom and found Turquoise and Rachel eating at the round dining table. The whole floor smelled of grilled meat. Hamburgers.

Rachel patted her hand on the rickety wooden chair next to her. "Come. Sit. Eat. You were in there more than an hour."

David stared at her in disbelief. *Over an hour?!* "I was in there maybe ten minutes."

Turquoise shook her head.

Rachel smirked but said nothing more. Her humanlike motions continued to startle him.

David took a seat at the table, his mind confused, reality stretching at the seams. He decided not to think anymore about reality or where they were or what they were doing here. Instead, he focused on sitting, breathing, eating. Resting.

The night went long. After eating, he and Turquoise asked Rachel many questions, most of which she attempted to answer to the best of her ability.

She had been built long ago, on another planet called

Spectrum. She was supposed to be the most advanced AI in the entire universe, imbued with a strange presence of life that was found in a dark and uninhabited corner of the galaxy. Sadly, she did not perform to her creators' expectations and was sent for dismantling.

She wouldn't tell David or Turquoise exactly what her creators' expectations were, but David read between the lines and assumed they wanted her to do something—or somethings—against her will. If it was possible for her to have her own will.

She would have been completely dismantled had Spectrum not been attacked by multiple alien species at once. War broke out on Spectrum, and Rachel watched most of it from the confines of a glass cage created to keep her on display until the time of her demise.

When Spectrum was about to be destroyed, the planet's council members initiated an emergency protocol that dumped all their knowledge into the only AI they had to protect it—Rachel. Then they cast her into space. Her abandoned vessel landed on Earth. She couldn't remember much of what happened on Earth, as if her memories had been wiped. She somehow made it from Earth to here, and she was found by Rick who tried to nurse her back to life, repairing her circuits, cleaning her parts.

"Rick lured sentries to our den and killed them. Then he used the more intricate pieces of their armor to repair my circuits. Their armor has incredible conduit power and can be soldered to my circuit boards with ease. And their technology works much, much better than copper."

"What's with the daisy on your coat?" David asked as he took a sip of bottled water.

Turquoise was still working on her food, her gaze alternating between David and Rachel as questions and answers were thrust across the table.

"I don't remember. I was part of a military force…" She looked sad, David noticed. Incredibly sad. Her blue eyes turned bluer, and actual tears seemed to leak from the corners of her eyes.

"A military force? Like an army?"

She wiped the tears from her eyes and laughed. "I apologize for bringing such a somber mood to the table this evening. Drink your water, and then it will be time to rest. We have much to do tomorrow. The vehicle in the garage needs minor repairs, but it will be able to take us to Carrie Green."

"But I have questions."

She grinned a motherly, all-knowing grin. "Answers will come when they should, David Corbin slash Lazerblade." Her voice, David noticed, suddenly sounded more natural. She had pitches in her voice which David had never heard a robot or electronic device replicate before.

David finished his food as Rachel started to clean the table of dinnerware. "What happens after we get to Carrie?" he asked.

"Everything will play out the way it should in this reality," she answered without making eye contact with him.

"What does that mean? I want to find Carrie—possibly even Serenity—and go back home, to my reality."

"Serenity is out of our reach. You must know, David, that all realities, all times, affect one another. Weave through one another. Everything is connected." Rachel started the water in the kitchen sink, pouring a bit of green soap from a bottle into the water. "Everything we do in this world, in this reality, is connected to your reality. And all of it—all realities, all possibilities—are connected to the same future. A future that cannot be changed."

"That's depressing," Turquoise mumbled. Finished with her dinner, she set her fork on her plate and leaned back in the chair. "So, we have no way to change the future. If it all ends up the same no matter what we do, then what is the point?"

"A philosophical question? I see. I am not at a point where I can answer those…yet."

"What do you mean, 'yet'?" David asked.

Her eyes blinked, and the blue in them seemed to sparkle a bit. It was hard to admit, but David felt as if he were falling for the robot woman. Not in a romantic way, persay, but he could see how she could become a good friend. An inanimate, soulless friend.

She pursed her lips and then smiled. "I am an Artificial Intelligence, David Corbin slash Lazerblade."

"Please," he said, putting his hand up in protest. "Just call me David."

She nodded. "Very well. David, I am an Artificial Intelligence. By design, I am constantly learning, processing, and expanding my knowledge and my features. When I was given life again, when you switched me back on, my core essence rebooted itself. My memory wasn't wiped, but it has been partitioned into various sections which are slowly and surely coming together as I continue to function. They were partitioned so that no one person could steal the information I contain within my databanks."

"What kind of information?"

"Everything learned on Spectrum. The planet was the most technologically advanced civilization in the entire galaxy. The most advanced in almost every reality. They built an empire, and they did so stealing technology from other planets. Their intention was to prepare for a war with Legion, but the war was so much greater than anyone could have anticipated. Alien entities from all over the galaxy participated in a concerted effort to defuse and dismantle Spectrum for good."

Turquoise shook her head. "Absolute power corrupts absolutely."

Rachel nodded as she took Turquoise's dishes from the table and carried them to the kitchen sink. "Yes. It can."

David sighed. "What do you mean there's only one future and that it can't be changed?"

Rachel paused for a moment, and her eyes closed as if she was thinking hard about the answer. When her eyes opened, her shoulders relaxed, and David saw a sparkle in her pupils again. "One future. The very end of the line, the line of this reality and all realities. Where everything intersects. The End Point. The opposite of the Grand Origin Point, where everything began."

"Doomsday?" Turquoise asked.

Rachel did not answer this. Instead, she began scrubbing their dishes with an old, brown sponge that had been resting upon the counter near the sink.

David watched as Turquoise slumped over in her chair from exhaustion. She finally stood up and went to the couch and spread herself out across the cushions, falling asleep almost immediately. Again.

21 Time

"Your friend is loyal," Rachel said as she finished washing dishes, placing the still-wet dinnerware on the counter on strips of paper towels.

David nodded. "She is." He briefly wondered why Rachel was bothering to wash dishes in a gas station she 'stole' from another reality, but realized there were more pressing things to try and figure out.

"You two were meant to be together, in the friendship you are engaged in."

"Maybe."

Rachel finished setting all the dinnerware on the paper towels and then turned toward David. "No maybe."

He chuckled innocently enough, but then he feared Rachel might take it as an insult. "I doubt you can see all futures. All timelines." And then he lowered his voice, disbelieving he was even buying into all of this. "All possibilities."

"I can."

"We'll see."

Rachel took a seat the table across from him. He was again stunned by her beauty. For a piece of mechanical and electrical engineering, she had been made to look as human as possible. And she continued to look more and more human the more time he spent with her, though he wondered if that was actually just his imagination.

She narrowed her glowing blue eyes at him. "You are a skeptic, David. I can appreciate that."

"Can you?"

"You sound bitter."

"I have to admit that I've been bitter ever since I learned that Carrie is supposed to be some Chosen One."

"Why? Because it changes the plans you had with her? Because it gives hope to those who need hope the most?"

"For the most part, but I wouldn't put it that way."

"You're selfish." She said the words, but they didn't come off quite as insulting as David figured they would. Instead, it felt like she had stuck a rod of truth through his chest and told him to accept who he was. The pill was hard to swallow, but he swallowed it anyway. *Selfish...*

"Maybe."

She grinned. "It's understandable selfishness. You love Carrie. You have always loved Carrie in differing degrees."

"I've always loved her with all of me."

Rachel shook her head. The way her hair spilled across her shoulders brought a realism to her features that actually scared David. "Not all of you. Not all the time. You love her when it is convenient to love her. When you have time to love her."

David stood up from the table abruptly, nearly knocking his bottled water over. "I don't have time to argue with a machine. I'm going to get some sleep."

"I'm not trying to upset you, David." She lifted her eyes toward him. "Understand that because I can see all paths, I can see each part of those paths—the beginnings and the ends. I have memory of every single interaction you have had with Carrie in all realities."

"Fantastic." David headed toward the bedroom. He felt a wave of guilt for taking the only room when he had two ladies—make that a lady and a robot—that he probably should have been putting first. But he washed the guilt away with the thoughts of Carrie and why he was doing everything he was doing.

"I have seen your love for her fluctuate," Rachel continued. "When you have saving the world to keep you busy, you put her to the side. Yes, she's always on your mind, but never at the top of your priority list. Then, when things settle down, you want her because she is all you have left. What if I told you there was more. More to this life you live, more purpose to everything you do?"

He huffed. "I'd say that's great. I'm going to sleep now. Wake me when it's time to get out of here." He went into the bedroom and shut the door. He found a lock on the knob and engaged it. He battled within himself with both the desire to be close to Rachel because she somehow knew everything, and the desire to stay distant from her because she was supposed to be a machine, an intelligent AI that couldn't possibly understand everything to do with human emotion.

David reached behind him to the wall near the doorframe, felt for the light switch, and flipped it on. A small lamp on a nightstand on the other side of the room lit up, allowing David to see a simple bed, wooden dresser, and a wall-length mirror.

David went to the window and peered out at the gas pumps. He then gazed out further across the desert landscape. Night had fallen, and though he couldn't see very far even though there was light from a full moon and a starry sky, he could see enough to know they were in the middle of nowhere. Literally.

His mind tried to constantly wrap itself around the fact that Rachel had pulled this gas station from another reality. He still didn't completely believe it.

He sat on the bed and wiped his eyes. Tiredness was taking its toll, as was whatever slip sickness Rachel claimed he had. He felt the pulling, the stretching, the very effect that time—and him being out of his own reality—was starting to have on him. He believed her about slip sickness killing him if he didn't get back home soon. He just didn't know how that would happen or when.

He figured if she had settled them down for the night and told them to sleep, then she wasn't too concerned that he might be close to death from the slip sickness. David tried to find comfort in that theory, but then he remembered that she was an arcane and ancient piece of technology from a planet he had never heard of, and that she had just barely been rebooted earlier today. She was unreliable as of yet, and untrustworthy.

David leaned back and rested on the bed, staring at the brown and black stained ceiling. His body wanted to sleep, but he knew his mind wouldn't allow it. There was too much going on, too much that hadn't been adequately explained yet. And his head was having trouble making sense of everything. He couldn't put the pieces together, couldn't figure out where the gaps and the margins were.

He turned on his side and spotted a magazine on the small wooden nightstand near the lamp. Against his better judgment, he sat up, took the magazine, and decided to do some light reading. *Maybe it will help me sleep.*

The magazine was "Time", one he had never heard of. The front cover had a photograph of a young blonde female dressed in a blue pantsuit, with thick black glasses.

Amanda Stone's Reign: How the United States' First Female President Is Making Waves

David had never heard of Amanda Stone. Or the United States. But he found it interesting there was a female president in this other reality that Rachel had supposedly pulled the gas station from. The woman on the cover looked intimidating. There was a slyness in her eyes, a cleverness that he had seen before in many of the criminals he had come across in his lifetime. But there was also a tiredness there, a look of wanting to give up, of surrender. But David didn't know what she would be surrendering to.

He flipped through the magazine, pouring over the ads and articles from another time, another place. There were models giving props to many different types of products: clothing, jewelry, vehicles. Even soda. So many of them had sexual appeal—half-naked men and women (mostly women), standing or sitting in provocative stances, revealing nearly every intimate part of themselves to sell an inanimate object. It was much like his time and his world.

He came across the article from the front cover. It was an interview and a commentary on President Amanda Stone, The United States' first female president.

Enera had never had a female president.

He skimmed the article, finding many of the questions and answers somewhat intriguing…

Q: Who was your influence?
A: Marilyn Monroe. It wasn't just her charm that people admired, it was her brutal honesty when asked a question.

Q: What do you think can help the American people the most under your presidency?

A: Honesty. Brutal honesty. The American people don't really know what they want. That's why they elected a leader, that's why we have our whole judicial system in place. It acts as a discipline, a boundary for those with no self-control—which is the entire American public.

Q: What do you think is the biggest problem facing America and possibly holding it back?

A: Religion. Blind attribution to a god that has never shown his face or revealed his presence. It's ridiculous, really, how many people have fallen for religious fanaticism. You would think we'd be smarter in this age, wiser, not prone to fall for dumb schemes or spiritual nonsense. I will find a way to do away with this, by first removing this invisible entity from the People's minds. After that, I'll act as the disciplinarian they have wanted and deserve. We will make America great.

David set the magazine on his stomach and thought about the religious system of his own world. They had the various gods that many attributed their victories to. Stalus's were set up for worship of these gods.

He didn't consider himself very religious. He worshipped the gods like everyone else. Well, when he had the time. But mostly, he just kept to himself. There were some fanatics he had come across on occasion, people absolutely obsessed with the gods and their ways and the fear they drove into people.

Though he didn't care for her dictator-like tone, David did wonder if this President Stone was actually doing some good by doing away with the spiritual fanaticism.

He fell asleep thinking about it.

22 Betrayal

The next morning, David opened his eyes to a bright sun pushing its way into his small, temporary dwelling space. He rolled onto his side, knocking the magazine he had been reading the night before to the floor. He felt a body next to him, warm and smelling of familiar perfume. He turned over and found Carrie lying next to him, most of her body buried under a thick comforter, her innocent face staring at him. Her green eyes sparkled in the sunlight. She took hold of his mouth and crashed her lips into his, kissing him long.

A knock on the bedroom door snapped him from his reverie, and he found himself alone, on the single bed, in the room in the quaint little gas station from another time and place.

He rubbed his eyes, confused. He was certain Carrie had just been here, in the bed beside him. Her body had felt real, the kiss had definitely felt real. He even remembered the warmth of her form.

The handle to the bedroom door jiggled and then the door swung open. Rachel walked in with a plate of breakfast. She had changed clothes, and now wore a simple blue blouse and blue jeans. Her long black hair flowed across her shoulders in curls, and her blue eyes lit up with the rising sun.

"I made you both some breakfast. Eat up and we'll continue on toward Carrie."

"I…"

"What is it?" she asked, setting the plate of breakfast on the nightstand. She noticed the magazine on the floor and picked it up. She stared at the cover for a moment, giving no indication of an opinion, and then set the magazine on the dresser. "What's wrong?"

He shook his head and took the plate of breakfast. She made scrambled eggs, toast, and bacon. The smell of bacon filled his nostrils, and so many memories of growing up in his home hit him all at once.

"I had a dream. But it wasn't a dream. Carrie was right here, next to me. She kissed me. I felt her warmth."

Rachel nodded. "Slip sickness."

"Why didn't we travel through the night? If Carrie is so important, if I'm 'dying' of slip sickness, why settle us here for the night?"

"Slip sickness is worse when you have no sleep. And Carrie's status is fine today. The dream you had, it was another reality. If you want something badly enough, sometimes you will inadvertently pull that thing into the reality you are in, temporarily of course."

"So that really was Carrie beside me?"

"In a sense, but not the sense you are thinking of. It's a version of Carrie, one of an infinite number of versions."

David found the whole business of alternate realities sickening. He took a bite of the scrambled eggs. They had the perfect amount of salt on them. The bacon could have been crispier. The toast was dry.

Rachel pointed to the magazine. He noticed her nails were painted blue. "You were reading that last night?"

David nodded, still chewing his bacon.

"President Amanda Stone."

David swallowed. "You know her?"

"Of her." Her gaze seemed lost, starstruck. There was something in her eyes. Hurt? Fear? "She's wound up in a variety of different earth-based realities. In 2007, Earth Time, she ran against Greg Mason for President of the United States. She won by a landslide, mainly because she was female. After she was initiated into Office, she began destroying civil liberties one by one."

"What happened to her?"

Rachel grinned. "There are stories to tell, David. In another time, another place."

He shrugged. "I just want to find Carrie. I want to get out of here."

"You minimize your destiny, young man."

"Please don't call me that," he said as he stared into her lifelike eyes. He stood to his feet and carried his plate out of the room. "I don't like it when people talk to me like I'm a child."

Rachel followed him into the kitchen area. Turquoise sat at the dining table, eating breakfast.

"Quite the contrary," Rachel said. "I imagine you have more on your shoulders than most adults."

"Great," David said as he tossed the plate in the sink. The ceramic hit the inside of the sink and shattered. "Can we go now?"

Turquoise stood to her feet. "Yes. I for one am ready to get out of here."

Rachel shrugged. "If you are both finished eating, then yes, we can leave now. It is time to find Carrie." She glanced sidelong toward David but said nothing more.

He tried to read her expression, but she had none. Those lips, those cheekbones, those eyes. David attempted to read her poker face but could discern nothing. He figured being a robot allowed her to bypass most human reactions—emotional reactions—that gave most people away in their lies and fairy tales.

Instead, Rachel led them down to the first floor and out to the open garage. The air outside felt cool and crisp, as if the season had changed overnight. David took in a deep breath of it and exhaled in a small cloud of frost. He suddenly wondered if his denim jacket and T-shirt was going to be enough to keep him warm in this sudden shock of weather.

The vehicle on the lift was a sedan with the name 'Jeep' on the back tailgate above the bumper. It was a brand David had never heard of. The sleek and stylish body reminded him of the Cobalt brand from his own reality. After lowering the lift, Rachel started the vehicle while David took the front passenger seat and Turquoise took to the back. The Jeep smelled of gasoline and age. The engine sounded rough and wanting.

They traveled across the desert toward the main city, taking the long stretch of road that they had started down the day before.

The day dragged on, and through it all, David had no concept of time. It seemed to stretch, pull at his very being, and it was reminiscent of a goat chewing on one's shirt. He remembered that happening at the Winter Festival many years ago.

He felt nauseous on and off, but gripping his boomerang seemed to have a strange, soothing effect on him. He wanted to ask Rachel about it but decided against it. The last thing he wanted was more disturbing facts about the space/time continuum.

When they reached the outskirts of Andradesta, they encountered a mile stretch of old abandoned factories and warehouses. David didn't remember seeing them when he had come through this way with Drax, but he was also racing to find one of his friends.

Drax.

David wondered if he had been brought back to life yet. Lexy would have been happy to see him, but probably not with a drained battery.

Rachel pulled the vehicle into the lot of a three-story brick industrial building. Large smokestacks pierced a low cloud line that had formed in the last half hour. The air was growing cold, and David wondered if it had something to do with where they were or if it had something to do with his very presence.

Rachel turned off the car engine and then just sat there, staring at the building.

"What is it?" David asked, gripping his boomerang. Something felt unsteady here. The pull at his very spirit, his very being, was stronger here.

Turquoise left the car without so much as a word.

Rachel turned to David and smiled, but tears ran down her face. He wondered how she could cry, being a conglomerate of electrical and mechanical parts. He wondered if it was just an illusion, like her female form and the clothing she 'wore.'

"There are decisions that will be made here that will impact many timelines, David." She took his hand in hers. Her limbs felt warm, but David had expected her grip to be cold for some reason. "I may be man-made, but I do have a soul."

"That's impossible."

She shook her head. "Nothing is impossible. My heart breaks at this point. I've seen this part of your journey so many times…and each time, I've had to look away."

His stomach turned. "Is Carrie dead?"

She neither confirmed nor denied his anxious inquiry. Instead, she looked out the windshield at the massive brick structure in front of them. "This is a place of great evil."

"Legion?"

She shook her head. "Worse."

"What could possibly be worse?"

"David, there are innumerable times and realities. In each of these, there are many similarities. But there are just as many—if not more—differences. President Amanda Stone is elected president in one reality, but not in another. Both timelines differ significantly after that point.

"In other realities, you die. Others, you live. Some, you are victorious, and others you fail. Branches and branches and branches of various timelines and possibilities and outcomes."

"This one?" he asked, pointing to the building. Whatever was inside the building seemed to pull at the skin at the tip of his finger, as if the forces inside were magnetic. Though, he had to admit, nothing seemed uncanny or malevolent from the outside of the building. It was made of red brick. It rose three stories. And whatever was inside was waiting for him.

"This one. This one is all ones. This scene, this incident, happens in every single reality I have ever seen."

He felt sick. It wasn't the slip sickness. This was a nausea growing in his core. "How is that possible with all of the various outcomes?"

Rachel shrugged for the first time and seemed to be genuinely confused by her own inadequate answer. "I don't fully understand these anomalies."

"Well," he said as he opened the car door, "there's only

one way to find out what's going to happen in there."

Rachel nodded but did not move. "Yes. Only one way."

Before David could make sense of what was happening, he felt the blue pulse beam smack into his chest and flood through his veins, closing off his nerves, shutting down his consciousness. The edges of his vision blackened, and the last thing he saw was Turquoise's gun pointed at him, and a pink frown upon his friend's beautiful face.

23 Remote Understanding

old air touched the back of his neck and snuck down his shirt, lightly teasing his spine as it moved. The chill was enough to wake him from his slumber.

His arms wouldn't move. His eyelids felt like weights. His legs struggled to shift.

He could hear the wind, but that was it. No car engine. No talking. No anything. Just clean, chilly air.

When he finally managed to open his heavy eyes, he was surprised to find himself in the same spot he had fallen. The car was gone, but the imposing brick building stood tall above him, the ominous, foreboding feeling just as strong as it was before he was taken out.

Taken out by Turquoise, of all people. A friend.

Confused, he simply lay there in the hard gravel, staring up at the building, watching lazy clouds skate across the sky in his peripheral vision. He pondered everything about this reality and wished he could simply wish himself out of here. The strangest thing happened though when he continued to stare at the brick industrial building. Something seemed familiar. Had he been here before? He couldn't quite remember. He knew that with the smokestacks, the building must have been used for production, but of what?

And what was its connection to Carrie?

David got to his knees and rested for a moment. The pulse blast Turquoise had used on him had been just enough to knock him out, paralyze him for a bit. It was taking a bit of time for the blood to rush back through his veins at a normal pace and for his thoughts to return to the forefront of his mind.

Where had Rachel gone with the car? Where had Turquoise run off to? Where was Carrie?

He stood to his feet as the blood rushed back into his legs. He wobbled a bit but found himself able to walk. He glanced around but could see no sign of any other life. It was just him and this building and the other buildings around him.

He had been abandoned here, even by Rachel. He remembered her ominous message before getting out of the car. She had said this was one point and all points. That what was to happen in the building was to happen in all realities.

Or maybe she meant what Turquoise did was what was to happen in all realities, David conjectured.

The pull on him was still here, and it grew stronger the more he observed the brick building. He sensed something inside the structure, but he wasn't sure what it was. He felt sick, he felt displaced. His hands hurt, as did the spot Turquoise had shot him: in the side of his ribs. His ribs felt bruised and sore, as if he had been punched and kicked in them multiple times.

He had been hit with a pulse before. A few times, actually, at various times in the past. Each time felt worse than the last, as if his body learned to hate the act more and more each time it happened.

This time felt the absolute worse. But there was something different about it too—as if the pulse had stayed underneath his skin instead of dissipating through his bloodstream. The soreness was unusual, and his skin felt as if it was on fire. He lifted his shirt and examined his ribs. Nothing visually alarming.

He let his shirt drop back in place and then he looked up at the building. Something told him to leave. To run. To flee from this place of evil. But he knew he couldn't do that. He needed answers to what was going on. He needed to find Carrie. If anything, he just wanted to put a stop to whatever was pulling at him from within this structure.

Everything about this reality felt different, new, and terrifying.

He started toward the building, and when he neared it, he noticed a small door had been propped open with a single red brick.

He gripped his boomerang, sliding it out of his holster. The item grounded him, anchored him to his thoughts on the current situation. It became a token, a bauble that his very life seemed to cling to. Ironic that it was his lifetime weapon of choice.

He peered inside the massive building. When he stepped in, the door slammed shut behind him. He looked down toward the floor and saw that the brick was gone. He had no idea what happened to the it, or what powers were at work in this place…

…but he knew there was something evil in this realm.

The building was empty of people. Bright lamps hung from the ceiling, illuminating the front passage to this liminal space. The cement floor offered up a myriad of various stains, adding to the character of the structure. The smell of oil and metal filled the atmosphere, while posters from another era covered the walls. Streamers hung from the rafters, and confetti covered the ground, adding a harsh beauty to the multitude of stains. Shadows hid in the back of the spacious room, concealing nothing and everything at the same time.

This place looked to have at one time been an industrial factory, and at another time, a dance hall.

The contradiction between the two was unsettling.

David walked across the floor toward a lone wooden table that stood in the center of the room. Across the table sat various objects, many of which David had never seen before:

A flyer for a high school dance.

A statue of a stalus, coated in a shiny black material.

A small flower pot with a single white daisy blooming within.

A book, *The Drifting Classroom.*

A pink watch, cracked at the face.

Another book, *The Holy Bible.*

A necklace of a red, upside-down cross.

A small shard of black metal, the tip of a possible weapon.

David fixed his gaze on each item in turn, confused as to their meaning or purpose in a place like this. Then he realized the streamers hanging from the ceiling and the confetti on the floor were all from the dance at the Silver Kangaroo hotel in downtown Lysallis. The night he was going to tell Carrie how he felt, before Ryc Waterford interrupted the evening with a bomb. Before he kidnapped Carrie.

The sound of footsteps did nothing to startle David. His hand was already on his boomerang.

"There's no need for that," the man said.

David turned as a tall gentleman in a black suit and red tie came around to the other side of the table opposite David. His black hair was parted on the side, a beard hung from his face, and he had a tattoo on the left side of his neck of clock hands stuck at a minute to midnight.

"You look confused," the man said.

"A bit."

"Please," he said, motioning to David's hand which rested on his boomerang. "Please, let's dispense with unpleasantries. I'm not here to hurt you. I could have shot you in the back or slit your throat by now if I wanted."

David kept his hand steady on the boomerang, both as an 'in case', and to steady himself. The slip sickness was washing over him again, and he couldn't afford to collapse here or now.

The man grunted. "Very well. Your distrusting attitude is not a good start for us. My name is Redford."

"I'm not here to make friends," David said. "I was shot by a pulse pistol and woke up to find my friends gone."

"Who shot you?"

David refused to answer the question.

Redford laughed. "Are they really your friends if they shoot you?" He motioned to the items on the table. "Do you recognize any of these, David?"

David glanced at each item again. "No."

"As I would expect you to answer. If you answered yes, I would call you a liar. Or maybe, if you answered yes, it would have meant things were too far along to even be worth a try at fixing."

"Speak clearly," David snapped at the man.

Redford smiled, but it was a sickly smile, like a rock under which spiders hide. "I'm here to fix things. Fix things that were broken long ago. These items here, they are artifacts of an age when rebellion ruled the day. When those who thought they were above time and space decided to change the course of a history that was already put in place at the beginning of

233

all things.

"This flower, for example," he said as he pointed to the daisy. "It represents Daisy Pierce, a young woman who was captured and killed for her beliefs. I admired her to a certain degree, as most of the world did at the time. But—" Redford gripped the daisy by the stem and ripped the flower out of the pot. The roots dangled from his hand as dirt scattered across the table. He took the pot in his other hand and swung it across the room. It hit the cement floor and shattered, sending shards of terra cotta across the industrial building like meteorites falling from the sky.

Something pulled at David's skin, like the sharp fingernails of an old woman trying to remove a splinter from underneath the surface. He felt the pull on his arm, in his chest. He fell to his knees and felt as if he might retch.

Redford came around the table and knelt to David's level. "Did you feel that," he said. He smelled of cheap cologne, and David felt a depravity within the man. Redford squeezed the daisy in his fist, ripped the petals as if they were made of construction paper, and then threw the daisy to the floor before stepping on it, smearing the white petals into the concrete floor.

David felt the pull again, this time in his knees and in his neck. The item—the artifact—seemed to possess some connection to him, some connection to his reality.

Redford returned to the table as David struggled to his feet. "I tried to fix time—many, many years ago. I tried to help humanity. I was one of the 'good guys.' But you wouldn't know that. You have forgotten the difference between good and bad. Your lines have blurred because time has blurred."

"What are these," David finally said as he used the table to prop him back to his feet, his chest aching. "What is happening?"

Redford stared at him. "Your destiny. The destiny that you deserve."

The man took the flyer from the school dance and ripped it into two, then four, then six pieces, and then he threw the pieces up in the air. They fell like giant chunks of confetti, and David felt the pull in his spine and his head. He threw up across the floor.

Redford grimaced, and then he held up the pink watch. "If only you had known the girl who owned this watch, David. I think you and her would have gotten along quite well. In fact, the man she was in love with reminds me a lot of you."

David grabbed his chest, the pain radiating through him, equaling at first and then overcoming the pain the pulse had left him with. "I don't have…time for…this."

The man dropped the pink watch on the ground and then stomped on it with his foot. David heard the watch components crunch under the man's shoe. David felt another tug, this one at his spirit, as if it was going to leave his body.

Redford smiled. "I did what I could, you must understand. Nobody listened to me. That—" Redford bit his lower lip, clearly stopping himself from saying something foul. "That damn brat, Nathan. He should have died."

David turned and started to walk toward the exit of the industrial building, toward the door that had slammed shut behind him. "Good luck with that."

He suddenly felt a gust, a pull, the same that he had felt back in the grocery store. He turned back toward Redford. The man had a small contraption in his hand that looked a lot like a car alarm dongle. Next to him though was a doorway. Framed in black, shimmering material, the door was open to swirling purple and black colors on the other side. Mesmerizing colors. Colors David felt himself being drawn naturally to.

"You feel it, don't you?" Redford asked. "That pull. That tug."

"I do." David found no reason to lie to the man about that.

"It's time. Collapsing under itself. Did you know that many believe a single holy entity created everything, including time? How absurd. Time has been here since the beginning. Time will be here in the end. Strangely enough, time will be the downfall of itself."

"How did you open that portal?"

Redford held up the small device in his hand. "This?" He shook it as if he was putting it on display. "It's a remote to control the Black Doors. This is the last thing I crafted before I was excommunicated from the Time Protection Society. You probably know nothing about us, David. And that's okay. You don't need to know what we're about to appreciate our effect on history. All you really need to know is that you've come to your end. *You*, the human race.

"I've grown tired of fighting against those who fight against time. I've grown tired of trying to put everything back in order. I've grown tired of doing a job nobody else will lift a finger to do. So, it's time to get a bit drastic." Redford walked behind the door and came around the other side with another person in his grip.

Carrie.

Her wrists were bound behind her back and duct tape covered her mouth. The Lysallis High School sweatshirt he had given her to wear what felt so long ago was torn in places. The strange ink marks had taken over most of her once-fair skin. Her eyes seemed vacant, staring listlessly at David.

David's hand went to his boomerang. Without warning,

Redford pulled a pistol from the back waistline of his pants and fired a shot off, hitting David in the right shoulder. He stumbled backwards and fell to the pavement.

"Don't touch that weapon of yours again. You're not going to stop this. Nobody is going to stop it. This is where I make my stand and put a stop to everything Nathan did. To everything you've been doing."

David sat up, gripping his wound as it bled out underneath his coat. The bullet had gone clean through. He was grateful for this, as dealing with an infection this far out of his own time and space would have made things so much more complicated. Pain blossomed across his shoulder and chest, and he fought to remain calm.

Redford grabbed Carrie's wrists and moved her in front of the door. His eyes seemed full of life and full of joy. This was a groundbreaking moment for him, although David didn't fully understand why.

David stood to his feet, his chest screaming for him to get back on the floor. He was careful not to instinctively put his hand on his boomerang. He believed Redford would shoot to kill if he had to. "Let her go."

Redford shook his head.

"What do you want?"

"This. *This* is what I want. There's no exchange to be made here. I'm going to throw her in. She'll land on the other side. I'll close this door, and you'll never find her again. You won't be able to access the weapon. You won't ever get your hands on the Codex. Order, David, will be restored. Time will be restored. It will heal, events will play out like they should have nearly a century ago, and the human race will be destroyed. Simple as that."

David's gaze shifted. Redford saw it. He knew David was thinking of what to do. But there wasn't much to do. Except go in after her, which David would…wherever it led.

The bleeding slowed, but the ache in his shoulder felt as if a pole of scalding rebar had gone through it. The dull ache kept him grounded to this reality in a way he didn't want to be grounded.

Redford yanked on Carrie's wrist binds and pushed her through the doorway. Before David could react, Redford shut the door and it disappeared, leaving David and Redford as the only two people in the industrial building.

David fought to calm himself. He wanted to make himself believe it had been a different Carrie. But he knew that look in her eyes. He knew the form of her frame. He recognized the Legion marks—the rack matter. It was *his* Carrie. And now she was lost.

He wondered if he could use Redford's remote to open it again, find out where she went.

As if reading his thoughts, Redford dropped the remote on the floor and then stepped on it, crushing it into pieces. "Just in case," he said. "In case you get any thoughts of going after her." He started toward the back of the building, toward those shadows, gun pointed back on David as he left.

And then he was gone through some doorway back there that David couldn't see.

David stood, holding his shoulder, his mind racing, his heart racing more.

Carrie was gone.

All he had left was gone.

24 Answers

It was nightfall when David gave up on trying to put the pieces of the crushed remote back together. He had watched Professor Grey put together dozens of machines—even helped him build the time traveling component—but the remote seemed to be made of materials David had never seen before. A metal that looked a lot like copper but was yellow instead of the usual brightened bronze color, lined the inside of the circuits. There were small LEDs inside of the remote that seemed to have no form or function but to light up the inside of the device.

What is the purpose of that?

A microchip inside was damaged beyond repair.

David gathered the small pieces together, wrapped them in an old vintage poster from a traveling circus, and placed them in the pocket of his coat, where the timepiece had been before Turquoise took it from him.

The bleeding from the gunshot wound had stopped, but David knew he needed to clean it out. The industrial building was void of restrooms or offices. It was almost as if it was built specifically for Redford to give his presentation to David.

That's ridiculous.

His shoulder hurt, but he was grateful Redford had let him live.

David walked out of the building the same way he walked in, and then he stood outside under the starry sky, confused as to where to go. Carrie was gone. Turquoise was gone. Rachel was gone. Where was he supposed to venture?

Lexy.

But the city was miles away, and he didn't want to wander out into this wasteland under the cover of darkness when he knew nothing about this reality.

He rubbed the bridge of his nose in frustration and then took a seat on a stack of pallets on the side of the building. He lay back, staring up at the stars, feeling as if he had finally reached a dead end in all things.

He would have normally felt panic overtake him in a moment like this. With Carrie being taken to who-knows-where, he didn't think he would cope so well. But a strange calm washed over him, easing his anxiety, easing his panic. He wasn't sure where the calm came from, but he accepted it. And he quickly fell asleep because of it.

An hour later, lightning flashed, startling David awake. He sat up as Vector took a seat next to him on the stack of pallets.

She drew her hood down and looked him in the eyes. Her face was bruised, her cheeks cut and bleeding, but she still seemed to hold the beauty she always had as Jennifer. David wasn't certain what she was doing here. He assumed her last visit was her last. But he didn't question it, as she was (always) a sight for sore eyes.

David huffed and wrung his hands together in his lap.

"Dead end."

She nodded and smiled. "So it seems."

David looked up at the stars again. He was mesmerized by the variety of colored planets and moons he could see. There was a violet-colored one that reminded him of Veronica. A green one that reminded him of Carrie. And a gray one that resembled the way he felt.

"I didn't really plan on this happening," Jennifer said.

"What did you think was going to happen when you left behind that portal?"

She shook her head. "I didn't plan on leaving that portal behind. I didn't think time was that weak…yet."

David nodded. "Well, now you know. And now it's too late. We're already on a path even you have no control over."

"I never had control over any paths, David. I simply guided you in the best direction I could. Helped you when I could. Helped you more than I should have."

"And yet, it was all for nothing. Carrie's gone—again. Turquoise turned on me for reasons I don't understand, taking the timepiece. And the android girl, Rachel—she's gone to who knows where."

"I didn't expect you to find Rachel here. It's strange that you traveled through a portal that was created by me *by accident* and yet you *still* ended up on the same path I had foreseen by simply leaving you at the grocery store."

"What was supposed to happen?"

"Serenity was supposed to open a portal back to Anaisha. You would find Rachel. Find Eden Ambersay. Everything would end happily ever after." She had a jovial tone in her voice when she said it, indicating to David that she didn't really expect everything to end happily ever after.

"Who is Eden?"

Jennifer didn't answer, only stared at him with a face that looked as tired as he felt.

"Serenity ate some food," he explained. "Poisoned her. Then we found the portal. She didn't have the power to get us out of there, so we had to go through it. All four of us were split up. Redford just tossed Carrie through a portal. Turquoise shot me with a pulse pistol and stole the timepiece. Rachel is...I don't know."

Vector took his hand in hers. Her fingers felt like thin heated rods of metal. "I didn't expect this. But it's not out of His control."

"Who?" David looked into her eyes and remembered the first time they met. They went on a date, and then he found out she was Mr. Big's niece. Kingpin of the city's criminal network, and David had to fall for his niece. Little orphan Jennifer.

She pulled her hand from his. "God."

David scoffed. "There's a lot of gods, Jennifer. You'll have to be more specific."

She said nothing. He turned to look at her again and found her smiling warmly at him. "It's been a while since I heard anyone use my real name."

He smiled back, but his smile was impatient, unwilling to remain for longer than a few seconds. He was at a dead end, and all he wanted to do was get out. Get back home. Get Carrie.

"There is one true God, David. Anaisha knows almost nothing about Him because that was the way it was deemed necessary when the planet was colonized. Earth folk traveled to Anaisha on starships. Memories were wiped. And a new order was created. The knowledge of God was wiped from the history books thanks to one man: Mr. Silver."

"*Another* religion?"

She had a strange look on her face, something between amusement and sadness. "Not religion, exactly. Faith. Relationship."

Jennifer stepped off the pallets and walked to the front of the industrial building. Lights had come on outside the building, illuminating the perimeter around the brick structure. David followed her to the doorway. She peered inside but said nothing before she walked away from the building and stood out where the beat-up asphalt street met the grounds of the industrial building.

"I'm going to break my own rules, David. Just this once."

"I doubt this will be the first time you've broken rules— even your own."

"You'd be surprised at how disciplined I've become."

"Didn't you tell me you were dying?"

She glared at him. "Turquoise is facing her own past right now. Memories that she has had locked away in her mind for so many long years. It's a struggle she must complete on her own."

"And the timepiece?"

"Carrie is in a place you cannot yet reach. And Rachel— well, she was taken. Taken by a different form of evil than any you've encountered before. A person you will meet soon. Whatever you do, do not allow him to leave this place, David. This reality's version of him must die. Eventually, all versions of him will have to die."

"What do you mean this reality's version of him?"

"He *must* die."

David shrugged, and then he nodded, thinking she was simply speaking gibberish. He seemed to have no qualms about killing now. This bothered him. "I'll do what needs to be done."

"He's not human, David. He's an AI that was created to protect this planet. He wants the knowledge, the precious information, stored within Rachel. You cannot let him have it. She is the key to Anaisha's salvation. She is the key to humanity's salvation. That is why I told you to find her and forget Carrie. Rachel is the one you need to protect and keep out of the wrong hands."

"You told me the Codex of Ra'f was…" It suddenly struck David that Rachel was Ra'f. That Rachel was the codex he had been chasing after.

Jennifer peered into his eyes, a knowing expression on her face. "Those gears are turning properly, it seems. She is the codex. She's the one you must protect."

"You could have told me that the codex was a being. You could have told me Rachel was a robot."

She chuckled, and David found it pleasing to hear her laugh again.

"She's more than a robot, David."

"She's made of gears and servos. She's a robot."

"I wish I could be as naïve as you. I really do. I don't mean to insult you, I just—sometimes how little you know about what's really going on underneath the surface is something I would treasure. I've seen too many things, I've experienced too many things. I wish I could forget so much of it, but I can't."

"Who is Rachel?"

"You will find out soon enough. Right now, you need to protect her. Protect her like you protected Carrie. Use whatever powers are manifesting within you and protect her with all of yourself. Your future—humanity's future, depends on it."

"Fine. How do I find her?"

"She's being held not far from here. There's an underground installation in the wasteland. You must be careful. Sentries guard the installation."

"Sentries?"

She nodded. Her beautiful green eyes caught the reflection of the moon, and for a moment, David was taken back in time to the first time they kissed. He remembered how sweet-tasting her lips were. They had just eaten dessert at the Cone Malone, and her lips had been covered in traces of chocolate.

Jennifer stared into his glassy gaze, an amused look on her face. "I need you to focus. Not on me, not on Carrie, but on Rachel. Save her. She may be able to help you find Carrie at some point."

At some point? He nodded. "Alright."

Jennifer pointed toward foothills a few miles from where they stood, across the barren wasteland, on the other side of the desert. "Two miles. You'll come to an abandoned school bus. You'll find a cement stairwell that leads into a bunker. There you'll find the AI. Destroy it. Save Rachel. She'll lead you home."

"And to Carrie?"

"Stay focused, please. You have more to do in our timeline, but first we must get you and Rachel back before something horrible happens to her."

"She seemed quite capable of protecting herself."

"She can. To an extent. But this AI you're about to go against, David…it's a confrontation I was hoping you could avoid until you were better prepared. Be on your guard. Do not have mercy on it. First chance you get, you destroy it. Understand?"

David nodded, although he *didn't* completely understand.

Jennifer wrapped him in a hug. "I don't know when or if I'll see you again. Stay the course." She rubbed her fingers across his left cheek, and he felt passion in her touch. Passion he hadn't felt in a long time.

He wrapped his arms around her thin waste and pulled her close to him. He could smell perfume on her person, but it was obvious it was masking a foul smell. She was mostly covered in bandages, so he could only guess her skin was infected and possibly festering underneath them.

For some reason, he didn't care.

He pulled her close and kissed her on the lips. The kiss electrified him. The voltage popped his ears, skipped his heartbeat, and sent waves of euphoric currents down his spine. Jennifer did nothing to pull away, so David kissed her for what felt like a lifetime. Love fell into that kiss, love that he had at one time, many years earlier, felt for Jennifer. The niece of his enemy, the love of his life. Forbidden fruit.

Forbidden destiny.

A blast of electricity tossed him to the ground.

When he came to, she was gone. Emptiness flooded him for a moment, slicing through his insides like the jagged edges of broken stained-glass.

He shook the feeling, the darkness, and stood to his feet.

He decided to scavenge the industrial building for any supplies he could find and came up mostly empty-handed. He couldn't even scavenge the watch which Redford had crushed under his foot. David did take the sharp, black metal object. The Holy Bible, a book David knew nothing about, had to be left behind because it wouldn't fit in any of his pockets. The book was printed in incredibly small front and packed with many words he couldn't make sense of. He assumed it was written in a foreign language, but he couldn't be sure.

The black statue of a stalus intrigued him, almost seemed

to call to him. But he left it behind as well. There was no purpose to it, except to hold papers to a desk. He could probably use it as a weapon in a pinch, seeing as it had a very sharp top, but it would do him no good against sentries.

What are sentries doing mixed up in all of this?

He walked the inside space of the building once or twice, his mind curious as to the origins of this building. Had it been a factory? Was it a place for parties? It seemed two realities had merged into this one place. The space felt strange. As he glanced around the massive room, it felt empty. Not only of things, but of life. The walls seemed like they stretched for miles, and almost seemed to repeat in certain patterns of stains and scratches. The cement flooring seemed inhabited, alive, as if the cement was wet and flowing instead of dry and stable. He couldn't properly explain any of it. It was almost as if the building was a live entity.

He dismissed the theory. Though he had seen some interesting and near-impossible things in his lifetime, he didn't think a building could be alive.

But something about it definitely felt off.

He ventured around the outside of the building as well, finding nothing but wooden pallets and bags of dry cement.

And then he ventured into the wilderness toward the facility where Rachel was being held. Where an AI needed to die.

And where Destiny would once again call for a reluctant hero.

25 Neon Lights

I t wasn't a jarring sound or a bright light that woke Carrie. It was silence. Utter silence.

Her eyes opened and she found herself surrounded by darkness. Dark fog, really, sliding like silk across the black asphalt she lay upon.

She turned onto her back and stared up at the black ceiling of sky above her, her eyes filled with thick sleep. She wasn't certain how long she had been asleep—or rather, been out of it—but she figured it had to have been awhile.

She tried to remember...

David.

Redford.

The tear.

She felt something press against her chest, her sides. A force. *A spirit?* Dark and heavy. Heavy and awful.

She turned onto her side and then pushed herself to her knees. Dim light glowed from the other side of the surrounding fog, all around her, slightly illuminating the circle she found herself in.

Black pavement. Asphalt. Black sky. Black fog.

She could smell something…strawberries. *And popcorn?* The scent was strange, but not all that alarming. After all that she had seen in her lifetime, the mixture of smells was somewhat humorous.

Carrie sat up, her will fighting against the heavy feeling that seemed to blanket her like heavy, water-laden sheets. She couldn't place the feeling exactly, except to think of it as…*dread? Despair? Foreboding?*

She took a deep breath, and her lungs suddenly felt heavy. *What's in the air?* It felt cold, like the moisture in pockets of fog. Her eyes began to adjust to the darkness, and she could make out the outlines of buildings around her. She was in the middle of a street? Yes—lights flickered in the distance, through the dark fog. Neon lights. Pinks, blues, whites.

She rubbed her eyes, took another deep breath, and spit off to the side, clearing her throat of heavy moisture. It tasted metallic, almost rocky. Stone-like. Panic crept through her chest at the possibility she could be inhaling some kind of foreign substance.

You can't think about that right now, she told herself. *Get up!*

She stood cautiously. There was so much darkness all around her, and she didn't want to spook someone or something that might be slumbering out there. Once she stood, she stretched. Her bones felt cramped, compacted, and it was a somewhat painful chore to get her flexibility back.

Taking another deep breath, she peered into the darkness, toward one of the neon lights she could make out through the fog. Bright pink and blue, it glowed with a blurry luminescence, beckoning her to its bright beacon.

249

She walked toward that light. Cautiously. Carefully. Silently as could be. Moving through the thick fog felt like cutting through levitating columns of wet sand. She held her right hand over her mouth in the hopes of blocking as much of it from getting down into her lungs, though she knew it was a mostly futile effort. She had to breathe. And breathing meant inhaling whatever was in this air.

She broke through the thick fog, her body feeling week, tired. She couldn't sense Viranda within her spirit, but she wasn't convinced that didn't mean she was no longer with her. She had apparently come through a doorway, one that brought her to a place of darkness. Viranda could simply not be attuned to this realm.

Carrie found herself shrugging.

The look on David's face...

Carrie stopped in the middle of her journey through the fog and replayed the moment in her head. The moment David had been forced to watch her get dumped through a tear in reality. The moment he figured he had lost her forever.

She shook her head and continued through the fog. She couldn't worry about David. Not right now. She had to find some way out of this place. Some way back.

Carrie drew closer to the neon lights, her breath becoming heavier as she moved deeper into the fog. There was a chill in the air, one that didn't feel natural. It brought cold to her bones, and it was then she gave up the idea that Viranda was still with her. Her presence—her symbiotic presence—had a way of almost keeping Carrie warm. The void felt within her now—first David's missing presence, and now Viranda's—left Carrie feeling quite lonely. Almost scared.

She pushed past the fear and reached the point of origin

where the blue and pink neon lights pierced the dark fog. At first, Carrie thought the blue and pink neon would have led her to a strip club. Or maybe a video store. She didn't expect them to lead her to a laundromat. The blue neon had been twisted into the shape of a box of soap, and pink neon bubbles 'floated' up from the box.

She looked to her right and saw a door. She took hold of the handle and pulled, half expecting the door to refuse entry. But it swung open with ease, allowing her entry into a pit of darkness. Though her eyes had started to adjust to the fog, as there were various neon lights scattered throughout the street, her eyes were not accustomed to the laundromat. There wasn't a single light shining inside the establishment. The scent of laundry soap and dryer sheets flooded her sense of smell, overwhelming her with memories of home.

She closed her eyes, took a deep breath, and reached her left hand out, running it along the wall in the hopes of finding a—*switch!* She swung upward, flipping the switch. Fluorescent lights popped on all across the ceiling, nearly blinding her. She entered the building, shutting and locking the door behind her.

She looked out the window and saw nothing but darkness. She turned back toward the laundry room, half-expecting to find some weird creature or something out of the ordinary residing within the small space. But all she found were washers and dryers. Stainless steel, non-moving.

She stepped further into the laundromat, finding metal baskets on wheels, a machine that seemed to make change from paper credits, and a healthy number of washers and dryers that looked to be brand new and never-before used. A machine on the wall to her right contained mini boxes of detergent and dryer sheets.

Carrie took another deep breath and found she could breathe easier here in the laundromat. Without the strange fog, which she was grateful hadn't found a way inside, she was able to breath normal air.

As she exhaled, she glanced down at her arms, confirming what she had pieced together only minutes before: Viranda was no longer with her. The marks on Carrie's arms—the rack matter—was gone. In place, her ivory-colored skin covered her limbs. She couldn't remember when she had last had normal skin that wasn't infected with Legion's symbiote. And as relieved as she would have been had she come upon this days earlier, she found this to be a very disheartening fact.

Viranda was gone. *But where did she go?*

Something caught Carrie's eye. Her attention darted to a washing machine tucked into the corner of the laundromat. Something about it played with her eyes. Tricked her mind. But she couldn't place what. Staring at it, it looked like all the other washing machines in the building. But…

She drew closer to the machine, her hands trembling. Without Viranda, without David, without even Veronica, she found her loneliness to be somewhat debilitating. In this dark world, in this place out of places, how would she survive? Would she find others here? Would she find a way out?

Pushing the fear aside, she approached the washing machine. Whirlpool was the brand affixed to the surface of the white-colored appliance. She had never heard of that brand before. She stared at the machine for a moment, unsure of what had actually drawn her attention to it to begin with. There was nothing unusual about it. It was a white Whirlpool washing machine. It—

It changed colors suddenly, flashing blue, then red. It

changed shape, from square to round. It changed size, from small to large to medium. It all happened quickly, almost quicker than could be perceived unless one were staring intently at it.

But then the machine started to crack.

Carrie stepped back, away from the washer. Thick black lines spider-webbed across the machine, and then the washer broke apart into pieces, chunks of metal and ceramic tumbling clumsily across the tile floor. One of them hit Carrie's shoe. She bent down and picked it up, observing the place where the piece had broken off—it glowed a dark blue color, as if it had been melted off, but by lightning?

As the washer broke apart, a strange black swirl sat suspended in mid-air where the washing machine used to sit. It was roughly the size of a person—Carrie's size—and it seemed to be stable and stationary, not growing like the portal David had led them through.

Carrie turned her back on the portal and made her way to the front door of the laundromat. She didn't dare step into another portal. Did she? *What if it leads home? What if it leads to David? What if it leads to someplace worse…*

She glanced out the window and peered into the darkness. *Are you out there, Viranda?* Carrie couldn't think of leaving the girl behind. Yes, she was Legion, but she was an ally. And she had helped Carrie so far, and Carrie had a feeling she would need Viranda's help for whatever was up ahead.

Carrie scoured the laundromat for supplies she could use in the darkness. Though at first glance there didn't seem to be anything but soap and dryer lint in the laundromat, after searching a maintenance closet and a small office, Carrie found a flashlight, a small handheld radio, a scarf, a small denim shoulder bag, a butterfly knife, a notepad and pen, and a broom. After some improvisation with some rope she also found, she managed to affix the butterfly knife to the end of the broomstick to create a makeshift spear of sorts.

Admiring her work, she smiled. Though the circumstances were not ideal, she found a strange hope in being able to at least arm herself. She stuck the remainder of the rope, the pen and paper, and the radio into the denim shoulder bag. She wasn't certain she would find Viranda, but if she did, she would need the paper and pen to communicate with her.

She wrapped the scarf around her mouth, using it as a mask to filter out as much of the thick fog as she could. The scarf was black with red stripes, and the silky material felt comfortable against her face.

Carrie opened the laundromat door, turning to glance over her shoulder at the black portal once more. A stone fell into her gut when she realized the portal had increased in size. Not by much, but enough to notice. Maybe by a couple feet. There were no dazzling colors in the portal either, no starry skies. Just darkness. Pitch black.

She took one more deep breath of the clean, unladen air, and then stepped outside of the laundromat and into the dark fog. She shined the flashlight in front of her, dismayed to find that the light did not pierce the fog at all. In fact, the fog seemed to swallow the light and make…new fog out of it?

Carrie shut the flashlight off and shoved it into the shoulder bag. She peered through the darkness, seeing a number of various neon lights glowing along the street, like beacons indicating places of interest. The only problem was, she had no idea where Viranda could have gone, let alone had any idea if Viranda was even here.

She closed her eyes and settled her mind. If her connection

with Viranda had truly been that deep, that symbiotic, then she should—*Yes!* She felt Viranda's presence as an image of Viranda entered her mind, white static across a black backdrop.

"Where are you?" she asked the girl.

She heard nothing back but pulses. She slid the handheld radio from her bag and turned it on. The small digital screen glowed blue with the numbers of the radio frequency. She heard nothing but static. The sound was strange, as it didn't bounce off the fog, but instead was absorbed by the fog. Sound didn't travel too far from where she was.

She turned a dial on the side of the radio, scouring the different channels of static in the hopes she would find a match for the pulses Viranda was putting out.

She landed on a station that sounded like someone speaking…

She refined the frequency and listened carefully, as the voice was still surrounded by a great deal of static.

"…arri….fin….fac…"

Carrie took another deep breath, the mask filtering out a decent amount of the fog to where she could at least breathe. She listened carefully, trying her best with trembling hands to fine-tune the signal.

"Carr…ind me…tory…"

Exhaling a deep sigh, Carrie tried her best to remain patient. She knew she didn't have much time to find Viranda, not if that black portal was growing larger every minute. *Where did it lead?* she wondered. She doubted that it would lead her back home, back to David. No, she sensed something on the other side of it. Something dark. She feared going through that portal, but she knew she might not have a choice. At least she could try to find Viranda. The girl might be able to help her on the other side, or maybe even help her avoid the portal altogether.

Carrie tried once more to fine-tune the small radio. Frustrated with her shaky hands, she nearly dropped it.

She decided it would help if she sat, so she took a seat on the cold, dark ground, unsure of what might be slithering or crawling across the surface of this place. Her jeans weren't a very good insulator against the chilly surface, but they would at least help protect her against whatever might be wanting to get a piece of her skin. She kept the shoulder bag close to her, straddling her left shoulder across her chest. She wanted to be ready if she had to make a quick getaway. She set the makeshift spear on the ground, close to her side, ready to snap up if need be.

She steadied her hands more easily now that she was sitting, and she went to work attempting to fine-tune the radio once more.

"arrie…find me…in the…actory."

She drew a breath and nodded. "Factory it is," she whispered. She crammed the small radio into her bag, stood to her feet, and snatched up the spear.

Unsure of which direction to go, she decided to head down the street, cutting through the fog between the intervals of neon lights. There was no time to investigate. She had to find this factory that Viranda was in before the portal became too big. Carrie would much rather have made it her own choice to leap into it rather than having that choice made for her.

She cut through the dark fog, stabbing at it with the tip of the spear, watching as it wisped left and right in smoky swirls.

As she drew closer to the neon lights, she realized each of the establishments the lights belonged to: a café, a pharmacy, a bookstore…

She wanted to poke into each one of them, as each would have their own various useful resources, but the clock prevented her from doing so. She wasn't sure why that portal had opened there in the laundromat when she just happened to be there. It reminded her of the portal that opened in the strange grocery store that straddled time. Only this portal seemed a bit more menacing. Felt more menacing. Felt wrong in all the ways.

As she ventured further down the street, Carrie was surprised to find no other creatures or beings around her. She heard no strange sounds, saw nothing besides the dark fog, the neon lights, and the suffocating lack of hope. It was an eerie feeling to be so alone in such a public place. The lack of life, lack of social markers, made the place seem dead, but also malevolent in a strange way.

Then she heard it. The chimes. A melodious sound that seemed to echo from every direction, surrounding her in a tune, in a melody, that seemed incredibly wrong for the setting she found herself in. The music, if one could call it that, was very much like the piano tunes that were usually played in the stalus's around Western Anaisha whenever weddings or religious gatherings—mostly hollow worship services dedicated to Anaisha's multiple gods—took place.

Carrie closed her eyes and tried to focus on the sound. It was coming from straight ahead of her.

She cut through the darkness, faster now, keeping her spear in front of her like the figurehead on a pirate ship. The melody grew in volume the further she went.

It wasn't too long before the dark fog parted completely before her, moving up in large waves to her left and right, clearing the center of the street to leave only road and empty space between her and a very large building a quarter mile in front of her.

Small flames flickered around various points outside the building, casting strange shapes across the surface of the structure. The building itself was a strange shape: a large rectangle, but with odd, warped curvatures coming off the sides and out of the top. The closer she drew to the building, the stranger it looked. Carrie noticed it was made of dark-gray-colored brick, but it didn't look as if the brick had been painted that color. Rather, whatever color the brick had at one point been—red, if Carrie had to guess—had been drained out of the building's pieces.

The dark fog had parted so much by this point that Carrie had nearly the whole street clear to the sidewalks on each side of the street. Nothing impeded her route to the factory, and that's what worried her the most.

26

Just Desert

ost of the desert was flat, with small hills scattered about here and there, easily climbed and easily forgotten. The air was cool, but not as freezing as it had been earlier. David was grateful for this, as he didn't think he'd survive out here if the nighttime temperature dropped too much. His shoulder ached. He couldn't remember when he had last eaten—probably back at the gas station with Rachel and Turquoise.

David tried to avoid thinking about Turquoise, but the thought of her inevitably continued to come back around again and again and again.

Why did she shoot me?

Where did she go?

Why did she take the timepiece?

What did Jennifer mean when she said Turquoise was facing her own past? Does that mean I won't see her again?

He hoped not. He liked Turquoise. Had actually grown quite attached to her. But the question remained: Why did she do what she did?

Maybe she had been aiming at someone who was trying to take Rachel and missed? But she had looked David directly in the eyes and shot him in the chest. If her gun had been turned from stun to kill, he would be dead right now, communing with whatever false gods inhabited the afterworld.

David made it about a mile and a half before he decided to stop at the top of a small hill and rest. The hill gave him a chance to see the path behind him, all the way to the brick building in the distance. The hill also gave him a clear view of the school bus a half mile in front of him. It sat in the distance, like a beached whale, a forgotten relic from somewhere.

The night was quiet. Kind. There was a calm about it. He had expected the wilderness to be filled with foul beasts and even fouler traps, much like the Wastelands of Western Anaisha.

He would have been at full peace out here if his shoulder wasn't in so much pain, and if Carrie wasn't missing, and if he knew of the fate of Jennifer...Vector.

He held his boomerang out in front of him while he stared up at the stars, his mind wandering to the moment he killed Agent Parks. His boomerang had never killed anyone before that point.

He watched the blue moonlight glisten off the weapon as he observed the dried blood stains splattered across the metal surface from his fight with the sentries. He couldn't help but look at the weapon as a violent machination now. A tool of destruction.

Don't be a fool, he reminded himself. *You used this to protect Carrie. To save her life.*

But at what cost? Another life?

Yes, he answered himself. *Parks' life.* The man who had hunted David across Western Anaisha. The man who had tried to snuff out Carrie's candlelight.

As David stared at the boomerang, his eyes grew heavy and he fell to sleep, dreaming of better days....

They were better days. The days he and his sister were inseparable...

"Did you see it, David?" she said, her pigtails bouncing up and down as she struck her small hand toward the TV.

Thirteen-year-old David turned to Cybil. His hair, unkempt and shooting wildly every which way, was a perfect personification of his spirit. There was something wild about those days, something free about those days of his youth.

Their youth.

Three years younger, Cybil's eyes were full of life, full of wonder. She was pointing to the television, where a newsfeed was scrolling across the screen, pushing through a story about Mr. Big—some big-time criminal who was robbing banks all over Lysallis.

"He robbed another one!" Cybil shouted.

David huffed. "He'll be caught soon. You can't rob that many banks and get away with it forever."

Cybil spit her lips at the television. "What if we run into him out there on the streets?"

David chuckled as he took a seat on the living room floor next to his sister. "We aren't going to run into him on the street. He's out robbing banks. We don't even go to the bank unless mom insists we run errands with her. But that doesn't happen because I'm stuck babysitting you most of the time."

Cybil blushed.

David sighed, wishing he hadn't said it like that. The truth was, he didn't mind watching his younger sister. She was pleasant to be around— for the most part.

"I didn't mean that," he apologized.

She shrugged and turned back toward the television.

"Mr. Big—as he has been labeled by local bank patrons—has robbed seventeen banks in the Lysallis area, stealing an estimated total of $1,000,0000. Local police have been unable to catch him or even produce any leads to his whereabouts."

Cybil's eyes lit up again. "What if we caught him?"

David chuckled again but stopped when he saw his sister's lips in a straight line, unyielding to his humorous attitude.

"I'm serious," she said. "You and me. We could capture him. Trap him. Then the police would be able to lock him up. Let's get him!"

David put a gentle hand on his sister's shoulder. "He's much too dangerous. Let the cops handle him."

"But what if he hurts someone before that?"

"He hasn't hurt anyone yet. No killings. No shootings."

It was Cybil's turn to huff. "Not yet. But that doesn't mean he won't."

David nodded. "Fair point. I'm actually more curious about why he is stealing so much money."

Cybil scratched her blonde head. "You think he's going to use it for something?"

David shrugged.

"Promise me if we ever get the chance, we'll catch him. Together."

David put on his best fake smile. "Sure, sis."

David awoke in a cold sweat, his shoulder in agonizing pain. He struggled to sit up, his heart racing, his eyes glancing frantically around to make sure no wild animals or enemies were nearby, stalking him.

He took a few deep breaths to steady his heartbeat. The dream felt so real. It was an event, an exchange, that had actually occurred between him and his sister many years ago.

But why would that come to his mind now?

Because she's dead, he reminded himself.

He stood to his feet, the world spinning somewhat. He closed his eyes, gripping his wounded shoulder.

David wished he could just rest. Just stop. Halt. Cease all of this action, this movement. He wanted nothing more than to settle down with Carrie, to enjoy whatever life still had left to offer.

But this would not be his fate.

Not tonight, anyway.

David opened his eyes and looked out on the school bus a half mile in front of him. There was something familiar about the shape bathed in blue moonlight. Most school buses looked the same: yellowish orange with black text on the side with the school (or the school district) name.

But there was something off about this bus. There was something distinct about the back end of the vehicle. The back part curved up just a little, something familiar of the school bus he rode when he was in junior high.

When he met Carrie, Veronica, even Sean.

The world started to spin again, and the bus started to change colors under the moonlight. Yellow to red. Red to purple. It looked as if it changed shapes too, from sleek and stylish to blocky and congruent. He couldn't exactly tell this far away.

He gripped his boomerang and the world stopped spinning. The colors stopped shifting. The night fell back into a calm stride.

David continued toward the bus, toward the man he would have to kill.

I can't do this, he told himself as he tightened the grip on his boomerang. The weapon hung in the holster on his side like a firearm, but one could argue this was more dangerous than a basic firearm. He used it to kill an agent. Used it against sentries. Would he use it again?

He nodded. He would, if for no other reason than Jennifer asked it of him.

He continued toward the bus, his mind racing through memories of his sister, of Carrie, of Mr. Big. What was that man up to right now? Did it matter? The world was starting to fall apart—this much, David could feel in his bones. Mr. Big was a simple blip on the radar at this point.

No, it seemed his bigger issue right now was Legion. Maybe even Redford? He didn't really know anymore.

Jennifer was telling him it was this Mr. Silver.

What if it's all of them?

David stopped and looked up, realizing he had reached the school bus.

Printed on the side in black text were the words: Lysallis Junior High.

What are you doing here?

He knew he recognized the back end of the bus. He examined the side of the vehicle closer and found a three-inch long gash in the surface, where he had outmaneuvered a metal blade that Darkrock had used against him in a battle from his youth.

David reached out to touch the gash, to lend credence to his belief that this had to be an illusion of some kind. When his finger touched the metal, he felt a jolt, and the bus burst into a blossom of yellow-colored light and disappeared.

He looked to where the bus had been and found a concrete staircase that led from the surface of the desert plains to a large metal door at the bottom, illuminated by a bright white light.

Scanning the area around him, he found nothing but desert, more desert, and even more desert.

No enemies. No friends. Just the calm night air moving through his hair and across his face like a tender caress.

He went down the stairs to the metal door at the bottom. The bright light flickered, as if it was fully aware of his presence. David pulled on the crescent handle, but the door would not open.

Locked.

He tried again.

Still locked.

"Okay, Jennifer. You led me here. Now how do I get into this place?"

No answer.

He stared at the door. Then he glanced up the stairs, into the starry night sky. Then back to the door.

Nothing happened.

David took a seat on the cement pavement under his feet and buried his face in his hands. More exhausted than frustrated, he dozed off, dreaming again…

"Of course I like her," he said, blushing.

Veronica flipped her hair and giggled. "Duh. That's not what I asked."

David set his can of Syn soda on the countertop and let out an irritated huff. "What do you mean?"

Veronica took a seat on the barstool and set her hands on the counter in front of him. Her nails were long and purple, and she carried the scent of lilac perfume. "I mean, do you love her?"

David turned away from her, shocked at the question. He had always known Veronica to be direct, but about everything other than his feelings for Carrie. He could easily admit that he liked Carrie. That much was already obvious to everyone around them. But to admit he loved her?

David shrugged.

Veronica narrowed her eyes at him.

"What?" he asked.

She shook her head, a warm smile on her face. "You can't admit it, can you?"

"What? That I have feelings for Carrie?"

"We already know that, David. You can't admit that you love her. Because you don't."

Her *last few words stung him with a venom he had never felt before, one that penetrated his bone and muscle and saturated his heart. Of course he loved Carrie. He had always loved Carrie.*

Veronica took a sip of her soda and then tapped her long fingernails against the surface of the can, making an obnoxious—but rhythmic— noise. "You want to love her. But you don't."

David scoffed, then lifted his soda can as if he were going to take another sip, but then slammed it down against the countertop. "Why would you say that?"

"Because it's the truth. You don't love Carrie. Not really…"

A loud click woke David from his light slumber. He jolted awake, breaking free from his vivid dream as he looked up at the metal door to find it cracked open.

David stood to his feet and stretched. His body felt as if it had been sleeping for hours. He glanced down at his watch, but the face was blurred, telling him nothing of value. He rubbed his eyes and checked again: nothing but blur.

That can't be a good sign…

He looked down at the door handle and found it busted off, small pieces of the crescent hardware scattered across the cement.

Had Jennifer come to open the way?

He looked up the stairs and saw only the starry sky, but with less stars. The sun was starting to bleed across the darkness.

He turned and pulled on the edge of the door, opening it to a long cement corridor. As he stepped in, he felt eyes upon him from every direction. All he found were cement walls and a cement floor that led down a long, cement hallway toward what looked to be another metal door.

David started down the corridor, one hand on his boomerang, the other pulling the front of his coat closed. The air was freezing cold down here, and the place smelled of mildew and dirt.

He wanted to think it was his imagination, but somehow he knew that as he moved further down the hallway, the walls were starting to come closer and closer together, tightening the space he had to move in, igniting his own claustrophobia.

By the time he reached the metal door, his shoulders were touching each of the walls on both sides of him. The door—which was tall and skinny—was locked. Before he could curse every object created under the heavens, a loud click echoed through the hall and the door popped open.

He swung the door open to a large antechamber made of cement, as a wash of warmth poured over him. The room was full of what he guessed to be servers, each encased in a protective tower of thick glass. David stepped into the room, his right hand still on the boomerang at his side. Thousands of red and green and blue lights flickered on the server towers, and a low humming sound vibrated through the air around him.

David strolled through the room, down a pathway that had been deliberately placed between the rows and rows of server towers.

Where did all of these come from? Who put these here?

He reached the other end of the room and found himself at a small receptionist desk devoid of anything but a flat screen monitor that sat on a large tripod taking the place of a chair and receptionist.

The screen flashed on and a flurry of static filled the monitor.

David's eyes glanced around the room, wary of the nest of servers. He scanned the rest of the room, finding no other doors other than the one he had entered the room through. He noticed a CCTV camera in the corner behind the receptionist desk, behind him. A little red light blinked on the camera, and David could only guess it was active and currently monitoring him.

"David Corbin," a tinny voice spoke from the monitor. David glanced down at the screen, but the static was still there. *"Nineteen years old. Five-foot-eleven. Green eyes. Brown hair."*

"Who are you?"

"Deemed Anaisha's greatest hero."

David's hand gripped his boomerang tighter as he fought to stay grounded in this reality. "Silver?"

"Having trouble keeping yourself in this realm of time and space?"

David glanced at the servers, watching the multi-colored lights do an electric dance in tune with the humming. He was grateful for the heat in the room, but he would almost rather endure the cold outside to avoid being here.

"I've waited a long time for you, David. A very long time. 100 years to be exact."

The static on the screen reminded David of the snow that fell while he sat in his sister's living room chair, attempting to end his life because of her murder.

"If I explained who I was, you wouldn't understand. Not completely. Not sufficiently to move forward from here with any kind of clear understanding of what you're involved in."

The screen went dark.

David pulled the boomerang from his side and jammed it into the monitor, smashing the glass. Sparks cast from the wound. Then he looked up at the servers, realizing those were probably Silver's true organs.

If he is an AI of some sort, he'll have electronic parts somewhere.

A low static hum came from the CCTV camera.

"You have only proven my point that you have no clear understanding of what you're involved in. You cannot kill me, especially not by killing one of my many hosts. Besides, Corbin, you came here for a more pressing reason. You want me to return the girl to you. The mechanical creature."

David looked up at the camera, fighting the urge to smash it with his boomerang. "Where is she?"

"You'll find out soon enough. But by that time, it will be too late."

David moved out from behind the receptionist counter and made his way to the first tower in a row of servers. He used his boomerang to smash the glass door, and then he took the tip of the boomerang and stabbed it into the server unit. He watched as sparks bled out of the machine, and then the red, green, and blue lights slowly faded as the server tower died.

He moved on to the next server, smashing the glass, stabbing the machine. He jumped back as the sparks leapt around his face like electric fireflies.

"You defy your purpose for being here. The girl waits for you."

David pulled his boomerang from the second dying server and then slid the weapon into its holster. He looked at the rest of the servers—six rows of them—and realized it would take some time to destroy all of them. But he told Jennifer he would kill this thing, this Mr. Silver, and he intended to do just that.

After he found Rachel.

"I'm here for her."

"Of course you are. Produce one damsel in distress, and you will undoubtedly produce one David Corbin to rescue her. It is the grand nature of things, is it not?"

"Is it?"

269

"You deny this fact about yourself? Jennifer. Carrie. Even Veronica. You have an insatiable need to protect, to guard, to save. To rescue. It's ingrained in you. A seriously defective trait. And yet, you can do nothing to save yourself. You rely on the kindness of females to get through life. Even their mere presence drives you forward, like a ship navigating a storm with the help of an hourglass-shaped lighthouse."

"Where is she?"

"Why do you think I brought you here, David? Just to play games with you? To tease you? You've traveled quite far—farther than you think—to get to this place. You've endured many sacrifices as well. So why would I waste my time now that you're here? I am not one to waste my time. Or my effort. Or my assets."

A blast of air shot out of the ceiling a few feet from him. The floor opened in a circular pattern below that, and David watched as a cylindrical chamber rose up out of the floor. Within the chamber, a body floated, suspended in transparent gel.

"Rachel!"

Her eyes were closed, but David could see her chest, could see the fatigue-colored jacket, rising and falling with her breathing motions.

"Here is your Rachel. Although, this is one female you will not be rescuing, David. No, I have other purposes for this one."

David gripped his boomerang. "I'm taking her with me."

"No." The chamber shook, and David watched as a purple electrical current ran through the water, electrifying Rachel's entire form. Her clothes flickered in and out, alternating from nude to dresses to skirts to pants. Her face flitted through a myriad of features, giving her a ghostly, otherworldly presence.

When the currents stopped, Rachel's eyes closed, and her form reverted to the jacket with the daisy patch, and blue jeans.

David placed one hand on the glass surface of the chamber, holding his other hand on his boomerang to steady him. "I will get you out," he whispered to her.

Rachel's eyes opened suddenly, her gaze swallowing David like a black hole.

"You see? She is perfectly fine."

David pulled his boomerang from the holster.

The camera moved to follow his motions. *"You think you can use that to destroy me? Many have attempted to kill me before. Both my once-human form, and now my immortal form."*

"You're not immortal."

"I sought immortality for years. You have no idea. I finally found it on my own terms. My spirit is embodied in these servers, and these servers have backups in the cloud. And that cloud has backups to that cloud. And so on. Destroy this building. Destroy everything in it. It doesn't matter. You will not destroy me."

David watched as another electrical current flowed through Rachel. And another. Her face twisted in pain. And even though she was a mechanical being, even though she was something created by man's hands, he felt a strange connection, a strange empathy and a deep sympathy for her.

David's knees buckled and he fell to the floor. He felt a pulsing in his chest, a burning in his eyes. The same feeling he felt when he defended Carrie...

"We cannot allow that today, David."

David heard doors open elsewhere in the room. Then he felt an electric pulse rush through his back, paralyzing him.

"Today, you are my prisoner. Today will be the first day you learn what it is to be humble before a true god."

Everything went black.

27 The Factory

C arrie expected the factory to have people within it. Workers, maybe. With all the flickering firelight that surrounded the outside of the color-drained structure, she figured maybe there were other humans here. Maybe even creatures.

But once Carrie stepped through the rusted iron doorway leading into the factory, she found nothing but darkness. She turned on her flashlight. This wasn't darkness like the dark fog, now at her back, flooding the street once again. This was darkness that was easily dispelled with her light.

The chimes continued, loud now, echoing throughout the building like a massive gong. It seemed they were trying to play a song, but there was a beat that would come around that sounded off. A few of them, actually. Enough to throw the 'song' off and resort the sounds to simply that: sounds. Noise. Melodious noise, but still noise nonetheless.

Inside the massive factory, Carrie found broken machines, covered in years and maybe decades of grease and dirt and age.

The machines were large, and Carrie couldn't place exactly what they would have done. They were massive iron structures that were bent at odd angles and had hooks dangling from the tops and even the sides. They almost looked as if they had held massive items in place, like airplane parts? They were the only kind of parts that her mind could compare these machines with.

There were other strange structures within the factory as well. With Carrie's limited light, she couldn't completely discern what these were, but they were affixed to the concrete floor and looked like giant cisterns. Maybe they had held metals at one point. Maybe melted metals? Like gold or iron or lead?

She could only guess at this point.

The factory had been abandoned for a long while, and the machines were in disrepair. Dust filled every space, and if there had been people here at one point, they were long gone. Carrie found comfort in this for some reason. Though she felt alone in this strange world, she would rather be solitary than surrounded by...anything, really. Except her friends.

She followed her flashlight beam throughout the factory, cutting through dust and darkness, making her way toward the chimes. Those off-tune chimes.

Carrie suddenly wanted to turn back, to leave the factory.

But she knew Viranda was here. She could feel her presence, up ahead, through the darkness.

Carrie stopped and found herself standing in front of a set of double doors made of dark oak. They looked completely out of place in the steel and concrete factory. The surface of the doors glistened with stain, and an ornate handle had been set into each door, making it possible to open both of them outward.

She shined the light to the right side of the doors and found a white piece of paper stuck to the metal wall with a round, black magnet. She took the paper off the wall and shined the light on it, reading it silently to herself:

Notice is hereby given on your eviction.

The rest of the note was written in a language she neither understood nor had ever seen before.

She focused on the doors again. The chiming was coming from the other side. But did she want to know what was through these doors?

Carrie closed her eyes. Focused. Felt Viranda on the other side of those doors. But also felt something else—another Viranda?

She placed her palm on the handle and clicked open the right side of the double doors. She pulled the door open, revealing a brightly lit room. She stepped in, shutting the door behind her.

The room she found herself in was nothing like the rest of the factory. It was a white room, the walls made of ceramic paneling. Glossy white. Glowing white lines traveled around each panel. The floor was made of the same paneling, but the panels themselves glowed a soft white, lending a good amount of illumination to the small, square room.

In the center of the room sat Viranda, her white hair and black and white polka dot dress. She wore black heels, and her skin was a bright white—paler than anyone Carrie had ever seen before.

Viranda was crying.

Next to her, on the floor, was a young woman, probably close to Viranda's age, laying in a pool of blood.

It was the stark color of the blood that made Carrie sick to her stomach. The bright red shined off the white floor like the feathers on a tropical bird. The coppery scent of the blood reached Carrie and turned her stomach.

Viranda looked up at Carrie, tears dripping from her pale cheeks. She shook her head.

Carrie set her shoulder bag on the floor and pulled out the pen and paper, handing it to Viranda.

The Legion girl did nothing with the items. She turned back towards the dead girl and continued to grieve.

Carrie could feel her despair. Taste her tears. There was a sadness that one could not easily describe short of feeling it. It was a heavy feeling, like multiple layers of clothing when its raining, or falling in a swimming pool with blankets wrapped around your soul. Carrie dropped to her knees, unsure as to why Viranda felt so much grief over this girl.

To Carrie's relief, Viranda lifted the pad of paper and pen from the floor and began scribbling out words.

It was then, while waiting for Viranda to answer the unspoken question, that Carrie realized the chimes had stopped. She tried to remember when they had stopped—maybe when she opened the dark oak door? She couldn't remember. She hadn't been paying attention.

She had been sure that whatever was originally causing the sound of the chimes would be behind these doors, but she had been wrong. Unless—unless there was something about the dead girl or Viranda that had caused the melodies. The broken, wrong melodies.

Between sobs and bouts of silence and inaction, Viranda finally handed the notepad back to Carrie.

She was me.

Carrie looked up from the paper, confused.

"What do you mean?" she asked, her voice sounding strange in the small room. When she spoke, a melody followed her voice, as if there was a bit of music accompanying her words.

Viranda didn't answer. She didn't even look at Carrie. Carrie set the notepad and pen on the floor next to the girl. After a few minutes of staring at the dead girl, Viranda picked them up and wrote again.

When she handed the paper back to Carrie, the message was much longer, but had been scribbled more hastily, making it somewhat harder to read:

You understand nothing of the origins of Legion. That is not your fault. I am sorry for being selfish. She is me. Another me. Another world? She died at the hands of my kind. Long ago. Her name was Jasmine. She was thirteen when she died. I hurt.

Carrie glanced up from the notepad to look upon the dead girl. She stepped closer, trying not to invade the space Viranda was taking up with the girl. The dead girl, Jasmin, did not look thirteen. She looked much older. Older like Viranda. Maybe in her early twenties.

"I don't understand. She looks older. Much older."

Viranda nodded.

"How can that be possible if she died in her teens?"

Viranda motioned for the notepad and pen. Carrie gave them to her.

You really don't know what Legion is, do you?

Carrie shook her head after reading the note. She tried to hand the pad and pen back to Viranda, but the girl refused to look at Carrie, let alone reach out for the items.

Carrie withdrew her hand. "What is Legion? Are you…You are many?" she said, remembering something Viranda had taught her back in the school of her soul.

Viranda nodded, but not toward Carrie, rather toward the corpse before her. Carrie turned and stared upon the dead girl, curious.

If the dead girl was only thirteen, but Viranda looked much older, then that meant that…

"She's from another time?"

Viranda stood to her feet, then brushed the hem of her dress down. Aside from the paleness, Carrie found Viranda to be very beautiful, in a strange gothic sort of way. The girl looked up at Carrie, her eyes no longer full of tears, but of anger. Anger toward Carrie?

No. Not me. Her own kind.

"You are many. Spread out across timelines?"

Viranda approached Carrie and took the pen and paper from her hands. She slapped the pad of paper against the white wall and started writing words, frantically, clumsily, across the page, as if she was draining her soul and mind on that pad of paper.

Carrie took the moment to step closer to the corpse. She walked around it to where she could see the face. It was indeed Viranda. But her skin wasn't pale. She had freckles. And a tiny loop stuck through her left eyebrow.

Carrie knelt and took in the sight, the smell. She inhaled the copper scent of blood, but this time her stomach didn't turn. The blood was indeed fresh, and that made Carrie more curious as to who or what had killed her.

Viranda shoved the small piece of paper into Carrie's hand. Carrie stood, glancing over the page.

Legion is strewn about many realities. All of them, in fact. We all started at the Origin and then split and multiplied every time something changed. There are near-infinite number of me. But each one that is killed destroys a little bit of me. Little by little. Until there is nothing left.

Carrie looked up at the girl. Sadness had returned to her eyes, replacing the flash of anger from only minutes earlier.

"Who killed her? Killed you?"

Viranda's arm went up and pointed behind Carrie.

Carrie turned, startled to find a figure in the open doorway. A dark figure wearing a mask made of glistening black stone, with ornate neon colors of bright green and bright pink splashed across the surface.

She—Carrie could tell by the shape of breasts in the figure's dark hoodie—pointed her finger at Carrie. "Verush partum rehala mehum."

"What?" Carrie whispered.

Viranda took Carrie's hand. "We should run."

"Where?" Carrie asked.

"Don't."

They both looked up at the masked figure.

"What?" Carrie asked, louder this time.

The woman put up a gloved hand. "Don't run," she said, her voice muffled by the mask. Then she pointed to Viranda. "She needs to die."

Carrie stood in front of Viranda, shielding her.

The figure pointed to the corpse lying on the floor behind Carrie. "I killed her. There are only three left." She pointed at Viranda again. "Two after her."

"You can't kill her," Carrie growled. "She is my friend."

278

The masked woman shook her head. "Enemies."

"No. No, not enemies. She is my friend. The others—they are enemies."

The woman lifted a sharp, foot-long blade in her other hand, the one that had been hidden in shadows up to this point. Carrie realized then that this woman's whole body was surrounded in shadows, shadows that engulfed her edges, blurred her framework. Her stone mask stared at them, but there was life, evil life, residing within that stoic face.

The blade dripped blood, and the horrible gravity of what had occurred moments before Carrie had arrived at the factory left her speechless.

This stone-faced woman had killed the other Viranda. And there were three others? Two plus the Viranda Carrie had come to know.

"You cannot let her live," the figure said, her voice neutral and unflinching.

"She means no harm. She is trying to separate from Legion."

If the stone-faced woman was surprised by the information, it was impossible for Carrie to tell with the mask hiding the woman's emotional expressions. There was a moment of silence, pure silence, in the white-walled room.

The figure swung the blade so fast that Carrie almost didn't dodge it in time. She managed to push Viranda to the side opposite her, leaving a small gap where the blade fell between them.

They both tumbled to the floor, but Carrie scrambled to her feet quickly and dove for the figure, ramming into her left side as she lifted the blade to swing again. The girl careened to the side and fell to the ground, her blade clashing to the floor.

Carrie grabbed Viranda's hand, yanked her up, and pulled her out of the white-walled room.

They entered the factory, but it was then that Carrie realized she left her flashlight in the white-walled room. They maneuvered hastily in the darkness, the orange glow from the flames outside the building leaking in at different points, casting some of the machinery in frightful shadows.

Carrie's mind raced, not only with questions but with anxiety. She imagined her or Viranda rushing into the wall of a steel machine, or impaling themselves on an iron hook dangling down.

They managed to reach the front entrance of the factory without issue, but before Carrie could pull Viranda outside, the rusted iron doors slammed shut, and the darkness was wisped out of the factory, leaving behind a cascade of blue light that washed across the open area.

Carrie glanced out toward the white-walled room but wasn't able to see the stone-masked figure. She was either still on the ground or she had fled. Or she was hunting them…

The blue light saturated everything within the factory, even—as Carrie glanced down and noticed—her own clothing. Viranda's pale skin was absorbed in blue light, and the brightness of the light was easily traced toward the ceiling of the building. Carrie strained her sight toward the rafters above, hoping to make out some kind of rescuer.

Instead, she saw a woman. One who was once old and decrepit. One who was now fully restored to her more powerful and evocative form.

"The Great Witch," Carrie whispered.

Viranda stepped behind Carrie, almost cowering at the site of the woman.

Evanescence floated down toward them, silver rod in her

hand, her blue high heels touching softly against the concrete flooring of the factory. She was dressed in a blue corset and gown, and a bright stone sat nestled between her breasts—the source of the blue light. The woman's raven-colored hair flowed behind her, almost like a cape, and her eyes shone like blue pearls.

When she finally found footing against the ground, the blue light washed away, and darkness crept back into the corners of the building. But around them, the blue light of the gemstone kept the small group illuminated.

"You," Carrie said.

The witch smiled, her black lipstick curving into her cheeks like slithering leeches. "Carrie Green."

Viranda tugged on the back of Carrie's jacket, in the direction of the shut doors. Carrie ignored the girl. She knew they wouldn't be able to leave while the witch was here. She carried magic, powerful magic.

Evanescence tapped her silver rod against the floor, and lights flickered on around the entire factory. The sodium lights in the ceiling—lights which would have normally taken minutes to come to full light— flashed on and washed the room in bright light.

"I have a history lesson for you," the witch said. She pointed toward the large machines Carrie had seen earlier, the ones with the hooks dangling from them. "I want you to know a little about what's going on."

"Why? What do you want with me?"

"Your death," the woman said, flashing her teeth at Carrie. They were bright white, and when contrasted with the woman's black lipstick, the combination reminded Carrie of the dead zebras she had seen at the Lysallis Zoo some years back.

Viranda yanked on Carrie's clothes again, but Carrie ig-

281

nored her. She could sense the girl's anxiety and her strong desire to leave the factory. But they didn't stand a chance against the Great Witch, and they didn't know what else may be lurking in the factory.

Viranda's thoughts, vague fragments of her thoughts, entered Carrie's mind. She was thinking of the dark portal that was growing in the city. Growing. Growing...

The witch stood, staring at Carrie, with that dead zebra grin on her face. There was something different about the woman, something more sinister that didn't exist when Carrie had last faced off against the woman.

They waited for what felt like an eternity, as the Great Witch, Evanescence, stood, staring at them. That stupid grin on her face, the lights in the factory alive and bringing a different tone to the building. Without the darkness, without the shadows, the factory was less menacing. Carrie feared the place less, though she knew it was a mistake not to fear what lay hidden within it.

"You are a traitor," Evanescence finally said.

At first, Carrie was confused at the comment, but then she realized the comment hadn't been directed toward her, but toward Viranda.

The girl peered around Carrie's arm, keeping her grip tight on her wrists.

Evanescence stared at Viranda, her grin vanishing like smoke. In place of her wicked smile, she wore a blank stare and a straight face. Like stone. "You betrayed us. It is because of you that Legion was nearly destroyed so many years ago. It is because of you that Nathan Pierce—"

Viranda seemed to shudder at the name. Not out of fear, but out of excitement. Out of joy. Carrie had never heard the name before, but there was something about Nathan Pierce that seemed to give great happiness—and hope?—to the Legion traitor.

Evanescence pointed to the machine with hooks. "There used to be much death here. Much destruction."

"Where are we?" Carrie asked. She found her voice catching in her throat. She wasn't afraid of Evanescence exactly, but she wasn't prepared to deal with the woman's dark magic. She didn't have Turquoise or David or anyone else around that could help her fight the witch, and Viranda didn't look as if she would be helpful in a fight. At least not right now.

Evanescence tapped her rod against the floor, and a strange blur appeared on the hooks hanging from the machine. A person, a body to be more exact, hung from the hooks, shredded and bleeding. There was a head on the body, but Carrie was unable to see the face because the figure had been beaten so badly.

"Torture," the witch said.

Carrie turned her head so she couldn't see the hooks or the mangled body hanging from them.

"You may turn from it, but it will find you. It will find all of you. You think I traveled the galaxy to simply conquer? To destroy? No. We enslave. We use…" She tapped her rod and the image vanished, leaving the hooks there to dangle alone, unfettered by hallucinations.

A figure stepped to the side of Carrie and Viranda, just feet from them. When Evanescence saw the figure—the stone-masked being—she grimaced.

"You!" She pointed her rod at the female figure.

Carrie wasn't sure if the witch was trying to use her magic on the creature, but she kept thrusting the rod out with no effect.

The figure seemed to chuckle, but Carrie knew it was her imagination. There was no humor with this creature, this being. The stone-masked woman waved her hand at the witch and spoke. "Your power no longer compels me."

Evanescence rested her rod in an upright position, the end flat against the floor. "You found it, didn't you? You fools actually found it." Her glare flitted toward Carrie for a brief moment, then returned to the stone-masked woman. "It won't help you in the end. The End Point will come, and nothing will prevent it. You know that."

The stone-masked woman said nothing, but Carrie could tell there was a story here. Maybe something that could help her and her friends.

Viranda tugged on Carrie's coat, motioning toward the doors again.

Carrie reached behind her, taking hold of the iron handle. The door wouldn't budge.

The lights flickered and popped, leaving all of them in the pale blue light of the witch's gemstone.

Carrie looked over to the stone-masked woman and noticed the bright green and bright pink neon paint splashed across her mask was glowing.

Evanescence's face, lit up in the blue light, looked menacing and awful. It frightened Carrie, and she suddenly wanted, needed, to get out of the factory.

Evanescence tapped her staff on the floor and Carrie heard something behind her, a sound like scraping stone. She turned and found the rusted iron doors gone. In their place stood a rusted iron wall.

"Your kind are all but destroyed," Evanescence said to the stone-masked woman.

The figure still said nothing. She stood there, her mask glowing in the darkness.

Carrie started toward her left, in the other direction away from Evanescence, away from the stone-masked figure, and away from the white-walled room where a young woman named Jasmine lay, her blood interrupting the quiet of the factory.

Evanescence suddenly appeared in front of Carrie, a wicked grin flashing across her face, her teeth blue in the light of the gemstone. Carrie turned to her right, and Evanescence was suddenly there, again, that grin on her face. Frightened, Carrie turned behind her, toward the iron wall, not sure how to escape the building. Evanescence was there, standing in front of the place where the doors once stood.

Carrie and Viranda stepped back slowly, away from the witch, away from the stone-masked woman. Behind her, Carrie could feel the dark presence of the machines. They had been responsible for unspeakable torture, not only of body but of soul. She could feel Viranda's fear, her panic at facing the witch again. This had not been the first time, and Evanescence had a special level of hatred for the girl because of something she had done in the past. Something Carrie had to know more about.

The witch drew forward, closer to them, and this caused Carrie and Viranda to move backwards, closer to the white-walled room.

There was nowhere to run. The windows of the factory were too high up in the rafters. The white-walled room had no exits. Only shadows lurked behind them, waiting to swallow them into oblivion.

David. He could help them. If he was here. He could rescue them.

A loud crash slammed into the ceiling. Carrie looked up and found that something had torn a huge gash in the roof. Bright light and a flurry of rose petals poured into the factory. Carrie had to shield her eyes at the entrance of a blinding figure that plummeted from the sky and landed with a loud snap and pop to the floor of the factory between Carrie and Evanescence.

The figure inhaled and the bright light streamed into her body, illuminating it. Bright cobalt wings extended for ten feet in opposite directions behind her. The woman's hair shone a blazing white, and her youthful features betrayed her actual age. There was just something Carrie was able to pick up on staring into the woman's bright blue eyes: a story, a lifetime, an eternity.

The woman wore a white T-shirt and blue jeans, a humble getup for someone so stunning. Black and white sneakers of the skater variety adorned her feet. A half dozen necklaces dangled from her neck, all made of various metals and carrying a variety of baubles such as marbles, dice, and—a cross? Her arms were covered by colorful designs, but in the dim lighting, Carrie couldn't make out what those designs were, just that they reminded her of graffiti.

The woman stood tall and smirked at the witch, flinching her cobalt wings with a good degree of confidence and courage. "You do not belong in this realm."

Evanescence sneered. "You're one to talk, bastard child."

Though Carrie's focus was squarely on the newcomer, she couldn't help but notice out of the corner of her eye that the stone-masked figure was slipping out of sight, off to the side of the building. Carrie wondered if she and Viranda could follow her and escape that way. But the witch and the girl were in between them, and Evanescence—though also focused on the newcomer—still darted her gaze Carrie's way multiple times, letting her know that she was still planning on dealing with them, regardless of the interruption.

Carrie's mind tried to conjure a way of escape. If these two were going to battle it out, she didn't want to interfere. She and Viranda had to get home.

Then she remembered the portal outside, in the laundromat. There was a slight chance, however inconceivable, that the portal would lead them home.

"You won't escape here, girl."

Carrie caught a look from the witch, realizing she was speaking to Carrie, not the newcomer.

"You won't be touching a hair on their heads," the woman said.

The witch flashed a bright smile, bringing to mind the dead zebras again. Carrie remembered vomiting when she first saw them at the zoo that day. She had been so embarrassed, retching in front of David…

"It is an entertaining irony that you now defend the one you were once so bent on destroying," the witch said to the angelic woman. "You're in league with Legion now?"

The girl refused to answer the question, which seemed a bit more rhetorical than one requiring an actual answer. Though Carrie wanted to know who this woman was. She had fought Legion? Could she help them fight Legion?

A stick of bright white light appeared in the girl's right hand. From the angle she stood at, Carrie couldn't tell what it was exactly, but she would place bets that it was a light sword of some kind.

"You think you can kill me?" the witch said.

The girl said nothing, but she turned and stared at Carrie for what felt like a full minute, before she turned back toward the witch and lunged at her.

The witch moved so quickly that Carrie couldn't track her motions with her own eyes. One second, the witch was standing in the path of the sword. The next, she was to the right. The girl sped forward, through the spot where the witch had been mere moments earlier. But instead of stopping, instead of halting her movements the woman continued forward, thrusting the sword at the rusted iron wall that had been put up in place of the doors Carrie first entered the factory through.

Carrie grabbed Viranda's arm and yanked her forward as she started in a run toward the front of the factory.

The girl struck the wall with her sword and swung downward, cutting a bright line of light in the wall. She cut another line to the left, then up, and then to the right. Once the rectangle of light was complete, the girl shoved her shoulder into the cutout and the iron crumbled, creating an opening to the outside of the factory.

Before the witch could figure out what was happening, Carrie and Viranda reached the cutout.

The angelic woman nodded toward the opening. "Go. There isn't much time left."

Viranda rushed through makeshift doorway. Carrie stopped and looked up at the woman. "Time left for what?"

She smiled grimly. "For everything."

28 Blurred

When David awoke, it was to nothing more than a room with cement walls. His arms were tied above his head to a chain that led up to the ceiling. His feet barely touched the floor. He had been stripped of his clothing, his weapon. Everything. Everything but the necklace Jennifer had given him, dangling from his neck.

A warm substance slithered down the side of his head and dripped to the floor.

Blood.

Memory came back to him in fragments, and it took effort to put them together to make sense of anything.

He remembered sentries had taken him out while he tried to harness the power that had enabled him to twice save Carrie. The AI—Silver—had gotten the drop on him, knocking him unconscious.

His shoulder wound had reopened and was snaking blood down his chest and across his bare stomach. His head throbbed. A dull ache resided in his skull, and he realized they must have beaten him once he had fallen unconscious.

Silver had taken the situation and flipped it all over David. Jennifer had warned him, but he never could have in his wildest dreams imagined that a computer would get the best of him.

But Silver was more than a computer. At least, to David, he seemed to be more than a computer. There was a person in there, somewhere.

Whatever Silver was, he took Rachel.

David had to get her back.

A draft from a vent in the ceiling skated across his naked skin like an unwarranted intrusion. He needed clothes. Weapons.

The door opened and a sentry in glossy black armor entered the room.

"All of you are going to pay for this," David said, his voice breaking like a prepubescent teen.

The sentry placed a thick folder on the aluminum table, the only piece of furniture in the room, and then approached David. "Yes. The great hero, David Corbin. Captured. Tortured. Imprisoned. This," he said as he lifted his arms into the air, "is how life is supposed to be."

"Let's get this over with," David growled.

The sentry laughed. "It is me, David. Silver. I am able to communicate through the network of sentries all over this planet and the planets elsewhere throughout the galaxy and the universe. I have eyes and intelligence everywhere, Mr. Corbin. You've been swatting at Mr. Big your whole life, attacking Mr. Nokei, and why? I was there the whole time watching you. Waiting. Waiting for you to come to me, to step foot into *my* home, *my* territory.

"I am going to make this simple. I am going to torture you until you can no longer stand. After that, I'm going to kill you.

290

I want you to suffer, David. Suffer for everything you have ever done to me, to Mr. Big, and to anyone else who ever tried to make this world a better place."

The sentry's black-armored arm swung at David, striking him in the ribs. David grunted, and then another swing of the metal armor struck him on the chin, rattling his teeth.

"You were swatting at flies when I—the beast—was everywhere around you."

He struck David in the ribs again, then kicked at David's left knee. The pain coursed through David's entire leg. Another strike to David's head nearly knocked him out as the chains tying his wrists up to the ceiling clattered together.

Another swing to his face, splitting his bottom lip open.

Another swing to the side of his head, blurring his vision.

Another swing to his ribs. He couldn't tell if they were broken or just bruised at this point.

The sentry's black armor changed colors, shapes. David longed for his boomerang, but without it, he couldn't seem to ground himself here—if here was reality. He could no longer tell.

Was this reality?

Was this an alternate form of reality?

Why had he come here?

The sentry struck his hand toward David, but instead of a blow, the attack slit the skin of David's left cheek. Blood slid out. Another slit to David's side. Skin split. Blood escaped.

"I never thought this would be so satisfying. To be able to inhabit a body again, to be able to take out my rage on such a noble hero."

David couldn't remember why he was here. The events leading him here were fuzzy, blurred. Distant.

The sentry stood still for a moment, staring with empty

eyes at David.

Blood leaked from David, pooling on the floor around him.

"Let's give you time to think upon your sins, David. To ponder all the good you've done for Anaisha."

The sentry left the room.

David closed his eyes, his body weak, his mind weaker. Everything blurred together in his mind, but he fought to make sense of it all, to straighten all of it out.

The years prior to this, he had fought off Western Anaisha's most dangerous criminals, including Mr. Big, Mr. Nokei, and a slew of others. He sacrificed a normal life to fight these villains. He sacrificed relationships, his free time, a career. Everything.

His sister was dead. And for what? Carrie was gone. David was certain he would never find her again. He had no control over time. He had no control over fate. Veronica was gone. Somehow, David knew he was never going to return to his time to see her. Turquoise had betrayed him, stolen the timepiece. And Rachel was in the hands of a psychotic artificial intelligence.

Everything was hopeless. Everything was pointless. Everything was gone.

He slipped into blackness, accepting the darkness as a reprieve from his running, his fighting, his torture. Maybe there would be some comfort in the end of things. Maybe he would finally find his peace.

The sound of the door opening startled him from the shadows, alerting him to the presence of the sentry. David's body tensed, and he sought solace in death.

David opened his eyes and watched the sentry approach the table, where the file folder had been placed earlier. The sentry picked it up and flipped through it. David had no idea what was in that folder, besides papers and maybe photographs, but of what, he had no clue.

"I see here you infiltrated a mental health facility to save Scarlet Rogue?"

"Just kill me."

The sentry turned to him and closed the file folder, holding it close to his chest. "Your record is impressive. I've never met anyone with such a remarkable record of feats against evil. Huh, that almost sounds like a book title, doesn't it? I'll make sure to make...note...of that. There we go."

David noticed the sentry was just standing, staring at David. No movement. Just that metallic black armor reflecting David's broken countenance back to him.

The sentry reached up, and David flinched. The sentry backed up and nodded. "Sorry. I'm not sure what they did to you."

"What?"

The sentry reached up again and used his hands to break the brittle chains that had been tied around David's wrists. David fell to the floor with a hard thud as pain rippled throughout his body.

The sentry stepped back a few feet and offered up his hand. "Come with me. I'll get you out of here and then we can get you cleaned up."

David retched, discarding the very last of whatever was in his stomach.

"That's delightful. Look, can you at least walk? I can get us out of here, but I need you to do your part."

David wiped his arm across his broken lip. It stung, and the scent of vomit made his stomach churn. "Who are you?"

"A friend," he said, waving his hand for David to take it.

David placed his beaten palm into the Sentry's metal-armored hand. The sentry pulled him to his feet. David stood, swaying. "A real friend? Or do you want something from me too?"

The sentry shrugged. "You do have something I want. But we can discuss that later. Right now, we need to get your stuff. Down the hall, in one of the rooms. I'll cover you because I'm pretty sure they know what's going on by now."

David sighed. "What exactly *is* going on?"

A loud alarm echoed through the building.

"That."

"What is that?"

The sentry opened the door, glanced down both sides of the hallway, and pulled David into the hallway and started to lead them toward what David assumed was his things. They reached a plain door, and the sentry used an ID card to open it. He pulled David inside and then shut and locked the door. "Get dressed. Your stuff is in that silver container. The door will keep them out for a bit."

David glanced around the room mostly filled with bunk beds and storage boxes and found the silver box nestled between a bunk and a wooden dresser.

After much stumbling and painful acrobatics to get his clothes on, David got dressed. The sentry tried to help as much as possible without making the situation more awkward than it already was. After David painfully slid on his black denim coat and his glove, he felt relieved to be completely dressed.

He found his boomerang and holster in the bottom of the storage container. He affixed the holster to his waist, letting it hang just a bit against his thigh. He grabbed hold of the metal boomerang within it and closed his eyes, feeling the smooth surface of his weapon.

It felt as if order had suddenly been restored. As pain

wracked his body, David found he could still stand, could still hold his own.

"Time to go," the sentry said.

David could sense the panic creeping into the man's voice. But instead of panicking, David took a deep breath and allowed the boomerang to ground him into this reality. He felt his mind returning to this place, to the here-and-now. His wounds burned, and almost every muscle in his body ached. But his mind seemed to right itself.

"Do you have the shard?"

David opened his eyes and looked at the sentry. "The what?"

The sentry held the fingers of his left hand up, putting his thumb and forefinger parallel to one another to indicate something small. "Small shard. Black. Looks like an arrowhead of sorts."

David racked his muddled memory to try and remember if he had anything like that. Then he remembered the items that Redford destroyed before he threw Carrie into the portal.

David reached into his jean pocket and fished out the small shard. "This?" he asked, holding it up for the sentry to see.

The sentry nodded. "I'll take that in exchange for your—"

The door suddenly blew open, hitting the sentry as he flew into the bunk bed behind David.

David watched three sentries enter the room. He slid the shard into his coat pocket. He maneuvered his way behind a bunk bed, peering across the room at the armored assailants.

"David Corbin," one of the sentries said. "Back from the dead, I see." He glanced at the sentry who lay motionless across the bunk bed. "And you had one on the inside. Clever."

David noticed the sentry who had been helping him was completely motionless. Dead.

Or empty.

"I underestimated you, Corbin. Even with all the time I spent observing you and your methods, I see you still have some twists to throw my way."

A blast hit the sentry in the back. He fell to the floor. David saw a steaming red hole in the man's back. He looked up and saw another sentry holding a shiny black sentry gun, which he used to shoot the other two sentries in their foreheads—dead aim—before they could respond.

The traitor sentry laughed. "I'll have to tell Eden that all that time in the virtual simulators paid off."

"Eden?"

"Yeah…about that."

David peered out the door and saw an empty corridor running in both directions. "Where is Rachel?"

"Um, I wouldn't leave that way. Let me access an escape route."

David stepped into the hallway and made his way to the right. The sentry quickly fell in step behind him. "Where are you going? I just…hold on…I just pulled up a route that will get us out of here. We have to go in the other direction."

"I have to save Rachel."

"Rachel? Who is Rachel? I didn't see you with anyone else. Look, man, I was instructed to guide you out of here. Then you give me that shard, and then we can all be on our merry way."

"You can have the shard if you help me find Rachel and get her out of here as well. I'm not leaving without her."

"I wasn't instructed to save anyone called Rachel."

David burst through a doorway at the end of the hallway, leading them into another corridor. He didn't really know where he was going. In fact, he wasn't even sure what floor he was on, if there were different floors here in the underground.

"Look, if you give me just a second, I can access the records for this place. I can lead you to Rachel, and then we can get you both out of here."

David stopped and turned toward the sentry. "Who are you? Really."

"It's me, David. Squirrel. Master hacker."

"Squirrel? What are you doing here?"

"Long story. Short version? I hacked Silver's AI, took over some of his programming. I'm not really here—just using the sentry's body as a...host...of sorts."

"Where is Rachel?"

Squirrel pointed down the corridor, toward another door. "That way. Other side of that door should be the maintenance room."

David continued down the corridor, wondering how expansive this was. It seemed to be nothing more than an endless chain of hallways. He reached the door, but found it locked. Squirrel used a sentry ID to open it, and David stepped in, finding himself in a small closet-sized room. A generator hugged the wall to his left, and a ladder stood affixed to the wall in front of him, leading up into a maintenance vent.

"Okay," Squirrel said. "Head up that maintenance shaft. Go left. Travel about four yards, and then you'll come to a grate that sits over another room. Records indicate that's where Silver is storing her— actually, he's pulling data from her right now."

"We have to stop him."

Squirrel handed David a small earpiece. "I'll keep in touch with this."

David stuck the communicator into his right ear.

Squirrel then handed David his sentry gun and pointed to the shaft. "Head up there. I'll meet you there."

Ignoring the gun, David started up the ladder. His body screamed at him with every wrung of the ladder he managed to climb up. He tasted blood from the split in his lip, felt the bruising from his beating. But he pushed through, knowing he didn't have time to sit and pity himself. Something about Rachel pulled him, beckoned him. Stronger than the pull Carrie had on him. Stronger than the pull of his own self-preservation.

He heard Squirrel's armored feet clap away back into the corridor, aware that Squirrel's sentry could very well get taken over by Silver's AI at any time, without warning. He knew he couldn't put his trust in Squirrel. Not completely. Though he had trusted in Squirrel when the LZR Project worked in taking down Mr. Big, this was (as far as he knew) a different version of Squirrel. The Squirrel from this reality. A Squirrel David actually knew nothing about.

David crawled through the maintenance shaft, careful not to drag himself across his wounds. Waves of pain pulsed across his limbs, and he wanted nothing more than to sleep, to heal.

He followed Squirrel's directions and came to a vent that overlooked a room. Peering through the slits in the vent, he could barely make anything out in the shadows. Dim lighting barely accentuated the space, making it impossible to know what waited below him.

Knowing he had no time to waste—and that Silver probably already knew David's goal—he pushed in on the vent and dropped down into the room, landing on his feet, pain coursing through his wounds. He half-expected to find himself surrounded by sentries, however, he instead found himself in a nest of cubicles. Desks sat nestled in the small workspaces, each one covered in two or three computers. Pockets of shadow filled the cubicles while faint fluorescent lighting attempted, to no avail, to chase the darkness away. The room was full of musty heat, and a bulk of multi-colored wires ran from the cubicles to a tangle of metal parts piled in the center of the cubicle nest.

Rachel.

He recognized her form and the slender arms that he had first seen in the warehouse where an injured Turquoise had still been his friend. Those arms were bent at awkward angles, jetting out of a mangled mess of her other parts. He knelt to her and found what he thought was her head.

"Rachel?"

Her eyes opened, blue pixels of light that no longer echoed human form. "David?" Her voice was tinny, robotic.

He nodded.

"You're hurt?"

He nodded. "But I'm alive." He wanted to put her back together but didn't know where to start. He awkwardly attempted to place one of her arms back into the socket where a cluster of dangling wires sat, but that did no good.

"Leave me," she said. "I will download my information into a databank for you. Take it. Save your world."

"I'm not leaving without you."

She chuckled, and the robotic sound grated in his ears like a scratched record. "Leave me, David. You know it's your only choice."

"No," he said as he tapped his earpiece. "Squirrel?"

"David? Did you make it to Rachel alright?"

"Yeah. I found her, but she's in pretty bad shape. She's connected to a bunch of computers, but I don't know how to put her back together or disconnect her."

"Be careful. We don't want to break her connection without knowing what that would do to her."

David followed the wires into the center of the pile of robot parts and found that they ended in her back. "Well...I don't have time to figure all of that out."

"David, don't do anything drastic! I'm heading there now, and I can help you."

"No time," David said as he yanked on the base of the wires coming from her back. A surge of electricity blasted out of her, knocking him backwards. He rolled onto his back and sat up, watching as her body twitched and buzzed. A piercing tinny scream rang out from her vocal device, piercing his eardrums.

"You would put this unknown being in danger to feed your impatience?"

David stood to his feet and turned toward one of the computers where the voice seemed to have broadcast from.

"Yes, David. I am everywhere. You cannot hide from me. I am in all of your realities. I am in all of your timelines."

David returned to Rachel. Her body had stopped convulsing, and now her parts just lay motionless, her eyes closed and void of life.

He looked up and found a sentry standing a few feet from him, a large rifle in his hand. The end of the weapon had a large canister attached to it, and David could only guess what was inside.

"You have lost. You and her. I've already pulled some of the information I need from her. A few more minutes, and I'll have everything I need."

David stood in front of Rachel's lifeless body, shielding it with his thin, broken frame.

"You want to test me? I'm your perpetual nightmare, David. I can replicate. I can multiply. I can invade. I am greater even than Legion because I cannot be killed."

"So you admit that Legion can be killed?"

The sentry laughed. "Every entity in this universe can be killed one way or another. Your female robot friend there—the traitor to us all—knows all about that. But she won't get the chance to show you." He lifted the rifle toward David. "I considered not killing you, to allow you to live beyond this reality, however, you might alter too many of my plans. I can't have that. This world can't have that."

A stream of smoke puffed out of the chamber at the front of the rifle. A black canister the size of a soda can exited the gun straight toward Rachel. Without thinking about it, without planning his moves in advance, David felt a force come over him. Something powerful buzzed through him like electricity, pushing through his chest and his arms and legs. He reached his hand out instinctively and grabbed hold of the grenade canister, catching it mid-air just inches from Rachel's face.

If the sentry's helmet had the ability to express emotion, David might have seen the confusion that coursed through Silver's AI systems.

David threw the canister at the sentry, then he huddled over Rachel's parts as the grenade smacked the sentry square in the chest. The explosion was instant, flashing bright and shooting a fiery blossom of flames up the sentry's body.

David felt the heat through his clothes, scorching his back, tickling his ears, reaching around to his face. He closed his eyes as he pulled tightly on Rachel's body, drawing her closer to him. In that moment, there was something about her that resonated with him—something about her place in all of this, in her place in his future. Her place in his reality.

The heat suddenly stopped. Coolness washed over him. He looked up, eyes burning as if they had been hit with chili pepper. Rachel stood above him, a shield of crystal blue light erected over the both of them. Her face was just as angelic as it had been earlier, and her eyes shone that same exotic blue. Her figure had been completely repaired and restored.

He looked down in his arms, realizing then that he was holding a pile of junk computer parts.

Rachel reached down for his hand and helped him to his feet. He glanced over to where the sentry had stood only moments earlier. The sentry was completely gone. The entire far wall and flooring where the sentry had stood had collapsed. The doors were blocked by debris, and the vent David had used to access the room had collapsed into the room from the explosion. Smoke and the scent of gunpowder engulfed the room.

"You risked your life to protect me."

David's cheeks felt like they had been blasted with 10,000 grit sandpaper. His nose bled slightly, and his eyes burned. He grunted.

She reached her hand out. A portal tore open in front of him, distorting the reality around them. "Let's end this and go home," she said.

David gripped his boomerang, steadying himself.

Through the portal, David could see the server room. "I thought we couldn't destroy him."

A smile appeared on her face, almost instantly. The speed at which it appeared frightened him a bit and reminded him she was a mechanical being. There was nothing live or human about Rachel. He was an idiot for feeling so connected to her.

"We can destroy this version of him. Piece by piece. And we have to be careful how we do it. Silver is integrated into some of these reality's systems so well, that if we were able to pull the main plug on him, doing so would most likely collapse some of the civilizations he is involved in. Including Western Anaisha's."

David stared at the servers on the other side of the portal. "But we can't kill him here? Not completely?"

She shook her head. Her brunette hair moved with such fluidity, she gave off an uncanny valley feeling, as if her hair was trying too hard to look real. "Destroying him here will help."

They stepped through the portal. The sensation David experienced—or lack thereof—was nothing like what he had experienced by falling through the dark portal in the grocery store. Nothing pulled at his body. Nothing tore at his skin. It was like walking through a doorway into another room. Nothing more. Nothing less.

The server room was just as they had left it. Some of the servers were smashed in from when David attacked them with his boomerang. The room still buzzed and beeped, and there was a coldness to it that felt unnatural. Evil.

Rachel rubbed her thigh. Her jeans split open at the spot her hand touched, and her leg split open. She reached in and pulled out a small silver disc the size of her hand.

Rachel rubbed her thigh again, closing her leg. She walked to the computer console at the front desk and set the disc on the countertop, right next to a tall blue cup of soda.

David couldn't remember the cup of soda being there. He grabbed hold of his boomerang, steadying himself as the cup started to shift, taking various shapes and colors. Vague logos flashed across the surface of the cup. His mind reeled with questions about that cup: *What does an AI need with soda, or any food for that matter? Why would sentries be drinking soda? Where did this come from?*

Rachel took David by the arm. "We have to leave." She led him to the stairs that led up, out of the facility.

"Wait!" David tapped his earpiece. "Squirrel?"

Seconds later, David's earpiece erupted in static, and then Squirrel's voice came through. *"I'm here. Safe on the outside. Sorry I couldn't make it to your room on time. I got sidetracked."*

David saw the debris from the crescent door handle as they made their way outside the facility. They climbed the cement stairs, and when David came out of the shadow of the stairwell, he entered into obnoxiously bright sunlight that nearly blinded him.

Day had come.

A large tremor moved through the ground under him. He stumbled, but Rachel caught him and steadied him on his feet. Dust puffed out of the stairwell, shooting up into a column in the sky, dust blossoming all around them.

"Looks like you both got out of there just in time."

David turned to Rachel. She stood, staring out at the desert wasteland, her uncanny hair blowing in the breeze, dust populating the air around them. "Yeah," he said to Squirrel. "We might have hurt Silver a bit too. Thank you for your help."

"I'm glad I could be of assistance. You do still need to repay the debt, David. My employer wants that shard. How about we meet and discuss things. Fred's Diner, in Arlington? Two hours?"

Rachel turned toward David and nodded. "We can do that."

"How did you know what he said? He's in my ear."

Rachel tapped the side of her head. "I can tap into communications, David. One of my built-in accessories."

"Alright," Squirrel said. *"I'll see you both at the diner in two hours."*

29 Dark Realms

A washing machine. That's all it took. Something that had been residing within the Whirlpool brand washer had escaped through cracks in time or reality or the ozone. Carrie understood none of it.

But that washing machine.

When Carrie and Viranda fled the factory, Carrie expected to take Viranda back to the portal and see if they could just take their chances that the portal would take them home.

But the portal had come to Carrie. By the time they escaped the factory, the portal had grown to such a large size that it now took the place of the street Carrie had wandered to find Viranda. It had swallowed everything Carrie had encountered when she awoke here: the laundromat, the buildings, the neon lights...

The only thing that seemed to stop the portal was the factory itself. The very building seemed to have halted the growth of the portal, as the swirling maw now stood hundreds of feet high, and hundreds of feet wide, at the end of the factory driveway.

Carrie and Viranda stopped and stood, staring at the portal. Carrie's heart felt something dark emanating from within. Something off. The same strangeness she felt from the darkness around them, but stronger.

Wind swept through her hair, gusts of dark currents that seemed to slip in and out of the maw. Viranda said nothing about the portal, just stood and stared at it with Carrie.

Behind them, Carrie could hear the sounds of fighting. The young girl—the Eternal, Carrie decided to call her—was battling Evanescence. Probably keeping her busy so Carrie and Viranda could escape.

But escape to where? Escape to when?

The portal stood there like a big dumb washing machine, swirling around and around. Otherwise, unmoving. Otherwise, inanimate.

It couldn't cross the boundary line of the factory, but Carrie couldn't figure out why. She felt that information would be invaluable to them right now, but she would have no chance to investigate it further. She could go back into the factory and find out what was so special about it that this portal of darkness couldn't trespass against it…but the witch, and the Eternal, and the girl named Jasmine, and the stone-faced figure, and the torture-victims on hooks—they all prevented her from venturing back inside.

And all that stood before her was the portal. Just like in the grocery store. There was no way around it. No way from it.

Is something directing us? She asked the question in her mind, almost hoping Viranda would hear it. But that was silly, because Viranda stood by her side now, and she could hear Carrie's voice.

Something is directing us, she heard Viranda communicate

with her mind. *But where?*

Carrie was more concerned with *who* or *what* was directing them.

She stared up at the portal, her heart sinking. What if it took her further from David? What if it took her further from home?

But they didn't have a choice. Did they?

Carrie turned back toward the factory. Flashes of light and peels of thunder filled the space of the seemingly abandoned building. The Eternal was fighting the witch to buy them time. But was it time to escape all of this or time to reach the portal?

Viranda took Carrie's hand, causing her to look at the girl.

We have to go, she said to Carrie's mind. *We can face whatever is on the other side of that together. There's nothing for us here. You know that.*

Carrie nodded. She did know that. She tightened the strap on the denim shoulder bag and took a deep breath, squeezing Viranda's hand as they both moved toward the portal...

***

When Carrie stepped through the portal, she immediately felt a strange sensation of something entering her body, her mind, and then her spirit.

Viranda.

The Legion girl had entered Carrie once again, merging with her, melding with her. It was immediate once they crossed the portal's threshold.

The other sensation Carrie felt was that of falling. Fast. Hard. Out of control. She fell through pitch darkness. Through cold air. Through violent winds.

She closed her eyes as she fell, realizing this was probably how she was going to die. She scolded herself for not taking a chance at fighting the Great Witch. At least then she would have gone out of this world in a battle of glory. Not like this: falling, flailing, through the darkness. No control whatsoever.

Viranda?

Yes?

What is happening?

I don't know. This realm…

What about it?

I'm not sure. I feel like I've been here before. It feels familiar, and yet…

Are we going to die? Am I going to die?

I don't know, Carrie.

Carrie said nothing more to the girl. Thought nothing more of the girl. She opened her eyes, curious where her life would ultimately end. Would she slam into a slab of pavement and splurge into a puddle? Would she career into the side of a building, her bones smashing into fine dust?

She shook such morbid thoughts from her mind. Why would that angelic being allow them to flee through the portal if they were to die? Wouldn't the Eternal being want as much help as she could get going up against the Great Witch? She could have used their help.

Something flickered up ahead. It was a light, faint, white. It lingered in the distance, off to her right, in the darkness. She couldn't tell what it was. A star? A light bulb? As she passed the light, she realized it was a headlight. A single vehicle headlight, shining into the darkness, pointing directly at Carrie and Viranda.

She passed it without incident, falling in a more controlled manner now.

She crossed another light, a stoplight. The green, red, and yellow lights all glowed brightly in the distance, off to her left.

She passed it and continued on in the darkness.

Another headlight, this one attached to a crumpled SUV,

floated in the air above her.

Another stoplight, this one flickering haphazardly as if it had ingested too much caffeine.

What does this stuff have to do with anything? she wondered.

Viranda had no answer to give.

It's almost as if there was an accident here. A car accident…

Viranda seemed to shudder.

The name Nathan Pierce flew through Carrie's mind. The witch had spoken his name back in the factory, but Carrie still knew nothing about who he was.

Do you know who Nathan Pierce is?

Yes.

Who was he?

A friend.

From long ago?

Viranda didn't answer right away, and Carrie felt sorrow pulsing from the girl. Sorrow at Nathan's departure? But mixed with that sorrow was hope at the mention of him.

Carrie's body slammed into something hard, jolting her from her thoughts. She felt the impact in her bones, and the pain seemed to scatter quickly through every part of her being. She lay there, on a hard, flat surface, her lungs trying desperately to catch up with her.

Viranda seemed just as surprised when they hit the solid surface, though she didn't seem to feel the same pain Carrie did.

Carrie's hands felt the surface under her. Cement. Cold cement. It wasn't smooth either. Instead, it rose and fell in strange, jagged points that were rough to the touch. She felt them digging into her knees, into her stomach. She knew she had cuts from the impact, and she knew she had to be bleeding. Her jaw felt as if she had been punched in the mouth, her teeth aching.

We need to get up, Viranda said.

Yeah. You'll need to give me a minute, Carrie replied, her body aching with every movement she made to try to sit up. She pushed from the ground with her arms, finally sitting up, her legs bent beneath her. She ran her hands through her hair and brushed her arms and elbows, feeling cuts and scrapes from the fall.

She looked around but could see nothing. Everything was darkness, and everything was silent. She could hear no water, no wind, no shuffling of feet.

Where am I?

I don't know. But it feels like…home?

Home? Your home?

I don't think it is. But yes, it feels like home to me. Something familiar, something I know of.

Carrie slowly stood to her feet, her knees buckling at the motion. She stood up straight, locking her knees, and then brushed herself off. It was more of a routine gesture than anything practical, as she had simply landed on stone or concrete, not in dirt or sand. She took a few deep breaths to steady her mind, steady her nerves. The darkness was almost too much, but the silence nearly paralyzed her.

"Hello?" she called out. It was strange to hear her own voice in this silence. It sounded crystal clear, unhindered by white noise. She listened carefully for an echo, but her voice never came back to her. It left her mouth and vanished into the darkness. Into the silence.

Be careful, Viranda stated. *I feel I should remember something about this place, but I can't seem to…I can't seem to fathom what I should know.*

Carrie took a few steps forward, finding the solid ground underneath her. She didn't want to keep moving forward. She had no idea if this solid ground went on throughout the darkness as a whole, or if there were cliffs or pitfalls or creatures or people here as well, ready to greet them.

She looked up and around in the hopes of maybe spotting headlights or stoplights or any kind of light in the darkness. A beacon of some kind. A flicker of hope.

Nothing.

She took a few steps forward, traversing more solid ground.

"Caution, child. You know not what awaits you in this darkness."

Carrie stopped. Her gaze shifted. The voice seemed to come from everywhere around her but also from nowhere at all. She couldn't make anything out.

"Your human eyes are not accustomed to the Dark Realm. You will not be able to see here unless I give you the power to do so."

"Who are you?" she asked.

"Arnasted. The greatest of the Twelve."

"The twelve what?"

The creature hissed, but Carrie could not pinpoint where in the room—or rather, the open space—it was in. She could smell rotting eggs and could feel warm air move from different areas of the room, skating across her neck with a slight moisture that made her nauseous.

"Where am I?"

"You both are outside the boundaries."

"What boundaries?"

The creature hissed, and this time the sound was much closer to Carrie.

"Why won't you answer my questions?"

"I don't answer to humans. I am above you. So much higher above you."

Carrie narrowed her eyes as much as possible and peered

deeply into the darkness, trying her hardest to develop the accustomed sight that would have allowed her to see in a dim room in her reality. But she could see nothing.

This is one of the Ancients.

The creature hissed louder, and Carrie felt a gust of air sweep across her face, leaving behind a thick film on her cheeks, eyes, and mouth. The substance left a taste on her lips that reminded her of vomit. She turned to the side and dry heaved into darkness.

"All you humans are inconsiderate of other species. Of those above you."

Carrie took a deep breath and steadied herself. "You still won't tell me who—or what—you are."

"I answer to nobody. I am exalted."

"It's a simple question. If you do not fear me—if you feel you are above me—there is no reason you shouldn't be able to give me information about where I am or who you are. If you are as exalted as you claim."

The creature did not reply.

Carrie took a few deep breaths, steadying herself again. The darkness was forcing her into a claustrophobic panic.

At least now the silence has been broken, she thought.

"I am Arnasted. I am the greatest of the Twelve. We rule everything."

"And yet you reside here in the darkness?"

The creature's bellow knocked Carrie to the ground. She felt the sharp points of the ground's surface slice and dig into her elbows, palms, and back, and she screeched in pain.

"You insolent being! I exist outside of time and space. I exist outside of reality, and thus I have control over all realities."

Carrie stood to her feet and brushed herself off once

again. The routine seemed to ease her mind. She took a deep breath and started to march forward through the darkness, uncaring as to what she might run into.

What are you doing? Viranda asked, her tone more of a growl than a question of curiosity.

The only thing I have control of. Moving. We have to move. We have to find a way out of here.

Arnasted controls this place.

What are the Twelve, Viranda?

They are the Twelve essences of the Dark God. Arnasted is one of those essences.

Do they have to do with Legion?

Viranda seemed confused by the question. Carrie shook the confusion away, focusing on the steps in front of her. She could hear the creature in the dark air above her, grumbling and groaning.

Carrie suddenly felt the ground slide out from under her feet, and she fell again, tumbling through the darkness.

She could hear the creature's voice slithering through the void all around her as it spoke.

"Ignorant to think you have any control here. This is my realm. My home."

Carrie closed her mouth and continued to fall, steadying her nerves, readying herself for another impact against sharp stone.

But after what felt like minutes and possibly hours, that impact never came. She just continued falling. Falling through the darkness. Falling through oblivion.

It wasn't until she opened her eyes, not realizing she had actually closed them a while ago, that she saw the faint light up ahead or below or whatever direction she was coasting toward.

But as she drew closer to the light source, she realized these weren't the same light sources from earlier.

No headlights.

No stoplights.

No smashed vehicle.

No, this light was daylight. A tear in the darkness, revealing day behind dark.

She heard and felt the creature groan a hideous groan that seemed to shake the darkness within this realm.

What is that? Viranda asked.

Carrie didn't answer. She simply moved toward the tear, unsure what had caused it or where it was going to lead to. She figured for all that it was worth, any source of light would be welcome at this point.

The creature stirred in the darkness, its very presence moving the blackness, shifting the void. It seemed upset, angry even, at the intrusion into the boundaries of its domain.

Carrie felt a strong pull, something trying to yank her backwards, to prevent her from reaching that tear. But the light—whatever was on the other side of that tear—was stronger, more insistent.

"No. You are not welcome here!!!" the creature screamed. The sound shook Carrie's insides, caused her to tremble from the inside out. She couldn't yet fathom why the creature would be so upset.

Or who the creature was screaming at.

"This is my domain. You agreed to stay out of the darkness. You agreed to leave me be."

Who is he talking to? Carrie asked.

Viranda had no answers. She seemed to be focused on something, motivated toward something: that bright light that they were now closing in on. The daylight. The escape from this dark prison.

Carrie could smell warm air. The desert. Heat.

She could hear sounds. People talking…

A woman's voice: *"How long have you been working with the DMV?"*
An older gentleman's voice: *"Turn left here….Go."*
"I can't see around that truck."
"Go! You're fine."
"I don't know."
"Go!"

That last word seemed to hang in the darkness with them, filling the space with a wave of heat that breathed across Carrie's skin with summer sun.

The sounds of crunching metal and shattering glass pierced the silence that finally followed.

Viranda seemed excited. Eager to reach the tear in the darkness. Eager to reach the light.

That point of illumination was mere feet away now, but it felt as if it was taking them too long to reach it.

That force, probably the creature or the darkness, pulled on Carrie, pulled on Viranda, did its utmost to keep them here, tethered to this dark realm.

But another presence, one Carrie knew nothing of, was pulling them forward, *toward* the tear. Toward the light. Toward their escape from this realm.

"I will not allow you to go."

"Sorry," Carrie whispered as she closed her eyes. She summoned Viranda to pour all of her strength into moving them forward, toward that light. "I don't think you have a choice in this matter."

They pulled free of the creature's grip and hurtled toward the light, escaping the Dark Realm.

30 Shards

Two hours later, David and Rachel arrived in Arlington. They found Fred's Diner fairly easily as Rachel's internal navigation system took them straight there. The diner looked unassuming from the outside. Little care was given to the property. It was run down, with a bright red neon sign that screamed from thirty years ago. The windows were fogged up with dirt and grime, and the parking lot was littered with trash and cars from twenty years earlier.

The place felt strange to David, as if they had entered yet another pocket of another time. But Rachel assured David they hadn't traveled through time or space or realities again. They were still in the reality Serenity had taken them to.

Before arriving at the diner, Rachel led David to a nearby grocery store where he washed up in the restrooms, cleaning out his wounds to the best of his abilities. His body felt mangled, torn. His spirit even more so. Rachel bandaged some of his wounds with grocery store gauze and antiseptic, and even stitched up the gunshot wound in his shoulder with a sowing kit.

When they entered the diner, they found it nearly empty of people, save for the handful of diner staff all dressed in black and red uniforms, and a handful of people scattered about the booths around the restaurant. Everyone turned and glared at them when they entered the building.

David steadied himself with his boomerang again as various objects on the walls and pieces of random furniture chose to change shapes and colors. The transformations were worse there than any other place he had been to in this reality so far. Objects turned into people, people turned into objects. There was a pull here, an invisible one, tugging at his skin, his hair. He even felt his clothes gravitating toward some unknown source in the middle of the diner.

He fell to his knees, his head throbbing.

Rachel grabbed him under his arms and pulled him to his feet. "You doing alright?"

David fell over in a booth, his eyes burning. "I can't stay here. There's something about this place."

"It's a nexus." David heard the voice from across him. He pulled himself up and saw a sentry sitting in the booth across from him. Rachel took a seat next to David.

"A what?"

Squirrel spoke through the sentry's helmet, but the voice was monotone and lifeless. "A nexus."

Rachel turned to David, her eyes flashing blue. "A midpoint between realities. A nexus point. They are known only to a select few. They act as hubs, places where the barriers between a collection of realities is weakest, so it is easier to travel between them."

David dropped his face into his hands and let himself fall back into the thick red cushions of the booth. "I need to return to my reality. *We* need to return to my reality."

"Here are your cheeseburgers."

David looked up and found an old woman standing over their table, precariously balancing three plates in her arms. She set one down in front of each of them, wiped her hands on the towel sneaking out of the pocket of her apron, and walked away.

Squirrel pointed to David's plate. "Eat up. You need it."

"A cheeseburger?"

Squirrel nodded.

"And how are *you* supposed to eat?"

"I'm not. Well, not here, anyway. I am going to have a nice meal later tonight, here in my home, once we are finished conducting business."

"Then I take it you can't smell the dirty mop water?"

Squirrel shook his head. "No."

"Great." David looked down at his food and realized he was suddenly extremely hungry. He wolfed down the large cheeseburger. Rachel did not touch hers, nor did Squirrel. David found himself becoming more and more disconcerted with the fact that he was surrounded only by technology. He missed Veronica. Carrie. Even Turquoise.

"David," Squirrel said, "Silver has been wreaking havoc in our world for some time now."

David swallowed the last piece of cheeseburger, took a long drink of ice water, and then leaned back in the booth, already feeling somewhat better. "You mean *your* world?"

"No. I'm not in this reality, David. I know this seems strange, but I'm communicating with you outside of this realm. I'm in your original reality. The one Legion is about to attack."

David's head swam. "I'm having a hard time grasping some of this."

"I know," Squirrel said. "You don't have to understand all of it. I just ask that you listen. Silver isn't the greatest of your— or my—problems right now. He's a threat, sure. But not one that we need to focus on at the moment. Legion is. Legion is the entity that can end all life. All creation, really."

"So I've heard."

"Silver cannot be destroyed—yet. I'm working on a solution to that problem. Right now, though, Legion needs to be neutralized. By any means necessary."

"What do you want from me?"

Squirrel held out his sentry hand. The black armor glistened under the diner lamps. "The shard."

David reached into the pocket of his coat and pulled out the black shard he had collected from Redford's warehouse. He set it down on the table between them. Rachel said nothing, just stared at the shard.

Squirrel reached his hand toward it, but David clasped his fingers around it and slid it back toward himself. It seemed to hum in his possession. "Why do you want this so bad? How did you even know I had it?"

"I have my ways of knowing many things. That's not important right now."

"It is to me."

Rachel put a gentle hand on David's wrist. "You can trust him."

David froze there for a moment. There were few people he knew he could trust right now, and most of those people were elsewhere. Did he trust Rachel enough?

He slid the shard off the table and back into his pocket. "I don't want to alter this reality—or any reality—any more than I already have."

Squirrel pounded his fists on the surface of the table,

knocking Rachel's soda over as it spilled its liquid over the edge of the table and onto the floor. "You made a bargain. I expect you to keep your end."

He moved to scoot out of the booth, but Rachel tightened her grasp on his arm.

"David, I said he can be trusted."

David turned toward her. Those blazing blue eyes seemed so human, so full of life. *But she isn't alive. Is she?*

Squirrel huffed. "I need that shard. We ALL need that shard."

David turned toward Squirrel, toward the helmeted sentry sitting across from him. "What does it go to? Where did it come from? What does it do? I'll tell you something, Squirrel. I'm tired of not getting answers to anything. Everyone keeps piecemealing things to me, and I'm never given the full picture of what's going on. Carrie is missing. Someone who I thought was a close friend betrayed me and ran off with the timepiece. I'm not sure who I can trust right now."

Squirrel's sentry sat there, lifeless, staring at David for a few moments before he finally leaned back in the booth and let out a long, labored sigh. "I get it. I do. I'm sorry, I just…our future leans heavily on things like this shard. It has the potential to slow down and possibly destroy Legion."

David slapped his hands on the table and ground his teeth. "Who or what is Legion?"

Rachel set her palm on the top of the small television set at the end of their table, and the screen which had been showing an old episode of a game show, suddenly turned black.

"I will show you who Legion is, David," Rachel said.

The black screen turned white, and images played across the screen. Images of dark clouds, and people, and fighting…

"One hundred years ago," Rachel started, "Legion attacked a planet called Earth. Before that time, Legion had already consumed many planets in the universe, swallowing them in absolute darkness. But when Legion reached Earth, it…they…encountered resistance. A young man by the name of Nathaniel Pierce took a stand against Legion. Others joined him of course, but it wasn't just Legion they were fighting against. Legion had partnered with the Dark Army, a force of unimaginable evil. Both groups fought the humans. Ultimately, a final confrontation between Nathan and Legion ended with Legion weakened, forced to take refuge within a vessel you know as Evanescence, the Dark Witch."

David watched the image of Evanescence—a young, powerful version of the woman—stroll across the screen, approach a young man with dirty brown hair, and battle against him. Nathan pierced her chest with a blackened sword, but she did not die.

"What happened there?" David asked, pointing to the screen.

Rachel paused for a moment, letting the image switch to Nathan fighting a large sphere of darkness in the middle of a city street.

"That, David, is Legion. The core essence of it. Nathan fought it valiantly. He lost one of his greatest friends that day, when the Dark Army continued to interfere, and an entity you know as Chaos took the form of the Dark Dragon and killed Nathan's closest companion, Heather."

David watched as the dragon's tail—full of black harrowing spikes—struck Heather in the chest, piercing her, and then swung her up into the air. The girl, David thought, looked a bit like Veronica.

The image switched to Nathan stabbing the dark spherical entity with the blackened sword.

The television screen went black.

The waitress returned, taking everyone's plates. She refilled David's ice water, and then disappeared into the back.

"What happened?" David asked. "Nathan didn't kill Legion?"

Squirrel shook his head. "No."

Rachel turned to David, her bright blue eyes somewhat darkened by the mood. "The sword has a name: *Shadowbanish*. It comes in pieces, shards. The blade will engrave upon itself symbols of its wielder's life. It is a living blade. *Shadowbanish* was found by Nathan Pierce, and he wielded it valiantly against Legion."

"However," Squirrel interjected, "Nathan was missing a shard from Shadowbanish. He didn't know it at the time, but with the shard missing, it ensured that Legion would not be mortally wounded by Nathan's attack with the sword."

David pulled the shard from his pocket and set it on the table in front of them. "This was the missing shard?"

Squirrel nodded. "Yes. That's why I've been trying so hard to get it. To piece together Shadowbanish."

"I still don't understand why Redford had it."

"In the warehouse?" Rachel asked. "You found that in the warehouse?"

David nodded. "I found all sorts of things in there. The shard. A daisy. Other strange items."

"Reality breakers," Rachel whispered.

"That's impossible. There's no such thing," Squirrel said. He put his armored hand close to the shard. "May I, David?"

David shook his head and clasped his palm over the shard again. "Hold on—what are reality breakers?"

"Items that can travel through different realities, different timelines," Squirrel said. "But they don't change. Some items that move from one reality to another will become altered. Because an item from one…environment, we'll say…moves to another environment, some items become unstable. Some break. Some are physically altered in some way. Some begin to act…unseemly."

"What about humans? Animals?"

Squirrel shook his head. "Not a lot of research has been done on humans or animals, but it is theorized that humans and animals can adapt to changing environments naturally, so they are better suited to survive while crossing realities. Objects have no control over the changing environment. When these reality breakers are broken, it is said that a fragment of the reality they came from is broken, so that particular reality is damaged."

David said nothing, just let his mind try and absorb all of this information. He didn't understand everything about multiple realities and reality breakers. He found that he understood very little. He thought he knew what there was to know about time travel from his adventures with Professor Grey, but it was quickly dawning on him that he knew little to nothing about things outside his own realm.

He wondered if his boomerang was a reality breaker. "You said something about Origin Points earlier."

Rachel stared out the window at the darkened parking lot. "Everything has an Origin Point. And an End Point. That is unchanging, regardless of the reality or timeline one is in." She turned toward David and Squirrel and picked up an empty white coffee mug, setting it in the middle of the table. "Take this mug. It was probably created in a factory here on Anaisha. Somewhere. That's where it originated from. However, in another reality, it may not exist at all because the factory that makes them does not exist. Or maybe the mug exists in another reality, but it was made with inferior materials, and the mug is brown. Or blue. Or the mug could be square. The same principle applies to humans…for the most part."

David's head reeled. "Hold on. What if there's a reality where I'm not born? What if my parents decided they didn't want a child? What if my parents were killed before I could be conceived?"

"But there was always at least *one* reality where you were born," Rachel said.

David shook his head. "But wait, what if I was born in multiple realities? Then which one is my Origin Point? What if there is a version of me born disfigured or as a female?"

Rachel's blue eyes flashed. "You are looking at this from the wrong perspective. The term, 'Origin Point,' refers to when you were decided to be crafted by Creation. You were formed, by the Almighty."

"Who?"

"God."

"Jenni—Vector mentioned something about a 'one true God.'"

Rachel nodded.

Squirrel huffed. "God? Anaisha has many gods, none of which I find fascinating."

"I need to get to Carrie," David said as he began to slide the shard off the table again.

Squirrel swung his hand out, slamming it down on top of David's, trapping the shard near the edge of the table. Rachel's eyes burned toward Squirrel, but she made no movement to stop him.

"I need this, David. This shard—this piece of *Shadowbanish*—can tip the balance in our favor. Legion is coming. I don't know when. I just know it is. It's been dormant for decades now, but it will awaken, and when it does, humanity will be wiped from the face of Anaisha and eventually all other planets we reside on."

David slipped his hand out from under Squirrel's and pocketed the shard again. The surface of the shard was smooth, almost cold. There was a connection he felt with it. Something strong, powerful. Something destined for his hand.

But not yet...

A voice, a whisper, echoed through his spirit, saying, *"Give him the shard."*

Rachel turned to David. "You give him that, you'll be altering your future. I cannot predict what that alteration will be. Something is..." She held her head with her hand. "Something is clouding my vision—my calculations—of your reality. I don't know what it is."

David slid the shard out of his pocket and set it on the surface of the table. "Take it, Squirrel. Do what you need to with it."

Squirrel let out a heavy sigh and clumsily picked the shard off the table with his clunky armored hands. "Thank you, David. Thank you. You don't—may never—realize what you've done here today. This is..." he held the shard in front of him. "This is epic. This will change everything."

David slid out of the booth, gripping his boomerang as he stood. "Can we leave, please? I need to find Carrie."

"Carrie is no longer in this reality," Rachel said.

"Then we need to get back to Lexy. I made a promise to her. We get her, and then we try to find Serenity, and then we get out of here and try to find Carrie."

Rachel nodded.

Squirrel waved at them as they left the diner.

31 Accidents Will Happen

Carrie opened her eyes only to find herself on the ground, eating asphalt. Summer heat poured across her face, and thick black smoke surrounded them, pouring out from an upside-down SUV to her left. A pickup truck, a car, and a garbage truck were all situated as pieces in this strange accident. She could smell burning rubber and oil-laden smoke. She felt no pain but the scrapes and scratches she had incurred in the Dark Realm, though her head ached, and her jaw was still sore from the impact it had made against the stone ground in the other realm.

Carrie slowly got to her feet, her head swimming with dizziness. She inhaled summer heat and smoke and coughed it out in a burst. She glanced around for Viranda but remembered the girl was back within her, a symbiote with no other home but Carrie's subconscious.

I am here, Viranda said.

Carrie watched as firemen rushed to the overturned SUV with a giant jaw-like contraption she assumed was meant to pull the vehicle open. People started exiting the other crashed vehicles, shocked demeanors quickly turning to panicked states.

Carrie glanced down the street and saw an older gentleman hobbling toward an intersection.

Him! Viranda squealed.

Carrie started after him. She felt faster in this realm, in this reality. She had no idea though where she was or what she was doing here. Something had pulled her and Viranda here. *But what? Who? Why?*

The older man vanished into a small business complex. Carrie slowed her run, her sides aching from the heat and exercise.

Catch him! Viranda screamed in Carrie's spirit.

I know that's what you want, but I don't know why.

Viranda pushed Carrie forward, forcing her to move further down the street, toward the business complex. *Go!* she said. Carrie felt her legs move beneath her, but she couldn't recall moving them herself. It was as if she was skating on smooth ice, traversing the street like a ghostly entity.

She reached the suite the man had ducked into and found herself swinging open the door to go inside, even though she could hear a car down the street in front of them smashing through the windows of a coffee shop.

Viranda pushed Carrie into the office building and straight into a reception desk where Carrie's chest slammed against the marble countertop.

"Ouch! Careful!"

Sorry, Viranda said, though Carrie felt no remorse in her tone. Viranda pushed Carrie to the right and ushered her down a narrow hallway, dim with emergency lighting. Carrie could hear the old man up ahead, moving through the building, rifling through one of the back offices. She couldn't imagine who he was or what he was searching for.

But it was unusual. Had he left the scene of the accident? What did that accident have to do with anything at all? *Why are we here?*

Viranda ignored her question and shoved Carrie through the hallway. Carrie skidded her feet into the thin carpeting and halted her movement by slamming her hands into the walls of the corridor, anchoring herself in place.

Stop, she said to Viranda. *Please. I will go after him, but I don't like you trying to control me like this.*

Viranda stopped controlling Carrie. Carrie could sense regret from her symbiote.

I apologize, Viranda said. *But we need to catch up with him. We HAVE to.*

Why?

Silence for a split moment. Then, *I don't know.*

Carrie lowered her arms and moved down the hallway of her own volition. When she reached the back of the building, she found an office with an open window leading outside. Sighing, she crawled through the window and landed her feet on small rocks near the base of a tree.

Something shoved into her, and she fell to the ground. She looked up to find the old man looking down on her, his eyes wide in surprise.

"Grey?" Carrie whispered.

Grey! Viranda shouted in Carrie's head.

The old man reached a bandaged hand down to Carrie to help her up. As he lifted her to his feet, a smile broke across his face. "It's about time," he said.

She brushed herself off and then stared inquisitively at Grey, disbelief filling her spirit. "What are you talking about? What are you doing here?"

328

Professor Grey waved his bandaged hands around. "Here? Do you know where 'here' is?"

Carrie glanced around the business park. The sound of sirens wailed close to them. Carrie briefly wondered if everyone in the accident was alright. "No."

Grey nodded. "I will explain. I don't have much time, but I will explain."

"Where are we?"

"We're on Earth. Well, we're in another time. Another place." Grey's gaze wandered down to Carrie's arms, which were covered in the moving rack matter flowing across her skin with code. She took notice of his look and pulled the sleeves of her sweatshirt down. It was more out of instinct than any kind of distrust of Grey. He was a grandfather to her.

And in her reality, he was dead.

But that reality seemed too long ago. So far away. She could barely remember what had happened days ago. Years ago?

Grey nodded. "Come with me." He turned and headed into the parking lot of the business complex. He found a dark gray sedan and, using his bandaged hands, smashed the driver's side window out. He reached in, unlocked the door, and gained access to the car.

Carrie approached the car, taking full notice of the way Viranda seemed to be fangirling over Professor Grey. Viranda didn't say anything about him, but Carrie could feel Viranda's excitement—and hope—at just being around this man.

What is your obsession with him?

Not obsession, Viranda answered. *Wonder. Amazement. This one man is responsible for altering everything.*

What are you talking about?

You'll find out. I hope.

The engine started and Professor Grey motioned for Carrie to get in. She moved into the front passenger seat as Grey took them out of the parking lot and onto the street. He took them in the opposite direction of the car accident, passing a coffee shop called Starbucks where a black van had careened through the front windows. A half dozen onlookers gathered around the accident, and Carrie wondered, briefly, if everyone in the van was alright.

"What is going on? Why were we—was I—brought here?"

Grey said nothing. Didn't even look surprised. He simply drove the car down the street, checking the rear-view mirror every so often.

"Where are we going?"

"Someplace safe."

As Professor Grey drove them through a suburban area, Carrie closed her eyes. This was the first time she could remember having peace. Quiet.

Grey said nothing during their drive. Carrie felt no need to speak. Her instinct told her Grey already knew about what was going on in her world. *But how?*

We can trust him, Viranda whispered.

I know, Carrie whispered back. *I've always been able to trust him.*

Carrie fell asleep, her mind blacking out, her spirit resting in darkness.

When Grey gently shook her shoulder, her eyes bolted open in panic. But there was nothing to panic about.

Grey motioned for her to get out of the car. When she stood up out of the passenger seat, she found herself in the driveway of a one-story house. "Where are we?"

Grey walked up the three small steps to the front door without saying anything. He pulled keys from his pocket and entered the house, motioning for her to follow.

Carrie shut the car door and took a deep breath of the warm afternoon air. She was sweating from the intense heat. *Where are we that it's this warm this late in the afternoon?*

Viranda didn't answer, but Carrie didn't need an actual answer.

She stepped into the house. The smell of apples and cinnamon hit her full force. She found the scent comforting, and she suddenly realized she hadn't smelled that scent in years. *The last time was back when mom and dad got along?*

Carrie shook the thoughts from her mind. Her parents were the least of her worries right now. The very least. She had to find a way back to David. Back to Veronica. Back to her own world.

Grey led her through the kitchen. The sink was full of dishes, and the counter was covered in food stains. He led her into a living room full of laundry piles that populated the couch, the two recliners, and most of the floor space.

They continued into the back of the house. Through a dark hallway that made Carrie shudder for some reason. They entered a small bedroom where someone had setup a makeshift workbench out of two-by-fours and iron posts. On top of the workbench was a thick book bound in black and purple leather, a half dozen drink cups from a local gas station, and a strange piece of silver metal in the shape of a moon.

"We will be safe here while we talk," Grey said. "After that though, I have to leave."

Carrie continued to eye the items on the workbench. The book was thick, and various scraps of paper stuck out between the pages in haphazard angles. "Where are you going?"

Grey took a deep breath but didn't answer the question.

"You sure are quiet, Grey. Considering what's happening

right now, I'm surprised you aren't full of wise ramblings." She looked at the older gentleman. His eyes were tired, with black bags drooping down underneath. His body wasn't frail, but his frame seemed…deflated. Tired. Worn out.

He stood up straight, but only for a second before he went to the workbench and slid the moon token off the unpolished planks of two-by-fours, handing it to Carrie. "This is very, very important."

Carrie took the medallion. The silver was cold in her hand. "What is this?"

He shook his finger at her and then picked up the thick book. He fanned the book to a specific page brimming with sideways scraps of paper. "I haven't found a way to activate that. But I'm sure you will."

"What?"

Grey slammed his book shut and slammed it down on the workbench before he picked up one of the soda cups and took a few sips.

"What is going on, Grey? Why are we here? Where is here?"

He stopped sipping, shook the nearly melted ice in the cup, and then just stared at her, his eyes full of age and tiredness. Carrie couldn't remember him ever being this reserved. This quiet. The stray gray hairs that usually danced upon his head were dormant, sleeping, unmoving. This wasn't a different Grey from the one she knew—this was simply a nearly-defeated Grey. *He has been fighting something*, she told herself. *Something dark. Something much bigger than himself.*

"This is Earth. Phoenix, Arizona. Well, technically Gilbert, Arizona."

"Earth?" She remembered hearing that name before.

Grey nodded, taking another sip of his soda. "Your rack matter," he said, pointing to her covered arms.

By instinct, she wrapped her arms around herself. "What about it?"

"You have a symbiote. I had heard rumors."

She nodded.

He took another sip, the short bursts of liquid making a ghastly sound as he finished off his drink. "The symbols on your arms. They are coordinates."

She pulled her sleeves up and exposed her arms to him, watching as the black ink splotches moved across her skin with a silky essence. "I think so."

Grey set the drink cup on the workbench. He reached toward a shelf that had been screwed into the wall above the bench and took a small silver box from it. He blew the dust from the box and Carrie watched as the particles scattered through the light beams piercing through the window blinds. She imagined stars and galaxies and celestial bodies dancing around the room.

Grey set the box on the workbench and then put his hand out to Carrie. "Go ahead. It's yours now."

The box looked identical to the one she had taken from the Harpwillow, with black ornate designs surrounding the base and lid. She could see a faint greenish-blue glow slipping out from under the lid and out the bottom of the box.

"Where did you get that?"

Grey huffed. "Nevermind that. I did. Long ago. You need it, Carrie. You will need it. For what's coming."

It's another key fragment! Viranda shrieked.

I know. But how did he get it?

What does it matter?

It matters because this all seems too coincidental. That's two keys I have just HAPPEN to run into. What are the odds?

There are no odds involved in these things, Carrie. This is all meant to happen. We are being directed. Where, I don't know. But we ARE being directed SOMEWHERE.

Carrie opened the box. Inside lay the solid silver fragment, the arm of the key that the teeth would attach to. Once she found them. She reached in and took hold of it as it vanished in a mist of greenish-blue light.

The box immediately lost its luster and sagged across the workbench in a heap of brown decay.

Grey let out an extended breath. "I am relieved to be rid of that."

"Really, Grey. Where did you get it?"

He went to the blinds and peered through the slats to something—or nothing—outside. "I don't have time to tell you everything, Carrie. And the more you know, the more I risk. You and I aren't from this place or time. We're from Anaisha. From a hundred years beyond now. To be honest, very few things are relevant to you or your future right now. Our future." He turned from the blinds. "I have to leave in ten minutes. Before I leave, I will tell you what I believe is pertinent, what I believe will help."

And so Carrie took a seat at a chair that had been pushed in underneath the workbench. As impatient as she was to know everything, she knew Grey had a point. And he had a mission that he had to attend to, something she would probably never know anything about. She let him talk, while he crunched on the leftover ice in his drink cup, while he flailed his arms around, telling her the story of Legion and the destruction of their world.

While Grey spoke, Viranda seemed to tremble inside of Carrie, but Carrie couldn't perceive if it was out of fear at the story being told or out of excitement hearing Grey speak.

"In the reality I left, Legion consumed everything," he said. "Everything was covered in darkness. Evanescence led her hordes of the Dark Army across the majority of the planet. You and David and Sean were killed in various ways. You didn't stand a chance against all of that."

Carrie took note that he hadn't mentioned Veronica. Had she survived somehow? Carrie knew she was a tough girl but didn't think she was *that* tough.

"We lost everything because we weren't prepared. We weren't ready for Legion. For the Dark Army. For the chaos that ensued.

"I barely escaped that reality, with the help of my time component."

Carrie felt excitement in her heart at the mere mention of one of Grey's own contraptions. She remembered David spending hours with Grey, late into the nights, helping him with his experiments and inventions.

"I escaped here. I did what I could to start changing things."

"Such as?"

Grey looked at the floor as if there was a coin down there that someone had mistakenly dropped. "I caused that accident you saw."

"The one you were running away from?"

He nodded, shame filling his eyes as he looked up at her. "I had to do what I did." He extended his bandaged hands out toward her. "I did what had to be done."

Carrie said nothing to this. She trusted Grey and his judgement, even if she knew he was holding something back from her.

He seemed lost in his thoughts, his eyes staring at the floor.

Carrie said nothing for a few moments. She allowed him his reverie as she soaked in the moment, the time. She was standing before a man she respected above almost all others. A man who died in her reality. A man who had changed everything.

Grey snapped out of his stupor and motioned to the moon pendant in her hand. "The time will come when you'll figure out how to use that. I promise you, Carrie, it will turn the tide for you and the rest of the Lazerblades."

Carrie rubbed the pendant in her hand. Despite it sitting in her fist this whole time, the silver icon was ice cold and even seemed to sweat condensation into her palm.

"It's cold," she said.

Grey ignored her as he went to his workbench and took the book in hand.

"What is that?" she asked.

He glanced quickly at the book, but ignored her question as he shoved the book into a dark gray backpack that sat on the floor, against the workbench.

"Why won't you answer me," she said. "I know—"

Grey cut her off with a waving motion with his hand. "I know you have a ton of questions, my dear, but now is not the time. There won't ever be a time, really, when I can answer them all. You have to understand that I am changing everything that I believe will make significant alterations to your— our— future. A hundred years from now, I hope we are all in a better place to fight Legion and the Dark Army."

"How do...How did I die?"

Grey shot a glare her way, his wrinkled lips pursed in a disappointed formation. "You know better than that."

She slid the pendant into the pocket of her sweatshirt, feeling the cold against her stomach. "I know. I just want some answers." She motioned to her arms and the rack matter slithering across her skin. "What is this? What is all of this? And

336

not just what, but why? Why us? Why us, Grey?

"You know what David and I have always wanted? Each other. But not each other in a world of chaos. We have wanted each other in a world of peace. A world without Big, a world without criminals."

Grey nodded, his eyes softening on her. "I know, my dear. I know you two care deeply for each other."

"But?"

He smirked and then opened the top drawer of a corner dresser, pulling out some shirts which he shoved into the backpack. "But there are bigger things than your love for one another. And please, before you scold me for saying that, please understand that I don't say it lightly."

"I do love him. I think I've always loved him." Her gaze wandered to the floor. The teal carpeting was ugly and tacky, but it seemed to calm her mind.

"I know."

"I don't want to lose him."

"I know."

"How did he die? In the old timeline?"

Grey gathered other various items from around the room and shoved them into the backpack: toiletries, clothes, notebooks. When he tried to close the bag, Carrie thought the zipper was going to break.

"David was—is—a good friend of mine, Carrie. As are you. Because of that, I won't share the horrors I had to experience in the original timeline. You don't want to know of them. Believe me. I am sure you have enough to haunt your dreams for a lifetime. You don't need to add what I know onto it."

Carrie sighed, resigning to take his warning. She had seen things—the Harpwillow came to mind— that she would not easily forget. But what was still to come? What if Legion and the Dark Army invaded Anaisha to the point where they destroyed it?

Grey slung the backpack over his right shoulder. "I must go. I have other things to accomplish here."

Carrie stood in his way, blocking him from leaving the room. "I *need* more answers."

Grey stared into her eyes, saying nothing, making no movements. He was a man of iron will, Carrie knew this much about him, but she had to get more from him. She had to—

"How will I get home?"

Grey sighed. "I don't know. My machine is broken, so I can't even get myself home...yet."

Carrie pulled the pendant out of her sweatshirt pocket and rested it in her palm, in front of Grey. "What is this, really?"

"A key," Grey said, eyeing the artifact. "A very, very important key."

Carrie sighed, annoyed that she had to rake the information out of him. "A key to what?"

Grey put his hand over the pendant, his large hand easily covering Carrie's small, inky palm. "You'll find out when it's time. It's not time yet, though."

Grey slung his overstuffed backpack over his shoulder. "I must go."

"I have to get back to David."

"You'll wind up where you're meant to," Grey said matter-of-factly.

Carrie moved to the right to block him from leaving the room again, but he moved too fast, and he was too big. He was already halfway through the hallway toward the entrance of the house by the time she turned around fully.

"I need more answers."

He said nothing, only waved behind him and then disappeared from view into the foyer.

Carrie thought to chase him down, but somehow knew he had told her everything he was going to tell her.

"Where do we go from here?"

Viranda sighed. *I don't know.*

Carrie grasped the pendant in her hand. She wondered what good the small piece of jewelry could do against Legion, against everything that was coming up against them.

She turned to look at the room once more, hoping Grey had left something behind. But she knew nothing ever actually slipped his mind. If he had forgotten something, he hadn't actually 'forgotten' it.

She turned and looked over his makeshift workbench. His cup, empty of soda and harboring only a handful of crushed ice fragments, sat there, forgotten, along with other drinks he had consumed.

The black and purple bound book, filled with notes and random scraps of paper, sat on the bench. 'Forgotten.'

Carrie approached the bench, her heart excited to see that Grey had at least thought to leave her something other than a currently unusable talisman.

The book seemed to glisten under the dingy ceiling lights. Carrie lifted it off the workbench, surprised at how heavy it felt. She contributed its weight to the amount of scrap paper and notes that Grey had added to the volume.

How do you know he added all of that?

"You're right. I don't know." Carrie flipped open the cover of the book. A large black butterfly had been hand-painted in crude ink on the first page. "What is this?" She flipped the first few pages which were all covered in scribbled handwriting in various colors of ink, mostly purple.

"I see." A voice slithered from the shadows of a closet not ten feet from her.

Carrie slammed the book shut and jumped back a few feet, peering toward the dark closet. The door stood open, giving full view to a pool of darkness and two glowing red eyes peering out at her.

"Who are you?"

"I see that Grey has decided to interfere in our affairs."

That's not Legion, Viranda said.

If it's not Legion, then what is it?

I don't know.

Carrie waited for the creature to step out of the shadows, but it did not move.

She reached forward and took the book from the workbench, certain the entity would lunge at her. With how close she was to the closet, the creature could have easily taken her down.

"I want that book."

Carrie glanced down at the blank cover. Something in the book resonated with her. She knew she had to protect it. She had to care for it, as Grey had left it for her on purpose. For a purpose.

The creature hissed.

We need to leave, Viranda said. *I don't know what that is, but I know it isn't associated with Legion or with the Dark Army.*

Carrie backed up to the doorway leading to the hall where Grey had fled only minutes earlier. She peered down the hallway, but only looked straight into darkness. No light permeated the hallway, only the actual absence of all things.

The door slammed shut and the doorknob vanished, leaving behind a solid plank of wood.

Carrie turned toward the closet, at those red eyes peering at her from the darkness.

"You should not be here," the creature said in an exasperated tone. "You do not belong in this thread."

"Well, I'm here," she said, hugging the book tight to her chest.

"Yes."

The room, Carrie realized, had started to empty of light. The windows could no longer be seen, with their blinds and the piercing rays of sunlight that were here when Grey stood in the center of the room before her.

Darkness crept in along the edges, closing the room in on itself.

Carrie hugged the book and grasped the talisman, her heart beating rapidly. This darkness was unlike anything she had ever seen. Worse than the darkness in the Dark Realm. Worse than Legion's darkness. This was pure and utter absence of light. Of life.

The red eyes started to move out of the closet space toward her.

She felt the talisman in her hand grow colder as the darkness moved in closer. She could no longer see the workbench or Grey's soda cups or the mess of filing papers around the room.

"You must be dealt with. The others have escaped the grasp of our allies. But you have been left to me. And I will snuff you out like a candle wick."

Carrie felt the talisman burn in her palm. She tried to open her hand, but the icy heat from the medallion would not allow it. She tried to scream, but her throat caught, and those red eyes moved in closer and closer and closer. The darkness was all around her now, leaving her in a small spotlight of dim lighting.

She closed her eyes, wishing to be far away from this place. Far away from this new kind of evil.

Something cold slithered across her skin, biting her with its icy fangs. Then she felt warmth. Sunlight?

She opened her eyes. Large doors loomed over her, rising high into the air above her. The darkness was gone. Sunlight poured down from a blue sky above. She found stone bricks underneath her feet and felt a cool breeze moving through her disheveled hair.

What is this place? Viranda asked.

Carrie walked up the set of seven steps leading to the massive black and red-painted doors. Ornate decorum was emblazoned upon the surface of the black steel doors, a fanciful work of curved lines and branching threads that made the door look like it had the roots of a red tree painted upon it.

The symbol of an oak tree was set into the place the door handles would normally be. Each tree was painted red and was triple the size of Carrie's fist. All of the roots that were painted across the doors led to the tree handles.

Carrie looked down at her palm and found the talisman there. It was neither hot nor cold. And her palm looked unblemished by what she was sure had been a burning earlier.

She shoved the talisman into the pocket of her sweatshirt and then pressed her palm against the tree on the right door panel.

The ground shook as glowing red light burst out of the tree and then carried through the roots of the tree, causing the door to glow with red lines across a black backdrop.

The doors made a snapping sound, as if something had been loosed on the other side. The massive structure moved inward, opening up to a large space within.

What now? Viranda asked.

We venture forth, Carrie answered, hugging the Black Butterfly book close to her chest as she moved forward into the massive chamber.

32 Sacrifice

David and Rachel took a rundown city bus back to Lexy's prison rehabilitation facility, courtesy of Rachel's internal mapping software. It was just another useful gift of hers that said much about the person who designed her. Whomever that may have been. With how intricate she was, David wouldn't have been too surprised to find that Professor Grey crafted her, but Rachel had already admitted that she was created on another planet, on Spectrum. And Grey had never been to Spectrum.

As far as David knew.

Lexy's lab was in a plain-looking building, something that surprised David when he left to head out with Drax to hunt down Turquoise. But now, as he took a good, long look at the outside of the building, he realized it could—and probably commonly was—mistaken for a mature apartment complex, snuggled between a battered pawn shop and an even worse-looking ice cream parlor.

David and Rachel entered through a plain white doorway

and headed up a narrow flight of stairs. On the second floor, Rachel placed her hand upon an access panel to the right of another white door, allowing the machine to scan her palm.

"*Access granted, Lexy Parch,*" a tinny female voice chimed from the panel.

"How did you do that?" David asked as the door slid open.

Rachel turned to him, her neck motion ridiculously fluid. "I'm able to replicate security protocols, in certain situations."

They both entered the hallway, the same hallway David had appeared in when he was coughed out the other end of the corrupted portal. He recalled being blind and disoriented. He recalled meeting Lexy for the first time.

"Life signs are negative," Rachel whispered.

"Life signs? Who's—" And then David saw her body at the other end of the hallway. He ran down the corridor, Rachel keeping pace directly behind him. When he reached Lexy's corpse, he nearly choked on his own breath.

She was balled up in a fetal position, her white lab coat shielding her back. Blood soaked the carpet underneath her. The stench of death permeated this end of the hallway. Blood streaked the walls and carpet along a morbid trail that led back through the doorway into the other rooms.

"She struggled," Rachel mused. "She crawled out here for a reason."

David grabbed Lexy's side and gently pulled her toward him. Her body shifted onto her back, her arms opening, something glass dropping to her chest. Her face was a mask of blood, part of her hair adding texture to her cheeks and jaw-line. He could see gashes carved into her flesh, as if metal blades had cut deep into her face.

David caught his breath and veered his gaze toward the

344

item on her chest.

Toward the crystal timepiece.

"She's been dead for exactly four hours and eight minutes," Rachel said in a soft tone.

He grasped the timepiece with his right hand, grasped Lexy's cold, lifeless palm in his left. "I'm sorry this happened to you," he whispered. "You didn't deserve this."

He took the timepiece and looked it over briefly. It was more sleek in design to the one he had taken from him, but it had a clock in the center, stuck at 12, and glowing green. He slid it into the pocket of his coat.

"You knew her well."

David turned to Rachel, shaking his head. "No. Not really."

"It wasn't a question."

"I didn't know her at all. I arrived here, in this hallway, through a corrupted portal. She was the first to find me."

"I apologize. There are other realities, David. Sometimes I speak of them without realizing it."

He stood to his feet and faced Rachel. "Was there a reality where Lexy and I were together?"

"Four, actually. Three of which wound up benefiting your life."

He scratched the stubble across his face.

Rachel pointed toward bloody streaks along the wall and the edge of the doorway. "She fought someone."

A sense of dread fell into his stomach. "Are they still here?" He wanted to run, but the rage he felt for what had happened to this poor girl made him want to destroy whomever—or whatever—was responsible for this.

Rachel put her hand on the floor, sinking her fingers into the carpet. Then she closed her eyes. "He's still here." Her eyes shot open, and she sprung to her feet. "We must leave,

David. Now!"

Rachel took David by the hand, pulling him toward the hallway's entrance.

David knew something was wrong as soon as he felt time shift around him. The hallway, stretched before him, changed colors. The walls turned from white to black, the carpet from white to red. Rachel was the only constant, pulling him toward the other end of the long corridor, her body moving fluidly as if she was made of liquid.

Time shifted, colors shifted, and then a doorway appeared, a doorway with a black frame.

A Black Door!

Rachel and David passed into it.

It wasn't a fantastic world they slid into. It was darkness. Dark sky, dark ground. Rachel and David stumbled through the doorway and tumbled into dirt. David's first instinct was to spring up from the ground and turn back to the door in the hopes he could keep it open for them to return through, but by the time he got to his feet, the door was closed and gone, leaving them in utter darkness.

He brushed the dirt from his coat and pants. "Rachel?"

Her glittering blue eyes shone from his right, enabling him to take hold of her hand and help her up. "Thank you," she said, her voice seemingly calm, but with an edge of panic that David could only discern because of all the time he had spent with Carrie over the years. He had been able to pick up on the tone of panic, of anxiety, of worry.

"Where are we?" When he spoke, his words did not echo, but ended abruptly after being spoken.

Rachel did nothing to answer his question. Instead, light shone from her eyes and illuminated the path in front of them…a long road of dirt that led to nothing but more darkness. "Come. We have to get through this next part before we can make strides to save the End Point." She led him down the path, using her eyes to light the way.

David followed her, cautiously. All around them, the darkness encroached. No buildings. No people. No animals. Just darkness and the dirt path they walked along. "Did you bring us here?"

She shook her head. "This was his doing."

"Redford?"

She nodded. "The Black Doors, David. They exist in many places now. They are usually incredibly dangerous."

David felt the claustrophobia creeping in around him. It was as if he was trapped in a box made of black walls. No sunlight existed here, and he couldn't hear their footsteps, the dirt—or sand, maybe?—was so soft underneath their feet. "Where exactly is here? What is the End Point?"

"Time," she started, "has an Origin Point and an End Point. The Origin point is when the original you was born. The beginning of *your* time. The End Point is the final point where all realities intersect and end at."

"You mean everything will eventually come to the same end?"

She stopped along the path and tilted her head, the beams of light vanishing into the far darkness. "Yes, that's one way of putting it."

"That's one way of putting it?"

She continued walking, the light revealing more dirt and darkness. David started to take note that the dirt was in fact sand, and the sand was in fact black, like fine gunpowder.

"All realities have one Origin Point and one End Point. It's the nature of things. And these points are immovable, and unchanging. We can do nothing to alter them. They are fixed. Anchors."

If time has only one fixed start and end, and they cannot be changed, then what is the point of every—?

"The point is life, David."

Startled, he stopped following her and suddenly regretted that decision. The darkness began to swallow him as her light drifted along the path. He skipped to catch up with her and quickly rejoined her side. "Life?"

"Yes. The beginning and the end are fixed points. But what you do in the middle...that's life. That's all your doing."

"But what is the point of striving toward anything if the end is already determined?"

He couldn't see the rest of her face directly under her eyes, but he could swear she was smiling with the tone of her voice "We'll discuss this more later. Right now, we have to find Carrie. Once that happens, I can get a fix on her location."

"Where are we, Rachel? Are we in another reality? Another dimension?"

Rachel stopped walking and stared straight ahead at a black brick wall directly in front of them, ending the path they had been walking along. "We're in the Dark Realm."

David looked out to the left and right—as far as her light would reach—and saw nothing but the wall stretching into more darkness. "The what?"

"A place outside of reality."

"How can something exist outside of reality? And how could a Black Door take us here?"

Rachel stretched her arm and lightly touched the surface of the black wall. The brick she touched crumbled at her touch, exposing more brick behind it. "You understand so little, David." She coughed, and the sound came out both humanlike and as if a machine had manufactured it. "The Black

348

Doors can take one *anywhere*. They do not adhere to space or even time. They were created by accident. At Babel."

He watched her move her fingers into the hole she created. More brick fell apart, and she continued to move her hand forward, burrowing a hole in what seemed to be an incredibly thick wall made of nothing more than bricks of black dust.

"Babel?"

"Focus, David. The Black Doors are not a concern right now. This place is. And getting out of this place more so."

"What is this place?"

"It's the Origin Point of all darkness. Not natural darkness, but…"

"Evil?"

She pulled her arm out of the hole and shook the dust from her sleeve. "There are words for it." She reached both arms out and pushed her weight into the brick wall. The surface crumbled at her touch, allowing her to move forward through the thick wall and create a makeshift tunnel of sorts that David followed her through. She coughed again.

"I don't understand all of this."

Rachel let out a laugh, but it wasn't a funny laugh. She seemed concerned that he didn't understand what they were currently dealing with, but how could he? A Black Door brought them to a place outside of reality. David had never heard of such an outlandish thing, as if something, anything really, could exist outside of reality. One reality, let alone the dozens and hundreds and millions that most likely existed.

He followed Rachel through the brick as he mused about time and his own existence. He wondered about every choice he had ever made, every action he had ever taken, every small and seemingly insignificant decision that somehow created a new path, a new direction, a new reality.

An infinite number of them.

The thought sobered him.

Rachel continued to burrow through the wall. "Don't think too hard about it, David. There's much you don't understand. And that's normal for a human being."

"And you think you understand more, just because you're a machine?"

She coughed. "Do you really think I'm a mere machine? You've seen what I can do. You know better than that."

"Maybe." And he did. But he didn't fully understand it.

"I feel something inside of my programing. Something wrong."

David glanced around at the darkness, wary of something ambushing them. "What do you mean wrong?"

She wheezed. "Something in this place. It's corrupting my programming."

"Open a portal. Get us out of here. What are we even doing here?"

Rachel broke through the other side of the wall into more darkness. She moved out of the walkway and shined her lights on a figure ahead of them. David came out of the path and squinted to make out what her lights revealed: a young girl, bound to a chair, unresponsive to the darkness.

Her brunette hair glistened under Rachel's lights.

"Carrie?"

Rachel held her arm out against David's chest, preventing him from moving forward any further. "Don't."

"Is that her?"

Rachel scanned her light across Carrie's unconscious form. "It's Carrie. But not *your* Carrie."

"A Carrie from another reality?"

"Yes." A sickening retching sound flowed out of Rachel's mouth, and her whole form twitched.

"Are you okay?"

Rachel shook her head. "We must leave this place soon."

"Is she alive? This Carrie?"

Rachel nodded. "The darkness was too much for her at first. She fainted. I've already run a scan on her, and her life signs are somewhat normal."

"Somewhat?"

"Her body is dealing with being pulled out of her reality."

The creaking of a door echoed in the distance. When it slammed shut, a bright flash of light illuminated the area they stood in, revealing nothing more than white fog, Carrie's form, and the black sand underneath them.

David glanced up into the bright sky but could find no source of the light. It was as if it was coming from everywhere and nowhere all at once.

The lights in Rachel's eyes turned off.

A figure emerged from the fog. His trademark black suit and red tie told David that Redford never changed his clothes. The man stopped near Carrie's form and extended a hand toward David. "I need you, David, to please, please, please understand the gravity of this situation right now." He grabbed Carrie's jaw and lifted her head. Her eyes were shut, and her mouth drooped in a depressed manner.

David had no intention of moving any closer to Carrie. He had dealt with many of Chaos's illusions, and his gut told him not to trust Redford. At all. For any reason.

"I want the timepiece. Give me that, and I'll give her back to you. Simple trade."

"Simple?" David said. "Is this why you brought us here?!"

Redford motioned to Carrie. "I brought you here to get your attention. Again. To speak with you without worldly distractions. Or any distractions, really. Listen, David. She's trapped here, and I'm the only one who can release her into your care. Once you understand that, you'll know that giving me that timepiece is your best option. Your friend, Turquoise, took the other one. I figured I would allow that event to run its course, as it was highly unlikely you would get it back. But then you stumbled on another one. So I have to step in and take matters into my own hands."

David reached into his coat pocket and gripped the crystal piece. He felt a connection to it, something divine, maybe. He couldn't bring himself to release it into anyone's care. Not Turquoise's, not Rachel's, and certainly not Redford's. And even though he would fight to the ends of the planet—of all the realities in existence—to save Carrie's life, he couldn't bring himself to trade it for her, even if he did believe Redford would keep his end of the bargain.

Especially a different Carrie. But did it matter? Was one Carrie better than another?

Lexy died to make sure David had this second chance at the timepiece. It was fate—or something more—that obviously wanted him to have this item.

Redford crossed his arms, staring at David with the look his father used to give him when he wouldn't do as he was told. He motioned to Carrie. "She'll die here, David. A slow, painful death where her sanity will be lost forever. Even if you get her back, eventually, she'll be gone upstairs. A shell is what she'll be. Do you want that for her? For you? For your friends?"

"You already tossed my Carrie through a Black Door. Back in the brick building."

Redford grinned. "I should have known you could tell the difference between your Carrie and one of the other infinite number of Carries throughout the multiverse."

A low rumble echoed through the space between them, and something unseen shifted the wisps of fog, trailing them through the air like torn cotton balls. David sprung back, bumping into Rachel, who gripped his shoulders tight and held him steady.

"What is that?" David gasped.

Redford stood completely still, his face unchanging in the mysterious light. "It seems you need to be educated on where you're at."

The movement through the fog stopped, and David could hear heavy breathing somewhere off to his right, in the darkness.

"An Ancient One," Rachel whispered.

David didn't want to know what an Ancient One was. He focused his eyes on Carrie, sitting there, unconscious in the chair. He fought the urge to save her.

"Pay attention, David," Redford said, pulling David's attention back to him. "I'm going to open a Black Door that will toss her into the worst place you can possibly imagine. Unless you give me that timepiece."

David felt the timepiece in his pocket, the crystal shell cold in his grip. Something about it seemed to ground him even better than the boomerang.

A low groan rumbled from the darkness.

Redford held out his hand, and a Black Door opened behind Carrie. Redford moved his hand and the door swung open wide, revealing a deep darkness on the other side. "One more chance, David. The timepiece. Give it to me. I'll end all of this, and you and this Carrie can go achieve what you were always meant to achieve if that damn Nathan Pierce hadn't done what he did!"

David felt the broken pieces of Redford's remote in his pocket. "I thought you destroyed the remote."

Redford smiled. "I have some degree of control over time. I just went back and grabbed another one." He held up the remote he had in his hand.

"What is this timepiece to you?"

"The question, David, is what is it to you? It powers a weapon, right? Is that all it does? Do you know how many realities have been altered because of that thing? It needs to be destroyed, just like those items you saw in the warehouse needed to be destroyed. They are thorns in the side of creation, and they must be plucked. If I destroy that piece, it will set some things right. Not all, but some. And every little bit counts at this point."

David felt the crystal timepiece in his coat pocket, chill in his palm, sending a cold shiver along his right arm. "Rachel, what is the significance of this timepiece?"

Rachel fell to her knees, her vocal machinations emitting weird wheezing and coughing noises. "The timepiece's purpose is hidden from me."

David turned his neck to look on her. "What?"

She shrugged tiredly.

The Ancient One groaned again, this time from David's right, closer than he would have liked.

He pulled the timepiece from his pocket, unclear of which path to take. If he handed it to Redford—and if Redford kept his word, David could walk away with at least a version of Carrie. But if he didn't, this Carrie—a version that very well could have no knowledge of anything going on—could be tossed into further darkness. Into further insanity. Could he knowingly allow something horrible to happen to a hapless Carrie?

But...

So much had been sacrificed for the timepiece already. It was important, incredibly important. But why?

Redford lifted Carrie out of the chair. "Time's up, David." He kicked the chair over and positioned Carrie in front of the open doorway.

David gripped the timepiece harder, feeling its connection to him and to the multiple realities it seemed to encompass. Something in his spirit, in the very core of his soul, told him not to give up the crystal object, as small and seemingly insignificant it seemed to be. His future—all of their futures—were tied to it, somehow, even if he didn't understand how. Or why.

He slid the timepiece into his coat pocket...

...and Carrie was thrown in the outer darkness, into a place David knew he wouldn't be able to follow after her.

The door shut.

"Then I will allow you and the timepiece and your sick friend there to be destroyed." Redford and the light disappeared, and David and Rachel were left in complete and utter darkness.

33

This Evil Place

houghts flurried around him like wounded butterflies looking for a place to land and die. Thoughts of the past. Thoughts of what the future might have held, had David saved that version of Carrie.

But he hadn't. He let her go, in exchange for a crystal paperweight he clung to like some long-forgotten family heirloom. He found a strange irony in the matter, in the fact that he had complete control over saving her life this time. All he had to do was hand Redford the crystal and Redford would have given Carrie back. David knew, deep in his heart of hearts, that Redford would have kept his end of the bargain. The man was on a mission, not a killing spree, and the end point of that mission was obtaining the timepiece, destroying the timepiece, and setting things right in his own mind.

Now David sat in near-darkness, a corrupted AI next to him, her lights flickering on and off. Natural light did not exist on this plane, and neither did hope, apparently. Redford was gone, as was his ability to open the Black Doors that could enable them to escape this fathomless darkness.

"I'm sorry," Rachel whispered, her voice hoarse and without melody. "I don't have the energy to open a portal."

David sighed. He could do nothing to stop the corruption within her programming, and so another would lose their life—rather their existence, because of his decision to keep the timepiece.

As they sat in their stillness, David could still hear the Ancient One moving around the space near them. It did not approach them, nor did it speak to them. It simply moved through the darkness, making its presence known with groans and rumbles. It was a powerful creature, that much David could tell just by being within proximity of it. It was old, definitely living up to the 'Ancient' adage in its moniker. It wasn't part of Legion, though David had thought so at first because of its dark nature. No, David felt and sensed this was something different, something that had been around before or maybe at the same time as Legion. Maybe...

These thoughts, this knowledge, seemed to come to him naturally, though he did not know or understand why. It was pure darkness he sat in, and it took every ounce of his self-control not to panic in the claustrophobia he felt within the lightless walls. But while he sat, while he absorbed the darkness around him, he suddenly knew things about this place.

This evil place.

This was indeed the birthplace of something evil. Not all evil, but a very specific evil. An evil that had managed to create a place outside of time to hide from a being greater than it. This reality between realities was somehow a house to creatures almost older than time itself.

This Ancient One that roamed the darkness was powerful, but it used to be more powerful. It used to be worshipped, and it used to be revered and feared. But now it was a shell, a moving cocoon of its old self. It could destroy David in a hurry, but something—a force David could feel but not explain—prevented anything from touching David or Rachel.

This was a strange place indeed.

"I have two hours left, David, until the corruption eats away at the shielding protecting my vital components. I'm sorry that I could not help you rescue that Carrie. Or your Carrie. In many realities, I did. In many realities, she died from the darkness around us before having the chance to go through that doorway. And in one reality...she..."

"Save it, Rachel. Save your strength. I don't want to know about the other realities. All I care about is this one. It looks like we won't be here long anyway."

She coughed, and it was a strange cough, because it was human and full of mucus and huffy. "You speak of our end."

"Yes."

A low rumbling moved the air in front of them. "I control the beginning and the ending in this realm."

"Ignore it," Rachel said. "Nothing it says will matter here."

The rumbling continued, like small bursts of thunder. David felt it across his cheeks, felt it within his chest. "Who are you?" he asked, even though he already knew.

Rachel sighed, unnerving David with her humanlike qualities.

"I am the god of this realm."

"You are not," Rachel groaned.

The rumbling increased, and David felt it shift through his ribcage. He felt sick, but he refused to sit. He faced the creature, who he heard breathing in front of him. "Are you one of the Anaishan gods?"

The creature laughed, its voice rolling through the air in front of them like fast-moving city buses. "I am One of the Twelve."

Rachel managed to stand, her lights flickering, her form shaky. David grabbed underneath her arm and helped support her. She spoke to the creature as if she could see him. "You are an abomination. Your kind are filth. Putrid filth."

A violent gust of wind whooshed past David's face, and Rachel was taken from him, suddenly plunged into the darkness.

"Rachel? Rachel!?"

Silence stood beside David. He wondered when all of this was going to end.

"It will end when I say it ends," the creature bellowed. "Who are you here, David Corbin? You enter my realm and insist on demanding that I tell you who I am? You know nothing of the darkness. You know nothing of true evil."

"Then enlighten me."

"You already know. You know this is the birthplace of the Twelve. We were gods who controlled the mere existence of humanity for eons."

"You don't seem like a god to me. At least not now, not here."

"Yes." The being moved around David, circling him in random gusts of wind. "You would not recognize me now. But that does not mean that my power is any less potent. Redford brought you here to fix things, and he failed in that regard. He only left you as meal for me."

"I'm nobody's meal."

The creature laughed, and David felt spittle splatter across his face. It smelled of dusty tomes and musky candlelight. "You are what I say you are here. You are nothing. NOTHING!"

David closed his eyes and gripped the timepiece in his pocket. In one moment, he felt the protective barrier keeping the creature from him. And the next, he felt that protection vanish like wind. If the creature sensed that the shield had vanished, it did not mention it. David reached out to his right in the hopes he could find Rachel in a last-ditch effort to flee the darkness and possibly even flee this realm.

But all around him, the darkness felt thick, like clouds made of cotton. His fingers only found solid, spongy material all around him.

"You are unprotected, human."

"So I am."

David felt large talons swing through the darkness in front of him and furrow along his chest, cutting him open. He fell backwards and hit the ground. He gripped the burning wound and felt torn flesh where the nails ripped through his shirt.

"My prey."

David struggled to his feet. "Rachel?"

The talons swung at him again, but he rolled and felt them barely miss his back.

"Rachel?!"

Wind swept past David's cheek, and he felt the creature closer than before. "You will die here."

David felt talons rip at his back, and then rip at his right shoulder. He felt razor-sharp teeth tear at his right ear, and he dropped to the ground, pain biting every part of him. He groaned as he cupped his bleeding ear and embraced his wounded shoulder, where the stitches had broken.

"This is mere play for me, human. You will die here, but when I say it is time. I have not toyed with someone in a very long era."

David reached his arms out for Rachel. "Rachel?"

"She is gone!" the creature shouted. Talons swung, but they coasted above David's head, sweeping through his hair and chopping a clump off.

"Rachel!" He reached out and grabbed fingers. Cold, metallic fingers. He felt the talons sweep across the back of his head again while he pulled on those fingers. Rachel's body slid across the ground toward him.

"Mortals do not belong in this realm. Mortals are a plague upon life, upon all of existence."

David pulled Rachel's body close to his. Her lights were out, and she wasn't responding. He moved his hand around her form, hoping to find a switch of some kind that could reactivate her or activate something that could help him out. He felt both human skin and metal surface.

Pain flowed through his wounds, and he could feel warm blood slithering across his skin underneath his clothes.

"We control all realities because we exist outside of all realities. Time is not a restraint to the Twelve."

David precariously rolled Rachel onto her stomach and began to run his hand across her back. It felt somewhat awkward feeling around the body of an AI like this, especially one who had so many feminine features.

Thunder boomed through the space around him. Lightning flashed, and a terrible screech filled the air. David had to cup his ears as the noise intensified. He imagined glass shattering, mountains crumbling. His nose began to bleed, but he ignored it in favor of keeping his ears covered, though it did little to block out the terrifying noise.

Light filled the space, infinite light that stretched in all directions, horrible light that forced David's eyes to close. This light pierced his eyelids and filled his head, his body, his soul with a strange darkness. A heavy weight settled in David's spirit, a wet blanket that embraced his heart and pulled him toward the Depths, toward a darkness few knew.

David never knew light could be so horrible. This light wasn't bright, it wasn't pure, it was tinted with a tan or yellow color, and it burned through him like a wildfire. It smelled of rot, of urine, of everything grotesque.

The light tore at him, gently at first, and then with a strange intensity that made David wonder if the light was a living entity that was feeding off him.

He forced his eyes open, and they burned with the fantastic light. The screeching continued, rattling David's brain, shattering any confidence he had in fighting the creature. Instead, David ran his hands down the small of Rachel's back. His fingers found a small imprint near her spine. He pushed in on it in the hopes he had found a switch that could turn the tide of the battle. The imprint sunk into Rachel's back, leaving a hole roughly the size of his fist.

David closed his eyes, his body shuddering under the fierce velocity of the light and sounds. They wracked his body with pain, tearing at the fabric of his being and of the wounds he had already been inflicted with. He felt blood streaming from open wounds, running down his arms, his back, the back of his neck.

The timepiece pulsed in his pocket. David reached into his pocket and slid the object out into the open, into the horrible light. The screeching seemed not to affect the crystal timepiece, even though it felt as if David's skull was being pushed upon in a crushing manner by the terrible noise.

He slid the timepiece across Rachel's back and dipped it down into the small groove in her back. He felt the timepiece click into place. He rolled her onto her back so she was facing the dark, endless ceiling above them.

"This is where you die!!!!!"

That horrible light pricked at David's skin like the points of a thousand fishing hooks. He felt tearing, and he could feel hands inside of his face, crushing his head with reckless abandon.

Then, like an unexpected interlude in the midst of a concerto, a powerful bellow echoed out of Rachel's mouth, shattering the horrible light like glass, burning the sounds away in a blue fire.

Silence. Darkness. Stillness.

With the pulsing gone, David's head rested on the ashen ground of the strange, otherworldly realm. His eyes closed, and he tried to think back to how all of this started. With Amber having him tossed into that security room at the mall. The demon hybrid showing up at his apartment. To Carrie being kidnapped by Jerad.

The events of the past few days, the past week, played in his mind, one after another, like a movie. And all that stuck out in each and every event was Carrie. Whether or not she was a part of every event, David's mind placed her in every event. It was overwhelming at first but then it became quite pleasant to have Carrie in each and every daydream of his.

But now…now she was gone, and there wasn't a thing he could do about it. No effort, no act of strength, no toss of his boomerang could end things and bring his life back to what it was long ago, with Carrie by his side.

He could do nothing. Say nothing.

"Are you alright?" he heard Rachel ask from his right side.

He opened his eyes and found her figure shining in a bright, green glow. "What?"

She reached her hand down toward him, her smile sparkling and intoxicating. She was an emerald in the darkness, a lighthouse in the mist. "It's time to leave this place."

He reached up and took hold of her hand. It was warm.

She pulled him to his feet, and he felt his head swim with the quick motion.

"Where is he?" David asked.

Rachel looked around the darkness for a moment before answering. "It's on the ground, twenty yards in that direction," she answered, pointing.

"Can you get us out of here?"

She nodded. "The reality around us is unstable and tearing. I can open one of those tears and get us back to where we came from."

"And Carrie?"

She shook her head.

"Where is she?"

"She's in another place. A place I don't have access to."

David took a deep breath. There was nothing he could do about Carrie right now. He would have to concede to the fact that Carrie was lost to him—for the moment. "Get us out of here."

She pointed toward the same spot the creature was currently in. Her light grew, and the entire area around them, though void as it was but for the black sand, glowed with a bright green.

David could make out the creature now. It looked like nothing more than a massive brownish whale, slumped over on its side. Dirty white and green secretions slithered across the surface of its body. "It would be wise to kill it, David."

"Is it still alive?"

"Of course, David. I am one of the Twelve."

"Open a tear to get us out of here," he told Rachel.

She nodded, and then she turned and reached her arms out straight in front of her. She pulled her arms apart, and a bright blue and purple tear opened in the air in front of them. On the other side, David could see the sun rising on some

364

mountains. Rachel craned her head back toward him, holding the tear open. "Do what you need to, David. Just know that every action has a consequence."

"But if we're outside of reality, how would killing this thing impact our reality?"

"Arnasted's death will resonate throughout all realities, and his siblings will feel it as well."

"Arnasted? Siblings?"

The creature wheezed. "So, you have learned my name?"

"Will killing him help our reality?"

"Helping our reality is inconsequential now, David. All realities are tearing apart, and soon, there will only be one. The End Point."

"What does killing him accomplish?"

Rachel's face went blank for a moment before a slight grin crept across her face. "There are too many consequences to killing and not killing him. I cannot narrow it down for you. Do what you feel is right. Arnasted is an anomalous type of evil, one that should not go unchecked."

David nodded and turned toward the area she had originally pointed in. He slid the boomerang from the sheath at his side, feeling the weight of the grounding object. It had been a truer friend to him than most, and now it would put an end to a portion of the evil that had been plaguing creation for so many millennia.

The air around the creature stunk of putrid feces and spoiled milk. There was a heaving, bellowing breath exiting from the creature's face—which David had trouble distinguishing from the rest of its body. When it spoke, the front end of the creature rippled, like the surface of a bowl of pudding. But no teeth showed, and David could not find a nose or eyes, just brown, leathery flesh illuminated in Rachel's green glow.

"So, you would kill a creature you know nothing about to satisfy the want of an inorganic being?"

David reached his hand out to touch the creature. His hand fell upon a slimy blanket of flesh, one covered in a mass of pustules and jagged cuts—bits of rock, he guessed. This creature had at one time been heavily armored but the years, maybe even this place, had worn it all away.

"Many have fought me, human. Many have died."

"Not me."

"No, not you," the creature mused. There was a tone of respect in its voice, something David didn't expect. "You are valiant. Admirable. A hero, in your own right. But you know nothing of the consequences of your actions. You see the world in black and white, in right and wrong. You see in absolutes. But there are no absolutes. There are only actions and reactions. Actions and consequences. Can a 'right' action create a 'wrong' consequence? Wouldn't that defeat the purpose of taking the 'right' action?"

"I can't hold this portal open forever, David."

David ran his hand along the surface of the creature. He could feel something pulsing from it, something tied to David, tied to David's past. Something familiar. Something...wrong.

He took the tip of his boomerang and touched it lightly to the blanket of flesh. "I know that you're evil. I've seen your evil. I've felt it."

"Ah, yes, you label my actions evil because they fit YOUR definition of evil."

"You've killed countless people before me. And you would keep killing, if given the choice."

"But I've been given no such choice, so how do you know? I've been banished here by my siblings, forced into this

366

darkness that I have made my home."

David pondered the creature's words, wondering if this thing was indeed evil or if it was simply mistaken. He also thought to take into account the fact that this was an ancient, alien being. What could he—and others—learn from it? Would it be wise to kill it? Would it be wise to destroy another life, like he destroyed Agent Parks?

He turned to Rachel, who continued to hold the sunlit portal open. "What do I do, Rachel?"

"I cannot tell you what to do, David. But I can tell you that this creature is not innocent of bloodshed and destruction. Four years ago, it was responsible for the destruction of the Anaishan Pier, resulting in the death of thousands."

David remembered that event. Remembered thinking about all those people who died at the hands of some strange sea creature that wreaked havoc on all of those poor, defenseless people. "What? That was this thing?"

She nodded, her eyes blazing a vibrant green. "There are so many more forces behind the events you would consider 'ordinary,' David. So many."

David closed his eyes and put all of his weight on the boomerang. The metal tip pushed through the hardy layer of flesh, and David heard a sizzling sound like bacon on a skillet. He gripped the boomerang and pulled it to the right, making a rough cut through the creature's exterior. The sound it made was moist, unnerving. David's stomach did a turn as mounds of innards spilled out around his feet. He kept his hand steady, slicing the creature open for a length of three feet before stopping.

The sound of slapping intestines and bubbling blood forced David to almost retch. He quickly swallowed the bile.

"David…"

He lifted his head, every part of his body screaming at him in pain. On the other side of the portal, he saw a man and woman standing against the backdrop of beautiful wintery foothills. The sun shone bright and warm, and the multitude of scents from wildflowers poured into the darkness. The man had a striking resemblance to David, only a bit weathered, and with a well-trimmed beard. The woman was stunning, with ivory-colored skin, bright blue eyes, and flowing white hair.

David gained an uncanny feeling that he knew these two people. From another time, maybe another where.

He wobbled a bit as the fumes from the creature made him nearly want to vomit again. Rachel pulled her arms wider and the portal widened. David stood in front of it and stared at the man and woman. They said nothing, did nothing. Just stared back at him. And somehow, someway, David knew it was destiny for him to step through this portal. There was a connection, a bridge, that only Rachel could have created.

That only the timepiece could have made possible.

So he took a step through the portal, expecting to meet someone new.

Instead, he fell.

Through a bright blue sky, clouds passing him like fleeing spirits.

His stomach passed into his throat as his body veered toward land below. And when he hit the cement, he felt nothing. It was like landing in a pile of foam bricks.

He scrambled to his feet, his nerves shot. He looked up into the sky expecting Rachel to come down on top of him. But she wasn't up there. Nothing was up there but blue sky and clouds.

He took a look around and found himself in the empty driveway of a one-story house. His parents' house. The same house he had grown up in. The iron bench stood sentry over the front door, a piece of furniture his mother had installed years earlier.

Earlier, when he had arrived here after his sister's death, snow had covered the property. The snow was gone. The sun shone above, and a pleasant breeze moved across him. It felt like spring.

He glanced around him. The rest of the neighborhood was gone. The horizon shot outwards in all directions, at lengths he could not see the ends of. Into nothingness. Blue sky could be seen miles beyond the house in all directions, but it looked as if all of the land he stood on ran straight out to cliffs.

It reminded him of the grocery store that stood between realities, the one Serenity had brought them to. Him to.

He was alone, and the sudden realization startled him. Panicked him.

He turned to the house. At second glance, he realized it was worn down. Panels hung off at various points. The tan trim was chipping away. The chimney was crumbling, small fragments of bricks lying in a pile at the side of the building. The iron bench was rusted.

David glanced around at his surroundings again. Cliffs. Sky. And this lone house. His childhood house.

Why had he come here? He had clearly seen the other side of the portal Rachel had opened for them. There was a man and a woman on the other side. Something so familiar about them. Something linked all of them together. It felt right and natural.

So then why had he stepped into actual sky? And why hadn't he died when hitting the ground?

Why was he home? More importantly, what forces were strong enough to pull him here.

Because as David closed his eyes and took a few deep breaths, he was acutely aware of this place and what may have happened here not too long ago. A time in his childhood. A time he had forgotten. The events were blurry in his mind, covered in streaks, unable to be seen clearly.

The same knowledge that had come to him regarding Arnasted now came to him concerning this place that was disguised as a childhood sanctuary.

This place was ancient.

This place was powerful.

This place was misunderstood.

The front door swung open.

David waited for what felt like an eternity for someone to stroll out of that doorway, but nobody did. The door had opened for him to enter, not for someone to escape.

He started up the driveway, knowing this was the only way to go.

He was alone now. No Carrie. No Veronica. No Turquoise. No Rachel.

Just a house full of childhood mysteries.

The dwelling place of all realities…

The adventure continues…